Lucky

Barbara Cutrera

Published by On My Way Up, LLC

Cover Photography: Sherri Proctor
www.SherrisIslandImages.com

Cover Model: Aaron Mondon

This book is a work of fiction. The names, characters, places, and
incidents are the result of the author's imagination or are used
fictitiously. Any resemblance to actual events, locales, or persons,
living or dead, is coincidental.

ISBN: 978-1-944113-99-5
Second edition

For Brenda, who is the truest of friends and one of the best LSU fans EVER!

Chapter One

Aric was stunned when he caught a glimpse of his reflection in a wall of mirrors while hurrying through the Atlanta airport. The full-length view of himself made him stop and stare, despite the fact that he was going to miss his connecting flight if he didn't hurry. That suddenly became irrelevant. He wondered if he'd looked that exhausted and grim throughout the past five years since the D Plague and hadn't noticed. He'd devoted all of his attention to his work, following the worldwide health crisis in 2029, but that approach had obviously taken its toll. He was only twenty-seven, lonely, and depressed, but he was also inexplicably alive. That made Aric the most unusual person on Earth.

In the days following his revelation at the airport, Aric started getting more sleep, exercising regularly, eating healthier, and trying not to work eighteen-hour days. He also vowed to take a two-week vacation around the time of his birthday at the beginning of September. He was scheduled to attend a five-day business conference at a resort in Florida toward the end of August. So, he'd called the resort and extended his stay.

Weeks passed, and Aric was pleased to note that when he looked in the mirror his six-foot frame had filled out once more and his workouts had restored the definition of his muscles. Even his short brown hair seemed healthier, but his brown eyes remained shadowed by sadness. He supposed that would never change.

When he arrived at the Tampa International Airport, Aric gathered his luggage and went to pick up his rental car. Once his bags were loaded in the trunk, he climbed into the silver hybrid sedan, spoke the security code he'd been given by the Avis clerk, and was rewarded with the sound of the car's engine coming to life. He was looking forward to the thirty-minute drive that would take him from the airport to the Serenity Bay Resort and Spa. Settling back into the driver's seat, he rested his hands on the wheel, verbally directed the vehicle to shift first into Reverse, then Drive, and began his brief journey.

Once he was out of the airport parking area, Aric said, "Radio on. Personal identification number 211967-2221964. Give me most recent national and international news relating to my profile."

"Good afternoon, Aric," said a synthesized female voice that sounded human. "Today is Sunday, August 20, 2034. In breaking news, President Lakshmi Jitesh met with the head of the International Monetary Fund to discuss the resurgence in the U.S. economy during the first year and a half of her term and the 'Economic Recovery Ripple Effect' spreading throughout much of the globe. The global recession that dominated the past two decades caused the deceleration of technological and medical advances although growth in those areas did undeniably occur. It is hoped that the current period of recovery will allow for a return to the previous rate of development.

"Later this week, Vice-President Buddy LaFleur is scheduled to visit his and President Jitesh's home state of Louisiana to view the damage done by devastating tornadoes that struck the capitol city of Baton Rouge. Jitesh and LaFleur are the first U.S. political team born and raised in the same state and elected to the highest political offices on the same ticket. The –"

"Give me current health news," Aric interrupted as he steered the car onto the Interstate.

"My pleasure, Aric, the synthesized voice replied. "A recent study by the Harvard Medical School showed that the annual birth control injection developed by Rodrigue Pharmaceuticals and approved for public use by the Food and Drug Administration in 2032 has proven to be safe and 99.9% effective. According to Planned Parenthood, abortion rates have dropped by 40% since this option was made available.

"Researchers at the Mayo Clinic recently confirmed the effectiveness of another Rodrigue Pharmaceuticals development that is being hailed as the greatest weapon to date in the war against cancer. Although there is currently no method to prevent the disease, researchers feel that this new treatment will halt the progression of destructive cells in non-smoking patients. Cancer sufferers around the world are heartened by the trials that may make their survival rates skyrocket."

Aric smiled with satisfaction. The smile quickly vanished as the voice continued, "A data review sponsored by the United Nations confirmed that there is still no known cause of the biological event that killed over half of the world's population in 2029. The study also concluded that it remains undetermined as to why seemingly healthy individuals succumbed to the virus, although it is evident why those with compromised immune systems and others with debilitating conditions were affected. There has been no explanation for the swiftness of the event or why victims died within twenty-four hours and literally turned to dust. The D Plague, so named because it caused certain *death*, the *disintegration* of the human body, and the resultant *dust*, remains a mystery. Since no one who contracted the illness survived, researchers cannot predict whether there will be another plague like it and how to treat victims should one –"

"Play Mozart," Aric ordered quietly. He listened to the strains of the orchestra and the voice on the car's GPS as it steered him toward the Serenity Bay Resort and Spa, but his mind was elsewhere. What he'd heard was true and yet untrue. The D Plague had swept the world with unmatched biological ferocity. Over half of the Earth's population *had* been lost. People who contracted the disease collapsed and died within twenty-four hours, turning to dust. AIDs patients, premature babies, and others with severe health problems had been expected victims, yet healthy individuals had also died. Aric had lost everyone in his large family.

However, there was one thing the news people had gotten wrong, although it was not their fault. They had no way of knowing, because it had been one of the best-kept secrets in the world. One of the D Plague victims had survived, and his name was Aric Rodrigue.

Ever since, Aric had willingly submitted to top-secret government medical testing that would hopefully lead to discovery of the cause of the disease and a cure should it strike again. It was hoped that by studying him, the doctors could prevent a similar worldwide catastrophe. Aric had given blood, tissue, urine, and semen samples. He provided accounts of how he had felt during the two days he'd battled the excruciating bone, joint, and muscle pain and the high fever. He had no idea why he'd lived, and those who'd witnessed his survival had quickly been recruited to work on the government project.

Stop thinking about it, Aric told himself. *Look at the good your pharmaceutical company is responsible for by developing and perfecting things like the new cancer drug and the injectable birth control. Focus on the positives and on how the government's assisted you to help others while you've helped them. Think of all the lives you've saved and the deaths you've prevented.*

It wasn't enough. It was never enough for Aric. He had never understood why he'd survived the D Plague, but he figured there had to be a reason. He'd devoted his post-Plague life to using his money, abilities, and existence to saving others. He felt it was his calling. Well, that was what he told himself as he battled chronic depression and survivor's guilt.

Aric arrived at his destination and unloaded his rental car. Moments after entering the Serenity Bay Resort and Spa lobby, he began to release some of the tension in his neck and shoulders. He checked in, took the elevator to the top floor, and was soon standing at the entrance to his suite uttering the verbal command that would unlock his door. He stepped inside and savored the moment.

He was in a corner unit on the fourth floor that was painted in calming colors, just as he'd requested. The curtains had been drawn back on the floor-to-ceiling sliding doors that ran the length of the living area in front of him. He could see out across the water – even from where he stood in the foyer of his suite. The view was breathtaking.

The flooring throughout the place appeared to be bamboo. In front of him was a dining area that had a kitchenette positioned across from it. Closer to the glass doors was a living area that held a comfortable-looking, oversized couch and loveseat combination, a coffee table, a wall-mounted, paper-thin, flat-screen television, and a built-in docking pad that would allow him to charge all of his personal electronic devices.

Aric went to his bedroom. The furniture there was made of a dark wood Aric had seen when he'd visited Central America on business trips. A white duvet had been draped over the king-sized bed. Another wall-mounted, flat-screen television had been placed across from its foot. There was a walk-in closet and an enormous bathroom.

Returning to the bedroom, he moved over to the sliding doors that extended along the far wall and spoke the words, "Open doors."

After they'd slowly slid apart, he felt the breeze from the Bay and inhaled deeply. Stepping out onto the balcony, he surveyed the natural beauty of the land and water.

Aric returned to the bedroom and unpacked his bags, then walked over to the bed and fell back across it. It was then that he noticed the mural on the ceiling. It depicted what he assumed were native plants, birds, and animals. He studied it for a long time. It was delicate, classic, and beautiful.

Aric thought of his own apartment in New Orleans. It was stark and sparsely furnished. It was a place to stay, not a home. No one went in, except Aric and the cleaning staff. He was constantly with people because of his work, but he was very much alone.

After dinner at the hotel's casual restaurant later that evening, Aric went to the Concierge Desk. The concierge on duty was a woman who looked to be about eighty. Her name was June, and Aric would soon find out that she was extremely knowledgeable and friendly. This was, of course, her job. Still, she reminded him of other older Southern ladies he knew and used to know.

"What can I do for you?" she asked him with a smile that was infectious. "I'm here to help you schedule anything you need at the resort and anywhere else in the area. I also have a wealth of knowledge that can provide you with other hotel services you may require."

"Such as?"

"Laundry. You're here for three weeks. I'm thinking you won't be washing your clothes in the sinks or tub in your rooms. How often would you like your laundry done?"

"I saw a hamper in my bathroom. When it's full, then it'll be ready to be done."

She made a note on her computer then said, "The resort has tennis courts, a gym, horseback riding, three pools, a nine-hole golf course, masseuse services, and an on-site hair salon."

"I'd like a Swedish massage in my suite at 6:00 every morning."

"Certainly. Male or female masseuse?"

"Female."

"Got it," June said. "Do you have questions or requests regarding any other services?"

"What time of day will my rooms be cleaned?"

"What time would you like them cleaned?"

"Anytime between 8:00 and 5:00 is fine, as long as I don't have The Do Not Disturb message on."

She nodded and made another note, then told him, "If you have any special requests for the housekeeping staff, then I'd suggest you go through the front desk. The hotel chain prides itself on diversity and employs people of all different ethnic backgrounds and those with disabilities. Almost every single member of the housekeeping staff at this location is of Haitian descent and speaks only Creole."

Aric merely nodded. He didn't enlighten the concierge by telling her that he spoke Haitian Creole like a native. The woman who had lived with his family since way before he'd been born had been Haitian by birth and had raised him speaking Creole as well as the Cajun French that he and his family spoke in addition to English. She had been as much his mother as the woman who'd given him life. He missed them both. He missed everyone.

"Will you be cooking in your rooms?" the elderly woman was asking him. "Would you like someone to shop for you and stock your refrigerator and pantry or will you be doing that for yourself?"

He gave her a short list for the first week and asked her where the nearest grocery store was. After she'd given him directions to the market two blocks over, he thanked her and announced that he was heading for bed.

"Sleep well, Mr. Rodrigue," she told him before he departed. "Remember the name of this resort and why you're here. I know we live in a time where just about everything is voice-activated, and this makes it harder to resist the pull of technology. We use our voices to unlock doors, operate lights, appliances, phones, televisions, and computers, etcetera. We at Serenity Resort and Spa want you to make use of the conveniences we all take for granted but hope that our guests put down their phones and computers and shut off the television so that they can truly 'get away from it all' while they're here. Reconnect with your inner self and with others during the periods when you don't have to work. Life is too short not to make the most of it."

"Yes, Ma'am. Thank you, Miss June."

"I never miss anything," he heard her say as he rounded the corner that would lead him to the elevator. He fell asleep with a slight smile on his lips and woke ready to work.

Lucky

After taking care of some necessary company business, Aric went out onto his balcony and watched as the night gave way to morning. He returned to his rooms in time to hear the knock on his door. A tall, middle-aged, thin woman with short, blonde hair was waiting with a portable massage table. He ushered her in and offered to help her set up the padded table, but she declined and brought it out to the balcony.

"It is good to have massage outdoors," she said with what Aric suspected was a Swedish accent. He almost laughed. He'd never had a Swedish massage performed by a Swede before.

"Take off your robe," she commanded.

"I don't have my boxers on underneath."

"Good. That way, you won't have to take them off. One should always have massage in the nude. How else can the masseuse truly do her work?" When Aric hesitated, she ordered, "Strip. No one can see you because of the way your balcony is situated. Do not worry. I will not take advantage of you."

No one takes advantage of me, he thought. *Why should I care about this?*

He was soon lying face-down on the table with a small towel draped over his bare backside. He'd never had a massage outside or in the nude and found it extremely relaxing. He listened to the sounds of the water and the birds and felt the slight breeze. When his masseuse ordered him to turn over, he wished he didn't have to comply. He obeyed, and the towel was moved to his front. She continued her ministrations until she was finished and told him she was stepping inside so that he could simply "be" for a time.

Aric wanted to simply "be" for the rest of the day, but he knew he had meetings to attend and a business to run. With a sigh, he rose and slipped on his robe before going inside to thank the masseuse.

"That was the most enjoyable massage I've ever had," he confided. "Thank you...?"

"Olga."

"Thank you, Olga."

"You have many knots in your muscles. I will work on you each day to help you release them."

"I appreciate that. Let me help you fold up your table and carry it out so I can shower and get ready for the conference today."

"No. You should not disturb the aura of relaxation you attain during your massage. I will see myself out. You enjoy your day. I will be here again tomorrow."

Aric showered, shaved, and dressed before reviewing some business. He was walking toward the elevator by 8:00. As he went down the long hallway, he smiled and nodded to the Haitian housekeepers who were preparing to clean those rooms that had already been vacated. They all smiled and nodded back to him. Assuming he didn't speak Creole, no one spoke to him. That was fine. He might surprise them the next morning by greeting them in their native tongue.

He was almost at the elevator when he saw a stunning young woman with a cleaning cart. She was definitely not Haitian, although she wasn't 100% Caucasian either. The girl had fine features and small bones. Her skin had a light almond color to it, and she had blue eyes and chestnut-colored hair that fell in loose curls past her shoulders. She was the most exotic-looking person he'd ever seen. Aric estimated that she was approximately six inches shorter than he and was perhaps five years younger. Although somewhat underweight, she had a good-sized chest and backside. When he smiled and nodded to her as he passed, she smiled and nodded back, but the smile seemed forced. The woman quickly lowered her head and turned toward the door of the room that she was about to clean. Aric continued on to the elevator.

Something about the woman puzzled him, although he couldn't quite pinpoint what it was. When the elevator doors opened at the main floor, he hesitated before stepping out. He inexplicably wanted to go back to the top floor and talk to the housekeeper. He didn't. Pushing away thoughts of the woman, Aric moved toward the registration table and the work that he knew needed to be done.

Chapter Two

Anticipation was a feeling Aric always enjoyed. On his second morning at the hotel, he left his rooms and slowly made his way down the long hallway. This time, he greeted the housekeepers in Creole as he passed. The looks of delighted shock on their faces were priceless. He was glad his knowledge of their language made them happy.

By the time he'd almost reached the elevator, he spotted the mysterious young woman. She was bending down to get some towels from the bottom of her cart. Aric stopped and studied her nice, round, firm backside. He wanted to speak to her, but all he could do was stare.

"Don't you be scaring her," a gray-haired black housekeeper said quietly in Creole from beside him. "She's fragile, that one. We take care of her."

Aric looked toward the woman and repeated, "Fragile? I don't understand."

"No, and you won't be getting any explanations out of us. Miss Chelsea needs protecting. We all agreed to that, so don't you be hurting her!"

"I wouldn't dream of hurting her or you or anyone else."

"That's not what I mean. She can't take care of herself, yet. She may never be able to. You might hurt her without even realizing it. You keep that in mind."

"But –"

"No but's. You may have more money than I do, but I have more wisdom."

"Yes, Ma'am."

The woman smiled at him and asked, "Who raised you, Boy?"

"Her name was Tante Marie. She was my other mother."

"As most true tantes – or 'aunts' as the English word says – are. You Cajun? Hm. I thought so. I lived in that area for a long time. You mask the accent well, but I can hear it. You ashamed of your roots?"

"Quite the opposite. However, most other corporate businessmen wouldn't take me seriously if I went in speaking like I used to when I was growing up. They'd wrongly think I was some backwards hick, and that wouldn't help my business, would it?"

She sobered and shook her head before saying, "You'll be late for your meetings. Now, you remember what I said about Miss Chelsea."

"Yes, Tante…?"

The older woman grinned and said, "No white boy's called me that for a long time. I didn't realize how much I'd missed it. My name is Fredeline."

"One question before I go, Tante Fredeline. Does Miss Chelsea speak Creole?"

"Creole, French, and English. Now you get on to your work."

She turned and walked back in the direction of her cart. Aric began to walk forward again. When he passed Chelsea's cart, he greeted her in Creole, just as he'd done with the Haitian housekeepers. She looked up at him, the surprise evident in her blue eyes and on her face. She didn't smile. Instead, she seemed slightly fearful.

"I'm sorry," Aric told her in English. "I didn't mean to startle you. I know most white people don't speak Creole, but I was raised speaking it as well as English and Cajun French. Fredeline said you spoke Creole, so I thought I'd greet you like I greeted the others this morning."

He knew the other housekeepers were furtively watching him and prayed that Fredeline wouldn't interfere out of concern for this woman they were all protecting from…what? An abusive boyfriend? Had she witnessed some horrible crime and been emotionally scarred by it?

"Fredeline told you I spoke Creole?"

"Yes."

She glanced down the hall at the older woman then back to him. Aric realized he was holding his breath. He wanted to talk to her, to find out what was so different about her. Frankly, he wanted to touch her. He liked her face, her full breasts, the color of her smooth skin, the shape of her backside, the brown hair, and her blue eyes. Aric hadn't allowed himself to touch any woman since the D Plague and had isolated himself from intimacy with anyone.

"If Fredeline told you that about me, then you must be all right. Did she tell you anything else?"

"She told me not to hurt you."

Chelsea smiled slightly and said, "You can't hurt me. I'm nobody. You can't hurt someone who's nobody."

And with those words, Chelsea opened the door of the room she was to clean and left Aric standing beside her cart in the hallway. He frowned, glanced back at Fredeline, and then proceeded toward the elevator. Once he was downstairs and involved in meetings and discussions, he temporarily suspended his thoughts of Chelsea. It wasn't until his lunch break that he permitted himself to replay their conversation again in his head.

He was walking toward one of the hotel restaurants to meet several other conference attendees when he saw Chelsea standing at a floor-to-ceiling window that faced the grounds and the waters of the bay. She had her palms resting on the glass and was looking wistfully at the view in front of her. As he watched from a distance, she rested her forehead against the glass and closed her eyes for a moment before turning and walking away. He could feel the longing for whatever it was she wanted even from where he stood.

Aric joined some other conference attendees for lunch then went to the afternoon meetings. However, he found it extremely difficult not to think of Chelsea and of what he'd witnessed as she'd looked out through the window. He had to find out what her life had been like and what her present situation was. Perhaps there was something he could do.

The last meeting on the agenda for that day was canceled. Aric hurried back to his rooms and removed his suit; then he donned shorts, a knit shirt, and tennis shoes. He next set out to explore the grounds to hopefully find either Chelsea or Fredeline. As he wandered around the resort, he found neither, but he did manage to relax and enjoy the beauty of the place.

The following morning, after a thirty-minute run on the treadmill in the resort's gym and another wonderful Swedish massage by Olga, Aric showered, shaved, and dressed for the conference. The first thing he saw when he opened his door was Fredeline. She did not look happy. He invited her in. She was quickly standing in his foyer, lecturing him on how he shouldn't have hurt Chelsea.

"How did I hurt her? All I did was talk to her for a minute or two."

"Well, whatever you said made her cry all morning. We had to make sure the guests didn't see her like that. The hotel is very understanding, but the people who run this place wouldn't want their customers to see a staff member crying while the guests are here on vacation. That wouldn't look right."

"Please tell me what is going on with Chelsea. Something's not right with her. Is she mentally ill? Has she been stalked by someone? She seems so...lost."

"It's none of your business," Fredeline insisted. "It's not my place to be talking to you about what she's been through. If she wants you to know, then she'll tell you."

"Will she?"

Fredeline glanced toward the door and said, "I have to get back out in the hall before she notices I'm in here. I don't want her not to trust me or any of us. We're all she's got."

The housekeeper was quickly gone. Aric took a deep breath, held it, and then exhaled. Then he made his walk down the long hallway, greeting the housecleaning staff in Creole as he'd done the previous morning. They replied in kind, but he could feel wariness in them that hadn't been there the day before. When he reached Chelsea, he greeted her in Creole. This time, she replied in Creole and offered him a shy little smile.

Being mindful of the audience of Haitian women watching them, Aric didn't linger. He wished Chelsea a good morning and went downstairs. He was soon entrenched in networking with other heads of corporations, all wanting to do business with his company. His next three hours proved very fruitful and provided him without a spare moment to think of anything save his business and its past, present, and future success.

Not long before the allotted lunch break, Aric was standing in one corner of the resort's Atrium Ballroom, drinking a glass of iced tea and wondering if his afternoon meetings would prove as beneficial as his morning activities. That was when he saw Chelsea step in through one of the large doors that led into the hallway outside the enormous ballroom. She was holding an envelope in both hands and looked utterly terrified. As he watched, she slowly scanned the room, looking up, down, and side to side. She bit her lip and blinked rapidly. She took a step forward then stopped. Looking down, she seemed unable to go any further.

A plausible and likely explanation for Chelsea's abnormal behaviors suddenly presented itself to Aric. He moved swiftly to stand beside her and said her name. When she looked at him, he could see that her eyes were shining with tears. He asked her what was wrong.

"The new manager said I have to give this envelope to the man in the brown suit with the red tie." She indicated a man standing on the other side of the room and said, "He told me it was urgent."

"So, give him the envelope and everything will be fine."

"I can't."

"Why not?"

"Because I don't know where everything is."

"I...see. What if I take the man the envelope or have him come over here to you?"

"I think the new manager's watching on the cameras. I think he's doing this on purpose to get me fired. The other managers know I can't do things like this. He has to know, too. Why is he being mean to me?"

Aric's heart ached for her. She was suffering, and he wanted to make it stop.

"How about if I walk beside you?"

"The manager will see. I can't lose my job. I can't work anywhere else and be without Fredeline and the others." Staring down at the envelope in her hands, she said in a tremulous voice, "I don't know what to do."

"I do. Fredeline trusts me. Will you trust me?"

"I'll try."

Aric nodded thoughtfully and said, "I want you to take my hand and come with me."

She froze and asked softly, "You want to have sex with me? I don't...I don't think I know what to do."

Aric said firmly, "Chelsea, I am not asking you to come with me to have sex. I want you to trust me and take my hand. Then we're going to straighten out whatever is going on with this new manager."

"But I won't know what to say."

"I'll take care of it. You are *not* going to lose your job over this. I guarantee it."

He held out his right hand, and she took it with her left. He asked her to give him the envelope, and she complied. Then he led her to the front desk, identified himself, and requested to speak to the new manager on duty and the head of the hotel. Soon, he and Chelsea were seated in an office with two men: one old and friendly, one middle-aged and arrogant.

The situation was briefly explained to both men by Aric. As he spoke, he could see the smug man lose his confidence and the elderly man grow very stern. Chelsea sat mute beside Aric and appeared nervous and frightened. Once Aric had finished speaking, the older man turned toward the middle-aged man and told him to clear out his desk. He then called for Security to escort the now-former manager from the property.

When the manager was gone from the room, the head of the hotel looked kindly at Chelsea and said apologetically, "I'm sorry he put you through that. It was very wrong of him. No one here ever wants to see you distraught or in danger. I'm grateful to Mr. Rodrigue for assisting you. Believe me when I say that what happened this afternoon will never happen again."

Chelsea kept her head lowered and said softly, "Thank you, sir. I know you say it won't happen again, but what that man did scared me. Would it be all right if I left for the day?"

"Of course. Would you like another employee to drive you home?"

"No, Sir. I only live a couple blocks away. I'm sorry that there was trouble."

"*You* have nothing to be sorry about. We want all of our employees to feel safe and happy here at the resort. Please, let me know if you have any further problems."

"I will. Thank you again."

Once they'd left the man's office, Aric offered, "I'll walk you home. You're upset, and I'd feel more comfortable knowing you made it back to your place safely."

While Chelsea got her purse and left a message for Fredeline, Aric checked in with his office. He then went to the person in charge of the conference and explained that something of the utmost importance had occurred and declared he would be absent that afternoon. He asked that his copy of all materials dispersed be collected for him and sent to his rooms so he could review them later. The woman hastily agreed and assured him that everything would be sent to him at the end of the business day.

14

When Aric stepped out into the August heat with Chelsea, he removed his jacket. He draped it over one arm and asked her which way she lived. She indicated that they needed to cross the street and walk straight. He observed her as they got to the corner. She didn't seem capable of crossing the street.

"Fredeline and her granddaughter walk with me every day to and from work," she explained. "I've never had to cross alone before."

"You're not alone," he reminded her. "Take my hand again, and we'll cross together."

The longer Aric was with Chelsea, the more certain he was that he knew what was wrong with her. He was going to find out that afternoon if he was right, no matter what he had to do to get an answer. If he was correct in his assessment, then Chelsea was being greatly shortchanged by those who were trying their best to help her.

Main Street was populated by little shops owned by artists and florists and by small local restaurants. As they walked, he noticed the market Miss June had told him about when he'd visited the Concierge Desk that first night at Serenity Bay Resort and Spa. Chelsea's apartment was in an old complex located behind the market. Aric noted there were a dozen units in the building. Chelsea's was on the first floor on the far left end.

"Does Fredeline live here, too?" Aric asked.

"She and her granddaughter, Eve Rose, live next door to me."

"How old is Eve Rose?"

"Eighteen. She's a cook in one of the hotel's restaurants. She's a smart girl, but they don't have the money for her to go to college."

"Did you go to college?"

Looking up at Aric, she admitted, "I don't know. I think so."

"I see. May I come in for a little while?"

"You want to have sex with me now?" she asked nervously.

"I only want to talk. I think I can help you, if you'll let me."

"Why do you want to help me?"

"Because I do."

She gave the verbal command to unlock her door and led him inside her apartment. It was very tiny, furnished in a nondescript style, but well-kept. Aric sat on the couch, while Chelsea sat in a chair across from him.

"Do you want to help me so I'll have sex with you? Fredeline said I should be careful about men wanting to do that with me. She convinced me to take the birth control shot in case I had sex by mistake or got raped."

"Have you ever had sex?"

Chelsea looked away and said, "They told me I wasn't a virgin."

"They?"

"The doctors at the hospital."

Unable to restrain himself any longer, Aric asked, "Chelsea, did you suffer a traumatic brain injury?"

She appeared genuinely stunned and asked, "How did you know?"

"I didn't until just now. I started to suspect earlier today."

Chapter Three

"What made you think I's had a traumatic brain injury?" Chelsea asked. "Did you know someone who had a TBI?"

Aric nodded and suggested, "Why don't we both start from the beginning. I can go first if you want."

"That would be good."

"I was born and raised in New Orleans, Louisiana. My family had lots of money because of the oil industry, but neither of my parents wanted to continue in that line of work. Both sold their family's businesses and started a company that would focus on developing cures for illnesses and working on vaccines and things like the birth control shot."

"Were they doctors?"

"My mother was. My father was a businessman. They were a great team and formed a very successful company, which I've been running for the last five years."

"Five years. That's when the D Plague happened."

Aric nodded solemnly and said, "I lost my parents, my grandparents, my older sisters and their families, my aunts and uncles, my cousins, and my Tante Marie. Lots of friends, too."

"Were you planning on taking over your parents' company?"

"No. I'd graduated from Tulane and was supposed to start medical school the week the D Plague hit. I'd dreamed of becoming a neurosurgeon my entire life."

"So, why don't you go on to medical school? You still can."

Aric was not about to tell Chelsea about his miraculous survival of the D Plague and his resultant newfound calling. Instead, he told her an abbreviated version of the truth.

"My parents' company was amazing. They'd been on the verge of releasing the injectable birth control they'd perfected and were working on projects like the cancer-fighting drug that will be released soon. I decided I could save more lives by making certain that everything they'd developed was continued. I found that I had my father's head for business as well as my mother's head for medicine. I've combined the two and have done quite well. I'm glad I took over the company. I feel like I've done a lot of good.

Rodrigue Pharmaceuticals has continued to thrive in spite of the long global recession and then in the aftermath of the D Plague."

Chelsea digested this information before asking, "So, had you just read about TBI patients in college or did you actually know some?"

"Because I'd always been interested in neurology, I'd worked as a volunteer with all sorts of patients as an undergraduate pre-med student. Everyone is different, but lots of TBI patients suffer from similar challenges. I realized today that you were exhibiting some of those difficulties. Will you tell me what happened that caused your traumatic brain injury and what's happened since?"

Chelsea looked soulfully at him and said, "I have retrograde amnesia."

"Complete loss of memory beyond normal forgetfulness. You must have had damage to the hippocampus, the part of your brain that involves memory. That usually comes with an accident involving acceleration and deceleration."

"They tell me I was in a taxi in Orlando when it happened. The taxi was hit by a tanker truck. Both of the drivers died. Firemen pulled me from the burning taxi. I didn't have any broken bones, but I had a closed head injury and was in a coma for a month. When I woke up, I didn't know who I was."

"Your brain got jerked around and was probably injured by the rough areas inside the skull and by the pulling and stretching of the parts that were attached to your brain. Was anything else affected besides your memory?"

"I had trouble speaking and seeing clearly at first, but that got better quickly. My motor skills weren't so good, and I didn't have much strength. They moved me to a rehabilitation facility. I was there for six months. They did lots of tests and physical therapy."

"And what did they tell you?"

"That they suspected I was born around 2010. That I had an above-average I.Q. and was obviously college-educated, although they couldn't tell me in what. They could tell that I wasn't a virgin but that I'd never given birth. They said I had spatial issues and had trouble staying on task. I've gotten a lot better with that last one since I started my job here."

"Why are you working as a housekeeper?"

"I had no identification on me when I got rescued, and no one came forward to claim me. I don't know if it's because everyone in my family died of the D Plague like yours did or if they didn't want me. I don't know my real name, my real birthdate, my background, my education, my work history, or anything else. How can you get a job without a past?"

"You got the job at Serenity."

"Thanks to Fredeline. One of the cleaning women at the rehab facility became friendly with me when she found out I could speak Creole and French as well as English. Of course I don't know why I know how to speak those languages. Did I live in Haiti? Did I have Haitian friends or had I lived in a neighborhood with lots of Haitians?" With a shrug, she continued, "The woman introduced me to Fredeline when they released me from the facility. Fredeline told me I needed taking care of and said she wanted to help me. She said she was going to get me a job where she worked, which was a hotel in Orlando. She did, and we both got transferred here a couple of months ago."

"How'd you get your name?"

"I went through a list of baby names and picked the one I liked best, which was Chelsea."

"And Capra?"

"I heard it somewhere and liked the way Chelsea Capra sounded, so I picked that."

"And your birthdate?"

"I decided on June 8, 2010. The firemen rescued me on June 8, 2033 and the doctors who examined me said they thought I was born in 2010. I had to put something down on my official identification."

The magnitude of Chelsea's predicament was staggering. Aric temporarily pushed aside this thought and asked, "Have you had continual physical therapy since you were released from the rehab center?"

When she shook her head, he asked her to take his hands and squeeze them as hard as she could. She did so. The coordination was there, but the strength was almost nonexistent. He asked her to do several other simple physical tasks. Again, she was well-coordinated but weakened in her extremities.

"So, you've lost declarative memory, which is your autobiographical memory. What about procedural memory? What skills have you retained?"

"I'm really good with computers," she said brightly. "I worked on them a lot at the rehab facility during the second half of my stay there."

It was the first time Aric had seen Chelsea happy and excited, so he asked, "How good are you with computers?"

"Really good."

"Do you have one?"

Her smiled disappeared, and she lowered her head.

"Chelsea, do you manage your own money, or does someone help you?"

She began to cry and confided, "Eve Rose and Fredeline help me. I used to…I know I was beyond this before the accident. I can feel it. I was capable and smart and independent. Now I can't even walk through big, open spaces or cross the street by myself. I can't drive because I might not have the strength or reaction time needed in order to not hit a child if she ran out in the road. I can do complex math, but I can't figure out how much the tip is at a restaurant. I can't afford a Smartphone or computer because of my living expenses and the medication I need."

"What medications are you on?"

"Only one prescription, but it costs so much that it doesn't leave any money for extra things."

"What's it called?"

She told him, and he recognized the medication as an extremely expensive migraine medicine rarely covered by insurance.

"It's the only one that works for me," she explained. "Even then, it doesn't always work."

"Have you taken any antidepressants or anti-anxiety drugs since the accident?"

"No."

"Had any psychological counseling?"

"Not since the rehab facility."

Aric grimaced and said, "It may be 2034, but we still have such a long way to go to provide good healthcare for all. Someone who's been injured like you should have continual physical therapy for at least two years, continual emotional counseling as needed, and should have high expectations placed upon her so that she can regain as much of her past level of achievement as she had before the TBI. It doesn't sound like you're getting much of anything. Do you exercise?"

"Not outside of what I do for work. I'm afraid to do other things. The doctors told me I can't run or ride horses or do anything that might jostle my brain around or cause me to fall. It's very bad for TBI people to fall."

He nodded and withdrew the small, rectangular, black bar that was his computer from his jacket pocket and handed it to Chelsea. He asked her to show him what she could do with it and gave it the verbal command to turn on. The virtual screen appeared, and he ordered the computer to listen to Chelsea's voice then follow any directions she gave it.

For the following hour, Aric watched in amazement as Chelsea performed more complicated tasks using his computer than he ever had. Not only could she utilize it to perform any search on the Internet, she also knew how to manage its operating system and everything related to its functions.

Next, he did the same with his Smartphone, which was the size of an old-fashioned credit card. She proved just as facile with this. She smiled and seemed to exude self-confidence as she worked on the phone and the computer.

Aric excused himself to go to the restroom. He was so moved by Chelsea Capra, her circumstances, and her unmet needs. There was no way he was going to leave her in her current environment. She had clearly been a high-functioning woman and was well aware that she was not truly living, only existing. Her depression was palpable. He wondered why she hadn't already killed herself. Many people in her position would have committed suicide shortly after being released from the rehab center. Fredeline's intervention had probably saved her life.

Chelsea was completely absorbed by something on the computer when Aric returned to the living area of the apartment. He wondered how he should proceed. His cock was hard and ready, and he wanted nothing more than to make love to Chelsea Capra, but he knew that he couldn't. In her current state, he would definitely be taking advantage of her. Fredeline had been correct when she'd said that Chelsea wasn't able to take care of herself. The older woman had been right to insist that the nameless girl with no past take the birth control shot. If someone wanted to simply use Chelsea for sexual gratification, he wouldn't be faced with much opposition.

Chelsea looked up at him and asked, "What are you thinking?"

"I'm trying to figure out the best way to help you, but I'm worried about how to go about things."

"You like me."

"Very much."

"You feel sorry for me."

"Yes."

"You want to have sex with me."

"Yes."

"Why?"

"Because...because you're so unique and beautiful."

"And lonely and depressed like you."

Is it that obvious? Aric wondered. *Can everyone tell or just Chelsea?*

"I think I'd like to have sex with you, if I understood what sex is like. I don't know what it feels like to want anyone in that way. Fredeline says that's what makes me so vulnerable. Eve Rose says I'll remember someday, but I don't know. I haven't remembered anything, and it's been over a year. What if I never remember what it feels like to be normal?"

"If you let me help you, then maybe you can figure it out. Fredeline warned me not to hurt you, but she doesn't have to worry about that. I'd rather die than hurt you."

"Mr. Rodrigue?"

"Aric."

"Aric, I want you to help me. I want to find *me* again, even if I never know who I really was."

"I'll do whatever I can."

"Will you let me help you, too? You're so sad inside."

Aric swallowed the lump in his throat and nodded. He needed Chelsea as much as she needed him. Rising, he declared, "I should go. How about if I meet you here about 8:00 p.m. tomorrow? Maybe by then I'll have worked out a way for us to help each other."

She agreed and reluctantly turned off the computer and phone and handed both back to him. The purchase of such items for her would be first on his list after talking to Fredeline and assuring her that he wasn't out to harm Chelsea. He would work out the rest of the details later.

He stepped out of Chelsea's apartment – just as Fredeline and a young Haitian woman, probably Eve Rose, approached their door. The look the older woman gave him would have made most men turn tail and run. He knew what she must be thinking. He hurriedly assured her that he hadn't done anything improper with Chelsea and asked if he could talk with her about the girl before returning to the resort.

She brusquely introduced him to Eve Rose, who was tall and lanky, and told him to come inside where they could speak privately. He spent the following two hours detailing what he knew, what he thought, and how he wanted to help Chelsea Capra. By the time he left, Fredeline grudgingly admitted he was right but warned him that he needed to keep his desire for Chelsea in check for the present. He concurred and went back to his rooms to mull over his options.

That night, Aric didn't sleep much. He found himself staring up at the mural above his bed, thinking about Chelsea. What would it be like to have no identity? She would have low self-esteem and would wonder if she'd been good or bad, loved or unloved, a success or a failure. She wouldn't remember any details of her childhood, her teenaged years, or her life at college and beyond.

Aric thought of how his own memories of his past had defined the man he now was. What kind of man would he be if he didn't remember his large, loving family, his great times growing up with close friends, the types of food and music he'd always loved, and the culture he so appreciated? It was a frightening prospect to be a person and yet be no one. He realized that Chelsea Capra was living that nightmare every day.

Chapter Four

"You are very tense this morning," Olga chided, as she worked on Aric's shoulder muscles. "You look as though you did not sleep well either."

"I didn't."

"Let your mind go blank while I am here. You will find that you are more refreshed and can solve your problems more easily if you allow yourself to rest."

Aric dozed as Olga worked. At some point, she gently woke him and told him to move onto his back. He obliged, then slept again.

"Wake up, Mr. Rodrigue."

Aric opened his eyes. He felt utterly relaxed and refreshed.

"I sat in the chair here on the balcony and left you to sleep," the masseuse confided. "I did not want you to roll over and off the table, but you seemed to need the rest. I made an executive decision, as one might say. You will be able to shower, dress, and make it to your meetings."

Aric slowly sat up, being mindful not to let the small towel draped across his hips fall. He thanked Olga and asked her if she watched over her other clients as diligently.

"I care about each person as a human being. However, I feel somewhat differently toward you." She smiled when he seemed embarrassed and quickly continued, "No, not like that. It is only that you remind me of my son. He was thirty when he died in the D Plague."

"I'm sorry."

"Thank you. I am sorry as well. He was a great son and a wonderful husband and father."

"Did his wife and children live?"

"His wife. We have not spoken in several years. It is too painful."

He nodded and accepted the robe she handed him. He listened as she left his rooms while he prepared to shower. When he opened the door to leave for the morning meetings, Fredeline was waiting for him. She held a miniscule flash drive out to him.

"All Miss Chelsea's medical records," she said, by way of explanation. "She has her own copy, but I have the back-up. She asked me to give it to you. She's very protective of the one the doctors gave her."

"Thank you. How is she today?"

"Better and worse. You've given her hope, but you've also reminded her of how her life is now and of what it might have been like before."

"She needs to develop her new sense of self and new compensating strategies. She's got to have one-on-one therapy and attention in order to rebuild her life and learn how to function on her own as much as possible."

"You're going to take her away from us, aren't you?"

"That's up to you."

"Me? What do you mean?"

"Would you step inside for a minute?"

Fredeline glanced down the hall then came into Aric's foyer.

"I do want to take Chelsea out of here when my stay at Serenity is over in two and a half weeks. I want to take her back to New Orleans and totally revamp my approach to my work and everything else I do. Meeting Chelsea has made me realize how much *I* need to change my own life."

"And how do your plans involve me?"

"They involve you and Eve Rose. Being the victim of a traumatic brain injury, any change in Chelsea's routine is going to be difficult at first. She'll be in a new place with no old routine and no one she knows. I wouldn't feel comfortable leaving her alone yet while I was working or out."

"You want me and Eve Rose to come with you," she said quietly.

"Yes. You've taken great care of Chelsea since she was released from the rehabilitation facility. She's extremely dependent on you and Eve Rose and feels comfortable with you."

"What would we do?"

"In the beginning, I'd want you to watch over Chelsea and run the house."

"And Eve Rose?"

"Chelsea says she's a great cook. I was thinking she could cook when she's not in class."

25

"Class?"

"Chelsea says Eve Rose wants to go to college."

"We can't afford college."

"You could if you lived in my house and got paid good wages. You wouldn't have to pay rent or buy food or anything else other than what you wanted or needed."

"What about Miss Chelsea's medicine?"

"What about it?"

"We help her pay for it, but don't tell her. Since Eve Rose does her banking for her, she doesn't realize that we've been paying for some of the cost of the migraine pills. She can't afford them on her own."

"So that's why Eve Rose can't go to college? All of your extra money goes toward Chelsea's prescription?"

She nodded and said, "Eve Rose and I talked about it and decided that helping a human being in dire need was much more important than college. How can you compare the real suffering of one lost soul to going to school?"

"You're amazing, Fredeline."

"Just trying to be a good person and teach my granddaughter to do the same. I'd hope someone would do as much for me."

"Think about my offer," Aric told her. "I miss my Tante Marie. I'd like to have another Tante in the house."

"I could never replace your Tante Marie."

"I wouldn't expect you to, but it would make me happy to have Tante Fredeline in my house."

She left, and Aric quickly downloaded the medical information onto his computer before locking the tiny flash drive in his room safe and stepping out into the hall. He greeted the housekeepers in Creole as he passed, and they all gave him enthusiastic greetings in return. When he greeted Chelsea, she smiled broadly at him, and he could tell that her smile was genuine. She did look tired though.

"Is it still all right if I come to your apartment at 8:00 tonight?" he asked tentatively. "I don't think I can get there any earlier."

"I'd like that. I've been storyboarding to get ready."

"Storyboarding?"

"You picture what's going to happen so you can be ready. One of the therapists at the rehab center taught me how to do it. That way, if I know in advance that I have to alter my routine, I won't get so anxious."

"What do you normally do at 8:00? I could come a little later if that would be better."

"I read from 8:00 to 9:00."

"So, are you okay with not reading tonight?"

"I'm going to read while I eat my dinner at 6:00. If I do that, then I can still have time to read. I think it will work fine. I'll just have to remind myself to take a bite every few pages. I want to try it."

"What are you having for dinner?"

"A prepackaged meal. That's what I have every night on Mondays through Fridays. On the weekends, I eat with Fredeline and Eve Rose."

Curious, Aric asked, "Do you have the same prepackaged meal every night?"

"No. Monday is pizza. Tuesday is pasta. Wednesday I have something Asian. Thursday is poultry and vegetables. Friday is hot dip with pita bread."

"So, you eat different variations on those same dishes on those particular nights?"

"Yes. Today is Wednesday, so I'm having garlic chicken spring rolls."

He smiled and said, "Enjoy them and your reading. I'll see you at 8:00. I'm going to bring something with me that I think will make you happy." When she looked uncertain, he said, "You agreed to trust me, remember?"

"I'm kind of nervous, but I think it's good. It's not normal to be so focused on routine."

"It's normal for TBI victims."

Lifting a bundle of sheets from her cart, she said, "I don't like it."

"Me neither. We're going to work on that. Have a good day."

She smiled and wished him the same before turning away from him.

The day flew by without any break for Aric. It was immensely rewarding professionally, and the program he presented was enthusiastically received by the other businesspeople. He was thrilled and agreed to join several of them for a working dinner immediately following the last presentation of the day. That was also productive.

He returned to his rooms at 7:00, removed his suit, and put on shorts and a casual shirt. He had less than an hour to scan the complicated medical records of Patient #6.8.33.

The date she was rescued, Aric thought. *They couldn't even give her a name.*

The alarm on his Smartphone chimed when it was 7:30. He'd only had time to finish reading the summary of Chelsea's extensive medical files. Sighing, he shut off the computer and went down to the Concierge Desk. Miss June was waiting for him.

"Do you have them?" he asked her with anticipation.

"Just like you asked for," she replied sweetly. As she handed him a deep blue bag that held two small boxes, she said, "You let me know if you need anything else. I'm a resourceful woman."

"Obviously. Thank you so much, Miss June."

"It was my pleasure, Mr. Rodrigue. It was actually one of the easiest tasks requested of me in the last twenty-four hours. You have a good evening now."

"You, too."

Aric left the resort and walked down the street to Chelsea's apartment. He knocked on the door and waited. There was no response. He checked the time and found that it was 7:57. Since Chelsea was dependent on routine, he wondered if perhaps she wouldn't open the door until the precise time he'd specified. He leaned his back against the wall, waited until 8:00, and knocked again. There was still no answer.

Concerned, he tried the door handle and opened the door without resistance from a lock or chain. He was suddenly angry. Didn't Chelsea realize it was unsafe to leave her door unlocked? Someone could come in and hurt her.

It was locked when you walked her home yesterday, he reminded himself and hurried inside.

The curtains were closed, and the apartment was dark. Aric shut the door behind him, locked it, then turned on the lamp he'd seen on an end table. He scanned the room. Nothing seemed out of place. There were no bloodstains on the floor or signs of a scuffle. The living room and kitchen area were deserted. He moved toward what he assumed was Chelsea's bedroom and flipped on the overhead light. The full-sized bed was neatly made but empty. That only left one place to look before he went to Fredeline's apartment to see if she knew where Chelsea was.

When Aric turned on the light in the bathroom, he heard Chelsea cry out and caught a glimpse of her lying on the floor near the sink. She was barefoot but still wore her hotel uniform and was curled in a tight ball. Her back was to him. A part of him wondered if she'd been attacked or had fallen, but he sensed the true reason behind what was happening. He dimmed the light until it gave off a soft glow that allowed him to see but was not bright. Then he went to kneel behind Chelsea, who moaned softly. He said her name.

"Aric? I'm so sorry. I wanted tonight to be nice."

"When did the migraine start?"

"My head hurt a little all day, but it didn't get bad until about an hour before I left work. I took a pill right away – once I felt it coming on, but it didn't do anything. I took another one a while ago, but it hasn't helped. I need another pill."

Aric, who was well-versed in the world of pharmaceuticals because of his background and business, told her, "No." She whimpered and pleaded for him to give her a pill. He refused.

"But sometimes if it's not working and I take more, it eventually works," she insisted. "Please."

"Chelsea, that kind of medication is very strong and can be dangerous. You're only supposed to take one pill every eight hours. You've already had two in less than four hours, and you're asking me to give you another one? You could die."

"I've done it before. I haven't died." Wrapping her arms around her head, she said, "Maybe I should take them all. They should've let me die in that taxi. It would have been more merciful than leaving me like this. Someone should take me out and shoot me like a dog that needs to be put down."

Aric clenched his jaw and reminded himself that Chelsea was in terrible pain and was already in a precarious physical and emotional state. If he'd been in her shoes, he might be saying the same thing. Being angry with her for wanting a permanent end to her suffering would not help things.

"Has anything else worked in the past besides or in addition to the medication?"

"No bright light. If I'm strong enough, I crawl to the bathtub and get in. Then I take a rag and make it hot and put it on the back of my neck and wet another rag and make it cool and put it on my forehead. I keep doing that, and sometimes it helps."

"Do you ever fill the tub while you're in there fighting a migraine?"

"No. They told me I might have a seizure because of my brain injury and could drown."

"They were right. I'm glad you never tried that."

"Aric, will you please give me another pill?" she asked softly.

"No, but I will help you with the wet rag treatment you've used in the past. Do you *want* to be in the tub?"

"No. It's really uncomfortable to lie in there. I only do that because I can't keep getting up and down to wet the rags, and I get all wet because of the water."

"Why don't you call Fredeline or Eve Rose to help you?"

"They've offered, but I tell them I'd rather be alone when it happens so they don't feel bad and come over anyway. They do so much for me already."

Aric rose and rummaged around until he found a facecloth and a hand towel. He ran hot water from the faucet and soaked the hand towel then wrung it out. He folded it, lifted Chelsea's brown hair, and laid the towel across the back and side of her neck. She made a little noise, but Aric couldn't tell if it was one of relief or pain. He ran the rag under the cool water and crouched in front of Chelsea then gently wiped her face with it before laying it across her forehead.

"How often do you have migraines like these?"

"I get about two migraines a week, but I take the medicine and they don't usually get bad. I only have ones like these about once a month. I had them a lot more in the beginning."

"If I touch your skin or hair, will it make the pain worse?"

"I don't know. Nobody's ever touched me except at the hospital or during physical therapy. Well, Fredeline and Eve Rose hug me sometimes, but it's not while I'm having a migraine. Why?"

"Because studies have proven that skin-to-skin contact helps babies and young children who are in pain to relax. Other studies suggest the same is true for adults."

"But what if you touch me and it makes you want to have sex with me?"

He smiled down at her and said, "I already do, but I told you I won't unless we both think you're ready. I'm only trying to figure out what might make you feel better. How about if we try it?"

He stroked her hair and cheeks. She declared after a while that there was a slight lessening in her pain level, although it wasn't much. He rewet the rag and towel and replaced them on her neck and forehead. This cycle was repeated for the next hour, and Chelsea reported gradual improvement. Eventually, she slept.

Aric wondered what he should do. He didn't want to disturb Chelsea by moving her, but he didn't want to leave her lying on the hard tile either. He decided to let her stay where she was for a while, sat beside her, and switched on his computer. He was soon engrossed in Patient #6.8.33's files.

Chapter Five

Chelsea's files were fascinating. There was no way that she should have survived the crash between the tanker truck and the taxi she'd been riding in that early June evening. There had been an explosion, and both drivers had died upon impact. The unconscious survivor had been pulled from the wreckage with multiple contusions, abrasions, and a bruised brain. However, she had miraculously been spared broken bones and burns.

It was noted by one of the examining physicians that she suspected the patient might have been sexually assaulted. Someone had utilized a rape kit on the unconscious woman. Seminal fluid was retrieved but didn't match anyone listed in the national database of sexual offenders. There was no way to confirm or deny the supposition that the patient had been raped since she was in a coma. Aric did not click on the related links in this section.

Comatose for thirty-three days, the patient had awakened with retrograde amnesia and significant motor, speech, and vision problems. The amnesia seemed permanent, although the verbal and most of the visual issues had dissipated over the following two months. The motor skills had been refined at a slower pace, but the patient had been determined and hard-working, regaining control, if not notable gains, in strength.

While at the rehabilitation facility, she'd been given intensive speech and physical therapy and an array of intellectual and emotional tests. The results of these had led the doctors to conclude that Patient #6.8.33 was approximately twenty-three years old, had an I.Q. above 130, was probably a college graduate, and had been in good physical condition before the accident. The woman was not a virgin but had never delivered a child vaginally or via C-section. She had a strong will but suffered from the all-too-common resultant anxiety and depression that haunted those afflicted with traumatic brain injuries. She continued to have spatial issues, needed frequent reminders to stay on task, and required a set routine in order to function in any setting.

Six months after she'd regained consciousness, the prognosis for the patient was both positive and negative. With supports in place, she was expected to lead a productive life, although the professionals were unwilling to offer any specific outcomes. Aric wasn't surprised by this. No physician or social worker was going to commit to an absolute when it came to any closed-head-injury patient's recovery. He also wasn't surprised to read that there was not much optimism regarding the return of the patient's memories.

Many TBI patients had memory issues, although very few suffered from complete memory loss like Patient #6.8.33. The psychiatric evaluators considered Chelsea's loss of memory regarding the accident to be a blessing but were concerned about her long-term mental stability if she had no sense of self. The lack of knowledge regarding family background and ethnicity was also noted as a detriment. It was recommended that the patient be placed in a group home of some sort to give her a sense of belonging. A social worker would be charged with assisting her to get necessary identification papers and other documentation for government insurance. This social worker should connect her with someone to help her find a place to live, employment, and to make certain she had a job coach or a life coach.

So, what the heck happened? Aric wondered. *How did so many people drop the ball? They simply sent her out into the world without real supports, continued counseling and physical therapy, and appropriate procedural skills. She should have been placed in a business where she could work on computers and bolster the low self-esteem that came with having no identity.*

Aric turned off his computer and got stiffly to his feet. It was 5:30 a.m. He left the bathroom and went into the living room to call the resort in order to get a message to Olga and let her know that he would not be having his morning massage. He asked that she call his personal number in order to reschedule for later in the day, if possible.

Next, he phoned the conference organizer and apologized for his early call and for not being able to attend the programs scheduled for that day. As he'd done two days earlier, he told her something urgent had come up and requested that his copies of all materials from the meetings that he would be forced to miss be sent to his rooms. The woman assured him he would be sorely missed and hoped he would be able to attend the last day's meetings on Friday.

Aric rummaged around in the kitchen cabinets and found a box of granola bars. After eating two and drinking a glass of soy milk, he searched Chelsea's apartment for her phone. He wanted to call Fredeline and tell her that Chelsea had been very sick and wouldn't be in to work that day. He couldn't find the phone and didn't know Fredeline's number. So, he quietly left the apartment, closed the door without locking it, went next door, and knocked softly.

"Who is it?" he heard Eve Rose ask nervously.

"Aric Rodrigue."

The door was quickly opened, and Eve Rose and Fredeline stood just inside. They were already dressed in their hotel uniforms.

"What are you doing here?" Fredeline asked suspiciously. "You spend the night?"

"I went to Chelsea's last night to talk and found her on the floor in the bathroom crippled by a migraine. I did what I could to help her, then sat beside her while she slept. I read her medical files all night. She's still sleeping on the floor. I'm going to put her in bed, and then I'll sleep on the couch. She won't be at work today. I was going to call you, but I couldn't find her phone."

"She doesn't have one."

"What?"

"She can't afford it. Neither can we."

"How does the hotel get in touch with you if they need to?"

"One of our friends upstairs has a phone. They call her if they need to reach the rest of us."

Aric shook his head in disbelief. It was difficult for him to accept that there were working men and women in the modern age who couldn't afford to have *some* type of phone available to them.

"Did Miss Chelsea take too much medicine?" Eve rose asked. "I know she takes more than she's supposed to, but she says it doesn't work for her any other way when the migraines are really bad."

"Yes, she'd already taken too much, but I stopped her from taking more. There has to be an alternative. I work in pharmaceuticals. We'll figure it out."

"What if there is nothing?" Fredeline asked. "What if nothing really works on her?"

"I won't accept that. My people will start working on developing something if that's the case. She can't be the only person out there who doesn't respond to normal treatments."

"Were the medical records helpful?" asked the younger Haitian woman.

"Very. They were also very frustrating. I have other questions I need answered. I'll work on those today."

Fredeline looked Aric up and down and asked, "Have you always been like this?"

"Like what?" he asked blankly.

"A control freak," Eve Rose said frankly, to which her grandmother swatted her playfully on the arm.

"I guess I am sort of a control freak," Aric admitted. "I don't think I was as bad about it before the D Plague."

"We were all changed by the D Plague," Fredeline remarked. The older woman smiled at him and said, "You go back to Miss Chelsea and take care of her. We'll check on the both of you after work."

Aric returned to Chelsea's apartment and went to the bathroom. She remained asleep on the floor, facing the sink. After relieving his bladder, walking around her, and washing his hands, Aric crouched beside the sleeping woman. He needed to put her to bed, but he hated to leave her in the black pants and blue shirt that she'd slept in and worn the previous day. However, he was concerned if he undressed her that he wouldn't be able to stop himself from becoming aroused.

It had been five years since Aric had had sex with any woman, and there had been no other woman who'd stimulated and intrigued him as Chelsea Capra did. Before the D Plague, he'd been sexually involved with various women, although he'd never engaged in a "one-night stand" with anyone. That wasn't his style. If he was going to be intimate with someone, then he wanted to *know* her, to *respect* her, and to *appreciate* her.

He walked next door for a second time and got Fredeline and Eve Rose to help Chelsea. Olga returned his earlier call, and he stepped outside to talk with her and then called the Orlando hospital and rehab facility listed on Chelsea's records. He also checked in with his administrative assistant and told her he was going to switch off his phone for a while and would call her later.

When he returned to the apartment, Fredeline informed him that Chelsea was now clean, wearing pajamas, had brushed her teeth, and was asleep in her bed. Aric thanked the two women as they hurried off to work. He then removed his shoes, switched off his phone and placed it on the coffee table next to the blue bag he'd brought with him the previous night, and stretched out on the uncomfortable couch. He was instantly asleep.

When Aric woke, Chelsea was still in her pajamas but was sitting in the chair across from him. She was eating Ramen noodles from a small container. Her feet were tucked beneath her, and her brown hair was pulled back into a ponytail. He could easily see her nipples through the fabric of the snug cotton pajama top and wondered how much longer he could suppress his baser instincts.

He felt her stare before he lifted his eyes to look at her face. She was smiling slightly. He smiled back and asked her what time it was.

"2:49. I slept a long time. How long did you sleep?"

"Seven hours or so. I guess we both needed the rest." Sitting up, he rubbed the sleep from his eyes and informed her, "I read parts of your medical files while you slept last night and made a few calls to your doctors this morning. It was early, so I had to leave messages. I switched off my phone for once so it wouldn't wake either of us. I guess I should turn it on and see if anyone's called me back."

"I have a question before you do."

"Sure."

"What's in the bag? Is it the surprise you told me you were bringing me?"

"It is. Do you want it now or later?"

"Now," she said excitedly. "You said I'd like it. I want to see." Grinning, she added, "I think this is what it…what I used to feel like before the accident when I was waiting for something good to happen. It feels so nice."

"Any memories to go along with that remembered feeling?"

She shook her head but remained smiling and told him she was simply happy to be feeling something other than sadness or loneliness. She placed the empty bowl with the spoon resting inside of it on the coffee table and sat forward in the chair. Aric wondered if that was how she had waited for presents as a child.

A thought struck him that gave him pause. When children went missing, the Federal Bureau of Investigation often used computer programs to "age" their faces in photographs so that people might recognize the lost little ones and find them years after they'd been abducted. Was there a reverse program that could show what someone had looked like earlier in her life? That might open many doors for finding out something about Chelsea's past.

"Aric, may I please have my surprise?"

Pulling himself back to the present moment, he withdrew the two small boxes from the bag. Chelsea literally squealed with delight. She was ecstatic.

"Oh, Aric! A computer! And a Smartphone! And they're really good ones! Oh, my gosh!" Sobering, she said, "But I can't afford the data plans."

"You don't have to."

"But everyone has to pay for service."

"I want to talk to you about what I'd like regarding you, me, and the future and see if you'd like the same thing. Even if you don't, I'll still pay for your plans. I'm going to get a computer and phones for Tante Fredeline and Eve Rose, too. You all need them. It would make me very happy to know that I could do this for all of you."

She nodded thoughtfully and asked, "What about the rest? What do you want?"

"I want you, Fredeline, and Eve Rose to come back to New Orleans with me and live in my house. I'd like for you to work on getting stronger and figuring out who you are." When she opened her mouth to object, he raised a hand and said, "I don't mean who you *were*. I personally don't think you'll ever know that. You have to decide who you *are*. You have to be comfortable with that and know yourself. Otherwise, you're going to either have no self-image or someone else's image of what you should be. Either of those is wrong. You can literally reinvent yourself."

"When I woke up from my coma, everyone told me how lucky I was to have survived, how lucky I was not to have been hurt worse, and how lucky I was to be cared for by such great doctors. I didn't feel lucky at all. I hurt so much, and I couldn't move, speak, or see properly. I didn't have any memories of my own life, although I knew history from prehistoric times to the day before the accident. Really lucky." A tear slid down one cheek, but she smiled and said, "Maybe I was lucky. Maybe I was a horrible person no one loved, who hated her job and got beaten up by her boyfriend all the time.

Perhaps the accident gave me a fresh start. I had to be saved for some reason, right?"

"Right. Will you come with me to New Orleans?"

"I'll go with you on one condition."

"Just one?" he asked, raising a dark brow.

"Okay, more than one. I want you to see if you can love me, to have sex with me, and to take care of me. I won't go with you unless you let me do the same for you. I know what's wrong with me, but I don't know what's wrong with you. There's something that sets you apart, and it's good and bad. You're burdened with something, and you're so alone."

Unable to speak, Aric merely nodded. He desperately needed her, just as she desperately needed him. Chelsea looked as if she wanted to put her arms around him, and Aric wanted her to do exactly that. Instead, he suggested she set up her new computer and phone while he checked his messages. When he did, his blood ran cold in his veins.

Chapter Six

Later that Thursday night, Aric sat on his balcony staring out at the bay and told himself he'd had no choice but to lie to Chelsea, Fredeline, and Eve Rose earlier that evening. He'd told them he'd had no return messages from the hospital or rehab center. As he watched the sun set, he weighed his options in light of the information he'd actually received when he'd listened to the five disturbing voicemails.

All of Patient #6.8.33's records had "accidentally" been deleted from the hospital and rehabilitation facility's databases. Somehow, the back-ups had also disappeared. Chelsea's neurologists from the hospital had been killed in a small plane crash on their way to a conference eight months after her accident. The psychiatrist who'd overseen her psychological care had perished in a one-car crash a week after the plane incident. The doctor in charge of coordinating her physical therapy had overdosed on a prescription painkiller two weeks after that. Aric wondered if other people involved in Chelsea's care had died under suspicious circumstances. When he'd tried to reach the social worker, he was informed he'd disappeared while jogging six weeks after Chelsea had been released from the rehab center. Aric hadn't made any more calls.

Why? he wondered. *Why kill all those people if someone was really after Chelsea? Why not simply allow her to die in the hospital or kill her? Obviously, someone wants her alive. Who? What is his or her motive? Is Chelsea in danger even now?* Recalling their earlier conversation, he thought, *Chelsea certainly has me pegged. She makes me remember what it's like to really live. Perhaps that's why I'm so driven to bring her, Fredeline, and Eve Rose home with me. I can't take the isolation for another day. Plus, Chelsea is more beautiful and, seemingly innocent, than any other woman I've ever met. She's sure as hell got me under her spell. She's an enigma.*

Olga arrived for Aric's rescheduled massage at 7:00. As she worked on his knotted muscles, she scolded him for being so tense. When he didn't comment, she asked what was bothering him.

"I can't tell you. It's very serious and...complicated."

"Is there no one you can tell?" she asked, as she worked on his back.

"There is someone, but I don't want to get her involved. I trust her implicitly, but she has the weight of the world on her shoulders already."

"You should not rule this person out," Olga instructed him. "She may prove to be invaluable to you in solving this problem."

He considered this as she moved her hands to his left arm.

"How did you break this arm?" she inquired suddenly.

He lifted his head and asked, "How did you know that I broke that arm? It happened when I was in high school."

"In Sweden, I was a physical therapist for eighteen years. I can recognize when a person has had certain injuries."

"Why aren't you practicing physical therapy here?"

"I am over fifty years old. I did not want to have to go back to school and through the entire process involved in order to practice physical therapy in the United States. It was much quicker and easier to get my license as a massage therapist. I am still helping people to heal their bodies and minds but in a different way." As she urged him to lower his head back on the head rest, she asked again, "How did you break your left arm?"

"I used to work with my grandfather during the summers. He liked to buy old houses and fix them up then sell them. When I was sixteen, I was working on a house with him when the scaffold I was standing on gave way. They later told us it was a defective part that caused the collapse. My arm was broken in three places, and the doctor had to put in some pins. I did have physical therapy on it and regained my full range of motion. I'm impressed that you can tell it was broken."

"It is my job to know the human body and how it works."

An idea began to take shape in Aric's mind, and he thought wryly, *The owners of the resort are going to hate me.*

"Olga, how long have you been here at Serenity?"

"A few months."

"Do you like it?"

"It is a beautiful place to be, but I do not like the transient nature of my job. I would prefer a more stationary setting where clients came to me at one location and I had regular hours."

Chagrined, Aric apologized for asking her to provide her services so early in the morning and then later in the evening. She told him not to worry about it, that she had known when she'd accepted the position that wealthy clients did not always keep typical schedules. She was merely pleased to have a good job in a warm climate.

"I may be a Swede, but I have never liked the cold," she confided.

"What if you could remain in a warm climate but in one location with regular hours?"

"I would like that very much, although I would not do it if I had to leave the United States. I like it here." Realizing that he was offering her a job, she paused then asked, "Where? When?"

"New Orleans. When I leave in a couple of weeks."

"You wish for me to become your personal masseuse?"

"I want you to provide massage and physical therapy in my house."

"But I am not licensed as a physical therapist in the United States, and your arm is not truly in need of physical therapy."

"I'm not concerned about the licensing. You're a fabulous masseuse, and I'm confident you'll be an excellent physical therapist. The P.T. isn't for me."

"Please explain."

"Only if I can tell you in confidence."

"I am a masseuse. I am used to keeping things in confidence. It is sometimes like being a psychologist. People often share their secrets during their sessions."

Aric explained about his plans to take Chelsea, Fredeline, and Eve Rose back to Louisiana with him and Chelsea's unusual situation. He left out the parts regarding the missing records and deceased health care professionals. Aric asked Olga not to tell the hotel managers anything he'd shared with her, since Chelsea, Fredeline, and Eve Rose would not be turning in their two week notices until the end of the next day.

"I will not tell anyone," she promised. "So, you wish for me to provide you and the others with massage and to give Miss Capra physical therapy on a daily basis."

"Yes."

"Am I to live in the house with you and the others?"

"If you like. It's a huge house with plenty of bedrooms and bathrooms. If you don't want to live there, then I'll understand."

"Who lives there now?"

"No one has lived in it since the D Plague."

"Who lived there before?"

"When I was growing up, my entire family lived together."

"And that included…?"

"My parents, both sets of grandparents, and my older sisters."

"How many sisters?

Aric squeezed his eyes tightly shut in an attempt to hold back the tears and said, "Eight."

Olga stopped her massage and murmured, "Eight. All dead in the D Plague?"

"Everyone in my family, except for me. My sisters had already moved out of the house by that time, and most of them had married and had kids. All of their husbands and my nieces and nephews died during the D Plague, too. My oldest sister was eight months pregnant with her fourth child when…."

Aric couldn't finish his sentence. He usually worked very diligently at *not* thinking about his loved ones suffering as only he knew they had and then dying in the throes of agony and turning to dust. It made his own survival much more difficult to accept and caused him enormous guilt. He preferred to focus on the here and now and what he could do to help others.

Olga laid a hand on the back of his head and said softly, "I will come with you and live in the house, at least in the beginning. When Miss Capra has these migraines you spoke of, I may be able to alleviate some of her discomfort through massage." Withdrawing her hand and beginning to knead the muscles of his left calf, she asked, "Do you think it is wise to return to your previous home? Would it not make you too sad?"

"That's why I haven't gone back in five years. I don't know if I can live there again, but I want to try it. It was such a happy place until 2029. There was so much love and so many good times there. It would be a shame for it to stay empty with all that forgotten. Maybe if I go back and I'm not by myself, it could be a happy place again."

"And if you cannot live there?"

"I'll buy another house. My apartment is functional but for only one or two people."

"Mr. Rodrigue?"

"Aric."

"No," she said firmly. "Mr. Rodrigue as long as we are here. Even after that, you will be my employer. I do not believe in calling one's employer by his first name only."

"Mr. Aric then?"

"I could live with that. I do not comprehend your motives. I understand your wish to help Miss Capra and the rest of us, but you have only been here for four days and already the four of us are going to move with you to your house. Is this something you do often?"

"Never. I've been very alone since 2029. I've helped a lot of people but in a rather impersonal way. Chelsea made me look at life in a whole new light."

"Are you doing all of this just because you want her?"

"No, although I do want her. However, if that was all I wanted, then I could have had her here and moved on or taken her out without you, Fredeline, and Eve Rose. She's very helpless in certain ways, but she's an adult. I could have easily taken her to bed and gotten her to leave with me and do whatever I wanted."

"Why didn't you?"

"Because I'd like to think I'm a better man than that. I wouldn't be able to live with myself if I took advantage of her."

"Your parents and grandparents did a good job of raising you," Olga told him. "You are a good man, but you do confound me at times."

She finished her massage and told him she would turn in her notice the following Monday so that the hotel staff wouldn't be suspicious and become unhappy with Mr. Aric Rodrigue.

"One must always keep good relationships with those in business," Olga declared. "I would not want to cause future problems for you or for me by my departure from the hotel. I may need them as a reference one day."

"Very smart move."

"My son's father was a great businessman. I learned quite a lot from him during the years we were together."

"How long were you married?"

"We weren't. I was his mistress."

His look of shock must have shown on his face. Olga smiled and patted him on the shoulder before handing him his robe and leaving him alone on the balcony. Once she'd departed, Aric worked on company business until midnight. Then he went to bed and slept, waking at 6:00 to Olga's knock on the door.

"I overslept," he explained. "I never oversleep."

"It is not a terrible thing to oversleep."

"It is for me. I'll have to forego my exercise and the massage this morning if I'm going to finish the things I was working on last night and make it to my meetings today."

"You had your massage late," she reminded him. "Would you like for me to come tonight again as I did last night?"

"I have a better idea. If I give you the address, would you meet me at Chelsea's apartment at 8:00 p.m.? If you're going to come to New Orleans with us, then it would probably be good to make sure everyone gets along."

"I would be happy to come. What is her address?"

Aric was running late when he left his rooms that morning. He offered the housekeepers his now-customary Creole greetings to each of them as he made the long walk toward the elevators. They were all cheerful and told him to have a nice day. Fredeline gave him a huge grin and confided that Chelsea had been so excited with her new "toys" that she hadn't wanted to go to sleep. She'd had to be told she must if she was to work the following morning.

"She was like a little girl," the older Haitian woman said enthusiastically. "I've never seen her like that. It was a good thing."

Aric noted the bounce in Chelsea's step as he approached her. She looked toward him, radiating happiness and something else Aric had never before seen in her: self-confidence.

She thanked him again for the computer and phone but did so quietly. She told him Fredeline had instructed her not to tell anyone else at the hotel about anything that had happened over the past two days. She confided they were going to turn in their notice to the hotel at the end of the day and say they had other jobs.

"You do," he told her. "Your job is to get stronger and work on your sense of self, remember? Fredeline and Eve Rose will work at the house, and Eve Rose will go to college. Someone else will be living with us, too."

"Who?"

"You'll meet her tonight. I asked her to come by your apartment at 8:00 so she could visit with the three of you and make sure it was what you all wanted."

44

"I can't wait to meet her. Can I tell Fredeline?"

"Yes, but no one else except her and Eve Rose." Glancing toward the elevator, Aric said, "I have to go or I'll be late."

"I'll see you tonight then."

He nodded and told her to have a good day before heading downstairs. The last day of meetings and networking went well, and Aric was glad he'd been able to attend. Forced to take care of his own company business in-between meetings and afterward, Aric didn't have time to change into casual clothing before heading to Chelsea's place. Fredeline was waiting for him in front of the grocery store.

"Miss Chelsea wanted to cook a meal for you," she said with a slight shake of the head. "It didn't go too well, and she came over to our apartment in tears. I don't quite know what she did wrong. She had a recipe, but I guess maybe she skipped a step or two. Whatever it was ruined the dish. I've never seen the child cry so hard. We calmed her down, and Eve Rose brought her here to the store and got the same ingredients then went home with her to help her cook. I'm sure it will taste fine, but Miss Chelsea was awfully shaken by what happened. I think she was feeling real fine and thought she was...."

"Normal," Aric offered.

Fredeline nodded somberly and said, "It made her feel so bad to realize she wasn't doing as well as she'd thought."

"It can be very difficult for TBI patients to follow a list or a recipe. I think it'll get easier for Chelsea as time passes. She's already made great strides in her recovery. Relatively speaking, it's still pretty early in the healing process."

"I can tell you want Miss Chelsea real bad. Remember what I said and don't you go hurting her."

"I'm doing everything I can to *help* her, not *hurt* her."

"I know. I just worry. You are a man after all."

Chapter Seven

When Aric and Fredeline entered Chelsea's apartment, it smelled like garlic bread and some sort of pasta dish. Aric's stomach growled loudly, and everyone in the room laughed, except Chelsea. She excused herself and went into the bedroom and shut the door.

"You go talk to her," Fredeline told him. "Eve Rose and I will set the table for us and for this other woman you've got coming." Chuckling, she said, "Soon, you'll have the whole hotel moving to New Orleans to your house!"

"Oh. I forgot to ask how it went when you all turned in your two weeks' notice today."

"Fine. The manager said he'd be sorry to lose us, but there are plenty of others who are on a waiting list to come work at Serenity. It won't be hard to find replacements."

Relieved, Aric knocked lightly on the bedroom door. When Chelsea didn't answer, he slowly turned the knob and entered. She was sitting on the edge of her bed with tears streaming down her cheeks. He shut the door and went to sit beside her.

"I wanted to cook a meal all by myself," she explained. "I was feeling so good and so in control. I thought I could do it. It was terrible, and I don't know what I did wrong. I can't even follow a recipe!"

"That's not unusual for people who've had brain injuries. You'll get there. It may just take you a little longer."

"But I can do anything on the computer and can read all sorts of books and do complicated things. Why won't my brain let me do these simple activities?"

"Your brain is retraining itself to do certain functions because it got damaged during the accident. We're all going to help you. I have faith that you'll get most of what you lost back."

"Except my memories."

"They might come back."

"You said yesterday that you didn't think so. Why not?"

"The way your brain was hurt and what's happened since would lead me to believe that part was damaged beyond repair. Everything else has shown improvement. Knowing what I know, I don't think you'll remember. Stranger things have happened though."

He withdrew a tissue from a nearby box and wiped at her wet cheeks. She unexpectedly reached up to touch his face and said, "Your skin feels rough."

"I shave every morning. If I want my face to be smooth at night, then I have to shave again. What you're feeling is sometimes called a five o'clock shadow."

"But it's after 5:00," she said innocently.

Aric fought the urge to smile. Many TBI patients took all comments or expressions very literally. He marveled at the human brain and how complex it was whether it was healthy or damaged.

Chelsea tentatively lifted her mouth to his and kissed him. He kissed back, unwilling to stop himself. He put his arms around her and pulled her closer to him, and she slid her arms around his neck and opened her mouth. As their tongues slid back and forth across one another's, Aric's cock instantly grew rigid. Chelsea was an excellent kisser, and he enjoyed the taste of her mouth and the feel of her breasts pressing against his chest.

When someone knocked on the bedroom door, they quickly broke apart. Aric cleared his throat and announced that they'd be out in a moment. He looked at Chelsea and asked her if she was all right.

"I think I'm remembering what it feels like to want to have sex with someone," she confided. "I want…I want you to stay with me when everyone leaves and let me touch more of your skin."

"Excuse me?"

"I don't remember what it feels like to really touch another person's skin, except during physical therapy. I want to know. I *have* to know. I can't not know any longer."

"You're not ready for sex."

"I didn't say anything about sex. I just want to be close to somebody!"

She sounded desperate. Aric told her everything would be fine and that he'd stay once the others had left. She looked immensely relieved; then she went out of the room.

Olga had arrived while they'd been in the bedroom. The little group squeezed around the small dining table and ate shrimp fettuccine and garlic bread. Everyone praised the quality of the meal. Chelsea looked distraught by the unintentional reminder of how her attempts at cooking solo had gone.

By the time Olga left, there was no doubt in Aric's mind that he'd made the right choice when he'd asked her to join the others in their move. With their personalities and backgrounds, the group of women complemented each other well. He doubted there would be any trouble amongst them and felt comforted when in their presence.

Fredeline and Eve Rose departed shortly after Olga left. It was 10:15.

"Is it past your bedtime?" Aric playfully asked Chelsea while she washed the dishes in the sink.

"I don't have a bedtime on the weekends," she answered seriously. "During the week, I go to bed at 10:00 every night. On the weekends, I don't have any routine at all. It makes me feel sort of naughty, but happy."

"What's your routine like during the week?"

"I get up at 5:30, shower, dress, eat a granola bar, and drink some soy milk. I brush my teeth and fix my hair and make-up, then put on my earrings. I get a bowl of Ramen noodles to take with me to work, leave the apartment at 6:30, and walk next door. Eve Rose, Fredeline, and I walk to work. Fredeline and I start cleaning at 7:30. At noon we eat lunch. We get off at 5:00 and all walk home together. I eat my prepackaged dinner at 6:00. I watch TV until 8:00 then read from 8:00 to 9:00. Then I meditate from 9:00 to 10:00. Then I go to bed. I get up at 5:30 the next day and do it again."

"You meditate? What do you do when you meditate?"

"I kneel on the floor and hold my hands a certain way and repeat the words *"Nam-Myoho-Renge-Kyo"* over and over."

"What does it mean?"

"It means I'm taking refuge in the mystery of life. I'm sending out all the good in me and hoping to make the world better because of it."

"So, you're a Buddhist."

"I am?"

"I think so. Maybe you can research it on your new computer."

"I will. Now that I have a computer, I'll have to change my evening routine to add computer time. I'll probably quit watching television altogether."

"Would you show me how to meditate? I've never tried it."

Chelsea knelt in the center of the floor and placed her palms together as if in prayer. Then she began to chant. Aric watched in fascination. What she was doing was intense yet relaxed. He could almost feel the waves of positive energy emanating from her. Not only was this practice good for her body and soul, but the repetition of it was good for her injured brain.

After a while, Chelsea ceased chanting and asked if she could touch more of Aric's skin. He nodded, unbuttoned his shirt, and removed it and his undershirt, tossing them onto the chair where his jacket and tie already rested. Aric was highly aroused, and her scrutiny of his bare flesh was weakening his resolve not to make love to her.

She swallowed hard, stepped forward, and skimmed her fingers over his exposed flesh. Aric groaned, as she slipped her arms around his waist and rested her head against his chest. He felt his back press against one wall.

"This feels so right," she murmured. "It makes me feel safe."

He wrapped his arms around her and stroked her hair. She sighed with contentment. Then she stepped away from him and resumed her study of the top half of his body.

"You don't have hair on your chest, but you have a line of hair that runs from your belly button downward. Eve Rose told me when men have hair like that it's called a Happy Trail, because if you follow it then it leads to something that gives you happiness."

Aric wasn't sure if he should laugh out loud or express his surprise at the young Haitian woman's knowledge of such things. He doubted Fredeline would approve of her granddaughter's remarks and wondered if Eve Rose had received the annual birth control shot. He was going to talk to Chelsea about this, but he never got the chance.

"What the –?"

Chelsea quickly unzipped his fly then yanked down his boxers. She took the head of his erection in her mouth as if she'd done it on a daily basis for years. Not wanting her neighbors to hear, Aric gritted his teeth in order to avoid crying out as she slowly took him in all the way. Marveling at her lack of a gag reflex, he slipped his fingers into her hair. It was evident that she'd done this before and had done it well. It felt as though she wanted to suck him dry, and he never wanted it to end.

Chelsea made little noises of satisfaction as she drew on him. He saw how much pleasure she was getting out of what she was doing. When she grazed the skin of his veined shaft with her teeth, he came hard, his body jerking when he started to release. A groan escaped him, as he spilled into her. She drank him in as if she couldn't bear to break their connection. When he was finished, she finally pulled away from him and looked up at his face from where she was kneeling on the floor.

"That was so wonderful," she said quietly. "Didn't you think so?"

"It was better than wonderful," he told her. "I've never had anybody do it with such…passion before. You were phenomenal."

"You tasted so good," she told him seriously. "I liked it."

He grinned down at her and said, "Me, too."

As she got to her feet, she asked, "Can we have sex now?"

He refrained from explaining to her that they'd just had sex. He knew what she meant. This was not the time for a semantics lesson.

"No sex, yet."

"But that made me feel good, and it made you feel good. I took the birth control shot. Why can't we do other things with our bodies that make us feel good?"

"Because we should be taking things slower."

"I surprised you?"

"You sure did."

"Next time, you surprise me when you think I'm ready for something you want to do with our bodies."

After pulling up his boxers and zipping his fly, Aric put on his undershirt and his long-sleeved shirt and buttoned it. He kissed Chelsea, wished her a good night, and went back to his hotel rooms. Once he'd showered, he sat on his balcony and pondered how he was going to make it through the next two weeks without taking Chelsea to bed. He knew there was little chance that he would last much longer no matter what happened.

What would his father do if he were there in Aric's place? What would his grandfathers have done? He knew the answer. They'd all been good men with great zest for life. They wouldn't take advantage of Chelsea, but they wouldn't have hesitated to do exactly what he'd done by letting her pleasure him earlier that evening. She'd needed and wanted it as much as he had.

You know they wouldn't wait to pleasure her without using her. She may not remember anything about her life but she's so alone. She's wrapped herself in an emotional bubble to protect herself, but that's also kept her from feeling deeply. The bubble has obviously burst, and she's so starved for intimacy of any kind. Are you hurting her worse by not having sex with her, or are you trying to justify it with overanalyzing the situation?

Aric stopped thinking about it. The whole thing was making his head hurt. He would take things day by day and figure it out. He and the others would go back to New Orleans and see what this new phase of their lives would bring. He felt the anticipation and smiled.

Chapter Eight

For the next week, Aric spent his days swimming in the bay, playing piano in a hotel lounge that didn't open for business until noon, riding horses, and jogging around the resort grounds. He also explored the little town that surrounded Serenity, wandered through local shops, and ate at local restaurants. He found himself at Chelsea's each evening, although he made certain that the two of them were never alone for any length of time unless they were occupied with a specific non-sexual task. He read two books he'd been wanting to read for months. In short, he relaxed.

Of course, his relaxation time was interspersed with company business and mulling over how to proceed when it came to Chelsea's past and present. What he was doing was going to be life-changing for him, her, and the others, and he prayed that he wasn't endangering them all with his actions. Perhaps the deaths and disappearances of those who'd worked with her were merely coincidental.

You come from a State that was built on corruption, he reminded himself. *You know how things work when people will stop at nothing to get what they want. You know something is really wrong with this scenario.*

The biggest question about Chelsea was why she'd been allowed to live if someone was so intent on killing everyone who'd helped her. Aric couldn't imagine a plausible explanation and decided he was going to become paranoid if he spent too much time thinking about it. Instead, he tried to think about the future.

On September 4th, Aric awoke, acutely aware that it was his twenty-eighth birthday and that no one else in his family was there to share it with him. He longed for the frequent celebrations of his youth. With such a large group of relatives, it was always someone's birthday, someone's anniversary, someone's dance recital, someone's sports championship, or someone's graduation. There was always a crawfish or shrimp boil with tons of food, music, and laughter. As he stared up at the mural on his ceiling, Aric listened to the silence in the room. He thought of playing with his sisters and of being hugged and kissed by his Tante Marie, his parents, and grandparents. Feeling sad, he got out of bed and went outside on the balcony to stare out at the bay.

When Olga arrived for his morning massage, he told her he didn't feel like talking and found he was unable to even attempt to force a smile. She frowned but didn't press him for any information and merely went about her work as he lay on the massage table. After she'd gone, Aric put on his workout clothes and went to the exercise room. He pushed himself hard and lifted weights, ran on the treadmill, and rowed four miles on the rowing machine. He then went back to his rooms, slipped into his swim trunks, went down to one of the hotel pools, and swam twenty laps. By the time he returned to his floor, the housekeepers had come and gone. That was how he'd wanted it. He couldn't handle chatting with anyone that morning, not even Fredeline or Chelsea.

Aric was three steps from his door when he realized it was ajar. He tried to rationalize this by considering that one of the housekeepers had accidentally left it open. He knew that couldn't be the case. Chelsea had told him to do so would lead to automatic dismissal. Employees were extremely mindful about not being careless while at work.

His heart pounding, Aric approached the door. He had gooseflesh, and it wasn't because of his damp skin and wet swim trunks. He cautiously edged his way inside. The suite seemed deserted. A search of the rooms proved that they were empty.

Aric stood in the living area and ruminated over the situation. Nothing had been disturbed. Maybe the open door was merely an anomaly. Maybe....

The room safe! he suddenly thought frantically.

His computer, phone, and the flash drive back-up of Chelsea's records were all gone. Knowing it was pointless, Aric nevertheless went to the panel on the foyer wall, pressed a button, spoke to the person at the front desk, and reported the break-in and the theft of the phone and computer. He didn't mention the flash drive. Security guards were in his room within minutes. The local police arrived soon after.

He gave statements to the authorities and waited patiently while they searched his suite. The elderly man who ran the hotel personally appeared and apologized for what had happened. He assured Aric the security videos would be examined and that the police would have the hotel's full cooperation. He also promised to provide Aric with a replacement computer and phone and informed him that the last week of his stay at the resort would be at no charge to him.

Aric, who knew that the break-in had nothing to do with the hotel or its security but couldn't say so, thanked the man and the police for their help. Once they'd finished in his rooms, he returned to them, showered and dressed, and went downstairs to eat in one of the hotel restaurants. He wasn't concerned about the stolen information. He had a failsafe on his equipment that would cause it to literally self-destruct if anyone tried to access it besides him. As for the flash drive, he'd wiped it clean after finding out about the dead and missing healthcare professionals. All of his files and Chelsea's were secured in another virtual location known only to him.

What worried Aric was that someone had gone to such extreme lengths in order to take the items. Whoever had done it was obviously a professional, yet the door to the suite had been left ajar. Aric could only intuit that this was meant to alert him. Perhaps it was a warning. He was unnerved and felt violated by the theft. He was glad he'd convinced Chelsea to give him the original flash drive, which he'd immediately destroyed without telling her. The data was safe.

Miss June called out to him when he passed the Concierge Desk. For once, he didn't feel like talking to the older woman. She brightly insisted that he take a seat. He obeyed, mentally vowing not to linger.

"I'm sorry your Labor Day isn't going well. I've already ordered your replacement computer and phone. They'll be here this afternoon."

"Thank you."

"You're very welcome," she said with a sweet smile. "Now I'd like to talk with you about your future plans."

"I'm really not in the mood to schedule any more resort activities at the moment."

"That's good because I wasn't talking about resort activities. I was talking about your future plans."

"I don't follow."

"You're a bright man, Mr. Rodrigue. Follow."

He sat up a little straighter in his chair and narrowed his eyes. Was this pleasant, elderly, Southern lady actually intimating that she knew what was going on with him, Chelsea, and the rest? If so, was she working for the "good guys" or the "bad guys"?

"Now, I'm going to tell you what you need to do," she said politely. "And you are going to do it if you want to keep yourself and those women of yours safe. Do you understand me?"

Not willing to commit to any response, Aric mutely stared at her.

"You're going to go home to New Orleans with Chelsea Capra, Fredeline and Eve Rose Duplessis, and Olga Knudsen. You're also going to be going home with me."

"You?"

She extended her hand and said with a twinkle in her eyes, "June Penn. I'm going to be your new administrative assistant."

"What about the administrative assistant I have now?" he asked nervously.

"Well, she's just been offered an even better job and will be calling you later today to tell you that she's going to have to resign. Don't you fret about it. She'll be very happy and safe in her new location and position."

"Who *are* you?" Aric asked. "Do you really expect me to trust you? I'm not even sure what's going on and have no idea what your role is in any of this."

"My role is to watch over Chelsea Capra and make certain she stays safe. I was doing an awfully good job of it until you came along."

There was no reproving tone in her voice. She was simply commenting on the facts. Aric was mentally scrambling in an effort to figure out what was happening.

"Why are you protecting Chelsea? What does she know or represent? A lot of people are dead who helped her. Were you responsible?"

"We were not," she replied seriously. "We didn't even realize that Miss Capra existed until three months ago. As for who's after her and why, we're not certain. All we know is that it must be immensely important and that she needs protection."

"Do you know her true identity?"

"No. Her DNA doesn't match any in the national database of offenders or those who've been reported missing. She also doesn't look like anybody in the registry of criminals or missing persons."

"What do you know?"

"I can't tell you."

Aric rose from his seat and said, "Then I can't trust you."

Miss June gave him a grandmotherly smile before suggesting authoritatively that he resume his seat. When he did, she said, "We know via the taxi dispatcher's records that Chelsea was picked up from Disney Springs and was headed to Sea World when the accident happened. We also know that the accident was not an accident." When he asked how they knew this, she completely ignored the question and continued, "The entire situation is mystifying. Our people don't like to be mystified."

"Who do you work for?"

"A branch of a very large tree."

"Who's in charge of the tree?"

"Someone you've been very…intimate with several years ago. You're still close friends with her. It's amazing to me how powerful personalities are drawn to one another as if by an almost supernatural magnetism. You've got quite a presence about you, as does she."

Aric's lips parted slightly as he absorbed what Miss June was inferring. Did she really work for President Jitesh?

"Is the President in charge of this particular project?"

"She knows nothing about it. But you must admit it's a very big tree she's sworn to protect. Even the best of gardeners can't be everywhere in the garden at all times."

He thought about that for a while before admitting, "I still can't trust you."

"I wouldn't trust anyone if I were you. I have no way of proving that I'm your friend and not your enemy. However, if I was your enemy wouldn't I just have you and the others killed like the rest of those people? Why would I be talking to you and trying to help you?

"You have many friends in high places, Mr. Rodrigue. And I don't just mean the President and the Vice-President. There are quite a few people in various branches of the tree who want to see you live a long, healthy life so they can study you and learn from you. You and Miss Capra are quite valuable to quite a lot of people for different reasons."

Aric felt as if Miss June had punched him in the belly. He'd thought that less than a dozen people in the world knew he'd been a victim of the D Plague and had survived. He was at a complete loss as to how he should proceed. His head was spinning.

"It's your birthday," Miss June said kindly. "Please put your trust in me and know that I mean you no harm. I took an oath to protect this country – long before the current President was even born. I serve to safeguard what's right. I hope someday you'll truly believe me."

"We'll be under surveillance either way."

"Yes, although no cameras or data tapping inside unless it's deemed unavoidable. If that happens, then I'll let you know."

"What do you recommend? How will I explain this to the others?"

"Tell them that your administrative assistant resigned, and I told you I was retiring and wanting to move on to someplace new. You convinced me that I wasn't ready to retire and asked me to become your new assistant. They'll be quite understanding. I know and like all of them. They'll accept me without question."

"How long have you been at this?" Aric asked.

"Fifty-six years. I never tire of it. I find my work very rewarding."

Aric smiled and said, "I'm glad. If you're telling me the truth and have lasted this long, then I'm thankful you're on my side."

Later, Aric received his new computer and phone and proceeded to set them up with his preferences and to load them with his information. He took care of some necessary business, watched the news and a documentary about patients who had suffered damage to the temporal lobe of their brains, then walked to Chelsea's at 5:30. They had been eating dinner together for the past week, although he'd insisted on cooking with her each evening instead of eating prepackaged meals. They picked different recipes to try although Chelsea continued to struggle with following the instructions and often got frustrated. Aric was patient with her and helped her to work through her aggravation and anxiety. Because they were working on a task and not simply sitting around talking, Aric didn't worry about being alone with the woman and what might happen between them. Trying to cook demanded all of Chelsea's attention. When the food was ready, they'd call Fredeline and Eve Rose to join them.

Aric knocked when he got to Chelsea's door. She didn't answer. He tried the knob and found the door unlocked. He sensed instantly what was going on and headed for the bathroom. He didn't turn on the light when he reached the doorway and said her name. He heard her crying and asked her if he could put the light on low. She told him "Yes," but cried harder.

"I haven't had any headaches at all since the bad migraine when I first knew you," she sobbed. "I thought maybe they were gone. I thought maybe...maybe...it would be okay now."

"You're improving," he reminded her. "A week with no headaches is the best you've done since you woke up from the coma. That's great progress."

"But look at me today! What's wrong with me?"

He knew she wasn't merely referring to the migraines and gently shushed her. Then he wet a hand towel with hot water and a facecloth with cold water before bringing them to her. Once he'd put the towel on the back of her neck and the rag across her forehead, he sat beside her and asked, "How many pills have you taken?"

"One when I got home."

"Are you sure it was just one?"

"Yes. You said not to take any more than that every eight hours or I could die. I used to not care, but I don't want to die now that I met you." She moaned and added, "But I do *want* another pill. It hurts so badly."

He stroked her hair for several minutes before she asked him to stop, citing an increase in pain. He suggested she close her eyes and try meditating silently with her chant to see if that might help. For a long while, it did. Aric was relieved to see her visibly relax.

Suddenly, Chelsea's eyes flew open and she said, "I have to throw up. Please, Aric!"

He assumed she meant that she needed his help to rise and kneel in front of the toilet, and this was precisely what he did. He held her hair behind her head and supported her for several minutes. It was torture for him to see her in so much pain. When she was done, she sagged against him and trembled with fatigue.

"Maybe I should take you to the hospital," he suggested.

"I don't want to go to a hospital!" she declared frantically.

"Do you want me to call Olga? Maybe she could try massage to help you."

Shaking in his arms, she stammered, "O-okay."

He called Olga. While they waited for the woman to arrive, he gave Chelsea small sips of water then carried her to the couch.

As Aric wiped her face with a damp cloth, he murmured, "Everything will be alright."

"Can I hold your hand?"

"Of course."

Chelsea's fingers barely tightened around his as she took his hand. Aric pursed his lips and squeezed gently.

Olga came quickly. Once Aric let her in, she immediately went over to Chelsea and spoke soothingly to her. The Swede looked to Aric and said, "I want you to help me get her undressed and on her bed so that I can try to assist her. Go to her bedroom and see if you can find a comfortable nightgown I can put on her afterward."

He hurried to comply. He found something that looked extremely comfortable. It was a cotton knit blue nightshirt with a V-neck. A small white cloud was imprinted at the bottom of the V. He placed the nightshirt on one side of the bed then returned to the living room.

Olga already had Chelsea's blue uniform shirt unbuttoned and was in the process of unzipping her slacks. She ordered Aric to lift Chelsea slowly so she could remove her shirt, then they would take off her black work pants. Neither of those things proved difficult, and Chelsea was soon clad only in her bra and panties. Aric carried her to her bed and lowered her onto the mattress.

"Leave the room," Olga said. "I will take off Chelsea's undergarments once you are gone."

Aric sat in the chair in the small living room and stared dejectedly at the wall in front of him. He was weary, depressed, and confused. It was his twenty-eighth birthday. He had money, status, and was filled to the brim with longing, guilt, loss, and loneliness. He wanted his mother to hug him, to wish him a happy birthday, and to tell him that he was doing the right thing and was a good man doing good work.

Aric began to cry quietly. He allowed himself to do this for a while before forcing himself to suppress the tears. He went to the bathroom and washed his face, emerging just as Olga came out of the bedroom.

Chapter Nine

Olga looked closely at Aric, and he knew that she could tell he'd been crying. She said nothing about it and murmured, "She sleeps. We will see what occurs the next time. I believe I have isolated the proper pressure points and can aid her in minimizing the intensity of future migraines. I hope so. If not, then I will make adjustments. The poor girl was in such distress at one point that I thought we might have to call for an ambulance. She begged me not to, and the moment did pass." Frowning, she said, "She needs intensive physical therapy in order to regain her strength. Frankly, I am amazed that she is able to perform her housekeeping tasks at the hotel."

"If she wasn't doing that, then she'd probably have no strength at all," Aric noted. "At least it's pushed her to remain somewhat active simply through the physical labor that comes with the work."

Olga agreed and asked him if he wanted her to stay with him and Chelsea. He declined her offer and thanked her again for canceling on a hotel client in order to come to Chelsea's aid.

"What is a massage of one spoiled rich woman compared to alleviating the suffering of a desperate poor one? Besides, soon Chelsea will be my main focus. I am glad I was able to observe her during one of these migraines and to help. It gives me a better idea of how I should plan her therapy." Pausing, she asked, "Do you have a room with machines in your old house?"

"You mean a workout room? No."

"You will have to make one if I'm to help her. There are things she needs, some of which are simple and some complicated."

"We have plenty of rooms. A home gym wouldn't be a bad idea for all of us. Tell me what you need, and we'll get it."

"When we are in New Orleans and in the house, then we will figure it out. I will assume that you are not going to be in your rooms tomorrow at 6:00 for your massage. Call me if you wish to reschedule or if Chelsea needs me again."

After Olga left, Aric called the hotel and asked to talk to Miss June. He explained about Chelsea's current condition. He was concerned about her stress levels and knew she would be worried about missing work the following day.

"Have her call the hotel when she wakes. They'll let her know she can stop working without it causing a problem for the resort. Perhaps she can enjoy some of its amenities as your guest before she leaves with you this Sunday. You should take her to the beach. She's afraid to go but has wanted to do that ever since she moved here. She should visit it once before she moves to Louisiana. The beaches there aren't so good."

"No, they're not. The oil and gas industry destroyed them a long time ago. It's really sad. I'm glad my family got out of that business."

"It's a necessary evil," the older woman said. "There are always necessary evils."

"You know first-hand?"

"I do," she replied and disconnected the call.

After phoning Fredeline to let her know that they would not all be having dinner together that night because of Chelsea's migraine, Aric sat on the couch and turned on the old flat-screen TV that rested on a worn stand. The news was playing, and he stared blankly at footage of fighting in some devastated war-torn part of the world. Deciding that this was not going to improve his dark mood, he changed the channel several times before settling on a documentary regarding the rise of the current President and Vice-President of the United States to their respective political offices.

He knew Lakshmi Jitesh and Buddy LaFleur, both of whom were from his home state of Louisiana. He admired their politics and enjoyed being in their presence. He'd enjoyed very different relationships with each one.

His mother, who'd been a great supporter of then-Governor Jitesh, had introduced him to the graceful, petite, black-haired woman at a fundraiser when he'd been twenty-one. Aric had been quite taken with Jitesh, who was ten years his senior. She was intelligent, self-possessed, beautiful, and impressed by and attracted to him, despite his youth. They'd become friends and had gone to bed together six months later. Although their physical relationship had only lasted for several months, they'd remained close friends in the years that followed. Aric was one of the few people who had personal access to the President, although their conversations were infrequent. He still valued them and Jitesh herself, who had never married and was one of the youngest people to ever be elected to the White House. At thirty-eight, she was the most powerful woman in the world. And, in his eyes, she was also one of the most honest.

He'd met Buddy LaFleur seven years earlier when the man had been the Mayor of Baton Rouge. Large and bulky in stature, gray-haired Buddy was a former oil-rig worker who'd earned enough money to leave the rigs and follow his dream of attending law school. His cunning, wit, and charm combined with his intellect to propel him up the political ladder at astonishing speed. He was forty-nine, married, and had fathered three children, all of whom had died in the D Plague. Aric empathized with his loss and genuinely liked the man, but he didn't believe for one moment that LaFleur's political ambitions were anything but self-motivated.

Who am I kidding? Aric thought. *Human beings tend to be ego-centric at heart.*

But Lakshmi Jitesh was different. It wasn't that he idolized her. He simply saw her for what she was. It seemed as though almost every voter in the country had seen it, too. The woman was someone who wanted real change that could be realized through her direct actions and decisions. He'd heard a man in a crowd once call her a "Divine Being," and he didn't believe the man was making any reference to Lakshmi's physical beauty.

Whatever Jitesh and LaFleur were doing as President and Vice-President was working wonderfully well. On post-Plague Earth, their efforts had definitely had an impact. Things were looking better for the people and the planet than they had in decades. It wasn't perfect, but it seemed to be an inexorable wave of positive change that was slowly surging across the globe. Aric allowed his mind to wander and considered the state of the world in 2034.

"Aric?"

He looked across the room to where Chelsea stood in the doorway. She was wearing her blue nightshirt, and her brown hair was slightly tangled. He was relieved to note that the luminescent blue eyes didn't appear to reflect the pain he'd seen earlier in them.

"Feeling better?"

"Yes. I've never recovered from the pain so quickly after a migraine. I think Olga really helped me a lot."

"Good. I'm glad she'll be living with us and working with you. Maybe you'll actually be able to manage your migraines to the point where they're nonexistent."

She looked doubtful but simply said, "That would be so nice."

"Do you need anything?"

"We should start cooking. I'm sure we're late. Fredeline and Eve Rose will be hungry."

"I already told them we wouldn't be having dinner with them tonight. I'll just make us some scrambled eggs and toast or something."

"But we can't. We started a new routine. I need to follow my routine. I have to cook with you, eat, work on the computer, read, meditate, sleep, and then go to work tomorrow like always."

"You still look worn out. Our routine can be altered tonight. As for Serenity, call the hotel. See if you can stop work a little early."

"But they'll be short-handed."

"Just call them. Trust me. It'll be fine."

Chelsea sat on the couch beside him and phoned the resort. Within minutes, she'd ended the call and explained that she didn't have to go back to work and that everything would be all right. She seemed relieved, excused herself, and retreated to the bathroom. He heard the shower running and tried not to think of the woman's naked body covered in slick soap suds with rivulets of water running down her skin. After quite some time, she emerged from the bathroom. Aric looked in that direction, expecting to find her back in her nightshirt. Instead, she was naked. Aric was instantly on his feet attempting not to look at the lovely, nude woman with the almond-colored skin he wanted so very much who was standing in front of him.

"Chelsea, what do you think you're doing?"

She looked innocently at him and replied, "Getting clothes from my bedroom. I forgot to bring some in the bathroom. Why?" When his face reddened, she cocked her head, smiled, and merely said, "Oh."

Aric closed his eyes and forced himself to say, "Put something on before I can't stop myself from making love to you."

"Why do you want to stop yourself? You know we're going to do it eventually. Why are you holding back? I may not be normal, but I'm a grown woman who wants to have sex with you. I can't get pregnant because of the shot. I'm finally ready to look ahead. Why wait?"

Why indeed? he asked silently.

Aric soon had her in his arms. The feel of her damp skin under his hands was exquisite. Her mouth tasted like mint, and it registered somewhere in his mind that she'd brushed her teeth while in the bathroom. The brown hair was wet and clean, and he wrapped some loose strands around the fingers of one hand. She moaned softly as he deepened their kiss.

A few minutes later, he was lying naked on the bed with Chelsea. His mouth was locked around one nipple, and his fingers fluttered over the hard nub at the point of the damp triangle of curls below her belly. She cried out his name and climaxed.

Aric had thought he would enter her then. He'd always been the dominant partner during sex. Women seemed to expect it. Chelsea did not. He was soon lying on his back, buried deep within her. Although he was definitely participating in their lovemaking, he was under no delusions about his role in their current encounter. Chelsea had total control.

Aric had figured he'd run the gamut with partners, from the tigress prom queen he'd dated his senior year in high school to the tender Lakshmi Jitesh. He now realized how wrong he'd been. Being with Chelsea Capra was like nothing he'd ever imagined. All of her indecision had disappeared. She was insatiable, inexhaustible, and well-versed in how to please both herself and her partner.

"I'm going to hurt you, Chere," Aric managed to say at one point during a brief respite. "Oh, Chere," he groaned, using the Cajun French version of the word "dear" for males or females before continuing, "I know I'm – "

Chelsea placed two fingers over his mouth and increased the rhythmic movements of her hips before saying, "Long and thick. I know. You're not too big for me. Stop thinking and *feel* me around you. Come, Aric."

He came. Over and over, he came. Their positions changed, as did their techniques. What didn't change was the sexual connection that flowed between them. Aric marveled at Chelsea's expertise and stamina. She may not have great physical strength, but she didn't need it. She knew exactly what to do in order to maximize their pleasure.

Finally, neither of them was able to continue. They lay on the mattress with Aric holding Chelsea in his arms. She sighed with obvious pleasure and murmured, "That was very illuminating. I found a part of myself tonight, although I didn't regain any memories. Being with you makes me want to uncover what I'm really like." She pressed herself against him and asked, "Was I as good as other people you've had sex with in the past?"

"I've never, ever had sex with anyone like I did with you tonight. You're the greatest partner I've ever slept with. We actually did a few things I've never done."

"Maybe I was a prostitute?" she offered. "Would that make you not want me anymore?"

"I don't think it was just the physical part that made it so great. I think it was because you and I were meant for each other."

"I think you're right." Pausing, she said quietly, "If we go to your old house to live, then it will have all of your family's things in it. I have no memory of anything before last year. I have no family things. What if I try to make myself like what you're used to because I want to make you happy?"

"I had the entire house wiped clean. All of my family's possessions are packed in storage units for me to sort through when I'm able. I may never be able. Anyway, the house is bare, except for new queen-sized beds in each bedroom we're going to use. I want everyone to pick out what furniture they like and then we'll decorate the house accordingly. That way, it will be a new home and an old home."

"And it won't hurt so much?"

"That's what I'm hoping. Let's not talk about it anymore tonight. I only want to be with you and not think about anything else in the world outside this room."

Chelsea made a satisfied little sound and drifted off to sleep nestled in Aric's embrace. He quickly joined her, only waking when the sunlight streamed through the slit in the curtains on Chelsea's window and hit him in the face. She was no longer lying beside him in the bed, and the apartment was filled with deafening silence.

Chapter Ten

Practically leaping from the bed, Aric rushed through the doorway and almost tripped over Chelsea, who was kneeling on the living room floor, meditating. She yelped with surprise when he swore and narrowly avoided falling across her. Once they'd both recovered themselves somewhat, Aric crouched beside her and took her face in his hands before saying, "I was worried when I woke up and you weren't beside me."

"Why were you so worried?" she asked with a hint of suspicion in her voice.

Thinking furiously, he offered, "I wondered whether or not your migraine was back.

She smiled and said, "It's a good thing you're so cute and sexy. Otherwise, I might be more inclined to ask you why you're lying to me."

Aric didn't know what to say in response, so he kissed her. Although he was still naked, she had clearly showered and wore shorts and a purple shirt. She took one of his hands and brought it to the top of her shorts. Aric pulled back and told her that they were *not* going to have sex again.

"But why not? It was fantastic! You said so yourself."

"I did, and it was."

"So, let's do it again."

He grinned at her and said, "Later. Right now, I need to shower, dress, check in with my office, and eat something. Have you eaten?"

"A granola bar."

"I'll have the same; then we'll go on an adventure."

"What kind of an adventure?"

"I'll tell you on the way."

As Aric showered, he considered how he should attempt to take Chelsea to the beach. She was making progress at a breakneck pace, but her spatial issues were unlikely to improve rapidly, if at all. If he simply led her to the beach, she would be terrified.

You have to take her, he reminded himself. *Remember when you watched her looking out of the hotel window? Remember what Miss June said about her being afraid but wanting to go to the beach? You have to try to help her. Why not this morning?*

67

He didn't know if he should tell Chelsea or if that would make her more apprehensive. As he sat in the chair and ate his granola bar, he watched her work on the computer. It astounded him every time he witnessed her interacting with the device.

"You're so facile with technology. Did you try to use it to find out who you were before the accident?"

"After no one else could figure it out, I went on one of the computers at the library and hacked into as many databases as I could think of, but I found nothing."

"You did *what*?"

"I hacked into them."

"Which databases?"

"The ones that list criminals, missing persons, and government personnel. I know it sounds crazy, but I thought maybe I was a secret agent or something and that's why I ended up like I did and why all those other people who helped me died or disappeared."

Aric almost choked on his soy milk.

"You – you know about the missing and dead healthcare people?"

"Of course, I do. I tried to contact them a while after I got released from the rehab facility, and I found out they'd all been…they were dead or gone." Leveling her gaze at him, she said, "You obviously know. You weren't going to tell me?"

"I didn't know when I first met you. Once I found out, I wasn't sure how you'd take it. You seemed so…fragile. I was worried you'd fall apart or blame yourself or both."

"I did fall apart when I first found out. It can't be a coincidence, Aric. However, I don't think it's my fault. I didn't kill those people; someone else did. I just wish I knew why. Was it because of something I did before the accident? Was it because of who I was? Why not simply kill me and be done with it? It doesn't make any sense."

"No, it doesn't."

"Someone is protecting me."

He nodded.

"He talked to you?"

"She."

"But she doesn't know why all this has happened or who I am?"

"That's what she told me. All she knows is that you're evidently extremely important to someone, important enough to kill for. She and the people she works for want to keep you alive so they can figure it out. She said she worked for the United States government."

"When did you talk to this person?"

"Yesterday."

"And you weren't going to say anything about it?"

"Not until I thought you could handle it." Grinning sheepishly, he admitted, "I guess you can handle more than I give you credit for."

Chelsea looked away and said, "I may have brain damage and be totally incapable of doing some pretty simple things, but I'm also smart and able to think at an advanced level when it comes to others. Knowing you has made me access those parts of my brain that weren't stimulated before." Looking back to him, she said impishly, "You've managed to make me access various parts of me that needed stimulating."

He gave her a lopsided grin and said formally, "I'm glad I could be of service, ma Chere."

"Our life together is going to be very odd," she stated thoughtfully. "It won't be like the people I see on TV."

"No, it won't."

"That makes me sad. It would be nice to be 'normal,' but I don't have a choice in the matter, do I?"

"Not really."

"Do you think I should try to find out who I really am?"

"That's your call, not mine. My only concern is that you might draw unwanted attention if you find out the truth."

"Fredeline and Eve Rose don't know about the dead people. It didn't feel right to tell them. Do you think that's a mistake?"

Aric pondered this question for several minutes before saying, "I think the less they know the better."

"Will the people protecting me protect them, too?"

"I'm sure they'll protect all of us. I suspect I've been under similar protection for the last five years without even realizing it."

"Why?"

Aric rubbed at his eyes and said, "I can't tell you. I swore never to tell anyone. If I confide in you, then that might make your situation more tenuous."

She nodded resignedly and said, "Whatever happened to you wasn't your fault, Aric."

"A part of me knows that. The other part feels like it was. It's ridiculous, but it's the truth."

"Maybe you'll be able to tell me someday."

"I hope so. I want to."

She gave the verbal command, and her computer shut off. Pocketing it and her phone, she rose and extended her hand to Aric and asked him if they could go on their adventure.

"Only if you want to," he said hesitantly. "I plan to take you to the beach."

She appeared stunned and sat back down on the couch. She protested that she wanted to go but was immobilized by fear every time she thought of it. She had tried many times but had never made it past the buildings of the resort.

"Louisiana's beaches are muddy, rocky, and full of sticks and junk," Aric told her. "You should see what a beach is supposed to look like before we go. You should try to get in the water."

She swallowed hard and nodded.

"We don't have to do it today," he said reassuringly.

"Tomorrow won't be any different. I'd like to try."

"Then go put on your swimsuit, and we'll try."

"I don't have a swimsuit."

"What exactly do you have?"

"Two uniforms for work, two pairs of shorts, one pair of jeans, three short-sleeved shirts, two long-sleeved shirts, two bras, five pairs of panties, six pairs of socks, my nightshirt, a pair of work shoes and a pair of tennis shoes." Aric's disbelief must have been plastered all over his face because she added, "You said what *exactly* did I have."

"That's not...I'm...you did a good job of telling me. I'm just shocked that that's all you have for clothes."

"That's all I have, period. Oh, that and my earrings. I forgot about the diamond earrings."

She tucked some of her brown hair behind each ear, so he could see the half-carat diamond studs.

"You own nothing except a few articles of clothing but you have diamond stud earrings?"

"The earrings were in my ears when they rescued me, so I got them back once I was awake."

Aric scanned the living room and asked, "Are you telling me that nothing in this place is yours?"

"Yes. Everything came with the apartment, including the bed linens, dishes, glasses, utensils, and towels. It all has to stay here when I leave. It's okay. I didn't pick it out. I needed those things, but I don't think I would've bought these particular items even if I had the money to buy them. Fredeline and Eve Rose have more personal articles, but their apartment came furnished, too. None of us will have much to move."

"And the books you read at night?"

"They're from the library."

"And you have nothing else? No personal possessions at all?"

"Aric, I have no past. Whatever things I had were from my former life, the one I don't remember. I have me, some clothes, and my earrings. I don't need anything else."

"You need everything else," Aric told her. "And I intend to see that you find it all."

They walked hand-in-hand to Serenity. Aric led Chelsea straight to the Concierge Desk and introduced her to Miss June.

"Well, we've met before," the older woman said pleasantly. "But it's lovely to see you again. I suppose I'll be seeing a lot more of you soon."

"You will?"

"Miss June was telling me she was going to retire, but I told her I didn't think she was ready. My administrative assistant took another job, so I asked Miss June to try her hand at working for me. She'll be coming to New Orleans with us."

Chelsea brightened and asked, "Will you live with us, too?"

"An old lady like me likes to have her own little space. I'll probably find a place nearby. It will be so good to have a new, exciting job and begin a new chapter of my life."

"For all of us, I guess," Chelsea said. "I'm glad you're coming along. I like you, Miss June."

"And I really like you, my dear. Now, what can I do for you both today?"

"Chelsea and I are going to the beach, but she doesn't own a swimsuit," answered Aric. "Do you know where we can get her one?"

Miss June smiled broadly and said, "Right here at the resort. Why don't you put your swim trunks on, and I'll take Chelsea and make certain she has a nice bathing suit to wear?"

Since Chelsea seemed fine with this, Aric left the two women and retreated to his rooms. There, he spoke to his soon-to-be-former administrative assistant and handled some business matters that couldn't wait before changing into his swim trunks and slipping on some water shoes. He checked the time and noted with alarm that it had been over two hours since he'd left Chelsea with Miss June. He began to question his decision and worried about Chelsea's safety and the honesty of the older woman.

There came a light knock on his door. Aric hurried to open it. Chelsea stood in the hallway wearing a short, bright blue crocheted cover-up. He could see hints of bright pink fabric and her almond-colored skin underneath. An orange-and-pink beach bag was slung over one shoulder, and she wore pink flip-flops. She held a blue bag in one hand.

"My clothes, phone, computer, and tennis shoes are in here," she explained. "I have two beach towels and some sunscreen in the beach bag. Miss June said we would need those."

"Miss June is a very thoughtful woman," he told her. "Are you ready for this?"

"I'm ready to try."

He took her hand and led her to the elevator. When they reached the ground floor, she reluctantly followed him out through a back door of the spa area. Despite her lack of strength, Aric knew that she was gripping his hand as tightly as she could.

They kept to one of the trails that wound its way throughout the grounds. Aric had familiarized himself with the place during his stay at Serenity Bay Resort and Spa. He had an idea about where to take Chelsea so that she wouldn't be totally overwhelmed by the openness of the beach and the bay.

He led her through a grove of sea grape trees. It was both gratifying and heart-wrenching to see the woman so in awe of the natural beauty of the landscape she'd been unable to experience. He wondered if she was from Florida and had grown up in these

72

surroundings and couldn't remember or if this was the first time she'd viewed the environment up close. He knew she must be thinking the same thing, which made her separation from the average person that much greater.

When they reached the edge of the path, Aric asked Chelsea to sit on a fallen tree while he went ahead and spread out their towels. As he removed them and the suntan lotion from the bag, he noticed that Miss June had also slipped in several bottles of water, some hand wipes, and two wrapped sandwiches from one of the restaurants in the hotel. He smiled at her forethought as he spread out the towels near the water's edge.

Chelsea was visibly shaking when he returned to where she sat. She looked vulnerable, nothing like the woman who'd been so in control the night before as they'd made love. He asked her again whether or not she wanted to wait. She shook her head, even as she began to cry.

"I won't allow anything to happen to you," he vowed.

"Promise you won't let me go no matter what," she pleaded.

He promised and urged her to stand. Then he put one arm around her shoulders and guided her forward. When they stepped out onto the beach, Chelsea stopped and exclaimed, "I'm afraid!"

"I know, but you're okay. I'm holding you."

"But what if I fall? I can't fall! The more people with head injuries fall, the worse off they are!"

"I'm going to keep you safe."

Chelsea turned toward him and threw her arms around his neck as she cried.

"I put the towels and our bag near the water. They're about ten yards ahead of us. I'm going to hold you, and we'll walk to them. Focus on the towels and not on the beach or the bay. Give it a try for me."

She lowered her arms and slowly turned. Once she spotted the towels and bag, she calmed slightly and allowed Aric to put his arm around her shoulders again and walk across the sand with her. They sat on the towels, and Chelsea stared at her lap while Aric applied suntan lotion to himself. He then helped her to remove her cover-up and spread the lotion over her bare skin, admiring the bikini she wore as he did so.

"Aric?"

"Yes?"

"Does your company do blood work on people when they're doing research to develop new drugs?"

"Of course. Why?"

"Because I was thinking that I could find out what I am. I'm not white. I mean, I know I'm part white, but I'm something else, too. I asked them to figure it out at the hospital, but they said that was an optional test and that I'd have to pay for it. It was expensive, and I couldn't afford it. I want to know what my ethnic background is so that I can understand myself better."

"There is definitely a blood test for that. We'll do it as soon as we can once we're in New Orleans."

"Would it bother you if I was part-black or part-Arabic or part-Hispanic or something else?"

"Are you kidding?" he chuckled.

"No," she said seriously, and he reminded himself of the brain injury that would have affected her ability to filter certain nuances of speech, including intimation, sarcasm, and the like.

"You're exotic, beautiful, sweet, smart, and make love better than anyone I've ever known. Wherever that came from, I'm thankful for it." Looking quizzically at her, he asked, "Would it bother *you* to be part of a certain ethnic group?"

"No. It's only that I...." Her voice trailed off, and she suddenly looked out into the bay and admitted, "I wonder about my parents and family a lot. How was I raised? Were they nice to me? I do Buddhist chanting. Were they nice Buddhist people, or were they horrible to me and that's why I became Buddhist? What sort of neighborhood did I grow up in? Did I have brothers or sisters I played with and loved? Did we celebrate birthdays or religious holidays? All I have is...nothing. If I find out what my heritage is, then will I wonder more?"

Aric thought of his own large, happy family and then tried hard not to think of them.

"Are you ready to go out into the water?" he asked.

"Could we sit here for a while? I'm not so scared because we're sitting. Maybe if I take a minute or two, then I'll be ready to try the water."

"Miss June packed us a lunch. Let's eat and go out once our food's gone down."

Lucky

The paper-wrapped sandwiches Miss June had slipped into their beach bag held delicious turkey paninis that had some sort of spinach and artichoke spread on them. Aric and Chelsea ate and drank then sat and watched the water. It was a lovely day with a few fluffy clouds punctuating the bright blue sky. Dolphins surfaced occasionally out in the water, and birds soared overhead and dove into the bay for fish here and there.

"Are you ready?" Aric prompted.

"I want to be."

Getting to his feet, he directed, "Stand up and put your arms around my neck."

She complied, and he lifted her and began to walk toward the water. Chelsea buried her face against his chest and chanted softly as he got closer to the water's edge. She wasn't shaking, and Aric waded out into the bay. When he was waist-deep, he stopped and asked Chelsea if she wanted him to put her down. She nodded but asked him not to let her go.

Once she was on her feet, he put both arms around her and said, "You made it. What next?"

Still refusing to look away from his chest, Chelsea confided, "I don't know what I want to do. Could we stay in our current positions while I make up my mind?"

"I'd be perfectly happy to stand where we are all afternoon with you pressed against me."

As if to emphasize this, he pulled her closer and pushed his hips forward. She giggled, and he smiled.

Chelsea lowered her arms and hugged Aric's waist tightly before releasing him and turning toward the bay. He locked his arms around her and kissed the top of her head. She was suddenly grasping at his forearms and pressing her back hard against his chest.

"I'm scared, Aric!" she said in a rush. He tightened his arms around her, and she slowly calmed and admitted, "It's…it's so lovely and so vast. I want to go out further, but I can't. Will I ever be able to not be afraid of wide open spaces?"

"I honestly don't know."

"At least I did this," she declared with a mixture of resignation and pride. "Going into a pool shouldn't seem so scary after this."

"You haven't been in a pool since your accident?"

"No."

"Well, we'll have to try that next. There's a pool at the house in New Orleans. It would be nice for you to be able to enjoy it, although I want you to swear to me you'll never go in a pool or deep water without someone else around."

"I won't. I know the risks. I don't want to have a seizure and drown." Leaning her head back against him, she said, "I need to go now. This was good though. Thank you so much."

"It made me happy to do it. Being with you has made me realize how little has made me truly happy in the last five years."

Aric carried Chelsea back to shore, and she was able to walk beside him to their towels. Once they'd gathered their things, they retraced their steps to the hotel. They had barely made it into Aric's foyer before his swim trunks were off and Chelsea's bikini bottoms were lying next to them on the floor. She sobbed with what sounded like relief when he entered her. The sex was swift and explosive. When they were finished, she gave a little cry of despair as he withdrew. He carried her to the bed, lowered her on top of the duvet, and then stretched out beside her.

"I feel so empty when you're not in me," she explained after they'd cuddled for a long while. "Do it again, Aric."

"No. I'm pretty sore from that marathon session we had last night, and I know you must be sore, too. We can't do that all the time or else we'll hurt each other."

"But TBI patients like repetition," she insisted. "So, do it again."

She was smiling coyly up at him, and he laughed and startled both of them by doing it again.

Chapter Eleven

Aric arrived with his women at the New Orleans International Airport early the following Sunday morning. He knew that thinking of them as "his" women sounded sexist, but being chauvinistic was the furthest thing from his mind. He considered himself extremely fortunate to be in the company of Chelsea, Fredeline, Eve Rose, Olga, and Miss June. They weren't possessions; they were his salvation in various forms.

A driver in a hybrid SUV was waiting to take them to the Rodrigue family home. The atmosphere in the vehicle was tense. The others knew how uncertain Aric was about his homecoming and maintained a respectful silence. All was quiet as they cruised toward the house. Aric looked out of the window at the familiar cityscape and wondered how he was going to handle his return. When the driver turned onto the long road that led to his home, his heart grew even heavier.

Once the SUV was parked in front of the house, Aric asked the others to wait, got out, and went to the porch. He could easily envision his parents, grandparents, sisters, in-laws, cousins, nieces, nephews, and friends sitting, standing, chatting, playing, listening to music, drinking, and eating. They were all having a great time. They always had fun when they were together.

Aric envisioned the inside of the house as it had been during his pre-Plague life. He had lived there from birth until age twenty-two. He'd been more fortunate than most people in that his relatives were good-natured, loving, and had never been overshadowed by serious health issues or social problems. They'd had money but didn't take anything for granted and felt it was their responsibility to do as much good as they could in the world.

He looked directly at the front door then down at the WELCOME mat on the porch. His parents and grandparents had all died inside as he himself had lain in agony. When the medical people had made it to the house, they'd found him clinging to life and hadn't expected him to survive more than a few hours. They'd called in a team to clean up the remains of his family. His parents and grandparents were swept out of the front door as Aric shocked those present by not succumbing to death.

He walked around the huge house to the backyard and looked at the covered pool and the overgrowth that surrounded the patio area. He remembered a party his family had held for his Tante Marie's birthday the week before the D Plague hit. Everyone had a wonderful time, never suspecting it would be their last party. He remembered hugging his eldest sister and feeling her unborn son kick as they'd embraced.

Aric walked back to the SUV and got in. Not looking at the others, he said, "I thought I could do it, but I can't live here anymore. I'm sorry, but we'll have to stay in a hotel for a few days until we can find a new house."

He had wanted to say more, but he knew he wasn't going to be able to go on. Aric quickly climbed out of the SUV again and walked blindly toward the wooded area behind the house. He felt as though he was being crushed by his emotions and that if he could just keep moving, he wouldn't give in to the weight of his grief.

"Aric?"

He stopped when he heard Chelsea's voice but didn't turn around or speak.

"Did you play in these woods when you were a boy?"

He nodded.

"With your friends and your sisters?"

Another nod.

"What was it like to be a child?"

Aric looked back at her and said, "You're breaking my heart, Chere."

She came toward him and placed a hand on his chest before stating, "Your heart was broken five years before you met me."

"True enough, Chere."

"Chere. I like it when you call me 'Dear' in French, although your pronunciation of that word is different from regular French."

"I intend to do it a lot more often. And yes, in South Louisiana it sounds more like 'sha' because we speak Cajun French. It's not quite like the French Europeans speak. It's definitely less…formal."

Glancing toward the house, Chelsea asked wistfully, "Did you have a nice childhood? Did your family members love each other? Did you feel safe?"

"Yes."

"Will you tell me about it when you can?"

"*If* I can."

She kissed him and said, "You need to be away from this place. You'll never be happy here again." Taking his hand, she pulled him back toward the front of the house and told him, "You have to find a place where you can remember but not have it hurt so much."

Aric considered her words as they rode in the SUV. When the driver asked him where they were heading, he answered that he wasn't sure, yet. Then he turned to Chelsea and asked her to take out her computer and turn it on.

"What do you need?" she inquired curiously.

"A house."

"A house?" she echoed. "Aric, you can't mean to buy a house today."

"Why not?"

"Because that's a fool thing to do," Fredeline remarked. "You think we're going to be able to find a place you like this afternoon and move in by tonight?"

"Possibly."

"You're crazy!" Eve Rose exclaimed, but she was grinning madly at him.

"Not crazy," Miss June said kindly. "Tired, sad, and ready to be home is more like it."

"Do you know where you wish to live?" Olga asked with interest.

"I've always loved the Garden District, and the St. Charles Streetcar connects it with lots of amenities, attractions, and the converted warehouse where my company's headquarters is located."

"Where is it in relation to the apartment you already have?" asked Eve Rose.

"My apartment is part of the top floor of the company building. It's very convenient when I work long hours and need to catch some sleep."

"You can't do that anymore," Chelsea protested. "You have to be home with us."

"I plan on that, although it may be a necessity for me to sleep at work now and again depending on deadlines."

She didn't look pleased with his answer but merely pursed her lips then asked, "What do you want me to look for regarding houses?"

"I want to live in the Garden District in an historic home that is livable but needs restoration work. We'll need four to six bedrooms and as many bathrooms as possible. Everything else is negotiable."

"And the price?"

"Just see what's available that has what I want and don't look at the price."

Within five minutes, Chelsea had three prospective homes bookmarked. Aric called the realtor on the listing for the first one and immediately disliked her. That wasn't going to stop him from looking at the home. He set up an appointment with her for 1:00. The next realtor was nicer and agreed to meet him at 2:45. The last realtor was eager to meet and said he could barely wait until 5:00 to show Aric the mansion in question.

Aric and his women ate chicken at Cane's for lunch and talked about the things they needed to accomplish in the upcoming week. Afterward, they headed to the first showing. The realtor was unpleasant, and the Greek Revival-style house was obviously in deplorable physical condition. Aric declared the exterior was in such bad shape that he didn't have any desire to see the interior. They quickly moved on to the next place.

The second realtor was a great improvement over the first, but Aric was immediately put off by the location. The townhomes were situated outside his target area. They stood in the French Quarter and their doorways opened right onto the property lines. He apologized to the man and explained that he wanted something more private and removed from the street.

The final house was one block over from St. Charles Avenue. It was a Double-Gallery House, which was set back somewhat from the quiet street. It was appealing enough, and Aric agreed to take a tour with the realtor. He and the women climbed the few steps to the front porch and went inside.

Aric was disappointed. The lovely, old-fashioned exterior of the home had been ruined by a completely modern renovation inside. Everything was steel, glass, and concrete. In his opinion, it was a travesty.

He was about to voice his observations when he caught a glimpse of Chelsea out of the corner of his eye. She appeared frightened and was staring at the ugly metal staircase. He moved over to her and asked her what was wrong.

"I can't do lots of stairs," she replied shakily. "I might fall. I can't fall."

Aric grimaced. He hadn't even considered Chelsea's spatial challenges. He suddenly realized he'd never seen her climb a flight of stairs or go out onto the balcony of his hotel suite. Living in any house that had a staircase could increase her likelihood of falling and reinjuring her brain.

He assured her that he didn't care for the interior of this house and was not planning to purchase it regardless. Then he asked the realtor, a congenial young man, whether or not there were any large one-story houses for sale in the area.

"One block over," the man told him. "But it needs some work."

Remembering the first house they'd looked at, Aric asked how much work.

"It's livable," the realtor said encouragingly. "The outside's in great shape, but the inside needs a complete overhaul."

The feeling of anticipation Aric so enjoyed was suddenly there. He asked the man to walk with them to the house so they could take a look. They made their way through the sweltering September heat toward the property.

It was, ironically enough, a house fashioned in the Creole cottage style. A low white-picket fence ran the length of the property, which the realtor informed Aric was approximately a third of an acre in size. They filed through the gate and studied the house. It was a rectangular dwelling built at ground level and had a pitched roof with four dormers and a chimney that shot up through the center of the front part of the rooftop. Made of wood that had been painted a rusty red, the home had an old-fashioned door with an iron handle and four sets of French doors, flanked by full-length green shutters leading off the porch into the house itself.

"Will someone please inform me as to what Creole is?" Olga asked. "I understand that it can be used to describe a language and a people, but where did it come from?"

"Creole in Louisiana refers to colonial descendants of the French and Spanish settlers," Aric explained. "But you have Creoles of European descent and Creoles of Color."

"I used to hear stories of balls in the late 1700s and later in which rich white men would court colored Creole women both here and in Haiti," Fredeline put in. "Mixed-race women were real sought-after and groomed to please those who had money and power. Because of what they were, they didn't have many other choices in life."

"How interesting," Olga said thoughtfully. "And this was openly accepted during that time period? I would not have believed it."

"We could call this Creole House," Chelsea suggested. "Could we go inside? I like this place."

She was staring as if transfixed by the home, and Miss June observed that they should investigate its interior.

"How many square feet is this house?" inquired Aric, as the realtor led them toward the front door. "I doubt if there will be enough bedrooms and bathrooms for all of us."

"Then you'd probably be wrong," the man said with a flash of white teeth. "The entire house is fifty-six hundred square feet. In the main part of the home, you have a living area separated by the double-sided fireplace from the dining area and kitchen. Past the main part of the house are four bedrooms and two full bathrooms. Then there's the upstairs and the addition...."

"What addition?" Eve Rose asked.

"There's a door that leads to a hallway that connects the house to a smaller cottage that was converted into a master suite. The cottage and main house were built in 1810, but structural enhancements were made over the past couple of hundred years. According to Orleans Parish records, the cottage was connected to the main house in 2006. They did a magnificent job of making it look like it was part of the original construction, although there'd be no way any architect of 1810 would have done such a thing. Still, it looks great. You'll see."

They stepped into the main room of the house. It was an enormous space, separated by a huge, old, double-sided, free-standing brick fireplace. Aric looked worriedly at Chelsea, but she seemed to be doing well in the open area. He speculated that it was because the ceilings were only ten feet high, and the fireplace provided some delineation to the space.

The inside of the house was decorated in 20th Century Ugly. There were unattractive vertical blinds covering the lovely sets of French doors, worn, green carpet everywhere, and faded green-and-yellow striped wallpaper on the walls. The kitchen counters were white Formica that seemed to be over seventy-five years old, and the cabinets looked as though they might come away from the wall at any moment. All of the appliances were antiquated and not in a good way.

They moved on to the four bedrooms, all of which had threadbare Berber carpet and various, but equally unattractive, patterned types of wallpaper. The bathrooms were serviceable, but outdated. A set of French doors led out into the backyard from the center of the house, but the realtor asked the little group to bypass those for now and go to the solid wood door that was positioned at one end of the living room.

As they moved through the wide, windowless hallway, Aric asked, "What materials were used to construct this?"

"Concrete. If there's a hurricane, this is the place to be."

"Speaking of hurricanes, I can't help but note that the house isn't raised. Has there ever been any flooding?"

"Nothing. That's not to say it couldn't happen during a natural disaster, but the place has been spared since it was built. No damage has ever been documented or observed. It's like there's a protective shell around this property."

When they reached the end of the hallway, the realtor opened another thick wooden door and ushered them into the converted cottage. It consisted of a large master bedroom and bathroom combination that held potential but had worn wooden floors and peeling paint on the walls. Two sets of French doors opened onto a patio area. When they stepped outside, the two men and five women observed an overgrown yard filled with large trees and an overabundance of bushes, weeds, and plants. To their right was more of the same. To the left was the main part of the house. A kidney-shaped pool, filled with slimy green water, was surrounded by brick pavers and sat in-between the cottage patio and the primary structure.

Aric looked up at the dormers on the rear part of the house's roof. He asked their guide if he could examine the attic. The women all declined to participate in that facet of the tour.

"You can only reach the attic from the stairs at the side of the house," the man informed him. "There's a door with a lock on it. I'd be happy to show you."

Aric had expected to see a dusty, open attic space with exposed beams, the central section of the chimney that pierced the roof, and not much else. When the two men stepped in through the side door, he paused. This part of the house had furniture in it as well, and it didn't appear that the items had merely been placed up there for storage. Because of the pitched roof, a grown man could easily walk freely throughout the main part of the attic.

He wandered slowly, taking in the ancient crib, iron bed, rocking chair, battered dolls, old-fashioned wooden toys, and children's books. Turning back to the realtor, he asked soberly, "What is all this?"

The pleasant young man was no longer smiling. As he glanced around the room, he admitted, "I'd never been up here before. I think...I have a feeling this was a shut-away room."

"A what?"

The man sighed and said, "My great-grandmother told me once that centuries ago there were rich people who had disabled or mixed-race bastard children. Either was considered an embarrassment. So, they'd hide the unwanted children in a shut-away room with a nanny or with their mothers, depending on the situation. It was horrible. If the children were disabled, then they were kept there for their entire lives. If they were of mixed race, then they were often hidden until they were deemed old enough to put out on the streets or...given to someone to be used as a servant, for sex, or both."

"My God. I had no idea such a thing existed. How long ago was this?"

With a shrug, the man said, "1800s? I don't really know. It's not something that people tended to advertise. My great-grandmother said a lot of the children's births and deaths weren't ever recorded. It was like they never existed. They were literally shut away because they had the misfortune of being born."

Walking over to one of the dormer windows, Aric looked down into the backyard at the women standing near the pool. He focused on Chelsea. If she'd been born two hundred years earlier, would she have been sentenced to the shut-away room in the attic? Once she was old enough, would her father have given her to the highest bidder? If so, her fate would have probably included being forced to clean the man's house by day and then being molested by him at night. If she'd given birth to his children, would they have been shut away, too? Aric shuddered. He knew what he had to do.

Chapter Twelve

"How much is the owner asking for this place?" Aric asked the realtor.

"Well, the location and size of the house and property are extremely desirable, but the work required to renovate the interior will be considerable. The owner is asking five million."

"Do they own the property outright?"

"Yes."

"I'll give them three million in cash at the closing, providing an inspection can be done immediately and there aren't any major problems. I'd like for you to handle the sale of my other house, although I don't know what the market has been like since half the world's population was wiped out."

"You'd be surprised. Even with the reduction in population, real estate in New Orleans has been doing quite well since the D Plague. This place is actually a steal, even at five million."

The man excused himself and stepped outside to make some calls. Aric had worked on enough homes with his grandfather to know that there would be no major structural issues with the house. However, he wanted to know how much money he was going to have to sink into the property to tailor it to his needs and taste.

He looked around the attic, trying to imagine being a virtual prisoner in one's own home. He was dripping with sweat in the enclosed space. Even with the dormers open, it would be unbearably hot in the Louisiana summers before the invention of air-conditioning. He assumed that those living in the attics would be required to stay as quiet as possible when there were visitors at the house. How terrible to know that you were trapped in a room by the person who gave you life because that person was ashamed of you.

"It's called a 'throw-away room' where I come from," Miss June said from the doorway. "My grandfather used to say that it would have been better if those poor children had just been killed at birth rather than caged like animals."

"I can't believe anyone could do this to a child, especially not a special-needs child."

"Different times and different ways of thinking," she said matter-of-factly. "I think human beings have made a lot of progress over time, don't you?"

"Sometimes I wonder. I'm sure there's someone out there who has a child locked in an attic or basement as we speak."

"Those people are just plain sick in the head. The people who had these rooms were ignorant – no matter how educated they were. Sometimes they thought they were doing it to protect their children. Life was a lot more cruel for those with physical, mental, or emotional challenges." Coming into the attic, she said, "Girls in the South like Chelsea who weren't 'pure' would've either been pampered and cared for if they were lucky or more likely would've been outcasts in all ethnic communities. They'd have become prostitutes or been kept as…sexual slaves by their men. Their children would have suffered greatly. I thank God those days are past."

Nodding distractedly, Aric asked, "Do you think I'm crazy because I'm rushing into this?"

"I think you'd be crazy not to. It seems to me you've been so focused and isolated in your own way for the past five years that you need a little spontaneity."

"I'm certainly being spontaneous now."

"You should call your old friend in D.C. and have a long talk with her. You need to have a good conversation with someone who knows you well."

The realtor leaned into the attic and said questioningly, "Four million?"

"Three point seven," countered Aric. "Otherwise, I walk."

The man relayed this over his phone then nodded to Aric and gave him a thumbs-up sign. He stepped back outside, and Aric and Miss June hastened to follow. As they went down the steps, they discussed Miss June's new role as Aric's assistant.

"It's been decided by the higher-ups that I'll be your personal assistant here at home. That way, I can stay close to Chelsea, who is the focus of my assignment. You'll find a new administrative assistant at work when you arrive there tomorrow who's been hand-picked by me. His name is Jason, and he's excellent and trustworthy," she assured him. As they got closer to Fredeline, Olga,

Eve Rose, and Chelsea, she added, "I'll make certain everything runs smoothly while we adjust to life here."

"Then we're living here?" Eve Rose asked excitedly. "It's done?"

"It's done," answered Aric. "I'll insist on an inspection then I'll sign the papers. I'd like to move in and renovate the place myself, but I doubt if I'll have time. It's too bad because I love doing things like that."

"So, how will you do it?" Olga asked.

"I want Chelsea to work with me on fixing it up."

"Me? But how? I don't think I know how to renovate houses, and I'm certainly not strong enough to do the physical work."

"I know, but you're great with computers. If I tell you what I'd like, then you can use the technology to virtually design each room. I can decide what I like and dislike and then have projects done or get you to select things for the place." Looking back and forth between the women, he said, "I want you to design your own bedrooms, save for the flooring. They're your rooms."

"But we will probably not live here for the rest of our lives," Olga pointed out.

"No, but as long as you live here, this is your home, too." Turning to Chelsea, he said, "You and I can design the master suite together."

"But what if you get tired of me?"

"What?"

She repeated the question.

Aric asked the others to excuse them for a few minutes then led Chelsea through the overgrowth in the backyard until they almost stumbled over a concrete bench. He urged her to sit beside him then took her in his arms and kissed her. When he drew back, he said firmly, "I won't ever get tired of you. I've never felt this way about any woman in my life. You made me want to *feel* again. I love you, Chelsea."

"I love you, too. But what if you fall out of love with me?"

"What if *you* fall out of love with *me*?"

"I...I couldn't."

"And *I* couldn't fall out of love with *you*," he said with as much certainty as he could interject into his words. He meant it, but he wanted to make sure Chelsea believed him. "Let's stop worrying and just live our lives."

"It's…hard for me because…because I don't remember my life before last year," she said quietly. "It makes me less self-assured."

"I know. It'll be okay. It's barely been a year since your accident. Things will keep getting better." Sighing, he said, "I'm worn out. Let's find a hotel and get some dinner and sleep before I have to go in to work in the morning."

Aric walked with his entourage and the realtor back down the street to where the SUV and driver were waiting. After some further discussion between Aric and the realtor, the driver took Aric and the women to the Westin. They were all tired, hungry, and ready for a good night's sleep. After dinner, Aric had a talk with Miss June, promising he would call her when he left for work the next morning so that they could review what needed to be done while he was at his company's headquarters.

"I'm going to make a list," Aric told Chelsea while they got ready for bed. "I want you to follow it tomorrow and e-mail or text me with updates. I'll respond to them as soon as I can."

"But I can't follow lists! What if I mess something up?"

"You won't because you're going to work on that with Miss June. She's going to be your personal assistant as well as mine. She'll help you stay on track."

"She's one of them, isn't she?"

Aric put down the toothbrush in his hand and asked, "One of whom?"

"The people protecting me."

He shook his head in disbelief. Chelsea couldn't follow a list, but she could intuit that Miss June was part of the secret group of intelligence agents protecting her. All he could do was nod in confirmation of her suspicions.

"Should I trust her?" Chelsea asked.

"I decided I would. I can't see any reason why we shouldn't. If they wanted you dead, then they could have killed you many times over by now."

"As long as I'm nobody, then I think I'm safe. I guess it's a good thing I lost my previous life in that taxi. Otherwise, I'd probably be dead, too. I wish I knew who was after me."

Wrapping his arms around her shoulders, he said, "Come to bed. We'll think about it more tomorrow and afterward."

Chelsea was in rare form as they had sex that night. Always willing and capable when it came to lovemaking, she'd added it to her daily routine. She and Aric had at least one sexual encounter every day unless she was in the grip of a migraine. Aric, who'd been celibate for so long, typically had no complaints. That night, however, Chelsea was on top and was being so rough that she was actually hurting him. He had to halt her in the middle of the sex, and she looked lost and anxious.

"Don't stop me," she breathed. "Please, Aric."

"I need you to take things a little easier."

"But I don't want to. I need you to hurt me."

Aric froze and asked her to repeat what she'd said. She did.

"Oh, Chere," he murmured. "You don't mean that."

"I do," she insisted meekly.

"But why? Why would you need me to hurt you?"

"I – I don't know. I just do."

"You don't," he said in an authoritative tone. "Did someone hurt you before?"

"I don't know!" she cried, climbing off him and getting out of the bed. "I don't remember anything, Aric! Remember that? Maybe I liked to have men hurt me like that before the accident!"

"I don't believe that. You've never wanted me to hurt you until tonight, and we've been having sex regularly for a couple of weeks. What's different tonight?"

"I don't know! I don't understand!" Trembling, she begged, "Help me to understand!"

"I'm trying!" he yelled, as he got up and faced her. "You have to give it time!"

She covered her mouth with one hand and said, "Oh, Aric. I'll never be right and never know why. How can you love someone like me?"

Aric got control of himself, sat on the bed, pulled Chelsea into his lap, and wrapped his arms tightly around her. While she cried, he said, "I love you. One of my top priorities is getting you the help you need."

"What about you?" she sniffled. "You need help, too."

Kissing her on the temple, he said, "That's what you're for. You make me feel exhilarated and comforted whenever I'm around you."

"How?"

"Because you are the most complicated, yet straight-forward woman I know. You make me want to take care of you and make me want you to take care of me."

"Will you just hold me in your arms now and talk to me until I fall asleep?"

He stretched out on the bed and took her in his arms. She rested her head against his chest and said, "Tell me what it was like to be in school with other children and go to recess and do homework."

He was so sad for her that he wasn't able to speak for a full minute. A tear slid from the corner of each eye, but Chelsea couldn't see it from where she lay. He talked of life in parochial school, of teachers he liked and those he disliked, of school plays, of sports, and of homework, class projects, and field trips. Chelsea finally fell asleep, and Aric allowed himself to sleep, too.

When he woke the next morning, he and Chelsea were still in the same positions. He somehow managed to ease out from under her without waking her and hurried to shower, shave, brush his teeth, and dress. Then he called Miss June.

"What's the matter?" she asked immediately once he'd greeted her. "Something's happened."

"I can't talk to you about it," he replied quickly. "I'm not going to report to you about everything Chelsea does."

"No, but you can tell me when something has disturbed you enough to worry you. We're trying to keep her safe, remember?"

"Meet me outside my door in five minutes."

Once Miss June arrived, they moved to a small seating area down the hall. Aric very quickly and very quietly explained the previous night's incident to the older woman. She frowned and said, "More mystery. Just what we need. Perhaps she was the victim of an abduction, although we've already investigated things from that angle. Maybe she was someone's girlfriend, and they liked to hurt her during sex. She could have been the victim of a pedophile when she was a child. The list could go on and on." Sighing, she said, "I can't conceive of what her daily life must be like with no memory of anything before last year. When will you do the blood work that will determine her genetic background?"

"I was hoping you could take her and the others to the corporate headquarters this afternoon. Chelsea can have her blood drawn while she's there, and my people will send it off to the appropriate lab. Everyone will need certain security clearances, including you." Checking the time, he asked, "Is this Jason guy you've set me up with armed?"

"Of course."

"Licensed to kill?" he said in an attempt at humor.

"Why yes," Miss June replied seriously. "I'm also armed and am a darn good shot, if I do say so myself. You'll find that the people I'm going to hire to work for you around the house will also be armed and well-trained. We're here to protect all of you 24/7."

Impressed, Aric asked, "Did you ever have your own life?"

The elderly woman smiled and said, "I've had more lives than you can begin to know."

Chapter Thirteen

Aric took a taxi to Rodrigue Pharmaceuticals headquarters, which was located in a huge converted warehouse. The structure housed offices, laboratories, and his upstairs apartment. He was greeted on the sidewalk in front of the building by a brown-haired man, who was a few years his senior, a few inches taller, and in better physical shape than Aric would ever be, despite his exercise regimen. As they shook hands, the man introduced himself as Jason Duson.

"How much experience do you have?" Aric asked before they walked into the building.

"Twelve years."

"As an administrative assistant or...other experience?"

"Both. I'm very good."

"I'm sure you are. Otherwise, Miss June wouldn't have picked you to work with me." Stopping before he triggered the motion sensors that would open the sliding doors leading into the building, Aric asked, "Do you know about what happened to me five years ago?"

"Yes, Sir."

"How many other people outside of the research team know?"

"That I'm aware of? Twenty-three."

"Not a lot, but more than I thought. I wonder how many others there are, not that I can do anything about it."

"No, Sir."

"Are you always going to call me 'sir' when you talk to me?"

"Yes, Sir."

The two men smiled at one another before Aric said, "My life is literally in your hands. I should be calling you 'sir,' not the other way around. Please, don't call me that."

"Whatever you say. You're my top priority indefinitely."

"And if I die because you slip up?"

"Then my life is over, too. I might still be alive, but I might as well be dead."

"Damn. That's pretty harsh."

"It's good incentive."

"Have you ever killed anyone?"

"Yes."

"Did you enjoy it?"

"No. It was necessary but not satisfying."

"Glad to hear it. Come on."

Aric greeted the staff they passed by name and introduced each of them to Jason as the two men made their way through the enormous lobby with its high ceilinged, exposed brick, ducts, and pipes. The architects had decided to allow visitors and employees passing through the lobby to get a feel for what it must have been like to work in the warehouse that had originally been built in the early 1900s. Aric loved it.

The morning was hectic, but it went surprisingly well in light of Aric's three-week absence and the presence of the new administrative assistant. He and Jason enjoyed a working lunch, and Aric truthfully told the man that he was better than the previous administrative assistant, who'd been of extremely high caliber.

"It's good to know that the taxpayers are getting their money's worth," Jason joked.

"Speaking of payment, you're being paid by the government. What happens to the money I'm paying you? I know you have to be getting a paycheck. If you weren't, then my accountants would be suspicious."

"The checks are made out to me, but I don't get the money when I cash them. You're making a charitable donation to my actual employer, Uncle Sam."

"But what if I'd be paying you more than what the government pays you."

"I didn't decide to become an administrative assistant for the money."

"What did push you in that direction?"

"It runs in the family."

The men were interrupted by a call from the receptionist, who informed them that the women Aric had told her would be coming had arrived.

"There seems to be an issue," she told him. "Something about one of them not being able to walk through the lobby...?"

"Damn it," muttered Aric after he'd disconnected the call. "I should've thought about Chelsea's spatial issues when I told them to come here."

When he and Jason stepped out of the elevators, Aric easily spotted the women standing in one corner of the lobby. Chelsea was facing a window that looked out onto the street, and Miss June, Fredeline, Eve Rose, and Olga were clustered around her. Aric hurried over, nodded to the others, and immediately put his arms around Chelsea.

"I'm sorry, Chere," he whispered into her ear. "I didn't even think about you having to walk through this space."

"I tried," she said softly. "I held Fredeline's hand and Miss June's, but I couldn't do it."

"It's okay. There's another entrance on the side of the building. We'll walk around."

Each woman was soon processed by Security and had official identification that would allow them limited access to the building. None of the women was cleared to go into the laboratories unless accompanied by Aric. But they would be able to walk to his office and the restrooms should they visit him at work.

After Chelsea had submitted to withdrawal of blood by one of the phlebotomists, Aric asked her how she was doing with the list he'd e-mailed her. He was heartened when she brightened.

"I skipped only one line," she announced. "Miss June said I did a great job."

"Excellent. What did you find out about the house projects I need done?"

"After you sign the papers this afternoon and own the house, men will come and put in reclaimed pine floors throughout every room except the three bathrooms. I have several virtual bathrooms designed. I also picked out two different types of cabinets for the kitchen and some furniture like what you asked for. Olga has suggestions for the room that will be the home gym. After we leave here, we're going to go back to the hotel so that the others can design their rooms. You'll have to approve it all and make changes if you want."

"You got a lot accomplished."

"I did, didn't I? There's still so much left though. What do you want to do with the attic?"

"Make it something other than what it was."

"Why not make it a home office? Either that or you could turn it into a place for Miss June."

"Miss June said she didn't want to live with us. She said she'd find a place nearby."

"This is nearby and not with us. It's sort of separate. It could be like her own private apartment. You could put in a small bathroom and run air-conditioning and heat up there. It even has its own separate entrance."

"Ask her. I definitely want A/C and heat run up there, regardless."

Chelsea glanced across the room at the others, who were chatting near a vending area. She asked Aric if the two of them could go to his office for a few minutes before the little group departed for the hotel. He agreed to her request and told the others that he and Chelsea would return shortly.

They'd barely gotten into the office when Chelsea threw her arms around his neck and kissed him.

"I'm sorry for what happened last night," she said. "I still can't explain it. I've decided that it must have been due to the stress of our trip. Thank you for talking with me and helping me realize I didn't have to be hurt in order to feel relief."

Then Chelsea quickly undid his pants, pulled down his boxers, and took him in her mouth.

Aric had never had sex on the premises of Rodrigue Pharmaceuticals, but he didn't tell Chelsea to stop. Instead, he reveled in what she was doing and in the tiny sounds of pleasure she emitted as she pleased him. He came, struggling not to moan as he did so.

"You always taste so sweet," Chelsea told him, as he helped her to her feet. "I love doing that."

"I'm pretty happy with it, too," Aric chuckled. "Would it frighten you if I did something like this to you on the spur-of-the-moment somewhere outside the bedroom? I've wanted to but didn't want to startle you."

She grinned and said, "Startle me."

By the end of the day, Aric owned the Creole House and his family home was on the realtors' market. He returned to the Westin, ate dinner with the women, reviewed the virtual designs and rooms that were ready for him, and was happy that Miss June had agreed to live in what would be an upstairs apartment that would be created out of the old shut-away room. The renovation of the entire interior of his house would begin the following morning, as would the refinishing work on the pool and patio areas. A landscape architect would also visit the property in order to create plans for an outdoor makeover of the place.

Miss June asked Aric to stop by her hotel room before he went to bed. Chelsea, complaining of a headache, swallowed one of her pills before urging him to go talk to the personal assistant.

"Won't you be jealous if I go alone to Miss June's room?"

Taking him literally, she said, "No, I like Miss June and trust her. Besides she's probably fifty years older than you. So, I'm not worried."

Smiling down at her, Aric told Chelsea to call him if she needed him to return before he came back on his own.

"What changed your mind about living with us?" Aric asked the older woman once he'd taken a seat in the living area of her room.

"Chelsea did."

"She was that persuasive?"

"Unintentionally, yes." When Aric asked her to elucidate, she said, "I've been doing this for a very long time. I've pretty much seen it all or so I'd thought until I met Chelsea. Whatever happened to her or why she's been protected by this unknown person is confounding. I don't like to be confounded."

"And?"

"And it's very affecting to be personally involved with Chelsea. The aftereffects of her accident are mind-boggling to me. I've tried to imagine what it would be like to not recall being a child or young girl at all. It's almost impossible." Staring keenly at him she asked, "She'll never get her memories back?"

"I doubt it."

"That would be a lifelong struggle I wouldn't want to wish upon anyone." Miss June sipped from a nearby glass of water and remarked, "You come from a very large, loving family."

Aric nodded.

"You'll never be able to have children with Chelsea, will you?"

"Not as long as she's like this. Next year or the year after? Five years down the road? Who knows? People with traumatic brain injuries can make amazing recoveries over time."

"What if it never happens?"

"Then we never have children."

"That's a lot to give up."

"At least I can make the choice. No one gave Chelsea a choice in any of this."

There was silence between them for some time. Eventually, Miss June confided, "This will be my last job. I turned eighty in July and know that all good things must come to an end. But I'd like to see you and Chelsea safe and happy before I hang up my holster. They don't normally allow people my age to remain in the field, but I'm special."

"I can tell. What if this drags on for years?"

"If I'm not fit to continue working, then I'll step down and keep tabs on things from wherever I am. Jason will see this through."

"You're only eighty. I think you have at least another ten years left on the job."

"Thank you, but I hope everything is settled before 2044."

"Me, too."

"Did you make that call to your friend in D.C.?"

"Not yet."

"Make the call. You know it may take her a while to get back with you. Why wait?"

Aric left Miss June's and went back to his own rooms. Mercifully, Chelsea's medication appeared to have worked. She was sleeping peacefully. He shut the bedroom door and stretched out on the couch before initiating the call to Lakshmi Jitesh. After following the familiar procedure, he disconnected the call and yawned before going to get ready for bed. He had no idea where in the world Lakshmi was or how long it would take for her to find time to return his call. When she did, he would be glad to talk with her.

As he brushed his teeth, Aric thought of his brief romantic relationship with the woman who was currently the President of the United States of America. Despite the fact that she was about ten years older than he, they'd been very compatible and enjoyed their long conversations. A gentle lover, Lakshmi had shown Aric that sex could be powerful while being extraordinarily tender. He had enjoyed it, but he had to admit that he enjoyed sex with Chelsea more.

That's one reason why Lakshmi is your friend and you love Chelsea as your partner, he thought. *If there was one thing your mother taught you, it was to respect every person for his or her own contribution to the human race.*

Aric didn't want to think about his mother or anyone else in his family. Once he got started, he couldn't seem to stop. He experienced a brief flash of remembrance of swimming in the pool at his family home with his nieces and nephews and of kissing his youngest nephew's wet hair as the toddler giggled with delight. He loved that sound, the sound of a child laughing without a care in the world. It was the sound of innocence, something Chelsea would never remember.

Chapter Fourteen

Aric was working with Jason on corporate business the first Thursday in October when Lakshmi texted him to let him know that she was available to talk. He asked Jason to leave the room and told him he was not to be disturbed unless the building was on fire. He never knew whether his talks with Lakshmi would last five minutes or five hours. He wasn't going to waste a single second.

Lakshmi's image appeared on his virtual computer screen once he'd logged on for their face-to-face conversation.

"You look better than you have in years," she said with a genuine smile.

"Thanks. *You* look as lovely as the Hindu goddess of prosperity and beauty for which you were named."

"That's what you always say."

"Because it's true."

"How would you know? Have you met the goddess?"

They spent the next three and a half hours catching up on what had been going on in their personal and professional lives since they'd last spoken.

"That's quite a story," Lakshmi commented once Aric had finished his update. "Why didn't you call me sooner? It seems as though almost everyone who helped this woman in the first year after her accident has died or disappeared. Plus, you say that there are people telling you they're from the government protecting her. I would have expected a call earlier than this morning."

Aric stared dumbfounded at Lakshmi and said, "I called you when we returned to New Orleans. That was mid-September."

Now it was her turn to appear shocked.

"You followed the standard protocol for contacting me?"

"You know I did."

There was a protracted silence between them. Finally, Lakshmi said, "I'm going to look into this. It makes me extremely uneasy to know that notification of your call took over three weeks to make it to me. You didn't think it strange that I didn't call you sooner?"

"You're the President. I figured you were busy."

"Have I ever taken that long to call you back?"

"No, but I've been watching the news as always and seeing the upheaval in the Middle East and in South America. I knew you'd call when you could."

"If you ever contact me and don't hear back within forty-eight hours, then call again. I'm going to send you an encrypted e-mail with a contact person listed in case you still don't get a response. I don't like this, Aric. Something isn't right about it."

"To be sure."

After a moment, Lakshmi put aside the worried look he'd seen and said, "I can't wait to meet this mysterious woman who's...well...brought you back."

"Brought me back?"

"You haven't been yourself since the D Plague, and that's perfectly understandable. The man I've been talking to today is more like my dear friend Aric than the man I've been talking to for the past five years. Whoever this girl is, she's been able to reach you in a way none of the rest of us have. Buddy and I will be in Louisiana toward the end of next week for a four-day break. Let's get together at your new house."

"You can do that? Just drop by?"

"I wouldn't necessarily call it 'just dropping by,' but we can work it out. My Secret Service people will sweep the area, clear it of any threats, and protect the motorcade and us while we're there. Our day at the house will be normal for all intents and purposes."

"That would be great. Maybe we could have a cook-out, and you and Buddy could escape the Press. Will his wife be with him?"

"Yes, Nadine will be with him."

"You could bring a boyfriend."

She laughed and said, "Presidents don't have boyfriends or lovers. I'm in an exclusive relationship with the United States of America for at least another couple of years. After that, we'll see."

"I take it your people will contact my people?" he said with a grin.

"It sounds like they're all the same people, although I'm not aware of 'your people.' That's not surprising. I can't know everything every government agency does. I will check it out though and make certain your people are legit. I want you and those you care about to be safe. This situation with Chelsea's a real puzzler. Perhaps I can put someone on it?"

"That might make things more dangerous for her and all of us."
Leaning back in his chair, he said, "Just check out my people and
hold off on the rest. I hate to say it, but I don't really trust your
people. There are too many of them with their own agendas."

"Agreed."

"I'm looking forward to seeing you, Buddy, and Nadine."

"Say what you mean."

He laughed out loud and said, "I'm looking forward to seeing
you and Buddy. I wish Nadine was otherwise occupied. I hate to be
like that, but I've never liked her. Why Buddy married her, I'll
never know."

"That's because you're a man who has no designs on a career in
politics. Buddy LaFleur married Nadine Boisfantane because she
was a true Southern Belle with lots of old-school clout and money in
her family. She was beautiful, well-heeled, and the perfect wife for
someone who had his sights set on the White House."

"And Nadine?"

"She couldn't have missed Buddy's potential. He may not have
come from old money, but he was a smart cookie with personality
plus and lots of ambition. They did all the right things and had three
beautiful children. The only thing they didn't count on was losing
their girls in the D Plague. At least our stint as President and Vice-
President has gone well and seems to be leading to positive change
around the world."

"Will you run again for the White House?"

"I'd rather not, but I think I will. Buddy and I will run on the
same ticket and already have a phenomenal track record. Why not
do four more years of good while we can?"

"Then Buddy will run for President."

"I'm sure he will. Assuming we continue to do our jobs well, I
don't think he'll have any trouble winning. Hopefully, he'll have
two good terms and leave the country right where we wanted it to be
once we started all this."

"Which was?"

"Better off than it had been in forever." Sighing, she admitted,
"I have to go get ready for a dinner with the French President and his
cronies. I'll be seeing you soon. I'm looking forward to some really
good company and food. I wish my parents had survived the D
Plague and could be there with us."

"I wish mine had, too. I really liked your folks and always liked the LaFleur children and wish they were around to share in the fun as well. They were sweet kids."

"I'm glad you finally went home, Aric. You needed some finality, as much as any of us can have in our post-Plague world. Take care."

"You, too. See you soon."

At 6:00, Aric and Jason left the office, walked to the St. Charles Streetcar stop nearest to Rodrigue Pharmaceuticals, and caught the car that would take both of them home. Aric got off at his stop and wished Jason a good night. He knew from what Miss June had told him that Jason lived only two blocks away in the top half of an old Victorian home. It made Aric feel better knowing that the man was nearby in case of emergency.

As if other people aren't around to protect you. You're all probably under constant surveillance. Jason is one of many agents involved.

But Aric knew Jason. He and Miss June humanized the operation. Aric didn't think Lakshmi would find out anything bad about Jason or Miss June, but he was curious to see what results she was going to get when she launched what he knew would be a discreet inquiry involving the person responsible for Chelsea's protection detail.

When the Creole House came into view, Aric smiled. He couldn't wait to see the day's progress. The workmen were cleaning up as he walked through the gate. He greeted them by name as he passed them and wished them a good evening. Then he went into his house. He'd barely had time to close the door behind him when Chelsea called out excitedly, "Aric, come see!"

He scanned the main living area. The pine flooring was perfect, as was the taupe paint and white trim. The disgusting vertical blinds had been removed from the French doors, and a coating had been applied to the panes of glass that automatically darkened them when night fell, allowing those inside to see out but preventing those outside from seeing in. The couch and loveseat were white, and the end tables and coffee table were antiques that had been refinished to match the style of the house. The look of the place had been well thought-out, but the atmosphere was relaxed. That was exactly what Aric had wanted.

A paper-thin, flat-screen TV was mounted above the fireplace. Aric didn't like that but had conceded that there was no other suitable location for the television in the living room if he wanted the fireplace to remain the focal point of the space. At least the thing was not immediately visible to those entering the home.

"Aric!" Chelsea called out again. "In here!"

He moved to the kitchen. Restored wood cabinets lined the walls, and shiny stainless steel appliances gleamed in their designated spots. An enormous antique dining table and twelve chairs had been placed in the center of the floor, leaving plenty of room for those cooking to prepare meals and work while others sat and chatted with them or ate at the table.

He went to the exercise room, which was located in the corner bedroom off the kitchen. The walls in this room were a cheerful yellow, and cork mats had been placed under the equipment so nothing would scratch the pine. Chelsea was sitting on a weight bench looking very pleased with herself. Olga stood behind her and was smiling, but the look she gave Aric was one that said, "Be prepared."

Aric went over to Chelsea, bent to kiss her, and asked her what had her so excited. He watched as she lifted and lowered the leg lift part of the bench a dozen times. Then she accepted the two hand weights from Olga and lifted them a dozen times each. She appeared so happy that he couldn't help but grin and clap.

"I've been working on it since we got the equipment last week. I wasn't even able to lift anything more than once at first, but Olga showed me how to do it so I didn't hurt myself. I know it's only a few pounds, but it makes me feel like I'm getting better. I want to try the other machines, but Olga says all I can do is walk on the treadmill and do this for now. Well, that and the exercises I do with her and then her massage."

"Olga's right. You have to think about your brain and how what you do during exercise affects it. No running or lifting extreme amounts of weight, remember?" Glancing at Olga, he said, "This is great progress in a short amount of time."

"Yes, but that is making our girl here overly enthusiastic," Olga proclaimed. "She told me today that she wished to try the rowing machine."

"Absolutely not," Aric declared firmly.

"I'm not a child!" Chelsea protested.

"No, but you had a *brain* injury and almost died! You're doing a wonderful job of getting stronger, but rowing is very strenuous. You have to be in top shape to do that, and it may never happen." When Chelsea looked stricken, he added quickly, "I don't know if I could handle you in bed if you were that strong. You'd probably kill me."

Olga announced that this was more information than she needed to hear. Chelsea forced a smile then excused herself to go take a shower.

"How's she really doing?" he asked Olga once Chelsea had gone.

"Very well. She loves the repetition of the exercise but wants to do too much. I am telling her that too much might cause her more migraines, which is the truth. She has been very fortunate to have had only two migraines since we moved here last month, and those were relatively mild. She is still pushing herself. She wants to be stronger for you."

"For me?"

"She is highly intelligent but has so many challenges. She loves you and wants to please you and worries that you will tire of her limitations."

"But I've reassured her many times that would never happen."

"And you will be reassuring her about it until she feels comfortable with her level of achievement. Many women who are fully functional feel insecure or inadequate. Imagine you are Chelsea, who has great ability and yet is almost totally dependent on others. Do you not see my point?"

"I see it. We men are slow, but we get it eventually."

"Some do."

"I wonder if it would be damaging to Chelsea to…create a childhood for her."

"I do not understand," the Swede remarked.

"What if she went to school, to a Girl Scout meeting, or took a swimming class with children?"

Olga looked uncertain about this and suggested that he speak with a licensed mental health counselor before proceeding with those plans. He nodded and admitted that his return to work and the upheaval that had resulted from their move had temporarily derailed his efforts to find out exactly what Chelsea needed besides physical therapy and higher expectations.

"She should have a neurologist and a therapist. Now that the house is almost done, she needs to perform activities out in the community like shopping. Also, I want to start doing other things with Chelsea that normal couples do like visit attractions, attend events, and go out to dinner. Speaking of dinner, I'm starving. Are Fredeline and Eve Rose here?"

"They went to visit an old friend of Fredeline's she had not seen in many years since she left New Orleans."

"Is there any dinner in the fridge?"

"Some sort of Haitian stew. I ate earlier, but Chelsea has not eaten, yet."

"And Miss June?"

"Ate and went upstairs to her apartment. Now that Chelsea's workout is done for the evening, I believe I will go finish a book I was reading. Why don't you get her and eat? She is still too thin."

Aric walked to the wooden door at the end of the living room. The long connecting hallway was painted the same taupe color as the main living area and had the same white trim as every other room in the house. It was a boring hallway, and Chelsea had suggested they put up artwork when they bought other pieces for the house. He'd told her he couldn't have agreed more. The space was serviceable but uninteresting.

Aric went through the door to the private cottage. The walls in the bedroom were a deep maroon color that he felt gave the area a cozy atmosphere. The furniture was antique cherry wood, and a muted gold comforter was draped over the bed. As with the main living area and bathrooms, the walls were bare.

He walked to the bathroom, which was the only totally modern room in the house. A soaker tub was in one corner, and a walk-in shower that was defined by a curving glass block wall was positioned in the other. There were double sinks and plenty of storage as well as the typical water-saving toilet.

The shower was running. Aric stripped off his clothes and decided that now would be the right time for him to "startle" Chelsea as they'd discussed the previous month in his office. However, when he moved around to the inside of the shower, he found Chelsea standing under the spray of water with her hands and forehead pressed against the wall. His first thought was that she was having a migraine. He softly said her name.

"Aric, I'm so scared," she said shakily.

"Of what?"

"I don't know. It...I just got this feeling all of a sudden." Looking up at him, she said, "Let's have sex. I need to be in control for a while."

They had sex in the shower, and Chelsea calmed down. Aric admitted he was much more relaxed afterward as well. They put on comfortable but presentable pajamas, then went to the kitchen and heated up some stew. Aric devoured his, but Chelsea simply stared at her bowl.

"You have to eat, Chere," he urged. "You're already too thin."

"I don't feel like eating," she told him, as Fredeline and Eve Rose came into the house and entered the kitchen. "I'm not hungry."

"You listen to me," Fredeline said gently, as she took a seat beside Chelsea at the table. "You have to eat you some stew. You're skin and bones as it is, except for that nice top and bottom you got. It can't be helping your body or your head not to eat."

"But I'm too sad to eat."

"Sad about what?"

"Everything."

"You tell me what you're the saddest about right at this minute."

Her eyes welling with tears, Chelsea asked, "What if my mama's not dead and she's looking for me?"

"She's never going to find you if you starve yourself," Eve Rose pointed out. "If she's still alive, then maybe you'll find each other someday."

"But I won't remember her."

"She'd be happy to know her baby girl's safe," Fredeline told her. "You stop with all this supposing." Looking to Aric, she asked, "When are those blood tests going to be finished about Miss Chelsea's background?"

"Tomorrow, actually."

"So, that's a start." Stroking Chelsea's hair, she said, "You eat your stew; then we're going to make it all better for tonight."

"How?"

"I'm not going to tell you until you eat."

Chelsea ate the entire bowl of stew. Then Fredeline led her to the loveseat and told the younger woman to sit in her lap, while Aric and Eve Rose took their seats on the couch.

"But I'm too big," Chelsea protested.

"Nonsense. I'm old enough to be your grandma just like I'm Eve Rose's. You're never too big to sit in a grandma's lap."

Chelsea eased onto the Haitian woman's lap and put her head on Fredeline's shoulder. The older woman stroked her hair and told her about what it was like to be a child in Port-au-Prince during the latter part of the twentieth century. After a time, Chelsea slept.

Chapter Fifteen

As Aric lifted Chelsea, he glanced at Eve Rose and asked, "Would you go fold down the covers then get Olga and Miss June in here? I'll be right back."

Once Aric had placed Chelsea in the bed, he covered her with the comforter and stared down at her while she slept. Even if she hadn't been so intriguing to him, she was definitely a beautiful woman. The combination of the fine features, silky brown hair, almond-colored skin, and the currently closed bright blue eyes were striking.

As he walked back toward the living room, he couldn't help but wonder about the men Chelsea had been with before him. She was so experienced when it came to sex. Had she been a prostitute? Had she simply slept with multiple partners? Or had she been with only one man who'd taught her well how to please? Whatever the scenario, Aric was jealous. It was irrational but true.

When Aric stepped back into the living area, the women all turned to look at him. Fredeline remained on the loveseat, while Eve Rose was back on the couch now flanked by Olga and Miss June. For a moment, Aric thought of the "family meetings" his parents would often call to discuss schedules, important occasions, or upcoming events. His parents would sit on one couch, while his two sets of grandparents all sat on the other. He and his sisters sat on the floor or brought in chairs from the dining room.

"Mister Aric?"

He started guiltily and looked at Olga. Forcing himself to come back to the present, Aric lowered his backside onto the hearth, ran his fingers through his brown hair, and began, "There are a few very important things I want to discuss with you, some of which involve Chelsea and how we need to proceed. Since she's asleep, I'd like to go over those things with you now. Then we'll review the rest. I'll talk to Chelsea about all of it when she wakes up, but I'll approach it in a slightly…different way."

"She's still fragile but not nearly as much as when she met you," declared Fredeline. "And her headaches don't come so hard or so often."

He nodded and said, "But Olga pointed out to me earlier that Chelsea's still insecure and has little self-image."

"What do you propose to do about that?" asked Miss June. "How can she develop a real sense of self?"

Turning to the older Haitian woman and her granddaughter, he said, "Eve Rose won't start college until January. Until then, I'd like for you two to take Chelsea with you when you go shopping for groceries or do other things for the house. I don't want you to feel as if you have to take her with you everywhere, but she needs to get out and relearn how to function in regular activities of daily life. She needs to be with people outside the house."

Both women eagerly agreed to this and cited the need for one of them to be with Chelsea when she shopped, reminding Aric that the woman might be capable of performing complex intellectual tasks but still couldn't always follow a list or do simple math.

"I wish she'd use the Apps on her phone," he grumbled. "She has some great ones for those with TBI issues, but she won't use them."

"Once she gains some independence," Miss June offered. "Until that happens, she's going to doubt herself no matter how good the Apps are."

"We'll watch over her and help her," Eve Rose put in. "But there are some other things she needs to make her feel like a normal woman. I know she's bought clothes with us and has nice things, but she doesn't have any pretty skirts or dresses that are just for fun."

"I want to take her out to eat tomorrow night," Aric confided. "It's a casual place, but she could definitely wear a pretty skirt and top. Will you take her shopping, Eve Rose?"

The younger woman smiled and said, "Girl time! Sure. That'll be great!"

"Olga's doing a fantastic job of working with her on the physical stuff. Miss June, you've been a lifesaver with helping her regarding the directions she's needed to follow for all the house projects. She's excellent at it, but I know she still gets frustrated by her inability to keep the order of tasks straight. I'd like the two of you to keep up the good work and for you to take little excursions with her yourself."

"And you?" Miss June asked intently. "What else will you do?"

"Start spending my weekends exposing Chelsea to the experiences she doesn't remember. I'm also thinking about taking her to work as an IT person in the upcoming months. That would give her regular interaction with others and utilize her phenomenal computer skills. She still needs a local neurologist and a therapist who works with TBI patients."

"I'll locate a qualified neurologist and mental health professional for her," Miss June said hastily. "We want to make certain that her doctors will be around for a long while."

Aric instantly understood what the elderly woman was intimating and nodded.

"You told us there was also other important business to talk about," Fredeline said.

"The President, the Vice-President, and his wife will be coming here one day sometime next week."

"*The* President and Vice-President?" asked Eve Rose, as all of the women save for Miss June looked shocked. "Like, of the United States?"

"The very same. They're old friends of mine and will be taking in some R & R with us. Everyone here needs to keep quiet about it, be cooperative with the government people, and follow their orders. It's their job to protect Lakshmi, Buddy, and Nadine. You'll like them. Well, you'll like Lakshmi and Buddy. I'll leave it up to you to determine whether or not you like Nadine."

Miss June snickered, and the other women looked at her in confusion. Aric instantly realized that Miss June must have met Nadine. Judging by her reaction, she had the same impression of the Vice-President's wife as he did.

The impromptu meeting was adjourned, and the older women retired to their rooms while Eve Rose opted to remain on the couch and watch some television. Aric returned to his bedroom and climbed into bed beside the still-sleeping Chelsea. He fought his desire to wake her and tell her everything he'd just told the others. Instead, he gave in to sleep.

He woke in the middle of the night, sensing that something wasn't right. He quickly determined that Chelsea was not in the bed. One set of French doors stood open. He rushed outside and found Chelsea sitting in a chair next to the kidney-shaped pool, which was illuminated by underwater lighting. Forcing his heart rate to slow,

Aric took a seat beside her. He stared at her face and noted that she was looking up toward Miss June's darkened apartment.

"What is it, Chere?"

Without looking at him, she said, "Whenever I go up to the attic, it feels…familiar."

"I thought you were afraid of stairs."

"I am, but Olga makes me climb them every day to get used to them. I hold on tightly to the rail, and I'm okay. The going up isn't as scary as the coming down. I want to do it and not be so afraid."

"That's excellent."

Cocking her head, she speculated, "I wonder if I lived in an attic when I was a little girl."

Not knowing what to say in response to this, Aric talked of his conversation with the other women earlier that evening. Chelsea listened and commented, but her gaze never left the attic windows.

"You'll tell me about the blood test when we go out to dinner," she remarked, turning toward him at last. "I'm glad we're going. I want to know what it's like to go out on a date."

"I don't think *I* remember what it's like," Aric remarked. "It's been over five years."

As they returned to the cottage and Aric pulled and locked the doors behind them, Chelsea climbed into bed and asked, "Why don't you take drugs?"

Totally mystified by this seemingly nonsensical question, he said, "I've never taken illegal drugs in my life."

"I'm not talking about illegal drugs. I'm talking about antidepressants. You really need some medication. Something has made you so sad that you can't ever let it go out of you. Drugs would help with that."

"I can't take antidepressants."

"Why not?"

Aric said nothing.

"Do you really love me?" asked Chelsea.

"Yes."

"Then prove it."

"Marry me," he said impulsively.

"Okay," she responded, as if she'd expected his proposal. "Now prove that you love me."

"I just asked you to marry me. That's not proving I love you?"

"No."

"What will?"

"Telling me your secret, the one that weighs you down all the time. If you really love me, then you have to tell me so that I can comfort you like you comfort me."

Chelsea pulled off her pajama top and tossed it on the floor. When Aric protested that he didn't feel like having sex at that moment, she informed him that she was not planning on having sex with him. Then she put her arms around his neck and pulled him down as she lay back onto the bed. She scooted up slightly until his head rested across her ample bosom. He buried his face between her breasts and inhaled the comforting scent of her skin.

"I was twenty-two and close to leaving for medical school. The D Plague had started to spread around the world two weeks before, but its progression was erratic. There hadn't been any cases in Louisiana, yet. I think we all had a false sense of feeling like it was somehow going to pass us by. How wrong we were." Hugging her tightly, he said, "My eldest sister and her unborn baby were the first in our family to die. My Tante Marie, who'd gone to stay with her to help when the new baby came, was next. The rest succumbed one by one. All of my sisters, their spouses, and their children were gone within three days, but my parents, grandparents, and I seemed physically unaffected. Our house was like a mausoleum though. We were all in shock. No one spoke unless it was absolutely necessary, and all we did was cry from the time we woke up until we went to bed. The rest of our family was gone. Friends died, too. We were living a nightmare.

"Then it started in our house. My father was the first to fall victim to the symptoms. The moment the joint pain and fever started, we called 911, but they were so overloaded that they told us they might not get to our house for hours or days. We knew it didn't matter how soon they came. Once the D Plague symptoms manifested themselves, victims had about twenty-four hours to live. One by one, each of us developed the symptoms. We knew we were going to die and hugged each other and said our goodbyes. As the hours passed, I lay in my bed, listening to my parents and grandparents screaming as they died. I heard myself screaming and prayed for death. I thought about the rest of my family dying in the same way. Then all I could do was writhe in pain. I couldn't have formulated a coherent thought if I'd tried."

"How long did it last?"

"The government people determined that it took about forty hours for me from start to finish. Everyone else in my house had died and turned to dust by the time the medical personnel arrived. They took one look at me and figured they'd be sweeping me up soon, too. Imagine their surprise when I started to improve. I was transported to some secret U.S. Centers for Disease Control location. They tried to treat me with painkillers to help with the…to help. Nothing worked on me. So, I just suffered while they watched over me and took samples and did their best to comfort me. Within a few days, it was as if I'd never had the D Plague. To my knowledge, I'm the only person in the world who got it and lived, although I do wonder about that.

"I give samples of blood and bodily fluids once a month and fly to Georgia periodically for a complete physical performed by the government doctors. It's hoped that by studying me and trying to determine why I was able to survive, others might survive similar outbreaks or various diseases. I'm glad to help in any way I can. I figured that must be why I was left behind when everyone else I cared about was taken from this world. It wasn't only my family that was lost. So many millions are gone from their families, too."

"How awful. No wonder you're depressed. I still don't understand why you can't take antidepressants though."

"They don't work on me. No medications work on my post-Plague body."

"Nothing? So, if you got cancer or something like schizophrenia, then that would just be too bad?"

"I guess so. I've been lucky, so far. I haven't been sick with anything since I survived the D Plague five years ago."

"Did the government doctors tell you that there were any activities you couldn't engage in?"

"No. They told me to live my life as normally as possible and to let them know if I developed any strange health issues. Why? What would you think they would warn me about?"

"Sex."

"Sex? Up until I met you, I hadn't had sex with anyone since I was sick. Why would you think that would be a problem?"

She sighed with what sounded like exasperation and said, "I'm glad Fredeline made me take the birth control shot."

"Chelsea, what are you talking about?"

"Sex, Aric. When you have sex with someone, you exchange bodily fluids with them. Whatever made you different enabled you to survive the D Plague. You'd think the government people would warn you that you might inadvertently help or harm someone when coming into intimate contact with them. And what if you got someone pregnant? Who knows if your sperm would make super-healthy babies or ones that would never live or maybe kill their mothers with something like the D Plague? You were the pre-med student. You didn't think about these things?"

Aric was horrified to realize that he hadn't. He and Chelsea had been having sex at least once a day for the last several weeks. Had he already inadvertently poisoned her? Were the results of their contact negligible when it came to her health? What about his sperm? Could he ever take a chance on having a child with Chelsea in the future?

He tried to pull away from her, frantic to call his doctors at the CDC. Chelsea held him firmly against her, and he realized that she was stronger than she'd been before. He could have easily broken free had he wanted to, but it wouldn't have been as effortless as it would have been the previous month.

"We have to stop having sex," he declared. "And I want you tested by the same doctors to see if I've harmed you."

"Uh-uh," she retorted. "They can test me all they want and probably already have with the blood I gave three weeks ago for the genetics test. You'll have to forgive me if I'm a little suspicious of anyone and everyone, except you, Fredeline, Eve Rose, Olga, and Miss June. I'll play the government's game like you do if it helps others and keeps us safe, but we are *not* going to stop having sex. Ever. I love you, and I love you in me. If you've exposed me to something, then it's already too late. At least I'm not going to get pregnant. My shot is good until May." She paused then continued, "If we ever wanted to have babies, we'd have to really think about it. What kind of a risk would we be taking? Your children might be perfectly fine or they might be…well, they might not."

"I don't know that I'd ever be willing to take that risk," Aric confided. "I've got enough guilt on my plate without adding your death and the deaths of our babies to it. It's hard enough for me to make it through each day sometimes. Before you, I used my work as a tool to motivate me to keep going. Once I met you, I felt like you were sent to me in order to save me."

She laughed quietly and admitted, "I feel the same way about you. Make love to me, Aric Rodrigue."

He wanted to say no, but it was hopeless to try and refuse Chelsea when she wanted sex, which was pretty much any time. Their encounter was brief but intense, and both fell asleep immediately afterward. Aric dreamed of a mission trip he and his family had taken to Haiti when he'd been twelve and of the joy and sadness they'd experienced during their time there. He woke feeling torn between grief and comfort.

Chapter Sixteen

By 10:00 a.m. the following day, Aric had gotten a large amount of company business accomplished. He'd also made a call to the CDC regarding his concerns and questions but had been informed that his primary doctor was on vacation because Monday was Columbus Day, and she'd decided to take that Friday off. Aric left a voicemail for the woman, asking if she'd return his call as soon as possible Tuesday. An hour later, he'd had a heated debate with one of his brilliant but hot-headed researchers that had resulted in the man's storming away in a huff, although Aric knew from past experience that the researcher would calm down and come back later to apologize for his outburst. Aric had also finalized his selections for the team he was forming to begin work on improved migraine pharmaceutical treatments and reviewed the initial budget for the project with his accounting and marketing departments. Jason never left his side, not even when Aric took a break at noon to use the restroom.

"Is something up?" Aric asked, as they stood at the urinals. "You're a little more protective today then you have been in the past few weeks."

"We got word that the big boss was really...unsettled by whatever it was that the two of you talked about yesterday. We were told to step up our protection indefinitely."

"So, are you coming on my date with Chelsea tonight? We could double-date with you and Miss June."

Jason grinned and said, "No double-date. You'll be followed closely though."

When they returned to Aric's office, he noticed that he'd received an email from the genetics lab regarding Chelsea's testing. Aric glanced at Jason and then asked him to wait outside the office while he reviewed the information. He spent the next half hour reading over the report; then he rose and prepared to ask Jason if he was ready to walk with him to the restaurant down the street for lunch. That was when his phone alerted him that he had a text from Lakshmi. Aric resumed his seat and switched on the computer once again. Soon, Lakshmi's face appeared on the screen.

"I didn't expect to hear from you this afternoon," Aric told her after their customary greetings had been exchanged.

"I'm on Air Force One on my way back to the White House. I thought this would be a good time to call."

She sounded tense, which was out of character for her. He asked if something was wrong.

"I suspect so. The people protecting you and Chelsea are on the up-and-up. They work for the FBI."

"That's good, right?"

She smiled indulgently at him and said, "You're such a smart man, but you're so naïve about certain things. Way too trusting. You'd make a terrible politician and a worse operative. I'm glad you didn't want to be either. I value your innocence."

"I'm not that innocent."

"Did you realize that you've been under surveillance since you survived five years ago? My predecessor decided that you were one miracle who needed concealing and protecting for the good of mankind, and I agreed with that decision when I took over the Presidency. Please don't be hurt that I didn't tell you."

Aric refrained from speaking. Chelsea had been right in her deductions the previous night. He was a living empirical study for the government doctors.

"From what I've been told, you are the CDC's most valuable experiment. I knew that what you were doing by helping them was hugely important, but I never realized that they weren't being fully forthright with you."

"You mean like not warning me that having sex with Chelsea might harm her."

"They don't know that."

"No. They don't know anything. They're willing to risk someone else's life to prove their theories."

"Aric, they've been studying you and all of those samples and data for five years. Do you really think they'd let you put someone else's life in danger to prove a theory?"

"I'm starting to wonder. You say I'm naïve. You evidently aren't. Should I keep trusting these people? Do I have a choice?"

"At the moment? Yes, to the first question and no, to the second."

"And Chelsea?"

"I'd recommend she start following the same CDC procedures that you do for her own sake. It will give them valuable data and allow you to know right away if she's having an adverse reaction to being intimate with you." Looking rather uncertain, she said, "I...about having children...."

"I don't plan on it anytime soon. Maybe never."

She nodded sadly and said, "I want to return to the topic of Chelsea, since I'm on a tight schedule. She's also being protected by the FBI because of the deaths and missing persons incidents. The FBI is very dedicated to safeguarding her, but no one seems to know who issued the initial protection order. The agent who set it all up died of COPD not long after."

"So, this FBI guy died of COPD. Therefore, no one killed him to shut him up."

"No, but it appears he confided in no one before he died. My people can't find any documentation regarding the person above him who targeted Chelsea for protection. Anyway, no one's been able to figure out who she was before the accident either. Now that the two of you are involved, you have more security advantages. Do you plan to stay with her?"

"I asked her to marry me last night."

"You did what?"

He smiled and said, "You heard me."

"This woman must be the person for you. I've never known you to rush into any relationship, period."

"She fills the...emptiness in me and makes me happy, although it makes me sad to see her suffering physically or emotionally. I haven't been happy at all for a long time."

"I know. I'm sorry it didn't work out romantically for us, Aric. We needed each other."

"We still do. That's why we're such great friends."

"Yes, but it would've been nice if it had been more. It simply wasn't meant to be."

"Well, we've already established that I'd be terrible in politics, so I would've made a lousy husband for a President."

"True. You'll make a wonderful husband for Chelsea, I'm sure." Lakshmi turned her head slightly as though she were listening to something in another part of the room and said, "My phone is telling me I have a conference call with another head of state in five minutes. I should go."

"When will you, Buddy, and Nadine be here next week?"

"Saturday around 9:00 a.m., if that's okay with you. We're all so looking forward to some normalcy. The Secret Service people briefed us individually on the location and on those who'll be present. Buddy said he's very excited. Even Nadine said she can't wait. She seemed sincere."

He laughed, and they bid each other farewell. Then he went to get Jason and left the office for a while. The red beans, rice, and sausage they had for lunch made everything better somehow.

"Were the genetics' results illuminating?" Jason asked, as they rode the streetcar home that evening.

"Yes. Will your employer tell you about them or should I?"

Jason looked at him with appreciation and said, "Miss June will be told, I'm sure. She'll tell me if she thinks it's relevant."

"How long have you worked with her?"

"I was assigned to be part of her detail when I was twenty-seven, so it's been three years now."

"Are there many people in their eighties still doing your kind of work?"

"A handful."

"You fancy you'll be one of them someday?"

Jason shrugged and said, "It is a pretty elite Hall of Fame, but I don't know that I want to be part of it. I'd like to leave my options open."

Aric got off the streetcar, walked home, and instantly relaxed when he stepped inside and heard Chelsea call out, "Aric, come see in the kitchen!" He moved to that area not certain what would await him. The anticipation felt good. He only hoped that Chelsea hadn't forgotten they were supposed to go out to dinner.

She was standing in the middle of the kitchen wearing a long, full, pink skirt and a frilly white top that buttoned down the front. Sandals with thin white leather straps were on her feet. She wore her diamond earrings and minimal make-up.

"You look amazing, Chere," he told her before pulling her close to him and kissing her. "Even more amazing than you typically do."

She grinned and thanked him before asking, "Guess what I did today?"

"I have absolutely no idea."

"I spent the whole morning shopping with Eve Rose, and it was so much fun. We ate at Cochon for lunch, and I could eat the cornbread and aioli they serve at every meal and be so satisfied!"

"You'll have to take me back with you soon."

"I will."

"What happened after lunch?"

"When we got back, Miss June took me to Loyola University, and I talked with some professors at the computer science department. It was so refreshing! They understood what I was talking about, not like most people who only know the basics of how to use their computers. They were very intrigued by what I knew and had to say." Looking sheepishly at him, she admitted, "They did tell me I shouldn't hack into anyone's systems no matter what, because I could get caught no matter how good I am." With a hint of defiance that Aric had never heard before, she added, "I don't think anyone could catch me. I'm too good."

"Don't take a chance. I want you here with me, not in jail or dead."

"I know," she said resignedly. "That's what Miss June told me, too. I promised. No more hacking."

"Are you going to go back to the college to talk with the computer professors some more?"

"There and Tulane. I feel so powerful when I talk about that. Whatever I did before with my knowledge, the professors said I must have been a force to be reckoned with." Smiling, she said, "I liked the sound of that."

Unless that's what almost got you killed, thought Aric. *You may have been too good and gotten way too close to something big and bad.*

"Anything else I should know about your busy day?"

"Some government people came by to take my blood and other stuff. Miss June said you knew about it and that it was okay. They're going to test it all to see if our being together has done anything to me." Frowning, she added, "Miss June told me they had all my records from when I had the accident. That kind of weirds me out."

"I know how you feel."

"Sort of."

"I think you were busier than I was today," he told her in an effort to redirect the conversation. "Anything else?"

"Yes. Are you ready?"

"Maybe," he said cautiously.

"Close your eyes."

He obeyed.

"Okay, now open them."

When he did, she was standing before him holding a pan of brownies in her hands.

"I made them all by myself and followed a recipe without any help. Fredeline watched me to make sure I didn't forget anything, and she didn't have to tell me once that I skipped a step. She said they were delicious. Do you want one?"

Aric didn't hesitate to lift a brownie from the pan. Two were already gone.

"Who ate the other one?"

"Olga. She said I did great!" When he took a bite, she asked expectantly, "Were they telling me the truth? I haven't tried them, yet. I was too scared."

"Oh, Chere. These are soooo good." Aric meant it and asked, "What kind are they?"

"Chocolate fudge with caramel. It's really all right?"

He lifted a brownie from the pan and offered it to her. She placed the pan on the table and took a bite then chewed slowly. Her expression was impassive, and he wondered if she would cry, laugh, or be indifferent.

"They *are* good!" she exclaimed. "Oh, Aric! I *did* it!"

"You sure did. I'm proud of you. You should be proud of yourself."

"I am. I *did* it!" she repeated. "Oh, my gosh!"

They finished their brownies, drank some milk, and put the cover on the pan. Aric went to the bedroom, took off his work clothes, and slipped into jeans, a close-fitting plain black knit shirt, and boots. Then he and Chelsea bid the others a good evening and left the house.

The cab Aric had called appeared and took them to Moreau's, a restaurant and bar owned by an old college friend of his. It had a honky-tonk atmosphere, and there was a band playing blues and jazz in the main room. Aric and Chelsea were seated in a casual dining area.

"How long has this place been here?" Chelsea asked.

"My friend, Maurice Moreau, took over from his father when the man died in the D Plague. The place has been in the family for generations. In my opinion, they serve the best crawfish dishes in town here. You'll have to let me know what you think."

"I don't know if I've ever eaten crawfish."

"Well, tonight you can try some and see if you like it."

He introduced Chelsea to Maurice, who had a small, compact frame and a shaved head. When Aric explained that Chelsea was there to try crawfish for the first time, he thought the man was going to fall onto the floor in astonishment.

"You've never tried crawfish?"

"Not that I know of," she said anxiously. "I – I don't remember ever having it."

Maurice seemed to sense her apprehension and immediately set to work at putting her at ease. It was a useful talent for a restaurant owner. He told her not to worry and called for a pitcher of beer and a plate of boiled crawfish, potatoes, onions, and mushrooms. Then he sat at the table with them and reviewed the process involved in preparing such a meal.

"How do you eat boiled crawfish?" Chelsea asked Aric.

He showed her how to crack the shells with a special utensil in order to get to the meat. Since she didn't have the hand strength needed to perform this part of the process, both men set about cracking the outer carapace and claws and took turns giving the meat inside to Chelsea and eating it, along with the vegetables that had been cooked in the same seasoned water as the crawfish. As they were doing this, a waitress appeared with sample plates of crawfish dressing, a shrimp-and-crawfish jambalaya, and crawfish and crabmeat au gratin. Chelsea proclaimed her likes and dislikes for various items, and Maurice thanked her for her compliments and for her honesty regarding the things she didn't enjoy.

When Chelsea excused herself to use the restroom, Maurice turned to his friend and said, "She's beautiful, Aric. Smart, too. But something's a little off about her. What gives?"

Chapter Seventeen

Aric cleaned his hands with a hand wipe and said seriously, "Chelsea was in a bad car accident. She has some lingering challenges as a result. She's doing better every day."

"You seem happier than you've been since…right after we graduated from college. I'm happy for you. Glad to see you back around town, too. You've been working yourself so damned hard that I haven't seen much of you for five years."

"I know. I feel like Chelsea's brought me back from what happened with losing my family. I'm relieved you didn't lose all of yours."

"Only my daddy. I still feel awful about what happened to your family."

All that Aric could do was nod.

"Does Chelsea play pool?" asked Maurice.

"I don't know. She may not know."

"Let's ask. Fridays and Saturdays are my busiest nights, as you can imagine. Why don't the two of you hang out and dance. Then maybe we can go upstairs and play pool. We haven't done that since college."

When Chelsea returned to the table, the men asked her about the possibility of participating with them in a game of pool later. She replied that she wasn't sure if she knew how to play but was willing to try. Satisfied, Maurice excused himself and told them he would find them when he could spare some time for a game.

The band took a break, and the only sounds in the restaurant were that of customers' conversations, orders being put in and picked up by the wait staff, and the clinking of utensils. Aric decided that this would be as good a time as any to discuss the results of the genetic testing.

"Do you want to hear the test results here or in a more private setting?" Aric said.

"Now is fine."

"According to the testing, your ethnic heritage is 50% European, 25% Afro-Haitian, and 25% Native American. The European ancestry is French. The Native American portion is Choctaw."

"So, one of my parents was white, and one was of Haitian and Choctaw ancestry?"

"That's the way it appears."

"I probably am from Louisiana then."

"Your parents probably were. Where you were born and raised, who knows? It does explain how you know English, French, and Haitian Creole."

"I wonder which one of my parents was white and which one was mixed? Did they love each other or not? Did they love me? I'll never know, I suppose. At least I know what I am now, and that does explain a little. Thank you for getting the test done for me. It's nice to have some answers for a change."

When the band began playing again, Aric asked, "You want to dance?"

"I would like to try," she said, rising from the table and following him into the main room.

Chelsea did more than try. She was as good at dancing as she was at having sex. Aric had been told many times by his female partners that he was an excellent dancer, but he was in awe of Chelsea's abilities. Just as in the bedroom, she had no inhibitions when it came to movement on the dance floor. He allowed himself to relish being with someone who totally gave in to the music and the movement. He felt the stares of others but could not have cared less. All he wanted to do was be with Chelsea in the middle of the sound and the emotion. It was exciting and sensual in its own way.

Aric had no idea how much time had passed when the band stopped again. Maurice appeared with beers for him and Chelsea and suggested that they take a break and join him upstairs in his private room, so they could shoot some pool.

Chelsea gripped Aric's wrist as tightly as she could and held onto the handrail while they climbed the stairs. He noticed that she concentrated on what was in front of her and didn't look around or down. He kissed her on the cheek when they reached the top, and she smiled up at him as they entered Maurice's private room.

The décor was nothing like what was in the worn and homey restaurant and bar. This room was well-appointed with dark walls, masculine furniture, a flat-screen television, computer desk, and the large pool table with its rectangular Tiffany lamp suspended above it. There was a small full bath off to one side. The entire area was obviously soundproof.

"This is my hide-away," Maurice told Chelsea. "No one disturbs me when I'm in here unless it's a true emergency. You ready to try your hand at pool?"

As luck would have it, they were all superior pool players. They played four games. Maurice won two, while Chelsea and Aric each won one. They chatted and joked while they played. When Maurice asked Chelsea about her past, she flat-out told him that she didn't remember anything before June of 2033 when she'd been involved in a serious accident. Aric was pleased that she was comfortable enough with his friend to discuss her situation, and Maurice didn't hesitate to ask her some questions about what it felt like to have no memories.

"It sucks," she admitted. "But I can't change things. I just want to learn who I am now and be happy with Aric."

"He's happy with you, that's for damn sure," Maurice told her. "It warms my heart." Sighing, he said, "I've been away from my place for too long. I should get back downstairs. Why don't you two stay up here and shoot a few more games? Come down whenever you're done. The joint'll be jumpin' for at least another two hours. Take it easy and enjoy some private time. Lock the door behind me, and I'll knock if I need to come back in before you're ready to go."

Aric nodded knowingly to Maurice and thanked him then did as his friend had suggested. When he turned back around, Chelsea was sitting on the edge of one end of the pool table looking expectantly at him.

"I really like this game," she admitted. "I guess I was good at it before I lost my memories. Can we get one of these tables?"

"Where would we put it?"

"On the living side of the main area."

"There's not enough room."

"There isn't?"

"No."

She frowned and said, "I wish I were better at gauging the sizes of spaces."

"You did great in the main room of the restaurant tonight. That's a large space."

"But it was packed with people and the band, and it didn't seem so big."

"Good, because I want to come back here as often as we can and dance with you."

"You liked it, too?"

"Very much."

"I thought so. You felt really hard when I was rubbing against you on the dance floor. I liked it when you ran your hands over my body while we danced and when you pulled me close for the slow dances. I wish we could've had sex right there."

He walked over to where she was sitting, took her face in his hands, and tenderly kissed her. Aric unbuttoned her blouse and unhooked the front of her bra. As he urged her to lie back on the pool table, she asked him what he was doing.

"Startling you."

Her eyes widened, but she smiled. Within seconds, her bikini underwear was off. Her pink skirt was pushed up in the front, and he was making love to her with his tongue, lips, teeth, and hands. She made the wonderful little sounds of pleasure that she made when she had his cock in her mouth. When he repeatedly laved her cleft with his tongue, she arched her back, cried out, and climaxed. He waited until she came down and then unzipped his jeans. Soon, he was thrusting inside her, and she came again. Feeling Chelsea clench around him, Aric came, too.

He lay on top of her for a long time afterward, his head nestled against the cushion of her large breasts. He was drowsy, slightly drunk, and utterly relaxed. He didn't want to get up, but he knew they had to go home. Aric wasn't about to abuse Maurice's generosity.

Chelsea excused herself to use the bathroom; then it was his turn. When he emerged, something was different about the pool table. The green felt looked brighter somehow. When he asked Chelsea about this, she told him she'd freshened the felt.

"Freshened the felt?"

"I read somewhere that pool tables now have synthetic felt. You just use a certain type of disposable wipe to clean them. I figured Maurice would have the wipes around for that and found some in that cabinet over there. So, I freshened the felt after what we did. I thought it was the right thing to do. Was I wrong?"

"No. I've just never heard about that. We had an old pool table in my family's house. No synthetic felt on that one."

"So you have a pool table in storage? We should get it out and find a place for it in the Creole House. I really, really like to play, and it looks like you do, too."

"I've been playing since I was old enough to hold the cue, but I think we should just come back here or go to pool halls when we want to play."

"Aric, you should try to –"

"Chelsea, I can't!" he snapped. "Leave it alone!"

She shrank back, her eyes filling with tears. Aric instantly apologized and took her in his arms. She rested her head against his chest and cried. As Aric soothed Chelsea, he thought of Fredeline's warning that he could accidentally hurt her. She had seemed more "normal" that evening than he'd ever seen her, and he'd temporarily forgotten that she was still learning and adjusting. When he'd raised his voice, she'd looked as though she was afraid he might hit her. He wondered if she'd been abused as a child or by a partner when she'd been an adult.

Aric thought of the hospital report written up the day of the accident, the one that had mentioned suspicion of rape. Was that why Chelsea was in a cab? Had she been fleeing a rapist?

From Disney Springs to SeaWorld? he thought. *That doesn't make sense.*

"I'm sorry I was afraid," she said once she'd stopped crying. "I know you'd never hit me, but I guess I reacted instinctively. You've rarely gotten angry with me in the past."

"I wasn't angry with you tonight. I was scared. The thought of sorting through my family's things is too much for me to consider right now."

"I could go with you. Think about it."

He kissed the top of her head and said nothing. They walked hand-in-hand to the door. Once Aric had unlocked it, they stepped out onto the landing. There was still a crowd, although it had thinned considerably. Chelsea slid her arms around Aric's waist and said, "I'm afraid to go down the stairs."

"But I thought you were practicing with Olga on going up and down each day."

"I am, but that's outside during the daytime. This is in a darkened corner of a building. What if I fall?"

"I won't let you fall."

He put one arm around her shoulders and the other on one of her forearms. She was trembling. Maurice, who was standing behind the bar, caught his eye, smiled, and waved. Aric didn't smile back and shook his head. His friend sobered and nodded then turned slightly to talk to a bartender. Aric knew that he was watching their slow descent out of his peripheral vision.

When they made it to the bottom, Aric asked Chelsea if she'd call for the taxi while he talked to Maurice for a moment. He thanked his friend for his hospitality and assured him that both he and Chelsea would be regulars at Moreau's now that he was truly back in town.

"Chelsea likes you as much as I do," Aric told him. "I appreciate you letting us use your private room for some...relaxation. Everything was great until we had to come down the stairs. She's working on that, but she can't come down in the dark without being afraid."

"My MawMaw used to have trouble with stairs after her stroke. Healing takes time."

Aric nodded and shook hands with his friend. Chelsea came over and told Maurice how much she'd enjoyed the food, music, dancing, pool playing, and sex with Aric. Both men burst out laughing. It took Chelsea a moment to realize what she'd said that was so funny, but then she was soon laughing, too.

"Brain-injured people like me don't always have filters like regular people," she explained. "I didn't mean to embarrass you, Maurice."

"No problem. I'm glad you had yourself a good time all the way 'round."

The taxi let them off at the darkened Creole House at 2:00 a.m. They went in, quickly showered, got ready for bed, and were soon asleep. Neither of them stirred until noon the following day.

Chapter Eighteen

Aric and Chelsea sat at the kitchen table with Fredeline, Eve Rose, Olga, and Miss June and ate fried plantains and bowls of Diri Jon Jon, a Haitian rice and mushroom dish that Eve Rose had prepared for lunch. Everyone complimented the young woman, who thanked them and announced that she'd decided not to go to college after all.

"I love to cook and want to be a chef," she declared. "I'm going to apply to culinary school, if that's okay with my grandmother and with you, Mister Aric."

"Me?"

"You told me right after we moved to New Orleans that you'd pay for me to go to college, not culinary school."

"I'd be happy to pay for you to enhance your already fabulous cooking skills. As for your grandmother, you'll have to discuss that with her."

"I only want my girl to do what she loves."

Eve Rose practically leapt from the table and hurried off to begin applying to schools. Fredeline cleared away the dishes and told them to get out of the house and enjoy the unusually cool October day.

"I am going to the bookstore," Olga proclaimed. "Would anyone like to join me?"

"I'd be delighted," Miss June announced. "Let me get a sweater."

"If you can wait for me to finish the dishes, then I will come, too," Fredeline told the others.

"Of course, we will wait," Olga responded. "Take your time."

Aric turned to Chelsea and asked, "You want to go to the bookstore?"

"No. I want to ride the streetcar and explore places in the city."

Aric said, "Then you and I will ride the streetcar and explore the city together."

The couple spent the afternoon wandering around various parts of town and ended up in Jackson Square, going in and out of shops, and watching street performers. They had beignets and coffee at Café du Monde for dinner. Although Chelsea admired the architecture of the Saint Louis Cathedral, she told Aric she couldn't go in because of her spatial issues.

"All those vaulted ceilings in churches make me feel scared. They're so cavernous."

"Have you looked to see if there's a Buddhist temple nearby?"

"Not yet. I love my Buddhist chanting, but I don't think I'm a true Buddhist. I'm not a vegetarian, and I don't believe in reincarnation."

"That doesn't mean you couldn't go there for fellowship or to meditate or chant with others."

"Would you come with me?"

"Sure."

"Do you believe in reincarnation?"

"No. I'm not a vegetarian either. That doesn't mean I can't hang out with Buddhists and enjoy it."

"Do you believe in an afterlife?"

Aric thought about this for a while before stating, "I want to believe in an afterlife. I was raised a Christian, believing in Heaven and all that."

"But?"

"But I honestly don't know what happens after we die and won't pretend as though I do. I'll live my life the best I can and see what happens when my time is up. Either I'll drift into peaceful oblivion or find out there's a Heaven after all."

She nodded and said, "I'm glad we feel the same about that. I know a lot about Christian religion and about voodoo, so I think I must have been raised to learn both. I don't really believe in either, but I think they're good for what they were meant to do."

"Which was?"

"What all religions were designed to do, which is to make people feel like there's an order to things that doesn't always exist."

"Not a natural order but a supernatural one."

"Precisely." She smiled and asked, "Will you take me somewhere spiritual?"

He ruminated on this for a time as they walked then said, "I think I know the perfect place, assuming it's still there. I haven't been in years."

A five-minute walk and several turns later, they stood outside a shop that had a worn sign proclaiming Tante's Voodoo Market and

Christian Store. Aric took Chelsea's hand and opened the door. He breathed in the unusual fragrances of incense and herbs and felt instantly transported back to his youth. He'd come to this shop with his Tante Marie many times when he'd been small, but his trips to the place had tapered off as he'd gotten older and had what he'd felt were more important things to do with his friends and then with his girlfriends. He hadn't set foot in the store for at least a decade.

"Well, look at you, Aric Rodrigue!" a large, black woman proclaimed in Haitian Creole. "You were a boy the last time I saw you, and now you're a man!"

"Tante, you remember me," he said in her native tongue with pleasure and respect in his voice. "It's so good to see you."

He'd never known the woman's first name. Everyone, including her contemporaries, simply called her Tante. He suspected that she was perhaps Miss June's age but had no way of knowing.

"I have some things you need," she told him authoritatively. "Who is your beautiful woman here?"

Chelsea told the shop owner her name and said in Haitian Creole that it was a pleasure to meet her. Tante placed one palm on Chelsea's right cheek and said, "Sweet child. You are a Divine Being."

Aric froze. He recalled the stranger years ago saying those exact same words about Lakshmi Jitesh. Was it a coincidence that this old woman who was rumored to be a voodoo queen had just uttered the identical words about Chelsea? He thought it highly unlikely but had no other plausible explanation.

"You have no past," Tante murmured to Chelsea, her hand still on the younger woman's cheek. "You will never remember, my sweet girl, but you will find out the truth someday. Be at peace with who you are and love this man." Taking Chelsea's hand, she said, "You both come with me."

They obediently followed the probable octogenarian through a beaded curtain into a back room. Then they went through a black door and into what Aric assumed was Tante's home. It was colorful and made him feel at ease. Tante ordered them to sit on the couch, and she then disappeared through another doorway.

Aric wondered what was happening. He knew that his Tante Marie had believed in both voodoo and Christian traditions, as did many Haitians. His parents had no problem with her religious

132

beliefs, although she was never to practice voodoo in the Rodrigue home. He and his sisters had often speculated on what their Tante Marie did at her weekly Haitian gatherings, the ones they were never allowed to attend.

Aric pushed the thought of his sisters, parents, and Tante Marie away. The old woman reappeared in the living room with an ancient, tiny, black woman who had sparse white hair. The extremely elderly woman had spindly arms and legs and a wizened face. Tante helped her to sit in a chair and said, "I have to go back in the shop now. Old Helene has been waiting for you. You mind her, you hear?"

Once Tante was gone, Old Helene said in French, "You are both so strong and yet also weak." Holding out her bony hands toward Aric, she said, "I am one hundred and one years old. You listen well to me."

"Yes, Ma'am."

Once her cool hands rested in his warm ones, she said, "You have done great things and will do many more, but you must forgive yourself for living. This girl will be with you through it all. Take care of her, and she will take care of you."

"Can you see the future?"

"No, Boy. I can only feel your love for this one and the terrible sadness you hold in your heart. Such a heavy weight for so many years." When he nodded soberly, she added, "You are a good man and are on this Earth for a special reason. Never lose sight of that."

The centenarian slipped her hands from Aric's and turned toward Chelsea, who was seated too far from the woman to touch her. Old Helene motioned for Chelsea to come closer and sit on the floor beside her chair. The younger woman did this without hesitation and looked up expectantly.

Old Helene smiled gently down at Chelsea and said, "You don't remember me, do you?"

Aric sat bolt upright, and Chelsea looked shocked.

"I knew you?" she breathed. "Do you know who I am?"

"I met you once when you were a tiny girl. You were maybe three years old. You were with a woman who came to see me for advice about her mother."

"Was this woman white or mixed?"

133

"Neither. She was pure black, that one. You weren't her child. There were other children with you who weren't her children either. She was watching the lot of you while your parents or grandparents were working."

"Are you sure it was Chelsea?" asked Aric.

"Just because I am old does *not* mean I am senile. She may have been much smaller, but this child looked very much the same when she was little. What other mixed race child in Port-au Prince looked like this beauty? Who else had her color skin, hair, and eyes? She was the child."

"Port-au-Prince," Chelsea repeated. "So, you were in Haiti at the time?"

"I was."

"And what happened the day you met me?"

"I gave the woman the advice she asked for in exchange for an explanation about you. I could sense that you were a rare gem, and I was curious."

"What did she say?" Chelsea prompted.

"That your mama was a white woman and your daddy was part Haitian and part Indian. She said your mama loved your daddy, but her white family wouldn't stand for her having a colored child. They'd told her to have an abortion, but she refused. So, they ordered her to leave and either come back without her baby and pretend like she'd never had it or to stay with her colored lover. According to what your daddy had said to your babysitter, your mama went with him and stayed until after she gave birth to you and wouldn't let you out of her arms for the next month. Then, he woke up one morning and found her gone. The only thing she'd left behind were the beautiful diamond earrings she'd worn every day since he'd known her. The babysitter said he told her he'd locked them away and would give them to you when you were old enough."

"Did she say my parents' names? Did she say my name?

The ancient woman bent and kissed Chelsea on her forehead then said, "Your name was Sunshine. No one knew if that was your given name or a nickname your daddy had given you. The babysitter didn't tell me anything else about your parents, because it was time for her to go. I never saw her or you again, but I knew right then that one day you would find me and that I would tell you about our meeting."

"Was I happy when you saw me?"

"Very. You were like sunshine. You lit up the room. I could sense great power in you even then." Looking to Aric, she said, "He has great power in him, too. Powerful people seem to be drawn to one another."

Aric froze again. Her comment was reminiscent of what Miss June had said to him regarding his relationship with the President. Another coincidence?

"Can you sense anything about me now?" Chelsea was asking Old Helene. "I was in an accident and don't remember anything before June of 2033. It's hard not to remember anything."

Old Helene brushed some hair from Chelsea's face and said, "You have a lust for life and a lust for men. This man will always satisfy you and protect you. Don't be uncertain. Enjoy each day and each experience. Use the gifts you have and never stop learning. Let go of what fears you can. Some are in your brain and cannot be released. Some are in your heart and should be put to rest."

Tante reappeared and said, "The two of you should leave. Old Helene needs to lie down now. You kiss her and tell her thank you before you go back to the shop."

They each gingerly hugged and kissed the little woman on the cheek then waited in the store while Tante helped Old Helene to bed. People were milling about in the shop, selecting voodoo dolls, statues of saints, herbs, and other miscellany. Once Tante returned, she rang up several purchases for other customers then turned to Aric and Chelsea.

After placing a large bag on the counter, Tante said, "What I have in here is necessary for you. Don't discard any of it. Take it home, but do not look in the bag until tomorrow morning. Do not say a word to anyone once you arrive at your house – including each other – until you remove the contents of the bag. Then find the right places for what I've given you."

Aric reached for his wallet, but Tante shook her head.

"Not tonight."

"I don't understand."

"Old Helene has been waiting for this night for over twenty years. When I met her two years ago and asked her to live with me, she said she was waiting for a beautiful child she met once in 2013. She said she would live until the day that she was able to talk to this child and tell her important things. She said that would give her closure and allow her to have her final rest. It's past her time to go. You owe me no money for anything you get from me. Go, and be safe."

When they arrived at the Creole House., Aric was glad that Olga, Eve Rose, and Fredeline all seemed to be occupied in their rooms. He assumed Miss June was in her attic apartment. He and Chelsea went to the master suite. He put the bag from the shop in the corner and looked at the woman he loved. She stared at him numbly and bit her lip.

As Tante had ordered, neither of them spoke. They made love again and again until, exhausted, they had to stop. Chelsea slept, but Aric stared at the ceiling until the light of dawn filtered through the sheers on the French doors of the little cottage.

When Chelsea stirred, Aric rose and retrieved the bag from the corner. He reached into it and withdrew the first thing he touched. It was a large, wooden cross, painted in bright colors with various symbols and figures on it. Aric estimated the thing was over one foot across and two feet long.

"That should go in the living room," Chelsea declared. It will be perfect on the wall next to the door that leads to our little cottage. It's a great piece of art."

He agreed then reached into the bag again. He pulled out ten small, identical, white iron crosses that measured about three inches by five inches.

"These should go inside each room over the doorways for protection," he announced. "One for above the front door, one for each bedroom and bathroom, and one for the inside of the hallway. We had one over the inside of each doorway in my house when I was growing up."

There were bunches of herbs that obviously went in the kitchen, but neither of them knew exactly what to do with them. Chelsea suggested asking Fredeline, which Aric thought was a great idea. He put the bunches of herbs aside, along with a wooden bowl.

The final item in the large bag was a cloth pouch. Chelsea opened it and removed its contents. There were two small, octagonal amulets inside. The design on the amulets looked like pitchforks extending out from the center with dots around the edges. Aric frowned, but Chelsea smiled.

"They're amulets to protect us from evil and harm. If a person is in terrible danger, then you're supposed to call on Loa Eshu, who is very powerful, for protection. You should never do it in vain though. It should also be kept secret if you want it to work."

"Where does one keep it?"

"Some wear them on necklaces, but some carry them in their wallets or put them in safe places that are always near to them. Some people hang them in their homes."

Aric immediately slipped the amulet into his wallet. He didn't really believe in its power, but he respected the woman who'd given it to him and appreciated her thoughtfulness. He asked Chelsea where she would keep hers.

"I don't know. I'll have to decide."

They stared down at the items on the bed. Finally, Aric said, "About last night…." He sighed and admitted, "I don't really know what to say."

"It was good and bad for me."

"I know. Do you want to talk about it?"

"Not yet. Are you ready to go through your family's things?"

"Not yet."

"We should do both soon."

"Yes."

"But not today."

He kissed her, wondering how she was feeling about what Old Helene had told her regarding her abandonment by her mother. He knew she was trying to imagine the woman and her father. He couldn't help but imagine, too.

"Soleil," he said, using the French word for sunshine. "She said that was what you were called. Do you want me to start calling you that?"

"No. I'm Chelsea. Sunshine is gone. It's nice to know that I was a happy child, at least when I was very young. I hope I was happy my whole life until the night of the accident."

They spent the morning hanging crosses and getting a lesson from Fredeline and Eve Rose on the bundles of herbs. The wooden bowl was placed in the center of the table. Chelsea stated she was going to ride the streetcar the following day to get a stand so that the bowl could be displayed properly on the mantel of the kitchen side of the fireplace. No one objected, but Aric knew they were all concerned. He took comfort in knowing that Miss June would have Chelsea under surveillance and would monitor her every movement outside the home. Everything would be fine.

Chapter Nineteen

"How are you adjusting?" Jason asked Aric mid-morning on Monday.

"What do you mean?"

"Well, you went from solitary bachelor who was on the road for work 24/7 for five years to a homebody with a house full of women. Do you miss the old life?"

"Not for a minute. I already had a great staff here at Rodrigue Pharmaceuticals. I simply had to do a little reorganization to accommodate my new life. The business doesn't seem to have suffered for it. I know certain things will require my direct attention out of town here and there, but I can be home most of the time. I'm much happier with my life now, despite our...problems."

"Miss June likes it here."

"She told me this will be her last job. Do you think she'll stay in New Orleans once our unusual situations are resolved?"

"Yes."

It was one word, but the way Jason uttered it made Aric look shrewdly at his assistant and protector.

"Do you know something I don't?"

"I know a hell of a lot more," Jason replied casually. "That doesn't mean I can share everything with you."

Aric studied the man then said, "You're sad."

Jason nodded and got to his feet saying, "Your 10:30 appointment will be here any moment."

The meeting lasted for three hours. Once it was over, Aric withdrew a protein bar from his desk, unwrapped it, and wasted no time eating it then downing a bottle of water. He had another meeting with a potential distributor in fifteen minutes. A hearty meal was not in his immediate future.

Jason opened the door to his office without knocking. Aric thought this odd and was about to say something when Jason shut the door behind him and announced, "I just rescheduled your next appointment."

Aric wasn't sure whether he should be shocked, livid, or amused. He'd never had anyone rearrange his schedule without his express permission.

"We have to leave," Jason informed him. "Now. It's Chelsea."

Aric was out of his chair in a fraction of a second asking, "Is she okay?"

"Physically, she's fine. Emotionally, I'm not so sure. Miss June just called and said to get our asses back to your house right away. Chelsea's having some sort of crisis."

When they arrived at the Creole House, Fredeline was standing nervously outside the front door. She quickly let them know that Olga and Eve Rose weren't home and that Chelsea and Miss June were in the attic apartment. She urged Aric to go upstairs right away and asked Jason to wait inside.

Aric raced around the house and took the steps two at a time. When he reached the door, he paused, then tried to slow his breathing and calm himself. Whatever was going on with Chelsea, he needed to be in control. He knocked.

Miss June opened the door and stepped outside, so she could join him at the top of the stairs. After closing the door behind her, she explained that Chelsea had set out on her errand that morning to buy a stand for the wooden bowl and had done quite well. She'd taken the correct trolley, had found the appropriate store, purchased the stand and a couple of other things without incident, and had left the shop. She'd then taken the streetcar back home and had made it all the way to the gate before halting with her fingers on the handle.

"I was watching from the house," Miss June confided. "It was as if she was immobilized by panic. Fredeline was with me, and she said she could see it, too. We observed her for a moment to see what she would do, but she stayed where she was. That was when I called Jason and told him to get you home. After that, Fredeline and I went out to her, but she was very detached. Fredeline asked her if she could take her bag and purse, and Chelsea was pretty unresponsive. I reached over and undid the latch on the gate, and Fredeline took her things without getting any resistance. When I asked Chelsea what was the matter, she stared at me as if I weren't there. Then she walked past both of us and around the house to my steps here. She held on tightly to the rail, climbed up, and went through my door. I asked Fredeline to wait for the two of you and went to see about Chelsea."

"And?"

"She's huddled near one of the dormer windows. She let me put my arms around her but didn't seem to even notice. She isn't responding verbally to me either. I'm hoping you'll have more luck with her." When he reached for the door handle, Miss June stopped him and said, "I made a few calls. Chelsea has an appointment with a psychiatrist tomorrow morning at 9:00. She also has an appointment with a neurologist at 11:00."

Suspicious, Aric asked, "With whom?"

"Very good doctors who have been given all of Chelsea's records in advance. You'll meet them when you go with Chelsea. I altered their schedules; Jason's working on altering yours for tomorrow as we speak."

"So, these doctors are government people."

"Of course. Did you really think she could go to just anyone under the circumstances?"

"I don't really know what I think about any of this anymore," Aric muttered then went inside the attic and closed the door behind him.

Chelsea was sitting on the floor beside one of the windows that overlooked the backyard. Her right shoulder was pressed against the glass. Her knees were drawn up in front of her, her arms wrapped around them. She didn't acknowledge Aric when he sat beside her and said her name. He slipped his right arm around her shoulders and tucked some of her hair behind her left ear with his free hand.

"Come on, Chere," he murmured. "Talk to me."

"It happened again," she said quietly without moving.

"What did?"

"I had that feeling again like when I needed you to hurt me. One minute I was feeling so good. I did well this morning and was proud of myself. When I reached the gate, I felt so scared all of a sudden. I couldn't move. All I kept thinking was that I needed you then and there and that I needed you to...to...."

"Say it, Chelsea. I want to know, so I can help."

"You'll be disgusted," she declared. "I know I am."

"Things can't get better if you don't talk about them."

She laughed bitterly and said, "Well, if that's not the pot calling the kettle black."

Aric sighed and kissed her temple. She was right to imply that he was a hypocrite. His heart pounding hard, he said, "We both need to come clean. I'll start talking about my family, and I'll go through their things beginning this Sunday if you'll go with me. I can't do it without you there."

"You'll really do it?"

"Yes. Now, tell me what you were going to say."

Turning her face completely away from him, she said with shame, "I wanted you to rape me! That's so sick. Why would I need that? What's wrong with me? I felt like I somehow deserved it, but I hadn't done anything wrong."

Pulling her against his chest, Aric said, "Let's get one thing straight right now. No one *deserves* to be raped, whether they did something wrong or right. I don't know why you've had this feeling twice now, but I suspect it has something to do with the night of your accident. Did you read the reports? The doctors suspected you'd been raped. Perhaps whatever you're feeling in the present is subconsciously tied to whatever happened before you got in that taxi."

"I just read the main summary. I couldn't bring myself to review the rest and watch videos and see pictures of myself so messed up." Rubbing her cheek against his shirt, she asked, "What if you're right about the rape? If I can't remember it then how can I work through it?"

"I don't know. Miss June set up an appointment for you with a psychiatrist tomorrow. Maybe he'll have suggestions when and if you have any more of those feelings. You also have an appointment with a neurologist. Maybe that doctor's got some ideas." When she was silent, he asked hesitantly, "You're still feeling like you want me to hurt you?"

She nodded against his chest.

"Why did you come straight to Miss June's apartment?"

"I told you I felt at home up here. I guess I thought it might make the feeling go away if I came to the attic. It hasn't."

As uncertain as he was about how to proceed, Aric decided to take Chelsea back to their room and make love to her. Maybe having sex without violence would salve whatever was going on in her injured brain. He helped her to stand then put his arms around her as they walked out onto the top step of the outdoor stairs. They were halfway down when Chelsea stumbled. Aric caught her easily and said, "I have you. You're safe."

142

"I'm not!" she cried. "Everything is danger from without and within! What if it was my fault! Maybe that's why I feel like this! Maybe I want to be punished!"

She clutched at his shirt and sobbed. As he helped her down the remaining steps, he wished there was a way to get into their master suite without going through the house. He glanced across the yard toward the cottage and saw Fredeline opening one set of the French doors that led into their bedroom. Then Fredeline was gone.

They were soon inside. Aric led Chelsea to the bathroom and washed her face, which seemed to relax her somewhat. He removed first his clothing then hers and brought her to their bed where he tenderly made love to her. Afterward, she drifted off to sleep in his arms. Once Aric was certain that she wouldn't wake, he got out of bed, showered, and put on pajama bottoms. Then he retrieved his computer, set it on the desk in the bedroom, and accessed Chelsea's medical records from the hospital and rehab facility. He really didn't want to do what he was about to do, but he knew he had no alternative. He needed answers, especially before they saw the doctors the next morning.

He pulled up the original report and found the place in the notes, documenting the suspicion of rape. He clicked on the attachment that led him to the information detailing the use of the rape kit and the resultant negative match to anyone in the sexual offender database. There was one more attachment, part of the dictated report from the examining physician and related photographs.

Up until that moment, Aric had avoided this section and all photos or video images of the then-unconscious mystery patient. He didn't want to see Chelsea with such physical trauma and certainly didn't want to see possible evidence of sexual assault. It didn't matter what he wanted. What he needed was information that might help Chelsea.

Putting in an ear bud so no one could hear except him, he clicked on the dictation button and clenched his jaw as a female physician began her recitation of her notes. As he listened, he watched. He tried to pretend it wasn't Chelsea's body in the photographs showing that beautiful part of her bruised, torn, and bloodied.

Suspicion of rape? He thought with incredulity. *How could it have been anything but?*

The part of himself that had planned on becoming a neurosurgeon reminded him that, although major damage had been inflicted on the woman, it may have come from a consensual encounter. Some people did enjoy being injured during sex either by the use of body parts, fire, or one of a multitude of other implements. A doctor was there to examine the facts, not determine a patient's character or predilections.

However, as Aric continued to watch and listen, he could hear anger in the female physician's voice. Not only had damage been done to the cervix, the vaginal area, and its surroundings, but dark, finger-shaped bruises could clearly be seen on the mystery patient's thighs, wrists, and ankles.

Aric's blood was boiling. Whatever Chelsea had been in her previous life – hooker, salesclerk, IT worker, nun, or anything else – it was extremely clear what had happened to her before the accident. Several people had held her down while one person had repeatedly raped her. He wondered what sort of monsters had participated in her attack and how she'd ended up taking a taxi from Disney Springs after that kind of assault. It would have been difficult for her to stand and walk after such a rape, and the conscientious employees at the theme park would have quickly spotted someone in trouble and called for police and paramedics. He couldn't imagine anything like what had happened to Chelsea occurring at Disney. Perhaps she'd fled there, knowing that no one would expect her to be at one of the happiest places on Earth after being brutally raped.

When the presentation of notes and photos ended, Aric forced himself to return to the main page and click on the video images of Chelsea's arrival at the hospital and her treatment. He was grudgingly grateful that a law had been passed in 2030 requiring digital video cameras be mounted in all hospital rooms and in every room of rehab facilities and nursing homes. It was torture for him to see her lying comatose, her past completely erased less than an hour before. Her jeans, sweatshirt, and tennis shoes had protected her body from most of the glass and from flames. She did have some cuts and bruises, but she was in miraculously good condition if one didn't think of the brain injury and of the sexual assault and the finger marks on her soft almond-colored flesh.

He watched as they cut off her clothing and removed her diamond earrings and put them aside. Chelsea had been twenty pounds heavier at the time of her accident. It was a good weight for her. She was currently still way too thin in his estimation and....

Jeans and a sweatshirt? Why was she wearing jeans and a sweatshirt in Florida in June? It wasn't impossible but was highly unlikely that the temperature was anything but sweltering. Shorts and a tank top would have been more appropriate.

Going back to the beginning of the video, Aric scrutinized her clothing. The jeans appeared to be brand new. She was wearing a Minnie Mouse sweatshirt that also looked like it had been recently purchased. When the clothes were cut away, the patient was naked underneath.

Had she bought new clothes at Disney so that she could dispose of what she'd been wearing? Or had her attackers dressed her? Had the men kept her original outfit and undergarments as some sort of trophy? Or were they so torn and bloodied that they threw them away?

Over the course of the next couple of hours, Aric watched Chelsea wake from her coma, barely able to move, see, or speak. He caught video glimpses of her recovery and of her neuropsych evaluation, physical therapy, and her progress regarding adaptation to daily living. Her hair, which had been cut into a bob at some point by someone, grew longer again. Her recovery was incredible, but she remained withdrawn and anxious the majority of the time. More than once, she mentioned waiting for someone to come looking for her. Of course, no one ever came.

Aric closed the files and shut off the computer. After removing the ear bud, he went back over to the bed and climbed in beside Chelsea, who was beginning to wake. Opening her eyes, she looked pleadingly at him before asking for a migraine pill. He brought her one then told her he was going to dress and call for Olga.

"No!" she insisted. "I have to have a bath first!"

"Olga knows that we have sex."

"I don't care! She can't touch me until I've had a bath. That's just wrong!"

"A quick shower," he countered. "I'll help you."

Once Chelsea was clean, dry, and dressed in a nightshirt, she allowed him to call Olga. He could tell that this was going to be a bad migraine and hoped that Olga had come home during his time spent alone with Chelsea.

Unfortunately, the Swede was still away from the house, although when he reached her by phone she vowed to return as soon as she was able. He told her that Chelsea was getting increasingly worse and to hurry. While they waited, Aric tried the customary damp rag treatment, although this seemed to have no effect. He supported Chelsea as she vomited into the toilet, then held her in the darkened bathroom as she shook with pain and exhaustion.

When Olga entered the room, she knelt beside them and very lightly stroked the younger woman's hair. Then she directed Aric to bring Chelsea to the bed, remove the nightshirt, and place her on her left side. He did as he was told. When he began to retreat to the main part of the house, Olga stopped him.

"You must learn how to do this," she ordered. "I will not always be around. Perhaps she would not have gotten so bad today if you had known what to do to help her with the massage."

He agreed and nervously followed Olga's example and instruction. He was afraid of making things worse, but the masseuse was encouraging. After a while, Chelsea sighed with relief and sagged against the bedding. Not much later, she slept.

"Your turn," Olga said quietly.

"What?"

"You have not had a massage in five days. I can see the tightness in your muscles without even trying. Lie down."

Aric knew better than to argue. Without removing his pajama bottoms, he stretched out belly down next to Chelsea. Olga set to work, and soon he was able to relax. When he turned onto his back, Olga suggested he close his eyes and allow his thoughts to wander someplace pleasant. He did this and was barely aware of her hands kneading his knotted shoulder and neck muscles – until she exerted an extreme amount of pressure on one side of his neck. He found himself literally paralyzed and struggling to breathe. He was unable to open his eyelids.

All that Aric could think was, *If she kills me, they'll get Chelsea. I can't let them hurt Chelsea.*

Chapter Twenty

Aric strained to move any part of his body, but his efforts proved futile. He was getting light-headed. He suddenly thought of the cross above the door and the amulet in his wallet. Feeling rather foolish but desperate, he prayed for help from Jesus Christ and Loa Eshu. Olga's hand was gone from his neck, and he heard a horrific cracking noise and then a heavy crumpling sound.

"Aric! Aric, are you okay? Fuck!"

It was Jason. Aric wanted to answer but still couldn't speak. He did manage to open his eyes and looked up at the man's worried face then mouthed the word, "Olga."

"Is dead. I broke her neck."

"Chelsea?" Aric rasped.

Jason went around the bed and checked her pulse and breathing. Aric wished she wasn't lying naked on top of the covers. Jason was only human, and it might take him a while to get that image out of his head. With the way Chelsea looked, it was probably permanently imprinted.

"She's still asleep," Jason said with a smile of relief. "When Olga arrived home, she said you called her because Chelsea had a bad migraine. With the migraine, the meds you probably gave her, and Olga's massage, she's out. Let's hope she stays that way for a while."

Aric, who was now able to move, asked, "What the hell just happened?"

"Olga tried to kill you."

"Why?"

"No clue. We'll be working on that. Somebody screwed up big-time on our side. Everyone in this household was completely checked out by the FBI. Whatever Olga's game was, we'll have to investigate and see what we did wrong. You could've been killed."

"Don't go all out of your way to make me feel better."

"I'm just glad I came to check on you. I was going to ask if there was anything else any of you needed and found Olga in the process of killing you by compressing your jugular vein and some key pressure points. You need a doctor."

"I'll live. No doctor."

"Will you at least let me check you out?"

"Are you an M.D. as well as an administrative assistant and Federal agent.?"

"No, but I have had medical training. It's part of the job."

"Fine. Just keep your exam above the waist."

Jason snickered. It was somehow familiar to Aric, although he couldn't recall ever hearing the man snicker previously. He instantly forgot about the snickering and suppressed a groan as Jason probed the tender side of his neck.

"Olga did a real number on you," Jason told him. "Years of working as a physical therapist and masseuse certainly gave her enough knowledge and strength to know how to kill in a quick and efficient way."

"Again with the not making me feel better. And to think I trusted her and that she was alone with the others off and on all the time." After Jason made a call to Miss June and explained the situation, he asked, "What about Fredeline and Eve Rose? Now I don't know if I should trust them either. Hell, I don't even know if I should trust you or Miss June, but I don't have any choice there."

"Believe me when I say that Fredeline and Eve Rose will be triple checked-out by tonight. We'll be 100% certain they're who they profess to be."

Aric, who was trying not to look down at the dead woman's body, asked, "Do we tell them about what Olga did?"

"I think we have to," Miss June proclaimed as she entered the room and looked down. Frowning, she said, "Someone is going to pay for this with his or her career at the very least. If they knowingly aided and abetted Olga, the result will be incarceration or worse."

Aric nodded slowly before asking what was going to happen next.

"Olga's body will be discreetly removed very shortly," answered Miss June. "She conveniently fell on the area rug over here. She'll be wrapped up and taken away for an autopsy and a valid identification. We'll find out who she really was. Whoever orchestrated this spent a long time setting it up."

Jason excused himself from the room and stepped out through the French doors. Aric raised an eyebrow in a silent question.

"Killing is never taken lightly by any agent. To have to kill with one's hands was the most affecting form of extinguishing a life."

"So, why didn't Jason just shoot Olga?"

"He probably acted instinctively and realized every second counted. Even though his actions would be deemed necessary, Jason will be subject to a review. If he asked for a leave of absence or counseling, either request would be granted by his superiors."

Aric asked Miss June to get a thick, full-length blanket from the closet and cover the still-nude Chelsea before the FBI people arrived to spirit out Olga's body. As she draped the blanket over the young woman, he inquired as to Fredeline and Eve Rose's whereabouts. He was told they'd been escorted out of the house and were safe. They would be brought back once Olga's body was gone and their own backgrounds had been rechecked.

As FBI agents entered the room, Miss June directed them to work without speaking unless it was absolutely necessary. Aric turned his back to them and looked at Chelsea, who was beginning to come awake. He moved closer to her and took her in his arms, cradling her against his chest and blocking her view of what was going on behind him.

"Aric?" she mumbled. "There's someone in our room."

"Yes. Miss June's here, and there are others."

"Why?"

Tightening his hold on her, he replied, "Because Olga tried to kill me once you were asleep. Jason saved me, but he had to kill Olga to do it."

"I always wondered about Olga," Chelsea murmured drowsily. "She was very nice, but there was something about her that wasn't quite right."

"If you felt that way, then why didn't you tell me?"

"Because I'm kind of wary about most people. You understand."

"I do now," he admitted. "Are you wary of Fredeline and Eve Rose?"

"No. I think they're honest."

"What about Miss June and Jason?"

Aric wasn't certain why he'd asked her this question knowing that Miss June was in the room with at least half a dozen other Federal agents. He sincerely wanted to know what Chelsea thought and wanted Miss June to hear. Chelsea seemed to have an innate ability to tell whether people were being genuine or not, and he'd greatly underestimated it in the past.

"I think Miss June and Jason are good people, but I'm not sure about anyone else." She pressed her body closer to his and asked, "Are you hurt?"

"I'm sure I'll have a nasty bruise on my neck, but I'm okay. How's your head?"

"All better. I'm glad Olga showed you how to perform massage on me before she tried to kill you."

Aric couldn't help but laugh and said, "Yes, it was very nice of her to be so considerate before she attempted to murder me."

Once the room was empty, save for Aric and Chelsea, she kissed his jaw again and asked, "Did you think you were going to die?"

"For a few seconds."

"What was it like? Did you pray for death like when you were sick with the D Plague?"

"No. I was worried about what would happen to you. I didn't want to die, but I couldn't move to stop Olga. So, I prayed to Loa Eshu and Jesus and asked them to help me. Almost right after I did that, Jason saved my life."

"Did you thank Jesus and Loa Eshu? You should. It sounds like divine intervention to me."

"It can't hurt." Calling out into the silence of the room, Aric said, "Thank you for helping us! We may need you again. Keep us safe."

"That was very good," Chelsea said approvingly. "If they're really there, then I'm sure they appreciate it."

Moving to sit with his back against some pillows he'd propped in front of the headboard, Aric pulled Chelsea into his lap and tried not to think of her rape, her post-accident condition, her persistent migraines, her wish for him to hurt her, and Olga's attempt on his life. His neck was throbbing, but he knew there was nothing he could do about that since no medications worked on him. He would simply have to deal with it until everything healed.

"Aric? Earlier you told me you'd start talking about your family and that we'd begin to go through their things Sunday. Did you mean it, or were you just trying to get me to tell you why I was so upset?"

"You think I'd try to trick you? I'd never do that to you. I meant it."

"So, start talking."

"I have no idea where to start."

"Tell me about your sisters. How much older were they than you? Which one was your favorite? Which one was your least favorite? What kinds of things did you do together? What did they look like?"

"We all had brown hair and brown eyes. All of our names started with the letter A. My eldest sister was fifteen when I was born, and the one right before me was only a year older. I didn't have a least favorite sister, but my favorite was the oldest one. We all had a lot of fun together."

"Say everyone's name in descending order," she prompted.

"Aurelia, Amelia, Angelina, Amber, Audrey, Andrea, Anne, Alycia and Aric."

"Did your parents have names that started with 'A,' too?"

"As a matter of fact, they did. My dad was Allan, and my mom was Alexandra."

"What were they like?"

"Everyone in my family was smart, funny, and loving. I was very lucky to be born a Rodrigue."

"Your grandparents were nice?"

"Both sets lived with us, and everyone got along great. There were disagreements like in any family, but it was usually over one sister borrowing the other one's shirt without permission or what main course to have for dinner. Nothing major."

"Why was Aurelia your favorite sister?"

"She was very gentle but had great presence. However, I was probably closer to Alycia than anyone else. She was…eccentric, and it was difficult to understand her motivations sometimes. Yet, we had a deep connection. Perhaps it was because we were so close in age."

"And your Tante Marie? What was she like?"

"A lot like Fredeline, except she'd never married or had kids of her own. She'd been with our family almost her entire life and said we were her relations as far as she was concerned."

"Your earlier life sounds like it was idyllic."

"It was until the D Plague."

"You're still depressed a lot."

He was going to deny it but conceded, "I am, but at least I now recognize it for what it is and am so thankful I met you. You give me hope."

Before he could stop her, she had Aric's pajama bottoms down and took him in her mouth. For a time, he forgot about his beloved family, his concern about whom to trust, and the ultimate betrayal by Olga, who'd reminded him of a more reserved version of his mother. He stopped thinking and concentrated on *feeling*, and what he felt was phenomenal.

"So sweet," Chelsea sighed afterward. "I wonder if you tasted different before the D Plague."

"I don't even know if my other previous sexual partners are still alive. Well, except one."

"What was her name?"

He hesitated.

"Aric, you're doing it again. If you love me and trust me, then why aren't you completely open with me?"

"Her name was Lakshmi."

"Just like the President's name. That's very –" Sitting up quickly, she said, "The *President*? You had sex with President Jitesh?"

"She wasn't the President at the time. We were friends then briefly lovers then decided we were better off just being friends. Besides you, she's the one person on the planet I know I can trust implicitly."

"And she's coming here Saturday. Do you still want her?"

"You're jealous," he noted with amusement.

"Only if you still want her. How long has it been since you had sex with her?"

"About seven years."

"That's long enough," Chelsea observed. "Just promise me you'll never forget that she's your friend, and *I'm* your lover."

"You're the one I asked to marry me," he reminded her. "All I want is you."

Chapter Twenty-one

"What did you think of the psychiatrist and neurologist?" Aric asked Chelsea, as they headed to Moreau's after the two appointments. "You're very intuitive. What did your Honesty Barometer tell you?"

"I liked them and felt they were being forthright."

"Good. I've got to talk via the computer to my internist at the CDC when I get back to the office about some of my concerns. You and I will fly up very soon for our exams."

"When you talk with the CDC doctor, ask her about your sperm."

"What exactly should I ask about it?"

"If they've used any of it for in vitro fertilization."

Aric's mouth fell open. He was flabbergasted and asked her why she would even think that this would be a possibility.

"Because you give them blood and bodily fluids every month, including semen. You know they're testing it. You and I have talked about what might happen if you got anyone pregnant. Don't you think they're wondering, too? If there's been some sort of mutation and they could isolate it, then they could use that information to create healthier babies. If every egg they fertilize isn't viable, then that's the end of that. Literally."

Reeling from the implications of what Chelsea was suggesting, Aric attempted to look at this line of thinking in a clinical way and not from a personal standpoint. Were his doctors using his sperm to create life and destroy it without his permission for the ultimate purpose of saving lives? Did he already have children? If so, were they healthy and in good homes or were they sickly test subjects existing in a sterile medical facility without affection and normal human interaction? Had women been impregnated with his sperm thinking The Donor was a "normal" man or were they willing participants in an experiment?

"You should sit with me while I talk to the CDC doctor," Aric suggested.

"Only if you make love to me at Moreau's again. You need a distraction."

"We don't have time."

"We have time."

When they entered the restaurant, it was overflowing with people. Maurice called out to them and pushed his way through the crowd. Aric shook his friend's hand, and Chelsea gave the short man a hug that lasted a little too long. Maurice laughed loudly as they stepped apart and said, "You go ahead. I'll work on that." Turning toward Aric, he said, "You got yourself one amazing woman there."

As Maurice headed for the kitchen, Chelsea took Aric's hand and urged him toward the stairs that led up to the private rooms. Confused, Aric followed, unable to ask her what was going on in the middle of the crowd. When they were in the room with the pool table, he said, "What did you say to Maurice?"

"I told him to make us two crawfish po-boys to go so that we could come up here and have some quick and very much-needed sex."

Shaking his head but smiling, he said, "You didn't."

Looking triumphant, she said, "I most certainly did. Don't waste time talking. Make love to me, Aric Rodrigue."

They emerged twenty minutes later. Chelsea took her time, but she made it down the stairs on her own and appeared proud as a peacock. Aric kissed her and praised her for what she'd just done both upstairs and on her descent. She thanked him and tossed her hair over one shoulder in a mocking gesture of seduction, which made him laugh.

Maurice approached them with a bag, presumably filled with their po-boys. His expression was one of admiration and good humor at first. Then he sobered.

"What happened to your neck, man? I just noticed how banged up it is. You look like someone tried to kick-box you in the head and missed."

"That's exactly what happened, Aric lied. "My kick-boxing partner at the gym got a little carried away."

Maurice didn't look convinced but bid Aric and Chelsea goodbye and told them to come again soon.

"Again and again," Chelsea said with a mischievous smile as she pecked Maurice on the cheek. "Thank you so much."

Aric thanked the man as Chelsea walked toward the doorway. Maurice flashed him a grin and said, "Never a problem, Aric. You're an inspiration, my friend."

When they were back in the cab, Chelsea proclaimed, "Maurice didn't believe you about your neck."

"What was I supposed to tell him?"

"I don't know. You can't tell him, but I think you need to talk about it to me or someone else. Olga hurt you."

"Obviously."

"I don't only mean physically. You were fond of her. I think she reminded you of one of your sisters or your mother or someone like that. You trusted her, and she tried to kill you. Please talk to me."

"I'm trying not to think about it until at least the end of the day."

When they arrived at his office, they ate their po-boys at his desk. Once the remains of the meal had been cleared away, Aric made the call to the CDC. His doctor had texted him early that morning with a time when they could have a virtual conversation using their computers.

After Aric introduced Chelsea to the primary care physician, a trim woman in her early sixties, he said, "I won't beat around the bush. I have some serious doubts about the agency and need some straight answers to important questions."

The M.D. squared her shoulders and said, "Fire away."

"If the reason for my recovery was inexplicable, then surely the government people would suspect intercourse might lead to some sort of reaction for the other partner. Also, if pregnancy were to occur, there could be detrimental effects for the fetus and possibly the mother. Why wasn't this ever discussed with me?"

The woman looked uncomfortable and said, "I was told by my superiors not to broach the subject with you. Every test we've done on you since you survived has shown only healthy cells, fluid, and tissue. Your sperm seem healthy, and there are no motility issues."

"Have you fertilized eggs with my sperm?"

She paused then said resignedly, "Yes."

Aric felt as if he couldn't breathe for several moments. Chelsea took his hand and gave it a surprisingly noticeable squeeze. He gently squeezed back.

"What did you do with these fertilized eggs? Did you implant them in anyone?"

"No. That team studied them after fertilization, then destroyed the samples without implantation."

"Destroyed the samples," Aric repeated flatly. "You created human beings, studied them as long as you could, and then disposed of them."

"Potential human beings," the doctor said seriously.

"Did the women providing these eggs know what was going to happen to them?"

Her lengthy pause gave him his answer. Aric was so filled with rage that he couldn't speak. He was trying unsuccessfully to think of the other questions he'd intended to ask the doctor.

"What about me?" Chelsea asked. "What did the samples I gave last Friday show?"

"They show a marked improvement from the lab results provided in your records from the hospital and rehabilitation center. You're remarkably healthier than you were. That, in and of itself, isn't significant. What is significant is that you're much healthier than other women your age whether they've suffered severe physical trauma or not. I suspect the longer you're with Aric and the more you have intercourse with him, the healthier you'll be. I personally believe the contact you're having is leading to a positive reaction in your immune system. Of course, we have no way of knowing what the long-term effects are for either of you. That's why it's so important for us to continue monitoring your health."

"After what you just told me about the embryos?" Aric almost shouted. "I'm damn well never going to let any of you near us again."

"Who else will you let near you? If you hire private medical people, can you trust them any more than you trust us? How do you know they won't do other things with your samples? If you stop being monitored, what then? What if you begin to have issues you aren't even aware of? You might endanger your health or cause some sort of new plague without even knowing it. At least we'd give you medical attention and warning."

"Would you? Or would you simply sit back and allow your professional curiosity to be satisfied no matter what the result?"

"Your welfare and that of Miss Capra are our top priority. I've reviewed Miss Capra's previous medical records. We want to help you both."

"Tell me your impressions regarding her information, if you're so concerned," Aric snapped.

"I agree with everything, except the suspicion of rape. She was most definitely raped."

"How can you be so sure?" asked Chelsea.

The doctor looked at Aric and said, "I'm certain you've examined everything in the file. You'll have to explain it to her. Please, Aric. Don't walk away from us. I apologize for the agency if you feel we've wronged you. I have to go now, but I want to talk with you more about this. Promise me you won't make any rash decisions before we talk again."

"I'll make you no promises since you've already told me some lies."

"We never lied to you."

"No. You just withheld the truth."

Aric disconnected the call and switched off the computer. He was so disturbed by the conversation they'd had that he didn't know what to do or say next.

"Aric, how do they know for sure I was raped?" asked Chelsea in a small voice.

Shutting his eyes, he admitted, "It was very obvious. You'd been sexually brutalized."

"You know how I got the urge for you to hurt me those two times. Maybe I liked rough sex."

"This was more than rough sex. Also, you had bruises on your ankles, wrists, and thighs that looked like finger marks. It was pretty evident that you were held by several men and then assaulted by one of them."

She mouthed the word "oh" but seemed unable to say it. She asked him how they knew that only one man had penetrated her.

"There was semen from one donor and no evidence of spermicide or any sort of residue from a condom. Therefore, several men took part in the rape, but only one actually raped you."

She looked down and said quietly, "I'm glad I don't remember that."

He put his arms around her and said, "Me, too. If I ever meet the men who did that to you, I'll kill them."

"Aric, don't say that! They'd put you in jail! I need you with me!"

He assured her that he had no intentions of being separated from her; then he asked her about their conversation with the CDC doctor.

"I was surprised by how candid she was," Chelsea admitted. "She seemed to be telling the truth about all of it."

"I'm going to have to call Lakshmi," he said then sighed deeply. "I have no idea what to do. We need the CDC's help, but I abhor what they did by fertilizing eggs then destroying them without the consent of either donor. I don't care what other people might think. Once an egg is fertilized, I think of it as a person. That person just hasn't been developed and born, yet. Who knows how many of my children were created and destroyed so that they could get data for their studies?"

"I hate to say it, but did they have a choice? If they didn't do that, then how could they tell anything? What they learned might help us to have a baby one day if we want to or might save others' lives."

"They played God without permission," Aric said grimly. "It wasn't their decision to make."

"But if you call the President and she makes sure it stops, then what happens once her term is up? If they freeze your sperm, then it can last for a long time, right? What if they made embryos and froze them? After the President isn't in office anymore, the new President might give them the okay to implant the embryos in someone. You could have a bunch of kids and not even know it."

"I've thought of that. I'm stuck, and I hate being stuck. I need the government and wouldn't trust anyone else either. You and I do need monitoring, and I do want to see if what they learn from me and now you after you've been with me can help save people in the future. But should I allow them to create then dispose of innocents in the hope that it might save lives?"

Chelsea shrugged and said, "I don't know what to say. I'm still kind of fixated on the thing about people holding me down and raping me."

"Oh, Chere. I'm sorry. I wasn't thinking. My brain is pretty scrambled at the moment."

She pulled away and declared, "I need to do something right now."

"Chelsea, we can't."

"No, not that. Something else to divert my attention from all of this."

"How about if I introduce you to my IT staff and leave you to hang out with them? You could get a feel for the department and give me your opinion about how things are running."

Brightening, she agreed. He led her to the elevator, and they went down one floor to the IT offices. He left her there, happily discussing things he didn't understand about computer hardware and software. Then he returned to his office and called Lakshmi Jitesh, who called him back within ten minutes.

Aric explained about the incident with Chelsea and her migraine. He spoke of Olga's apparent helpfulness with Chelsea, then her attempt on his life and subsequent killing by Jason. He reviewed the appointments with the psychiatrist and neurologist. Finally, he told her of the conversation with his CDC doctor. He could feel his blood pressure rising with every word and was shaking with anger and emotion by the time he finished.

"What the hell am I supposed to do?" he asked his friend. "I'm so lost, Lakshmi."

"Aric, please take a cleansing breath. Let's separate the good from the bad and go from there."

"Good? What good?"

"Chelsea had a psychological episode. She's got a psychiatrist now to help her deal with her feelings and lack of a past as well as the rape, accident, and the mystery of the missing and deceased healthcare workers. Right?"

He nodded and tried to calm down.

"Chelsea had a bad migraine, and Olga showed you how to use the massage to help her in conjunction with her medication. That seems to be a good combination, and Chelsea recovered very quickly as a result. She now has a neurologist as well. Right?"

"Right."

"According to the CDC doctor, you are extremely healthy, and Chelsea seems to be healthier than she should be because of her intimate contact with you. Right?"

"Right."

Okay. That's all very good news. Now to the bad parts."
Looking sadly at him, she said, "Someone on our side missed a vital
clue that this Olga woman was a threat. You trusted her, and she
tried to kill you. Your protection saved you, but I know that must
make you uncertain regarding your security and also very wounded
by the betrayal of this woman you must have liked."

"Yes."

As for the business with the CDC...." Lakshmi shook her head
and said, "I need to think about this, Aric. I'll look into it. If what
the doctor said was true, then they're guilty of misconduct in my
eyes. However, should they be stopped? I'd have to know more
before I could give you my honest opinion. What they're doing may
be necessary for your sake and for the sake of others. As sickening
as I find it, if it would lead to a cure for future plagues or enable you
to know whether or not your children would be healthy or die some
horrible death then it might not be optional."

"It's been five years, and I've made a donation each month.
That's a lot of sperm for them to have at their disposal. I can't
believe I was so stupid that I never thought about what they might be
doing with it!"

"Aric, stop beating yourself up about that. All you wanted to do
by cooperating was to assist the government in helping others."

"And if I stop now, then that might cause further harm in the
future."

"Or it might not make any difference at all. You've provided
these people with lots of data. Perhaps it's more than enough."

"Or not! I could die of the D Plague tomorrow! Whatever
happened to me could only be temporary. I could now have infected
Chelsea with some weird strain of a mutated virus! If we have
children, then they could seem fine then one day just up and die! I
can barely live with my survival as it is! How could I live with
myself if that happened?"

"I don't know," she said frankly. "Unless someone can solve
this medical mystery, you'll never know. So, you either take
chances or avoid them. Anything you do will involve risk."

"Very comforting," he grumbled.

"Let me find out if there's anything classified you need to know.
For now, I believe you have to keep working with the government.
They have more resources than any private entity ever would. I

160

wouldn't trust them completely, but perhaps there's a way to get them to be more forthcoming with you about the specifics. I'll investigate and give you an informal report of my findings when Buddy, Nadine, and I come to your house this Saturday. Are you still up for our visit?"

"I need your visit."

"You need to cry, Aric. You know you do. I'm well aware that you battle depression and release a lot through your tears, whether others see them or not. I get the impression you haven't let yourself cry about any of the things you just described to me."

"I'm not crying until after your visit. I can't, Lakshmi. I'm really, really stressed and can't let myself fall apart. I don't think a short crying spell is going to fix this."

"A short crying spell doesn't really fix anything. I wish you could take antidepressants. The Gods know you need them."

"I wish I could, too. I was never chronically depressed before the D Plague, and I hate it. I'd welcome some relief." Smiling tiredly at his friend, he said, "I guess it's good that Chelsea enjoys sex so much. I get a release of all that pent-up emotion at least once a day."

"As a former sexual partner of yours, I'd rather not hear the details. I am happy for you though. You need this woman as much as she needs you. I can tell by the way you look when you talk about her that you love her. I can't wait to be introduced this weekend."

"She's looking forward to it as well, but I think she's jealous."

"You told her about us? Why?"

"You just said you didn't want to know the details."

"If it explains why you told her we were sexually involved, then I want to know. I thought we said we wouldn't really talk about that part of our lives after we became just friends again. So, talk."

Chapter Twenty-two

When Aric hesitated, Lakshmi said, "Aric, you're blushing! What is it?"

"Chelsea loves to have sex. She's very experienced and enjoys it on a frequent basis. She says...she tells me I taste sweet after..."

"I get the idea," Lakshmi said with a broad smile.

"You're enjoying my being embarrassed about this."

"Actually, I kind of am. Go on. I'm still waiting to hear how this led to your disclosure of our sexual relationship."

"Chelsea wondered if I taste sweeter since I survived the D Plague. I told her I only had one partner I knew of who was still alive, and she asked me her name. When I didn't want to share, she insisted I'd tell her if I really trusted her. I thought that was a valid point. I only used your first name, but it didn't take her but a moment to figure it out."

"Hm. I could try having sex with you again to compare before and after."

"Lakshmi!" he exclaimed, his face burning.

Smiling, she said, "I'm only kidding, Aric. I just couldn't resist seeing your reaction."

"Well, don't do it again," he said with irritation.

"I won't." Leaning forward in her chair, Lakshmi said, "And Aric? When I was with you, you didn't taste sweet at all. I found you nice and salty."

She disconnected the call before he could comment. He was infinitely relieved.

He worked on company business until 6:00 then went down to the IT department to find Chelsea. All of the offices were dark save one. Chelsea was sitting at a desk working on her computer.

"Did you have fun?" he asked, as he took a seat in the chair on the other side of the desk.

"I loved it. You have a great staff, except for the woman in the office right across the hall from this one. She's not very good and seems more interested in her upcoming vacation than about her job. She goofed off a lot this afternoon."

"How do you know?"

"Because I hacked into everyone's computers while they were working to see if they were doing a good job."

"Did you uncover anything else that I might find interesting?"

"Lots."

His curiosity piqued, Aric said, "What sorts of things did you uncover during your afternoon spent exploring my computer system?"

"Where do you want me to start?"

Surprised, Aric said, "Should I take notes?"

"I have a report completed already. I'm very thorough."

For the next hour, Chelsea detailed positive and negative activities occurring in various areas of Rodrigue Pharmaceuticals. Aric was relieved to know that his company was functioning at optimal efficiency overall but was disturbed by Chelsea's revelation that one researcher seemed to be compiling very restricted information for what appeared to be the purpose of selling it to a competitor. Aric remarked that he'd be talking to the police the following morning.

Chelsea had also uncovered a love triangle involving two men in his administrative staff and one woman who worked as a sales rep. Their e-mails, which had been sent through the company's private system, outlined the entire sordid affair. That would also have to be addressed the next day since one of the men involved seemed to be obsessed with winning the heart of the woman at all costs.

"I guess I should thank you for hacking into my computer system," Aric said wryly.

"Your system has pretty high security to stop people from hacking into it, but I managed to break through it in under an hour."

"Then I suppose I should upgrade the system."

"That's what I'd advise." Pausing, she said thoughtfully, "Maybe *that's* what I could do. I could be hired to see how secure people's systems are and then recommend safeguards for them. I'm just not certain how I'd get business since I have no proof of my abilities."

"How about if we talk to Lakshmi when she visits this weekend?"

"I assumed we were going to talk with her since she and the Vice-President and his wife are coming to the house."

There she goes taking me literally again, he thought. *Brain injury, Aric. Remember?*

"Let me rephrase that. Why don't we talk with Lakshmi about the possibility of you working for her doing the kind of thing you just described?"

"You mean work for the government hacking their systems on purpose? I thought you and I were both extremely suspicious of the government people."

"What better way to protect ourselves than to be accepted by them and infiltrate their organization? You could become a great asset to them if you proved to them how capable you are and what you could do to help secure their information. Plus, you could access what they have on us at any time."

"Thereby protecting you and me."

"Exactly."

"Or endangering us even more," she offered.

"Lakshmi will see to it that we're protected."

Chelsea smiled at him as if she were humoring a small child who had made an extremely simple, extremely naïve suggestion. She rose from her chair, came around to him, and took his face in her hands before kissing him. Then she told him how very sweet he was.

"You're so innocent," she murmured. "Do you think the President can protect us from everything? Even if she could, what about after she's no longer in office?"

"Do you have a better idea, because I'm all ears if that's the case."

"At the moment? No. The government needs both of us and will probably protect us and any children we might have for the rest of our lives so that they can learn from us. However, if we shut them out, they'll either pretend to leave us alone and continue to keep tabs on us without our permission or else they'll kill us."

"You truly believe that?"

"You have to ask after what's been happening since you survived the D Plague and I survived my accident?" When he rubbed tiredly at his eyes, she kissed him again and suggested, "Take me upstairs to your apartment. I want to see it before we go home."

He took her to the top floor of the building. Most of it was a storage unit for products, but a thousand square feet of it was his one-bedroom, one-bathroom apartment. He said his name, and the door to the unit slid back. He and Chelsea entered hand-in-hand.

There was a couch, a coffee table, and a television and other electronics in the living room. The kitchen was plain but functional. A café table with two chairs sat in the small room off the kitchen. Beside that was the full bath and the bedroom. Everything in the apartment was black or white.

"Where is the color?" Chelsea asked in bewilderment. "The walls are white, and everything else from the furniture to the cabinets to the bedding and towels is either white or black. It's so...."

"Minimalist?"

"Cold. Sterile. Defined."

"My life after the D Plague and before I met you."

Scanning the bedroom, she said, "There aren't even any windows in this whole place."

"No, there aren't."

She laid a hand on his chest and announced, "I don't like it here. I want to go. Promise me you won't stay here anymore."

"I don't plan on it, but I hate to get rid of this apartment. It's very secure and totally isolated."

"Very secure and totally isolated," Chelsea repeated distractedly.

"You're having that feeling again, aren't you?" he asked quietly. "The one where you want me to hurt you."

She nodded and said, "I need to be gone from here. Please, take me home."

Jason and Miss June were waiting for them outside the building. Aric asked Jason how he was holding up after what he'd had to do in order to save Aric the previous day, and the man assured him that he would be all right. Miss June eyed Chelsea with concern and suggested they take a taxi home instead of the streetcar. Chelsea practically plastered herself against Aric and insisted vehemently that she was *not* going to get into a taxi for any reason just then. They all agreed they could ride the trolley home.

"Olga's room has been dissected, wiped, and repainted," Jason told them. "My things have been moved in already."

"Are you sure you want to live with us?" Aric asked, as he held Chelsea tightly against him.

"Yes. I need to be in the house with you for the time being."

"What about Fredeline and Eve Rose?"

"They're completely cleared and back at home," Miss June confided. "I believe Eve Rose has made gumbo for dinner."

"I'm not hungry," Chelsea mumbled. "I think I need to throw up."

"We're almost at our stop, Chere," Aric said softly. "Can you make it one more minute?"

As soon as they stepped off the streetcar, Chelsea dashed for the nearest cluster of bushes and threw up her lunch. Aric gently held her against him afterward and asked if she would be able to walk the short distance home. She nodded and said, "I need to chant. I can do it to myself, but I need to concentrate on that. I can't...I can't think about how I'm feeling."

"Then you focus on your chanting, and I'll guide you home."

When they arrived at the Creole House, Chelsea hugged Fredeline and Eve Rose then immediately excused herself in order to go to bed. When Aric went to check on her thirty minutes later, she was already asleep. He kissed her forehead and pulled the covers up to her chin. He then returned to the kitchen and ate chicken and sausage gumbo with the others. Once the meal was over, he went with Jason to see the man's bedroom.

"It doesn't look like the same space," Aric declared, as he viewed the repainted room that held dark furniture and masculine bedding. New Orleans Saints football memorabilia was displayed in shadowbox frames on the walls.

After Aric and Jason had a brief discussion about the Saints and football in general, Aric left the man to finish unpacking his things and went back to the kitchen. Fredeline was standing at the sink, washing out the gumbo pot and singing a Haitian folk song titled "Wongolo" that his Tante Marie used to sing when she'd been alive. Aric sat in a chair at the table and watched the older woman and listened to her sing. It both pleased and saddened him.

When Fredeline finished, she dried the pot and put it away before turning to Aric. Without warning, she put her arms around him and hugged him to her, being mindful not to press against the bruised area on his neck. He closed his eyes and hugged back, imagining she was his Tante Marie and that he was a small boy again. Back then, the hug might have come after a badly scraped

166

knee. He never would've dreamed such contact would be needed in response to his attempted murder.

"You go sleep next to your woman and try not to think of anything except how much you love her," Fredeline told him. "You can't fix anything else tonight, so let it be and rest your head."

"Thank you, Tante Fredeline," Aric said, as he pulled away. "I needed that."

"I know," she said with a gentle smile. "We Tantes know best."

Chapter Twenty-three

The temperature in New Orleans was unpredictable between October and April. One day might be cool and the next steamy. Aric could remember Christmases where he'd worn a heavy sweater and coat and others where he'd been comfortable in a t-shirt and shorts.

For the October Saturday of Lakshmi, Buddy, and Nadine's visit, the high temperature was predicted to be in the mid-eighties. Aric hoped that his guests would bring their swimsuits. It would be a nice day to alternate between eating, lounging around, and taking dips in the pool to cool down.

Aric had asked Eve Rose to make a variety of side dishes of her choosing. He was going to grill shrimp, oysters, hamburgers, and sausage. It had been five years since he'd grilled anything, and he hoped he hadn't lost his edge.

The President of the United States of America arrived in a dark sedan at 9:00 a.m. Lakshmi was escorted inside by her Secret Service Detail. Of course, the Secret Service had already swept the house and surrounding area for potential threats and had coordinated everything with Jason, Miss June, and the agents Aric and the others knew existed but rarely saw. The Federal agents were not about to allow the President to be in any danger if at all possible. They would give their lives for hers. Although Aric found them annoying, he understood their need to control in order to protect. He admired their dedication.

When Lakshmi stepped into the main living area of his house, Aric gave her a friendly hug. She was five and a half feet tall, slender, and had long, black hair, dark skin, and dark eyes. She wore sandals, khaki shorts, and an orange top, and she had a maroon bindi, a dot applied between the center of the eyebrows, in deference to her Hindu upbringing. Lakshmi only wore the bindi on days when she had no public appearances to make, since she felt it would be unsuitable for the President to wear personal religious ornamentation when in public.

"Where is everyone?" Lakshmi asked him after he'd given her a tour of the Creole House and accepted her praise on its renovation and location. "Are they afraid of me?"

"They wanted to give us a few minutes alone since we hadn't seen each other in person for a while. They're sitting by the pool."

Aric led Lakshmi outside. Chelsea, Fredeline, and Eve Rose were sitting in chairs around an oblong patio table, chatting in Haitian Creole. He heard Eve Rose telling the other two women that she was very nervous about meeting the President and hoped she didn't trip over her own two feet and embarrass herself. Her grandmother declared that if she did, then she'd have an entertaining story to tell her own children one day. Aric noticed Chelsea's look of melancholy, but it disappeared the moment she saw him and the President. She beamed at Aric, placed her glass on the table, rose, and came toward them.

That day, Chelsea had opted to wear a brown cotton skirt and a blue top that had ruffled short sleeves. She wore her diamond earrings and brown slip-on sandals. He'd already told her several times how beautiful she looked.

"You look very handsome yourself," Chelsea had said. "I want to have sex with you right now."

"Let's wait until after our guests had left."

This had made her pout, which in turn caused him to smile.

"Chelsea, this is my friend, Lakshmi Jitesh. Lakshmi, this is my fiancée, Chelsea Capra."

The two women greeted one another and clasped hands. However, instead of a quick handshake, they held on to one another for a long moment. It was as if they were speaking without words. Finally, they released their hold on one another and smiled. As Chelsea went to get Eve Rose and Fredeline and bring them over to where Aric and the President stood, Lakshmi murmured to Aric, "She has a beautiful soul. I'm so happy for you, Aric."

He cocked his head and was about to ask her to explain when the other two women approached. Both wore brightly colored skirts and tops in Haitian fashion. As was always the case, Lakshmi instantly put everyone at ease once they were introduced. She was then introduced to Miss June and Jason. Within minutes, Aric, Chelsea, Fredeline, Miss June, Eve Rose, and she were all seated at the patio table and were drinking sweet tea.

Buddy and Nadine Lafleur and their Secret Service entourage arrived an hour later. Jason had been waiting for them in the house, and he led them out to the backyard. Everyone rose for the introductions, except for Lakshmi who merely smiled and nodded to her Vice-President and his wife. They both smiled back, but their smiles seemed forced. Although Aric expected this from Nadine, who was Lakshmi's height with small bones, blonde hair, and blue eyes, he was surprised to see it from Buddy. The large, muscular man was typically gregarious.

Maybe they had a fight on the way over, he speculated. *Their marriage hasn't been the same since they lost their kids in the D Plague.*

Aric glanced at Lakshmi, who shrugged and shook her head. Evidently, she had no clue as to the cause of the tension surrounding the couple. Aric decided that they might simply be having an "off" day. After all, they'd been married for over twenty years, and not every day would be ideal.

Buddy greeted everyone with a bit too much enthusiasm and accepted Fredeline's offer of tea. Nadine seemed a little too polite and reserved, even for her. She accepted the glass proffered her and took the empty seat to Chelsea's right. Chelsea hastened to assure her that she would welcome her company. Nadine continued to seem stiff but appeared relieved.

For the next forty-five minutes, the group talked, laughed, and debated various topics. However, Aric noticed that Buddy Lafleur kept stealing glances at Chelsea and Eve Rose, and Nadine seemed almost enamored of Chelsea.

Well, she is unusually beautiful, smart, and sweet. They know the general outline of her background, which is odd to say the least. Perhaps it's merely normal curiosity. But what's the deal with Buddy and Eve Rose?

Aric grilled the meat and seafood, and Eve Rose set out the side dishes on the counter in the kitchen. They ate at the large table near the fireplace. The others complimented Aric highly for his grilling efforts as well as Eve Rose for the side dishes she'd prepared.

"Miss Chelsea made the dessert for later," Fredeline told them, as she began to clear the table.

"I can prepare things from a recipe without any problems now," Chelsea declared with pride. "I seem to do well with desserts, so I'm sticking to those for now. I used to not be able to make anything because I couldn't follow a list of instructions. It's so nice to be better."

Nadine excused herself to use the bathroom, and the rest of them went back outside. When Nadine rejoined them fifteen minutes later, it appeared that she'd been crying. No one commented on the reddened eyes and puffy cheeks. Again, she chose to sit beside Chelsea.

"Did you bring your swimsuits?" Aric asked once they'd given their food time to digest. "It's getting pretty warm out here."

Everyone changed and went into the pool, save for Miss June and Jason. They all seemed to be having a great time, but Aric was acutely aware that Buddy was still paying a little too much attention to Eve Rose and Chelsea. Nadine remained in close proximity to Chelsea at all times. Chelsea chatted with the woman about her accident, her recovery, and the move from Florida to Louisiana. Aric was thankful that she omitted the parts about her rape, the dead and missing doctors, and the feeling she sometimes got that compelled her to ask Aric to hurt her.

Lakshmi asked Aric if they could speak privately about some business matters for a while, and Aric kissed Chelsea and excused himself from the pool. He and Lakshmi got two towels and went to the kitchen in order to talk. They simultaneously asked, "What is going on with Buddy and Nadine?"

After a brief discussion, they confirmed that they'd noticed the same odd behaviors but couldn't explain them. Lakshmi then moved onto what she'd found out regarding the CDC and revealed that it appeared that the primary care physician was telling the truth regarding what the government had been doing with Aric's samples. They discussed the pros and cons of continued cooperation with the government and agreed that Aric and Chelsea would maintain the status quo for at least as long as Lakshmi was in office and had the capacity to monitor the situation. Then they could reassess.

"Lakshmi, I need to discuss Chelsea and her remarkable computer skills with you. She and I have an idea as to how she could put them to good use. What if she worked for the government? That might be best for us, you and your people."

After a long pause, she said, "I'll have to think on that. I'm not certain if it would be beneficial or detrimental in light of what we've discovered and what we still don't know. Let me mull it over."

"Aric?"

Chelsea stood in her pink bikini and the blue, crocheted cover-up at the edge of the kitchen. She looked slightly panicked. Aric was immediately on his feet and put his arms around her. She was trembling.

"What's wrong, Chere?"

"I don't know. I'm scared all of a sudden."

"Scared of what?" Lakshmi asked with concern.

"The way I feel," Chelsea answered. "It has to do with my TBI. I get these bad feeling sometimes, and I don't know what to do. My new psychiatrist and I are going to work on them, but we've only met twice so far. We're supposed to focus on that next week." Burying her face against Aric's chest, she said, "I'm so sorry. Today is supposed to be a happy day, but I'm messing it up."

"You can't pick the times when these feelings strike," he pointed out. "It'll be all right."

Chelsea swallowed hard and said, "I need to chant."

"Chant?" Lakshmi echoed.

"I do Buddhist chanting almost every night – and whenever I have these feelings. It helps."

"How about if I teach you a Hindu chant that calms the mind?" Lakshmi suggested. Extending her hand, she said, "You lead the way to where you usually chant."

Chelsea walked with the President to the hallway that led to the master suite. Aric returned to the pool and told the others that Chelsea and Lakshmi wanted to get to know one another better and would return to the pool soon. An hour later, Lakshmi emerged alone from the French doors of the cottage.

"Where is Chelsea?" asked Nadine.

"She said she needed to lie down for a while. She hopes to be back soon."

"It must be very difficult for her not to remember her life before last year," Buddy offered. "I can't imagine it. Maybe she'll get her memories back."

"I don't think so, and neither do any of her doctors," Aric told him. "The damage to the temporal lobe of her brain appears to have permanently wiped out her past. She's coming to accept it, but it is pretty difficult not to recall anything about her family and what it was like to grow up. She has no idea what she did before the accident, although she's very good with computers. She's extremely

172

smart but has emotional and spatial challenges that will most likely never be completely resolved. I think the lack of identity has been the hardest thing for her to handle."

"So, she had to pick her own name?" Nadine asked with what sounded like horror in her voice.

"She didn't have a choice. She had no I.D. on her when the firemen rescued her and no memories. She said she liked the way Chelsea Capra sounded, so that's what she decided to be called."

"Very tragic," Buddy remarked soberly. "Hard to even think about such a thing happening to someone."

"It's horrible," Nadine volunteered. "She seems so giving and is obviously very intelligent. How terrible not to remember doing things like playing with other children, attending school, participating in hobbies she might have enjoyed, or being loved by her family! Maybe she should try to do some of those things now."

"We discussed that with the psychiatrist. We don't know if it will do more harm than good. Will it give her those experiences and fill that void, or will it make her feel even more alienated from others?"

"I'd like to help," Nadine declared firmly. "This is just intolerable!"

"How can you help?" Buddy asked irritably. "Our schedules are already so crazy. You don't have time."

"Buddy if *our* three girls were still alive, we'd make time for them no matter what. I want to make time for this girl. I know she's getting help and has good support, but I feel compelled to have a personal impact in her recovery. I could help at least once a month if that's okay with Aric."

Inwardly, Aric groaned. He and Nadine had never gotten along well, and he really didn't want to have to deal with her on a consistent basis. Why she had picked Chelsea to be her pet project, he wasn't certain. However, she did truly seem to want to help. He couldn't very well refuse.

"It's not my choice," he said. "Chelsea may have some issues, but she's a grown woman. You'll have to ask her what she wants."

Nadine was out of the pool and drying off in seconds. Aric bit his tongue and suppressed the urge to tell her to leave Chelsea alone for now. If he did that, then he was contradicting what he'd just said.

Let Chelsea tell her to go away, he thought. *She's an adult, even if she can't quite take care of herself all the time.*

Nadine slipped a red cover-up over her black, one-piece bathing suit and strode toward the master suite cottage. As the others watched, she knocked lightly on one of the French doors and then entered. Everyone stared at the door for a moment before conversation in the pool resumed. Buddy seemed downright sullen during the next half hour while Nadine was in the small cottage with Chelsea. His face brightened when Nadine emerged alone.

The woman slipped out of her cover-up and came back into the pool. She smiled with satisfaction and announced that Chelsea had readily agreed to spend a day with Nadine once a month. Buddy's expression soured for a few seconds, but he masked his displeasure quickly and told his wife that he was glad she was willing to help someone in need.

"I feel like we help so many people, but it's rather impersonal," Nadine remarked. "I think it's high time that changed." Touching her husband on the arm, she said, "I know you and Lakshmi don't really have time, but I can make time for Chelsea, just as I would have made time for our daughters if –"

Buddy hastily rose and got out of the pool before she could finish her sentence. Nadine's face flushed, and she apologized to the others and wiped at the corners of her eyes. Looking at Aric, she said, "I know we've never been the best of friends. Thank you for allowing me to do this. You said it's Chelsea's choice, but you could have stopped me from even asking."

"I appreciate that you want to help, and I understand."

Nadine bit her lip and blinked back tears. Buddy, who had gone into the main part of the house, came back into the yard and returned to the pool. Looking chagrined, he said, "I'm sorry. It's difficult for me to talk about our girls even now. I needed a minute." Turning to his wife, he said, "I get what you're saying, but I don't know if I can handle it. Our girls are gone. You can't replace them with Chelsea."

"That's not what I'm trying to do." Looking away from him, she said, "I have to do what's right."

There was an awkward pause. Chelsea picked this moment to reappear at the pool and ask the others if they were ready for dessert. Everyone dried off, went inside, and resumed their seats at the table. While Fredeline got each person something to drink, Chelsea sliced the chocolate raspberry torte cake she'd made the previous night. Aric put a fork on each plate and served the others.

"This is delicious," Nadine commented after she'd taken her first bite. "You did an excellent job."

Chelsea thanked her and smiled then asked, "Do you bake?"

"No, I've never been very good at cooking," Nadine admitted with what sounded to Aric like regret.

"If you come to see me once a month, then we could do whatever it is we're going to do for the day and then cook something before you leave. It's not hard if you can follow a recipe."

Nadine looked as if she was about to cry again but gave Chelsea a little smile and nodded. Aric was beginning to wonder if he'd been wrong about Nadine all along. Maybe she wasn't the self-centered socialite he'd always thought her to be.

"What will we do next month?" asked Chelsea.

"Buddy and I will be in Louisiana for Thanksgiving. I'm scheduled to go to a school and participate in a Thanksgiving lunch and holiday activities then read to the children. Perhaps you'd want to come with me…?"

Chelsea seemed slightly frightened by the prospect but said, "I'd like that. We could make a pumpkin pie as our first joint baking experiment."

Nadine said she thought that would be very appropriate and told Chelsea the date of the event. Aric knew the Secret Service people would soon be groaning. Adding Chelsea to this and future events would provide greater security complications for them.

Too damned bad, Aric thought. *It's their job. They'll have to deal with it.*

Buddy and Nadine prepared to leave just before 7:00. While Buddy made a trip to the bathroom, Nadine approached Aric, who had gone outside to retrieve some tongs he'd left by the grill.

"Thank you for your hospitality, Aric."

"Anytime. It was great to see you and Buddy."

"It's been too long since we've actually had a normal day like this." Glancing toward the house, she added, "We needed this distraction. Our youngest daughter would have turned fifteen today."

"Oh. I didn't realize this was her birthday. I – I'm so sorry."

Nadine shut her eyes and nodded rapidly. Aric had the sudden irrational urge to hug her. He knew exactly what she was feeling. He wondered if she was on antidepressants and once more wished he could take them.

Nadine startled Aric by saying, "You're a good man. Chelsea is a very lucky woman. I have no doubt that you'll always do right by her. You two appear to love one another very much. I envy you."

Aric didn't know what to say in response. Nadine must have sensed his discomfort and asked him when he and Chelsea were getting married. He admitted they hadn't set a date and bemoaned the fact that he hadn't even gotten her an engagement ring, yet.

"Well, you should do that soon," she advised. "Otherwise, men will assume she's unattached. I'm not quite certain if she'd be able to fend off an overly ardent man who didn't know she's engaged to be married."

"I never thought of that. Thanks for the advice, Nadine. I appreciate it."

They returned to the house together. Buddy thanked him for a wonderfully relaxing day, and he and Nadine bid everyone goodnight and left. Once Aric was certain that they were in their car, he turned to Lakshmi and said, "Cindy would've been fifteen today."

Lakshmi grimaced and said, "That explains a lot."

"Who's Cindy?" asked Eve Rose.

"She was their youngest child," answered Aric. "Their girls were really great kids. Nadine and Buddy lost all three in the D Plague."

"We all lost family or friends in the D Plague," Fredeline said quietly.

"I hate to say it, but I have to get going," Lakshmi announced. "This was such a fabulous day. It was so wonderful to see you, Aric, and to meet Jason and all of these lovely women. I'm sure I'll be talking with you all very soon."

Aric escorted Lakshmi onto the front porch and gave her a brief hug before thanking her for coming. The two friends promised to speak again in the very near future. Aric stood with one hand resting against a post and watched the President's motorcade depart. The taillights of the government vehicles disappeared down the road. He remained where he was for some time and thought about what an interesting day it had turned out to be. He tried not to think about what lay ahead tomorrow when he and Chelsea would go to the storage units to begin sorting through his family's things.

When he returned to the house, Eve Rose and Jason were watching television, while Fredeline and Miss June were drinking coffee at the kitchen table. Chelsea was nowhere in sight. Fredeline told him that she'd gone to the master suite to shower and get ready for bed. He declared his intention to follow her and wished everyone else a good night before going through the door that led to the hallway.

Chelsea was almost finished with her shower when he joined her. She stepped out and toweled off while he showered and washed his hair. By the time he'd toweled himself dry, she was no longer in the bathroom. He found her lying naked under the covers.

"You said we had to wait until tonight to have sex," she reminded him. "I've been waiting all day."

"Did the chant Lakshmi taught you help with your...uncomfortable feelings?"

"Yes. You want to hear it?"

"Sure."

Chelsea sat up, the nipples on her full breasts hard in the chill of the air-conditioned room. He tried to concentrate on what she was saying and not on her body, but he was finding it extremely difficult. He wanted to touch her very, very badly.

"Every decision I make is a choice between a grievance and a miracle. I let go of all grievances and choose the miracles."

"Do you know what a miracle you are?" he asked, as he leaned forward in order to brush his lips over hers.

"You're my miracle. Make love to me, Aric."

For a while, Aric was able to forget about everything except being with the woman he loved. There was no crushing sadness waiting for him at the storage facility that held his family's belongings as he held her. She was with him, and he was with her. Everything else was inconsequential.

Chapter Twenty-four

"Aric, what is this place?"

Without looking at Chelsea, he answered, "It's a storage unit for my family's things."

"This isn't a storage unit. It's a warehouse. It's huge. Your family's house was big but not *that* big."

"Everything that belonged to my family is in here. That includes all of the possessions from the Rodrigue home as well as each of my sisters' houses that their surviving in-laws didn't want. I gave the families of my brothers-in-law whatever furniture they wanted from their houses as well as any personal effects of their relatives. We worked out what belongings they wanted of my sisters, nieces, and nephews. I kept most of my sisters' things and whatever was left of the rest in this storage unit. When I thought we would move back into the family home, I had all of the things from in there moved in here with the other items."

Chelsea looked stunned. Coming around to stand in front of him, she asked, "So, you're telling me that the building behind me is housing articles belonging to everyone in your immediate family who died?"

"Yes. I've already had someone separate things into groups within the building. It won't take long to sort through most of it. I don't intend to keep much. I have electronic tags to mark what I do want."

"And the rest?"

"Will be donated to a local charity that helps abandoned children. The place runs a store. The profits from the store go toward funding the programs for the kids."

"Abandoned children," muttered Chelsea. "Like you and me."

He was about to tell her that this wasn't an accurate comparison when he realized she couldn't have been more right. His family had abandoned him although definitely not by choice. Chelsea's mother had abandoned her, and she had no idea whether or not her father had, too. They might be adults, but both of them were, indeed, abandoned children.

"How do you want to do this?" she asked him as she took his hands in hers. "The place looks huge. Am I going to be able to go in with you?"

"You mean because of your spatial issues?" When she nodded, he said, "There may be a lot of ground to cover, but the ceilings are only twelve feet high. The rooms are filled with all sorts of things. It's not a wide open space. I think you'll be fine. If you're not, then just tell me and we'll stop."

"Okay. It's 9:00 a.m. Where do we start?"

"I've reviewed the layout of the place. I want to walk through the area with the furniture first then the clothing. The boxes of personal effects will be the most time-consuming. That may take multiple trips to examine. I think the rest of what I don't want can be donated after today. Then I can downsize the amount of storage space I need."

Chelsea bit her lip and nodded nervously.

"What is it?" he prodded.

"I'm really worried about you and how you're going to handle this," she confided. "You're being very…clinical about it."

"I'm trying to be as clinical as possible. I'm scared to death."

She hugged him and asked whether or not he was ready to go inside. Clearing his throat, he told her he would never be ready but that it was time. They moved toward the door of the warehouse.

Once Aric had spoken the passcode, he and Chelsea entered and walked down the long hallway until they'd reached the first door on the right. He gave the passcode for this area, and the doors slid apart, revealing what appeared to be a large furniture showroom. He squeezed Chelsea's hand as tightly as he could without hurting her and stepped inside.

His heart pounding, Aric slowly walked through his family's past. He viewed living room furniture, dining tables and chairs, bedroom sets, toddler beds, cribs, china cabinets, end tables, coffee tables, rockers, pianos, and desks. Everywhere he looked, he imagined he saw the ghosts of his relatives sitting, eating, playing, and laughing. He had no idea how long he wandered through the enormous room. He figured Chelsea would be full of questions, but she remained silent as they made their way around the space.

He finally tagged six items in the room. Four were identical rocking chairs that had sat on the porch of his old house and that he planned to put along the front of his new home. Another was a baby grand piano that would fit perfectly in a large empty corner of the living area at the Creole House. The final piece was a long swing he'd made with his grandfather the month before everyone had died. They'd stained it but had never gotten a chance to build a stand and hang it before the D Plague struck.

Without speaking, Aric motioned for Chelsea to follow him out of the room. They moved to the doorway directly across the hall. Aric uttered another passcode, and the doors opened obligingly. Inside, there were racks of clothing. At the end of each rack identifying name markers had been listed. There were four empty racks near the front of the unit marked "KEEP."

Aric had decided he would select one piece of clothing from each family member's things. He asked Chelsea if she would take whatever he handed to her and hang the articles on the "KEEP" racks. She nodded very slightly and accepted the first thing he passed to her, which happened to be his maternal grandmother's favorite robe. The racks were soon filled. The only item of clothing Aric took from the rack with his name on it was the scrub shirt he'd been given by his eldest sister, Aurelia, upon his college graduation.

He slowly scanned the contents of the "KEEP" racks. He'd forgotten how beautiful his mother's wedding dress was and how delicate his favorite niece's Christening gown had been. He fingered the little t-shirt his nephew had loved so much, the one with the brontosaurus stitched in the center. His father's Saints Polo shirt made him think of games they'd attended together. For some reason, he found it most difficult to look at the "hippie" dress he'd kept that had belonged to Alycia, the sister closest to him in age. He fixed his gaze on one brother-in-law's LSU jersey and clenched his jaw.

Why are you saving these things? He wondered. *Who are you saving them for? Will you ever look at them again? They'll probably sit in a box somewhere, rotting away, unless they're hermetically sealed, and what would be the point in that? Perhaps we should put it all back.*

But he couldn't make himself do that. Leaving the racks as they were, he took Chelsea's hand and went to the last set of doors and uttered the final passcode. As the doors parted, Chelsea's breath hitched. There were at least a hundred boxes stacked in the room. Most averaged two feet by three feet.

"We don't have to go through them all," Aric assured her. "I simply asked them to put things in groups. I have no interest in any of the dinnerware, utensils, or glasses that belonged to my family members since none of it has historical significance. All of the old family things were destroyed during Hurricane Katrina the year before I was born. I also don't want any of the towels, bed linens, curtains, and the like. That knocks out a lot of boxes. Let's find those, so we'll know which ones to pass over."

They quickly located the cartons in question. That eliminated almost half of the room. However, it still left quite a lot of boxes.

"Where should we begin?" asked Chelsea.

"I guess at the edge of the piles we know I don't want. We can work our way toward the other side of the room and get as much done as possible. That way, the charity people can come in and clean things out in some sort of orderly fashion. It'll be easier for us and them."

The boxes nearest to them were marked "PHOTO ALBUMS" or "SCRAPBOOKS." Aric tagged them all without opening them. He also tagged a box labeled "DIGITAL RECORDINGS" without looking inside. The next grouping was marked "TOYS" and had the married names of his sisters inscribed underneath.

"Aric?"

"There'll be pictures," he said shakily. "My family loved to take photos. There'll be pictures of my nieces and nephews with their favorite toys. I don't need to keep them. Better that the abandoned kids get them or the proceeds from their sale."

"What about your toys and your sisters' toys? All these cartons are marked 'TOYS - RODRIGUE.' "

He shook his head and said, "The same. I'll have the photos and digital recordings. I can't keep all of this. I don't want to."

"You want to let go of your past as quickly as possible, and I would give anything to find mine," she said softly before reaching forward and opening a box labeled "TOOLS." Before he could stop her, she held his grandfather's hammer in one hand.

"Would you teach me to use tools?" she asked, as she studied the worn handle. "I think it would be nice to build things."

"Like what?" Aric managed to ask.

"Anything. Maybe we could make a stand for the swing you tagged in the other room. We could put it in the backyard and sit out there when the weather's nice."

"I'd like that very much."

Replacing the hammer inside the box, Chelsea took the electronic tags and marked that carton and several others marked "TOOLS." She also tagged several boxes labeled "JEWELRY" and "MEMENTOES."

"Chelsea, what are you doing? I may not want to keep all of that."

Holding the tags behind her back, she insisted, "You do, and you should. I won't allow you to throw away your memories. They're precious, Aric. You should cherish them, not try to give them away! Take it from someone whose memories were stolen from her."

Chelsea pushed him to tag more boxes than he'd intended. By the time they were finished, they had tagged thirty-two boxes. The only one they'd opened was the one that had held his grandfather's hammer. The rest remained untouched. It was after 4:00, and Aric felt completely drained. Although he and Chelsea had made sure to drink plenty of fluids and eat the sandwiches and snacks Eve Rose had put in a picnic basket for them, he was physically weary. At least the initial work had been done. Aric would have the rockers, piano, and swing delivered to the Creole House and have the clothing and tagged boxes moved to a small storage unit nearer to his home. Chelsea had made him promise to go through at least five cartons a week until he had sorted through everything.

"We'll need a shed or a workshop for the tools," he told her as he surveyed the room of boxes. "I want to keep all of those and will need a place to put them."

"That's seven boxes right there. That leaves you twenty-five to sort through. That's only a month or so if you do five a week. It won't be so bad."

It'll be hell, he thought sullenly. *But she's right. You need to take care of this now.*

"Do you want to buy some sort of shed or build one?"

"We've got space on the property for a good-sized workshop and shed. I'd rather have something done that would make it look like it was built at the same time as the house."

"Tell me what it needs, and I can make up virtual plans," she said excitedly.

"That sounds like a good idea." With a heavy sigh, he declared, "I'm ready to go. I can't believe we got all this done. I could never have been here without you. Everything would have stayed here for decades if you hadn't come along."

"Are you sorry we did it?"

"No…and yes."

As he turned to leave, Chelsea cried, "Aric, wait! There's one more box over here. It's pretty thin. I guess that's why we didn't see it."

The box measured about two feet by three feet and was only perhaps six inches deep. It was not labeled. With some trepidation, Aric opened one side and reached his hand in. His fingers touched bubble wrap. He eased the object out of the box. Whatever it was had been wrapped in protective cream-colored paper before the bubble wrap had been secured around it. He suddenly realized what it was, and his hands began to shake.

"Aric? Do you want me to do it?"

He nodded mutely, and she gingerly took the object from his hands. He licked his dry lips as she peeled away the tape, the bubble wrap, and the paper. When all of it had been removed, Chelsea emitted a small sound that fell somewhere between shock and wonder.

"When was this done?" she asked him in a barely audible whisper as she stared at the beautifully framed photographed portrait of Aric's family.

"The morning of my college graduation. My parents said they wanted a picture of the whole family, and everyone was coming to the afternoon ceremony. So, we met at the photographer's studio that morning and had pictures taken. This was the best one, the only one where everyone was smiling at the same time and no one was blinking or looking away. It was a great day, and we all went to lunch at Moreau's afterward and then on to Commencement."

"How many people are in the picture?"

"Thirty-six. Me, my parents, both sets of grandparents, Tante Marie, my eight sisters, my six brothers-in-law, my five nieces, and my nine nephews."

"You all look so happy," murmured Chelsea.

"We were."

"You should hang this in the hallway," she proclaimed. "It could be our first piece in there."

"Why? So I can have their smiling faces depress me even more every damn time I walk through the corridor to our bedroom? You want me to think about them dying horribly more than I already do? You can't imagine what it was like to suffer from the D Plague!"

"No, I can't! Only you can! But you can't sweep your loved ones under the rug like they were swept out of their houses because you want to forget their suffering! That was mercifully brief! They had a lifetime of love and joy, and you're dooming them to be forgotten by not celebrating all of those years they were alive!"

"Stop trying to tell me what the hell I *should* do! You have no idea what it's like to be me and to know that I'm the only person who was *lucky* enough to live when everyone else in my family died! You have no right to lecture me!"

Aric was furious as he stalked out of the warehouse and strode over to the car. Bracing his hands against the side of the hood, he gave the tire in front of him a swift kick. He didn't care that he was under protective surveillance and that others were witnessing his outburst.

They're probably enjoying the show, he speculated angrily and kicked the tire again. *Let them. Fuck them. Fuck everything!* Then, *What the fuck am I doing?*

He straightened and looked back toward the warehouse. Chelsea hadn't followed him out. Stuffing his hands into the pockets of his jeans, he went back inside to find her.

She was no longer in the room with the boxes, and the framed picture was nowhere in sight. Aric backtracked to the room that held the racks of clothing, but Chelsea wasn't there either. That left the part of the storage facility that housed the family furniture.

Aric called out Chelsea's name when he stepped inside. There was no answer, but he saw the family portrait propped on a nearby sofa. He moved forward slowly, becoming more alarmed with each passing second. What if someone had followed them in here and spirited Chelsea away while he'd been outside throwing his little tantrum?

Don't be a fool. Miss June and Jason would never let that happen. Chelsea has to be in here somewhere. Find her. Now.

Chapter Twenty-five

Aric found Chelsea hiding under a table in a far corner of the room. She had her knees drawn up and her arms wrapped around them. Tears were streaming down her cheeks. Aric crouched at one end of the table and apologized for his behavior. Chelsea said nothing and turned away from him.

"Come on, Chere. We should go."

Turning back toward him, she said, "Only if you will bring the picture home with us. Only if you look at it with me and identify everyone in the photo."

His jaw tightening, he asked, "And if I say, 'No?'"

"Then Miss June can take me home, and I'll stay upstairs in the shut-away room where I belong."

"You don't belong upstairs!" he shouted. "Didn't you hear what Old Helene said? You weren't a shut-away child! You were a happy little girl named Sunshine!"

"When I was three!" she practically screamed. "What about after that? Who knows what happened to me? Maybe somebody took me and sold me into some sort of child sex ring! Maybe that's why I'm so good at sex!"

"Chelsea –"

"What if it was my daddy?" she sobbed. "What if he got tired of me and sold me to the highest bidder?"

"Oh, Chere," Aric breathed. "You can't be thinking like that."

"I can be thinking anything because I don't *know* anything and never will!" Quickly scooting out from under the table, she stood and cried, "You know *everything* about your life! Everything! Yet, I practically had to force you to keep anything in this whole gigantic warehouse! All I have is a pair of diamond earrings from the mother who walked away from me because she cared more about her status than she did her own baby! One pair of earrings compared to all of this!"

With those last few words, she made a sweeping gesture with her hands. As Aric stepped forward and attempted to take her by the shoulders, she shrugged him off. He watched as she quickly removed the diamond earrings and then flung them across the room.

He heard two tiny sounds as they landed. Before he'd even had a chance to react, Chelsea turned and hurried out of the main entrance.

Aric didn't go after her. Instead, he moved toward where he'd heard the sounds. When he got close to where he thought they might be, he began to perform a methodical search. After twenty minutes, he found the first earring under one of the rocking chairs he'd electronically tagged. He pocketed it and went in search of the other. It took him forty more minutes, but he eventually located it near the crib that would have been used by his unborn nephew. He snatched the earring up and slipped it in his pocket with its mate. Then he went back to the portrait, picked it up, secured all of the doors in the building, and went out to the car.

Chelsea was sitting in the passenger seat of the vehicle with the door open. Aric carefully placed the framed picture in the trunk and went around to the driver's side of the car. Chelsea automatically pulled her door shut and buckled her seatbelt then twisted her body so that she was facing away from him as much as possible. She stared dully out of the window.

Aric wanted to talk to her but could think of nothing to say. When they arrived back at the Creole House, Chelsea unbuckled her seatbelt, got out of the car, and walked around the house. He knew she was headed to Miss June's apartment. He didn't go after her. Instead, he retrieved the picture from the trunk and went into the master suite through one set of the French doors. After he'd placed the portrait on the desk, he withdrew Chelsea's earrings from his pocket and put them in the only drawer that had an automatic lock on it. Once the drawer was closed, Aric walked down the hallway and through the doorway that led into the main living area.

There was movement in the kitchen, and he could smell something baking like lasagna and garlic bread. However, he heard no voices and was surprised to see Fredeline, Eve Rose, Jason, and Miss June all seated at the long table when he rounded the corner. They stared at him somberly as he poured himself a cup of coffee.

"Dinner will be ready soon," Eve Rose volunteered as he took a sip.

"I'm not hungry. Thank you though. Maybe later."

"Are you…is there anything we can do for you?" Fredeline asked gently.

"No, but thanks."

"Chelsea's upstairs," Miss June told him.

"I figured as much."

"Are you going up?" Jason queried.

"No."

He finished his coffee, rinsed out his mug in the sink, and left the room without another word to any of them. He knew they were all worried about how today's activities had impacted him, and he appreciated that they cared. That didn't mean he wanted to talk about any of it with anyone.

When Aric returned to his bedroom, he was startled to see Chelsea seated on the edge of their bed. Her back was to him, and her head was down. He sat beside her and took one of her hands in his. Without lifting her eyes from her lap, she asked, "Will you show me the portrait now?"

He rose resignedly and walked over to the desk. He brought the picture back, held it up in his lap with one hand, and began to point to and name everyone present and explain their relationships to one another – which man was married to which sister, which child belonged to which parents, etcetera. Being the only Haitian Creole in the picture, Tante Marie needed no such explanation.

The last person he pointed to was his eldest sister, Aurelia. Six months pregnant at the time of the photo shoot, she wore a stylish yet demure maternity dress and appeared calm and radiant as she stood flanked by her husband and Aric. Her two older sons stood grinning in front of her, while her beaming husband held their happy preschooler in his arms. Aurelia's sense of quiet joy had been captured in the photograph.

Aric thought of that last time he'd seen Aurelia at Tante Marie's birthday party. His sister had told him that this son would be her last, that she and her husband had decided they would stop at four. She'd also confided to him that she intended to name the baby Aric, after her baby brother. Aric had been deeply touched and had hugged his sister tightly as she'd prepared to leave. He'd felt the unborn Aric kick when he and Aurelia embraced and had smiled at the thought that he would soon be meeting his namesake. Of course, that was never to be.

He'd had nightmare after nightmare in the beginning as he'd envisioned all of them suffering and dying of the D Plague. It had been a nightly torture that went on for over a year. None of the nightmares were quite as bad as the one he'd had about Aurelia and tiny Aric. He knew from his post-Plague research that certain types of victims had suffered more than others, and one of these types was pregnant women. Because they were carrying a human being inside of them that was also dying of the D Plague, their own agony had been increased exponentially. He wondered if the helpless fetuses would have also suffered greater pain because they were trapped inside their stricken mothers' wombs. In every case, the mothers died first as their bodies did everything they could in order to protect their babies. All the doctors could do was standby helplessly and wait for the inevitable. Well, that was all they'd been able to do when it came to every D Plague victim – except, of course, for Aric.

"Thank you for sharing this with me," Chelsea said as she rested her hand on the back of his head and kissed his jaw. "It's such a beautiful portrait. You had a beautiful family."

"Yes, I did."

"We can put it away if you want," she offered. "That way, you wouldn't have to look at it all the time."

"No, I think you're right. It should be hung. I'm just not sure where I want to hang it, yet."

"You don't have to hang it today."

"I won't. I'll put it in the corner for the moment until I figure it out."

Resting her head against his shoulder, Chelsea said with longing, "I wish I knew what my parents looked like. If I had any brothers or sisters, then I wonder if they looked like me. After all, they'd be my half-siblings. Perhaps we wouldn't have looked anything alike."

"How do you picture your parents?"

"I don't."

"I was thinking maybe we could try an experiment."

"What kind?"

"They have computer programs that assist people in locating missing children by aging the images in photos."

"Aric, I know that. Computers are my thing, remember?"

"Of course, I remember. What I was wondering was whether or not there was a program that did the process in reverse. If we could take a picture of you now and get the program to go back each year of your life, then perhaps we might be able to identify you. You could run it through databases or we could actually have photos to show people. What do you think?"

"I don't know if it would help find out who I am, but it would be nice to know what I looked like while I was growing up. I'll have to see if any programs exist. If not, then the people in the computer science departments at the universities might be able to help or I could create a program myself."

"That's a great idea." Aric rose and placed the framed photograph of his family in the corner of the room near the desk and said, "I'm going to shower and go to bed. I'm wiped out. Eve Rose made dinner if you want some, but I'm not hungry."

"I am," she declared, surprising him. "I think I'll go get something to eat and read for a while then shower and come to bed. You're sure you don't want to join me and eat?"

"I'm sure." Aric pulled her to him and kissed her before saying, "Thank you again for everything today. I know it was stressful for you, too."

"In a different way."

Once she'd gone to the main part of the house, Aric decided he needed a long, hot bath. When he finally emerged from the tub, he put on pajama bottoms and brushed his teeth then returned to the master bedroom and was planning to simply lie down and go to sleep. The framed photo caught his attention as he sat on the mattress, and he couldn't resist going over to it and lifting it up. He smiled at the image, even as the tears began to flow.

Chelsea was suddenly beside him taking the picture from his hands. Instead of returning it to the corner, she placed it on the desk and propped it up against the wall so that the happy family remained in full view. Aric stared at his parents, sisters, Tante Marie, brothers-in-law, nephews, nieces, and himself. He sank onto the mattress, unable to draw his attention away from the photo.

Kneeling to his right, Chelsea placed her left hand on his back and cupped his left cheek with her right palm. She kissed him on the temple and urged gently, "Cry, *Bébé*. Just cry."

Aric wanted to tell her that he *had* cried for his family many times in the past. Being chronically depressed for five years, unable to take antidepressants, and not willing to enter into therapy himself, he'd cried quite a lot. He'd simply never cried in front of anyone else.

"Cry," she softly commanded. "I'm here with you."

Aric buried his face against her neck and wept. He held onto Chelsea as tightly as he dared. He had the irrational thought that if he released her even for a second, she would leave him, and he knew in his heart that he couldn't be alone again. The D Plague hadn't been able to kill him, but the loneliness and depression might if he lost Chelsea.

Chapter Twenty-six

Aric studied his reflection in the master bathroom's full-length mirror and smiled. He was dressed as King Arthur, replete with a period costume made mostly of black with a deep red cloak. He slid the realistic-looking Excalibur into its sheath, which was attached to the leather belt at his waist. He was pleased with the way he looked. He'd pretended to be King Arthur one Halloween as a boy, but he'd worn a simple child's knight costume. This one was detailed and made him feel as if he *were* Arthur. His smile became a grin.

It was Saturday, October 28th, and he and Chelsea were going to attend a Halloween charity event sponsored by his company and several others. They had coordinated their efforts with local homeless shelters, orphanages, and group homes in order to provide the children being served with a fun Halloween celebration. Each child would receive an equal allowance in order to purchase a costume and a toy. The children were to be taken to a local museum for Halloween-related activities like face-painting, games, and food. Someone from every company sponsoring the event was required to be in attendance and interact one-on-one with the children.

Aric had yet to see Chelsea's Guinevere costume. Miss June, who was going as Guinevere's maidservant, had kept all of the younger woman's attire up in her apartment. Jason was going as Sir Lancelot.

Fredeline and Eve Rose had declined Aric's invitation to join them at the event, citing a previous commitment with some friends in the Haitian community. Aric didn't ask, but Chelsea helpfully volunteered that they were participating in various rituals practiced around that particular time of year by those who believed in voodoo. Aric did not require elaboration. He wasn't afraid of such things, nor did he disapprove. He simply didn't believe in them.

Aric left the master suite and walked down the hallway toward the main part of the house. As he approached the door to the living area, he paused. Someone was playing the piano, and it sounded extraordinarily beautiful.

The week after Aric and Chelsea's trip to the storage unit, the designated charity had cleared out everything not tagged, and the rockers, swing, and baby grand piano had been delivered to the

Creole House. The four rockers sat along the front porch, and the swing rested on the back porch waiting for a stand. The baby grand piano had been positioned in the corner of the main living area nearest the hallway door, and a piano tuner had come the week after it arrived and tuned the instrument. However, to Aric's knowledge, no one had played it. To his knowledge, no one in the house besides himself even knew how to play. Obviously, this had been a misconception on his part.

He slowly opened the door and edged into the room. Chelsea sat at the piano wearing a dark blue gown that Aric imagined would've suited Guinevere very well. Chelsea's hair was pulled away from her face and held by some pins or clips he couldn't see, but the rest fell loosely around her shoulders. She wore delicate sapphire earrings that matched her gown and dark blue velvet slippers on her feet.

As Aric listened to Chelsea play, he realized that she was totally unaware of his presence. All of her attention was focused on the piece, which happened to be Debussy's *Arabesque No. 1 Piano Solo*. She was a magnificent pianist, far better than he.

Aric loved to play the piano and knew he had talent. Yet, he was under no delusions that he could have ever been a concert pianist. As he listened to Chelsea play, he was in awe. She had the skill, the touch, and the feeling that all truly great pianists possessed. He wondered how long she'd been playing, knowing that she would be unable to give him an answer.

When she finished, she stared at the keys for a moment then began to play Mozart's *Requiem Lacrimosa Piano Solo*. Again, there was a perfect balance of all of the elements needed in order to make the music come alive. Aric was about to shut his eyes and concentrate on the notes when he realized that he was not the only person transfixed by Chelsea's performance.

Jason and Miss June stood with stunned expressions near the fireplace. Fredeline and Eve Rose came up beside them and stared in wonder at Chelsea as she played. Five pairs of eyes were fixed on her, but she remained oblivious to everything except the piano. When she finished the piece, she lowered her hands into her lap and smiled.

"That was magnificent," Miss June said from where she stood. "You have amazing ability."

Chelsea appeared startled to see all of them standing in the room but quickly recovered herself and thanked the woman. She admitted that she hadn't remembered knowing how to play the piano and had merely sat in front of it to see what it sounded like when she touched the keys. Once she'd done so, the music had simply begun to flow from her.

"Do you know the names of the pieces you played?" Aric asked curiously.

"No. Are they famous?"

"Very, although from two extremely different composers. The first was Debussy, and the second was Mozart."

"Oh. I know who they are, but I couldn't tell you what I was playing. I just…knew what I was supposed to do. I really enjoyed it. I want to play more. I wonder how many pieces I know."

"With talent like that, I'm sure you know quite a few," Jason remarked. "I certainly wouldn't mind hearing you find out."

"I felt so peaceful while I played," Chelsea admitted. "I guess I had lessons."

"Another mysterious clue to your past," Aric offered. "Unfortunately, we'll have to talk about it later. We need to get going or we'll be late."

Chelsea rose quickly and said, "We can't be late. We'll disappoint the children."

Aric agreed, although he was inwardly very worried about how Chelsea was going to react to the night's activities. Would being around the children for the event be a positive or negative experience for her? Perhaps it would be a good indicator of how she would handle her trip to the elementary school with Nadine the following month.

When they arrived at the children's museum, Aric led the others through a side entrance. The entryway to the place was quite large and had a high, arched ceiling that would have stopped Chelsea in her tracks. So, he'd arranged to have a security guard let them in through another door.

The party wouldn't start for another forty-five minutes, and Aric took that time to introduce Chelsea, Miss June, and Jason to the other sponsors and their employees in attendance. Chelsea gripped his hand tightly but did admirably well in her interactions with the others. She'd told him that she and the psychiatrist had practiced role-playing in order to prepare her for the casual questions that others always asked at any party: Where are you from? What do you do for a living? Does your family live in the area? Are you married? Do you have children? What are your hobbies?

Aric listened to Chelsea's prepared responses as the two of them mingled with the others. She was from Haiti. She worked with computers. She had no family to speak of. She was engaged to Aric and had no children. As for hobbies, she'd been planning to say reading and exercising, but she now added playing the piano to the list. This pleased Aric more than he could have ever verbalized. She was improvising, something TBI patients were often unable to do. It was a very promising sign that Aric didn't miss.

Another sign he couldn't miss was the way the other men were staring at Chelsea. Her exotic looks always drew attention, but he was used to that from strangers. He knew these men and knew very well how many of them thought. They were rich, powerful, and used to getting what they wanted. He recalled Nadine's warning that he should give Chelsea an engagement ring as soon as possible or else she would be more vulnerable to advances by other men. He doubted if a ring would stop most of those at the event who had designs on her, so he put his arm protectively around her waist.

Like the other couples present, Aric and Chelsea posed for formal pictures for the society pages and business magazines that would no doubt laud those companies sponsoring the event. It was good publicity, although that wasn't the reason Aric became involved in such things. He insisted that Jason and Miss June take a formal picture together as well, knowing that their photo would not appear in any on-line magazine or newspaper but that each person who posed for a picture would be given a copy.

Once the children arrived, the fun began. The age range for the event was five to ten. The little ones seemed ecstatic to be doing what "normal" children their age took for granted and happily ran around in their costumes, had their faces painted, played Halloween games, ate, and enjoyed the museum. It made Aric feel good to know that he'd helped these little ones have what each child deserved, what he'd had growing up. He was enormously relieved to see Chelsea playing with the children as if she were one of them and having a wonderful time.

It suddenly struck Aric that every charity he contributed to involved aiding children. His family had always been directly involved with helping others, but they had worked with various demographic groups. Why had his efforts since the D Plague only been focused on assisting kids in need?

"Abandoned children," Chelsea had said, "like you and me."

Was that his subconscious motivation? Yet, not all of the programs he sponsored involved abandoned or orphaned children. Some of the kids had parents but were homeless, illiterate, poor, and/or neglected. They desperately needed beneficial organized afterschool activities.

"Aric," Jason said, "You all right?"

"Yes, I was lost in thought."

"You might want to come back to the present and see what Chelsea's up to. I'm not sure how she's going to do."

Aric scanned the room and was startled to realize that he'd lost track of his fiancée.

"Don't panic," his assistant said reassuringly. "You know we're keeping an eye on her, but I'm not really sure how what she's going to try will work out. I think you should be there. This way."

Aric followed the man to an adjacent room. Half of the floor consisted of dozens of squares that were programmed to randomly light up in varying patterns. As each square lit up, a musical note would sound. Those involved in this museum activity were expected to listen and watch the sequence of squares that lit up and then go to each one and tap on a button in one corner with a foot. As one level was successfully completed, the patterns and rapidity became more difficult to follow, although there was no time limit on the participant's replication.

Aric tensed. He had absolutely no idea how Chelsea would react. Her ability to follow lists and directions had improved greatly, but this was spontaneous sequencing and retention. She might be overwhelmed.

I should have brought her here before tonight, Aric realized. *I should have better prepared her.*

As if reading his thoughts, Miss June said from beside him, "You can't prepare her for everything. She's made great progress since she met you, but she's going to have successes and failures and have to learn to deal with both on her own."

Aric nodded and thanked Miss June for her sage words as he watched the happy children playing the game and urging Chelsea to try it. He was relieved to see that she didn't appear fearful, simply contemplative. Finally, she agreed to attempt the exercise but told the children she might not be any good at the game. Several of them commented that it didn't matter if she was good at it, that it was fun regardless.

Chelsea stood on the circle marked START and waited. The game began. The first few levels were extremely easy, and she had no trouble following along. She began to struggle at the Fifth Level and barely made it through the Sixth. As Aric wondered if she'd continue to play or admit defeat, something in her manner changed. A small smile played on her lips as she began Level Seven.

He watched in fascination as Chelsea moved slowly but effortlessly from one level to the next. He doubted whether or not he could have gotten past Level Twelve. As the crowd continued to increase in size, she passed Level Twenty-one. Someone nearby who worked at the museum remarked that there were thirty levels of the game, and no one had ever made it past twenty-seven.

By the time Chelsea reached Level Thirty, word had spread throughout the museum. The room wasn't large enough for everyone, but people were pushing and craning their necks in their attempts to see what was happening. Adults and children alike were cheering Chelsea on, although she appeared oblivious to everything except the game. Aric never took his eyes off her.

He knew the museum had digital recorders running in every room and that Chelsea's activities were being filmed. He would get a copy of the recording for himself, the neurologist, and the psychiatrist. Whatever was going on in Chelsea's brain, it was beyond the average person's capabilities.

The final intricate sequence played on the floor. Chelsea walked gracefully in her long blue dress from one square to the next and tapped the buttons as she went. When she reached the last one, she tapped it with her toes and smiled.

Unexpectedly, the entire set of squares began to light up and play notes around where Chelsea stood in the center. Aric didn't know the name of the piece, but it was definitely a work by Rachmaninoff. Chelsea appeared entranced and watched the light show for a few moments before closing her eyes, an expression of pure rapture on her face.

That's the same way she looks when she comes, thought Aric, growing instantly aroused. Smirking, he thought wryly, *Should I be flattered or am I going to have to compete with the piano now?*

Chapter Twenty-seven

When the music and light show ended, Chelsea opened her eyes to the applause and cheers of the crowd. She smiled shyly and looked at her feet. Aric hurried out to where she stood, took her in his arms, and kissed her. When they broke apart, he murmured, "You are magnificent."

She smiled up at him and swayed slightly. He steadied her and suggested she sit down and drink something. Leaning against him for support, she said, "I am kind of tired and thirsty."

"I don't doubt it. That took a lot of time and concentration. Do you realize you're the only one who's ever completed all thirty levels?"

"Really? It was so much fun and such a challenge."

As they sat on a bench, Chelsea accepted a glass of water and asked, "Do you want to know how I did it? I started to hum the notes. Once I analyzed the grid on the floor, I realized how the computer had been programmed to randomize the patterns. The formulas made sense, so I followed the notes in order to remember how the sequencing went. Both computers and music use math to work. I'd love to meet the person who designed this."

"I'm sure that person would love to meet you."

Miss June and Jason approached them and congratulated Chelsea on a job well done. Once Chelsea had rested for a while, they returned to the throng. They were in the middle of playing games with some of the children when Aric saw the curator of the museum. He excused himself from the group and approached the woman regarding his request for a copy of the digital recording that had caught Chelsea's actions. The curator immediately excused herself and returned fifteen minutes later with a tiny flash drive that held the recording. Aric pocketed it, thanked her, and went back to where he'd left Chelsea. She wasn't there.

He scanned the room in search of either Jason or Miss June. Neither was in view. He began to hurry from room to room, being polite to those he knew but not lingering. He was growing more alarmed with every second that he couldn't locate Chelsea and their protectors, although he was certain that Jason and Miss June were not the only ones providing surveillance at the Halloween event.

Aric rounded a corner and found Chelsea sitting on the floor looking slightly ill. He joined her and slipped an arm around her shoulders. She leaned against him and asked, "Do you have one of my pills with you?"

"I do. How about if you take it, and then we head for home?"

She nodded against him. Jason appeared from out of nowhere with a soda, and Chelsea swallowed the pill without hesitation. Aric helped her to stand and guided her toward the exit, offering their apologies to anyone they passed along the way. Miss June was waiting for them at the side door.

"You had quite a full evening," she told Chelsea once they were in the car. "That was a lot for you all at one time."

"How long were we there?"

"Four hours total. Most of that time, you didn't stop. It's not surprising that you're worn out and have a headache."

Chelsea whimpered softly, and Aric prayed that he would be as good as Olga had been at helping to relieve her pain. She hadn't had a migraine since the night Olga had tried to kill him three weeks earlier. He was still confused as to why the Swede had offered to show him how to help Chelsea if she'd planned on murdering him, but he was certainly grateful she had.

Olga's true identity and motive remained unclear. The FBI was no closer to determining her real name and agenda than they'd been on the night of her death. Lakshmi had confirmed that no one on her team had been able to get any more information than the FBI already had. The situation had everyone involved stumped.

When they returned to the Creole House, Chelsea was unable to stand. Aric carried her to their room and thanked the others before asking them to leave him and Chelsea alone. Fredeline and Eve Rose were still not back from their voodoo meeting, and Jason and Miss June informed Aric they would be in their rooms and to call them if need be.

Once Chelsea's gown and slippers had been removed, Aric took off his own costume and began her massage. At first, he felt clumsy as he worked on her neck, shoulders, and head but was soon awestruck by how quickly his efforts yielded a positive result. Chelsea was sleeping soundly within twenty minutes.

He watched her for a while then decided he was too wound up to sleep. Instead, he switched on his computer, loaded the digital recording he'd gotten from the museum, watched it three times, and emailed it to the psychiatrist and neurologist along with a written explanation. Then he went to a corner of the room and selected one of the boxes he was supposed to go through for the week. He carried it back to the desk.

It had been terribly painful the week before when he'd sorted through the first five boxes out of the thirty-two he and Chelsea had tagged at the warehouse. However, he'd been glad once he'd finished the first batch, had cried for a while, and had eventually felt better. He'd intended to examine the contents of the next five boxes the day after the Halloween party, but now he decided there was no reason to wait. The one he was going to open right then was labeled "JEWELRY – MEMENTOES."

Inside the large box were three smaller boxes. One was marked "MEMENTOES"; one was marked "COSTUME JEWELRY"; and one was marked "FINE JEWELRY." He wondered whether or not he would be able to look through any of it without Chelsea sitting next to him, bolstering his spirits and confidence. Glancing at her lying in the bed, he told himself to man up and get on with the task.

Aric sifted through the mementoes first, recognizing each piece as he did so. The variety was staggering. The items ranged from one grandfather's treasured belt buckle to his Tante Marie's favorite bookmark, the one he'd made and laminated for her during a school art project when he'd been in kindergarten. Wiping the tears from his face, he made himself look at each piece and remember. When he got to the bottom of the box, Aric saw eight small plastic boxes and had to stifle a sob.

He'd been three when his oldest sister had gotten the idea for them to each make a Christmas ornament for their parents. She'd taken all of her siblings to a pottery shop and instructed each of them to select an ornament and paint it in any way they liked. The personalities of the individual Rodrigue children shone through in their final designs and color choices. Aric lifted each one and studied it. When he got to Alycia's, the sister who was a year older than he, he admired the way the then four-year-old had taken all the colors of the rainbow and somehow blended them into a beautiful kaleidoscope pattern. His own piece was a star that he'd painted gold and then decorated with an awkwardly painted red heart.

Aric put all of the items back in the box and moved on to the costume jewelry. He recognized most of it but would only keep a few items that held sentimental value to him because of their significance to his sisters, mother, grandmothers, and Tante Marie.

Finally, he lifted the lid of the box that held the fine jewelry. Although his family had money, they'd never been ostentatious. That didn't mean they weren't appreciative of fine quality things. With so many women living in the house, there was quite a lot of nice jewelry in the box, including every wedding ring left behind.

What are you going to do with all these? he wondered. *Keep everything locked away in a bank vault...for what? For whom?*

Aric realized in that moment that he was never going to have children. No one would ever be able to predict what might happen to him as long as he lived, and no one would know what might happen if he tried to procreate. Because of her brain injury, Chelsea could endanger her life by becoming pregnant even if he hadn't been a biological mystery. He would never say it to her, but that same injury could also limit her ability to be a competent parent.

He was mildly shocked to find that he was relieved by his decision never to father a child. He loved interacting with kids and felt as if he was good with them, but he was not going to take a chance by trying to make a baby with Chelsea or a surrogate. He and Chelsea could live as they chose and devote their energies to helping children in need. If they ever decided they wanted a family, then they could look into adoption.

What if Chelsea doesn't agree? You can't make this decision for the both of you. What are you going to do if she tells you that having babies with you is a must for her?

Aric pushed that thought aside and replaced all the fine jewelry in the box except one piece. He decided he was going to take the rest to a jeweler he knew who made original pieces and then bring Chelsea back with him. He would suggest to her that she work with the jeweler to use the existing articles to make pieces designed especially for her. That way, he could combine his past with his present and future.

Aric took the box back to the corner and wrote a check mark on one side then returned to the desk and lifted the ring his sister Alycia had worn every moment for the last seven years of her life. It had been a Sweet Sixteen present from their parents. What no one except Alycia had realized was that her little brother had been the one to select it. He'd seen it in a shop window and texted a photo to his parents, who'd agreed that it would be perfect and had purchased the ring for their youngest daughter.

He shut his eyes and pictured Alycia as she'd been on the day of the party. Tall and thin with long, curly brown hair, she was wearing her favorite "hippie" dress, the one he'd kept at the warehouse. Her soulful brown eyes had been fixed on the ring, and a little smile had played on her lips. Then she'd looked directly at Aric and said, "Thank you."

Aric opened his eyes and looked at the ring. It was made of white gold and was set with a variety of precious and semi-precious stones that spiraled out from the center. It reminded him of a multicolored pinwheel that was quirky yet beautiful. It reminded him of Alycia.

He thought of the free-spirited Alycia, the sister who'd been so quiet and introspective. She'd been so focused on connecting with the forces of the universe that she'd set herself somewhat apart from the others in the Rodrigue household, who'd been a mostly boisterous lot. She only spoke when there was something important to say but did considerably more volunteer work than any of the others. When she wasn't in school or volunteering, Alycia liked to wander into the woods to read or think or commune with nature.

Aric knew that there was something else Alycia liked to do in the woods. One April day when he'd been fifteen and she sixteen, he'd been out for a walk on the family property and had unwittingly come across his sister having sex with a senior from their high school. They were too involved in what they were doing to have heard him approach. Aric had ducked back behind a tree then cautiously peered around the trunk. He wondered whether he should interrupt, leave, or stay hidden so that they wouldn't know he'd ever been there. In the end, he opted to stay and wait it out. What he hadn't planned on doing was spying on them, but he was young, filled with raging hormones, and had never actually seen anyone have sex. His burning curiosity overrode his good sense and his embarrassment. Both teenagers seemed to be experienced, and he inadvertently got what he would later come to understand was quite a lesson on how to have good sex.

Alycia had approached him about a month later and asked, "Have I done anything to make you mad? Why have you been avoiding me?"

His face flushed scarlet, he'd insisted, "There's nothing wrong."

"There is. Talk."

Aric had blurted out the entire story and then said, "I'm sorry. It was wrong to watch you doing that."

Smiling, his sister had said, "Don't worry. I'm not upset with you."

"You're not?" He said confused.

"Making love is the most beautiful thing human beings can do with each other," she'd told him. "When you do it with someone you care about, then it makes you feel connected to everything on the planet. You should try it. Just be safe and don't ever demean the other person or allow her to demean you. Making love should always be a magical thing." As she turned to go, she added, "Please don't tell Mom or Dad. I know they think I'm still a virgin, and I wouldn't want to disillusion them."

"I won't tell."

She gave him her little smile again and said earnestly, "I love you, Aric. I love everyone in the family, but you especially."

"Why *me* especially?"

"Because you love me even though you don't understand me, and you never judge me because I'm different. You don't know how much that means to me. I'm very lucky to have you as my brother. You let me be…me."

Aric stared at Alycia's ring for a long time as he debated how to proceed. Finally, he placed the ring on the desk and got into bed with Chelsea, trying not to wake her as he did so. Her eyelids fluttered open, and she asked him what time it was. He told her he didn't know and asked her how she was feeling.

"You did great," she told him. "I feel fine. Between the medicine and you, my migraine's gone. Do you mind if we talk about some important things right now?" When he shook his head, she announced, "I had a lot of fun with the kids tonight, but I don't think we should ever try to have any children. You'd never have a moment's peace if we did. You'd always be wondering if something terrible was going to happen every minute of every day. You're filled with enough emotional stress without adding more. If we just decide we're never going to have any kids, then you can at least let go of one worry."

"But what about you? Do you want babies?"

"It might be too much for me to have a baby because of the accident. Even if I didn't stroke out or have some other complication, I'm afraid I can't raise a child with my limitations. So, if we decide not to have kids then I can let go of one fear, too."

"Good points."

"Plus, if we don't ever plan on having children, then you can stop giving the government sperm donations each month. That will prevent them from experimenting with it and put your mind at ease about that particular quandary."

"That's one angle I never considered. That would be a relief in and of itself." Brushing some loose strands of hair away from her face, he asked, "Did you really have fun tonight?"

"Lots of fun. I don't think I'll be scared about being with children and doing things I don't remember from when I was little. It was exciting to do them for what felt like the first time."

Overcome by relief and love, Aric got out of bed, went over to the desk, and retrieved Alycia's ring. He brought it back to Chelsea and held it out to her. As she took it from him, he explained about Alycia, the ring, and spoke of what his sister had told him about making love.

"It's so clear how much you loved her. It's a beautiful and unusual ring," Chelsea remarked. "May I wear it as an engagement ring?"

"You really like it?"

"I love it. It's so…you."

He was about to tell her once more how much he loved her when someone rapped loudly on their bedroom door, causing them both to jump.

"Mister Aric! Miss Chelsea!" called Fredeline through the door. "You've got to come quick! It's Miss June! She's dead!"

Chapter Twenty-eight

Aric burst through the attic door and saw Jason, sitting on the edge of Miss June's bed with one of his hands resting on one of hers. The elderly woman was lying on her back with her eyes closed. She appeared to be sleeping. When Jason turned toward the door, Aric saw tracks of tears on the man's face.

"What happened?" Aric asked as he hurried across the large room toward the two agents. "Who killed her?"

"Nobody."

"What do you mean? Someone had to kill her."

"No, no one did. It's extremely doubtful that anyone will be killed here at the house or anywhere on the property since the President came for a visit, not that we'll ever let our guard slip."

"What are you talking about?"

"Why do you think President Jitesh came to your house earlier this month?"

"To visit with me, relax, and meet Chelsea, Fredeline, Eve Rose, Miss June, and you."

"Wrong. The President took a great personal risk by coming here, as did the Vice-President and his wife. The Secret Service bigwigs were about to crap their pants when they were informed of the plans for that day. They had to bust their asses even more than usual to ensure the security of Jitesh and the LaFleurs. It would have been much better for the President to have you and the rest of us meet with them somewhere more secure."

"Then why meet here?"

"To send a message loud and clear to anyone who was a threat to Chelsea or you. What better message than seeing that you were under protection from the Commander-in-chief and her sidekick?"

"So, Lakshmi, Buddy, and Nadine put their lives at risk – put the *country* at risk – for us? Why?"

"I'm not privy to the President's motivations. You'll have to discuss that with her yourself."

Aric glanced at the bed and asked, "But if no one is going to risk attacking us in the house, then how did Miss June die?"

"She had cancer. She told no one except me. No one. By the time the doctors diagnosed her with it, there was nothing they could do. It was everywhere. They gave her the choice of medical treatments that would've made her last few months a living hell or of having no treatment at all and enjoying what time she had left. She was in no pain, so she opted for the latter. I just don't believe she thought it would happen quite so soon."

"But what if it wasn't the cancer? What if someone really did kill her knowing that she was already dying?"

"You mean they hastened her death in some way?"

"Yes."

"That'll be for the coroner to determine, but I don't think there was foul play here. She told me a few days ago that she thought her number was going to be up soon. She wanted to work this case until the end. She wanted to die doing what she loved. She also didn't want the rest of you to feel sorry for her. That wasn't how she imagined spending her remaining days."

"So, why tell you?"

Jason shrugged and admitted, "Partially, because she wanted to position me to take over the case when she was gone. Partially, it was because I'm her grandson."

"Her grandson," Aric repeated slowly. Glancing at the dead woman, he said, "I'm so sorry, Jason. I had no idea that —" He stopped and said, "Well, maybe I had some idea."

"How?"

"Your snicker."

"What?"

"I heard Miss June snicker in this certain way when we were talking about Nadine. You snickered that same way once, and I couldn't figure out why I thought it was so familiar. Now I know why. Did your mother do that, too?"

Jason nodded and looked back at his grandmother's face.

"Was your mother an agent?"

"I told you it ran in the family. She was killed in the line of duty when I was twenty-three."

"And your father?"

"He owned a security firm. He died in the D Plague."

"Siblings?"

"One older brother, Julian."

"Did he take over the security firm when your father passed?"

"Actually, yes. Julian and I were never close. I wonder sometimes if he has any conscience. He's very good at running the security company though." Staring at the dead woman, Jason said wearily, "I guess I'll have to call and tell him about Gran."

Sighing and pulling up a chair beside the bed, Aric asked, "What now?"

"Your protection will continue, although I don't know if I want to bring a new person into the house."

"That's not what I meant."

"What then?"

"Your grandmother. What about funeral arrangements?"

"She didn't want anything. She always said it wasn't about her in life and shouldn't be about her in death. She'll be buried in a place of honor in Virginia." Wiping his cheeks, Jason said, "She had a great time at the Halloween party. It was a good send-off as it turns out. I'm really glad you pushed us to take that picture together. It'll be a nice way to remember our last evening spent with each other."

"What should we tell Chelsea, Eve Rose, and Fredeline?"

"The truth. She passed away in her sleep. I found her when I came up to talk to her about some things. I'm in charge of the protection detail now."

"But not that you were her grandson."

"No. I'd prefer it if you kept that part to yourself."

"Sure. Is there anything else I can do?"

"Talk to the others while I spend a little more time with my Gran."

Aric stood and placed a hand on Jason's shoulder before leaving and going slowly down the outside stairs. He went through the back doors and took a deep breath before heading toward the kitchen. As he entered, Chelsea, Eve Rose, and Fredeline all looked expectantly and nervously at him from where they sat at the table. He told them what he could and stayed with the women as they cried quietly. Eve Rose asked how Miss June could have been terminally ill with cancer and yet seem healthy and in good spirits.

"I know that people typically think of cancer sufferers as appearing sickly and being in pain all the time, but that's not always the case," Aric explained. "I remember one professor in college talking about how he'd attended autopsies as part of his medical training. He gave a lecture once about people who'd died in accidents or had been murdered, and then when the coroners performed the autopsies, they found the bodies riddled with cancer. The families and friends said they'd had no idea and that their loved ones had seemed vibrant and healthy up until the day they'd been killed. Their personal medical records didn't indicate that they had any knowledge of being terminally ill. It's certainly not the norm, but it does happen. I suppose if Miss June was unfortunate enough to be diagnosed with terminal cancer, then she was lucky enough to be asymptomatic until the end."

"Will there be a funeral?" asked Chelsea.

"Jason said Miss June didn't want one."

Fredeline suggested, "Funerals are good for the living, so we should have something to help remember and celebrate Miss June's life. Every person who loses someone should have that."

Aric stared at his feet and said nothing.

"Tell me you had a service for your family," Chelsea said quietly. When he was silent, she murmured, "Oh, Aric."

He rose and left the room without looking at any of them. Going to his bedroom, he sat at his desk and thought of his own grandmothers. They'd been much like Miss June and had that spunk that all great Southern women possessed. He tried not to remember hearing their screams as they'd died. At least Miss June hadn't had to die like that.

The door behind him opened and closed. Aric didn't turn. He expected that it was Chelsea. Instead, it was Fredeline who said his name. He asked her what she needed.

"I don't need anything. *You*, on the other hand, need help. Do you have any sort of grave markers for your family?"

"There's a commemorative plaque in the lobby of Rodrigue Pharmaceuticals. It lists everyone's names, birth dates, and death dates."

"Have you ever done anything to observe their passing?"

"You mean other than remembering their dying screams every day of my life?" he snapped. "Or maybe you mean devoting my life to continuing what my parents started instead of going on to medical school?"

Fredeline came across to him and rested a hand on his shoulder, much as he'd done with Jason earlier that morning.

"Whatever you went through while your family was dying must have been terrible."

"You have no idea."

"No, I don't. Taking over the family business is certainly a good way to honor your parents and the rest, but you need to have a way to honor them that will give you some real comfort."

"Like what?"

"November first is All Souls' Day. Do something for them every year on that date. Use the plaque as if it were headstones on their graves if they could have had graves. Just like going through your family's things with Miss Chelsea, it will help you to heal."

"Whom did you lose in the D Plague?"

"My son and his wife."

"Eve Rose's parents?"

"Yes. We'll honor them this Wednesday in our own fashion. You find your way of honoring those you lost."

Chapter Twenty-nine

That Wednesday, Aric stood with Jason in the lobby of his company and stared at the plaque he'd had made that was dedicated to June Penn. It had been positioned on the left side of the one dedicated to the Rodrigues. Between the two plaques sat a stand that held a large wreath of flowers.

"Thank you for doing this," Jason said quietly. "She would have appreciated it. I know I do."

"It's the least I could do. I wish we would have had more time to spend with Miss June before she died."

"Aric?"

Both men pivoted and saw Chelsea standing in jeans and a black sweater right inside the doorway. She looked terrified but began to walk forward. She never took her gaze from Aric's face. When he began to move toward her, Jason gripped his arm and told him to stay where he was.

"You're the one who said she needed to have higher expectations placed on her. Give her a chance to do this. She'll let you know if she can't make it."

Aric stood very still as Chelsea came slowly toward him. It seemed to take forever, but he wasn't going to rush her. The fact that she was combating her spatial issues with such determination made his heart soar. It didn't matter if she walked all the way across the lobby. Just attempting such a thing was a huge triumph for her.

When she finally arrived where he and Jason were standing, Aric took her in his arms and told her how proud he was of her. Holding him tightly, Chelsea confided, "I was scared to death, but I needed to do that. I can't be afraid of falling every time there's a big space. What if it's an emergency and I have to get somewhere in that kind of environment?"

"That was phenomenal. Why today?"

"Because I thought you might need me to be here."

Aric kissed her passionately, not caring who was watching. He did need her there and was inordinately pleased to see her. Once they broke apart, he showed her the plaques and the wreath. She nodded her approval.

"You did the right thing," she declared. "Do you feel better?"

Aric pondered this question and realized that yes, he did feel better, so he nodded and smiled at Chelsea. He kissed her forehead and told her that the little memorial had helped. She made him promise to do it each year, and he readily agreed. Relief of some sort was coursing through his body.

"Where are Eve Rose and Fredeline?" he asked. "Who came with you?"

"They're off doing their voodoo stuff. I came all by myself."

Aric could hear the pride in her voice and grinned at her. He escorted her to the elevators with Jason walking closely behind them. When they reached his office, Chelsea asked him if he wanted to see something amazing. He glanced uncomfortably at Jason, not knowing what his fiancée had in mind.

"It's not me naked," she announced, "although maybe in a little while."

Jason snickered, and Aric smiled and shook his head.

"Remember when you wondered if there was a computer program that could take someone's picture and make images of what that person looked like all the way back to when they were a baby?" When he told her that he did recall talking to her about this, she continued, "I found a program. I put a picture of myself in, and it only took one hour. I want you to see the results."

"Gladly."

She sat at the computer and typed in a series of commands. As Aric and Jason stood behind her, the first image appeared on the screen. It was a photo of Chelsea obviously positioned so that her facial features would be optimally visible.

"I had to follow directions and sit and look a certain way in order for the computer to take my picture just so," she told them. "It took me a few tries, but I finally got it."

The image on the virtual screen faded and was replaced with one that looked almost identical. However, as the three of them watched, that image was replaced by one that looked slightly altered. Every thirty seconds, a different "photo" appeared. Chelsea got younger and younger before their eyes. It was as if they were looking through a photo album that spanned from the present back almost a quarter of a century. The final picture was of a one-year-old child.

"You were amazingly beautiful your entire life," Aric murmured. "Does seeing yourself like this spark any memories?"

"No. It was very interesting to see what I looked like, but I don't recognize myself or remember anything because of these pictures."

"But maybe someone else will," Jason suggested. "I'd like to run each one through the database of missing children and find out if there are any matches."

"Sure."

"And I'd like to download this to my computer and phone and follow some other angles," Aric put forth.

"Done," Chelsea announced after typing in a few more commands. "Jason, I sent these to you, too."

The agent eyed her suspiciously and asked, "How?"

"Through your email. I located it before I left the house."

"How do you know my email address?"

Chelsea bit her lip and said, "Oh. I guess I should have asked you before searching for it. Sorry."

Jason checked his phone and said incredulously, "You sent this to my work email?"

She nodded.

"The system's encrypted."

Now chewing on her lower lip, Chelsea said in a small voice, "I know."

"How long did it take you to find my work email?"

"Forty minutes."

"Chere, you promised you wouldn't hack into anyone's systems again without their permission," groaned Aric.

"I kind of forgot," she admitted. "All I was focused on was that Jason might want me to give him this information. I didn't really think about how I was going about getting to his email."

Jason looked at Aric and said, "You have to call the President. I know you've broached the subject of having Chelsea work with the government, and she told you she'd have to think about it. Well, the time for debating that is over. If Chelsea can hack our system in forty minutes, then there's no question about what should be done. She has to be monitored for her own protection and everyone else's. I have a really bad feeling that whatever happened to her regarding the attack and accident was a direct result of her superior IT abilities."

Chelsea scrambled out of the desk chair so quickly that it fell over. Before either man could react, she slipped under the desk. When they crouched down and peered underneath, she was huddled in a corner with her knees drawn up and her arms wrapped around them. Her face was turned away.

"Chere?

"Aric, I'm so scared," she responded without moving. "Please, don't hurt me."

Finally, he thought. *Huge progress there.*

"Please, don't make me come out," she begged. "Please, don't take me upstairs."

"Upstairs?"

She nodded but continued to refuse to look at him.

"What's upstairs that frightens you?"

Aric hadn't thought that it was possible for Chelsea to burrow any further into the corner under the desk. He'd been wrong. He asked Jason to leave and close the door behind him. The man did so without question as Aric sat on the floor where he'd been crouching.

"We're not going anywhere, Chere," he said soothingly. "Will you come out, so I can hold you?"

She reluctantly crawled out from under the desk and fell into his arms. He expected her to tell him that they needed to have sex so that she could feel in control or to simply unzip his pants and take him in her mouth. Instead, she tucked her knees close to her body and trembled. He stroked her hair and told her that everything would be fine. When she eventually drifted off to sleep, he gently laid her on the carpet and went out to speak to Jason.

"You and I need to talk," Jason said quietly.

"We can talk until the cows come home. It won't help Chelsea."

"I think you're wrong. I've been an agent for a while. I have a theory."

"Which is?"

"You saw the way she reacted when I mentioned that I thought her attack and accident were linked to her computer skills."

"But she and I have discussed it. She knows that's a possibility."

"Did you ever talk about it while she was on the computer and had recently hacked into the Federal Government's system?"

"Of course not."

"Tell me everything about upstairs. What was she talking about there?"

"Are you a shrink now?" Aric snapped.

"No, I'm a Federal Agent! It's called the Federal Bureau of Investigation for Christ's sake!"

His anger quickly diminishing, Aric explained about Chelsea's unease during her tour of his upstairs apartment and her request that he never go back to stay there again. Jason absorbed every word, every detail. When Aric was finished, he looked pensive. He also looked angry.

"Consider this scenario: Chelsea's a computer whiz who breaks into someone's office to hack his computer. Why, I don't know. If she can hack Federal databases from home, then why risk going to someone's office?" Shaking his head, he went on, "For whatever reason, she's hacking into the system of someone very powerful and doing this in his office. The guy shows up unexpectedly. She tries to hide under his desk, but she's found. The powerful person is enraged and wants to kill her, but first he wants to teach her a lesson. He's got total control of the situation and decides what better way to punish her than to rape her? She's gorgeous, and he wants to hurt her and give himself sexual gratification all at the same time. He has goons with him, and they haul Chelsea to the guy's apartment in the building. The goons hold her while he brutalizes her. It's after hours, so no one hears her scream. Then, the goons either take her out and dump her somewhere with nothing but the clothes on her back, or she escapes and ends up at Disney Springs in an effort to lose them. Or maybe they take her to Disney Springs themselves and call a taxi. They pretend she's drunk or crazy and put her in a cab and tell the driver to take her to SeaWorld. The accident is supposed to kill her, but she somehow survives but with no memory. Lucky for her. If she had any knowledge of what had actually happened, they would have come back and finished the job."

Aric's hands were clenched into fists. What Jason was proposing was not only possible but plausible. It would explain Chelsea's irrational fears and some of the events. What it didn't explain was how the accident could have been orchestrated in such a short amount of time and why those who'd treated her afterward at the medical facilities had been killed. He inquired about this, and Jason shrugged and said he was going to follow some leads now that they had a more concrete theory about what might have occurred on June 8, 2033.

"What now?" Aric asked tightly.

"We work on fleshing out various parts of my theory. We have those photos of Chelsea when she was younger, so that might give us some leads. If I were you, then I'd get rid of that apartment space upstairs as soon as possible. Otherwise, she's going to have an irrational fear of coming here every time she thinks about it."

"Believe me, the place will be cleared by tomorrow night."

The door behind him opened, and Chelsea hesitantly stepped out and asked the two men what they were discussing.

Jason said, "I have some ideas about your case and believe that I know how we should proceed."

"Oh, I'm glad to hear you say that."

"I hope you'll also be glad to hear that I'm going to have my old apartment upstairs cleared out," Aric said, noting his fiancée's obvious relief. "It'll be useful as storage space."

"Could we go home now?" she asked. "Or to Maurice's restaurant?"

"I can't. I've got meetings all afternoon."

"I can call someone to personally go with you wherever you want," Jason offered. "You're always under surveillance for your protection, but if you want someone to walk beside you, that can be arranged."

"No, I want Aric to come so we can have sex," she said innocently. "It has to be Aric."

The two men shared a wordless exchange. Aric kissed Chelsea and reminded her that she really shouldn't talk so openly about having sex. He suggested that she go with one of Jason's people to have lunch at Moreau's or return to the house.

Pouting, she declared, "But I want to have sex with you, Aric. I want you to be...." She searched for the right words then settled on, "Tender the whole time. I want you to take care of me."

"I'll always take care of you." Tucking some hair behind one of her ears, he said, "And I'll do...the other tonight. I can't now. I have to work."

"And call Lakshmi?"

"Yes."

"But you'll make love to me later?"

Smiling, he said in Haitian Creole, "You know I will. I'll make love to you all night if you want. It would be perfect if we never had to leave the bedroom, wouldn't it?"

Her face brightened, and she kissed him and nodded. Squaring her shoulders, she said, "I think I'll run some errands and then go home. Try not to be too late."

"I won't be late. Promise me you'll eat some lunch while you're out."

"I will. I've been extra-hungry, lately. Will you be home for dinner?"

"I'm planning on it."

Aric put in a call to Lakshmi; then he spent the afternoon working hard but found himself extremely distracted. He was attempting to compartmentalize his job, Chelsea's new "photo album," and Jason's hypothesis about what had happened to Chelsea. At 5:40, he found himself sitting at his desk, staring blindly at a report about production quotas and imagining Chelsea sneaking into someone's office, being discovered, suffering the terror and pain of a horrific rape and somehow ending up in the taxi accident.

Jason suddenly flung open the door to the office and cried, "We have to get home *now*!"

Aric jumped up and raced after Jason. He knew better than to ask the Federal Agent anything until they were in a more private location. Once they were seated in a waiting car, he inquired, "What's the emergency?"

The man looked grimly at him and said, "Eve Rose and Fredeline."

"What about them?"

"They're dead."

"What?!?" Aric shouted, as all the blood drained from his face.

"They and their protection detail were found murdered after the detail didn't check in on time."

"Where?"

"I can't tell you."

"Why the hell not?!?"

216

"Because I can't!" Jason growled. "This is really fucked up! If whoever is behind all this is willing to kill Federal Agents in such a cavalier manner, then we are into some really deep shit!"

"So, FBI Agents' lives are more important than the lives of two Haitian women?"

"I didn't say that!" snarled Jason. "But people are less likely to kill FBI Agents than they are to kill ordinary civilians! It says something about the fucking murderers!"

Aric's mouth fell open. He had never seen Jason so enraged. As he watched, however, the man drew in a deep breath, exhaled, and got his emotions under control. While the car wound its way through the evening traffic, Jason confided to Aric that Chelsea hadn't been told anything and was waiting for everyone at the Creole House.

As Aric struggled to think of how he was going to break the news to Chelsea, he asked, "How were the others killed? Don't tell me it was in a traffic accident."

Jason simply shook his head and stared out of the window.

"Tell me!" Aric demanded. "Were they shot?"

Jason didn't give him a verbal answer but did nod almost imperceptibly.

"And?"

Raising one eyebrow, Jason looked questioningly at Aric.

"There has to be more. I know you'd be furious about something like this, but you're a little *too* furious. What aren't you telling me?"

The car stopped in front of the Creole House. As the two men hurried toward the house, Jason said quietly, "Eve Rose was raped. From what I know, it sounds very similar to Chelsea's rape. The main difference is that Chelsea didn't take a bullet afterward."

Aric stopped and muttered, "My god. You think it's the same guy?"

"Guys," Jason corrected. "Several to hold her down while someone sexually assaulted her. They'll use a rape kit on her body. I'm betting the semen will show that the rapist is one and the same in both cases. The monster," he hissed. His eyes dark and cold, he added, "I *will* find and eliminate him if it's the last thing I do."

Chapter Thirty

When they entered the living area, Chelsea was at the piano, playing a piece by Beethoven. The men stood watching her for a few moments before Jason excused himself to make some calls. Aric walked slowly to the piano and stood beside it. When Chelsea finished the piece, she looked up at him and smiled. Then her smile vanished, and her eyes widened. Somehow, she intuited what he was going to say.

His phone rang. He ignored it, even though he knew that it had to be Lakshmi. Gathering Chelsea up against him, he told her that Fredeline and Eve Rose were gone, but he didn't mention how they'd died or that the younger woman had been raped. He felt tears well in his own eyes as she cried against him.

"I don't understand," Chelsea sobbed. "Who is doing this and why? If they want to kill me, then why not just do it? Why kill all of these people who take care of me?" Breaking away from him, she insisted, "You have to leave me!"

"Never," he said firmly. "I'm in as much danger because of my unusual physical condition as you are because of whatever happened to you. Fredeline and Eve Rose might have been killed because of me. Olga tried to kill me. Both of those things may have been directly related to my perceived value to someone and not you." Kissing her on the top of the head, he murmured, "I'll be with you until the day I die, whether that's tomorrow or when I'm a hundred! Maybe you should leave me!"

"I could never leave you," she said softly. "Never ever."

Aric's phone rang again, and he sighed heavily. Chelsea told him to take the call and excused herself in order to wash her face. Once she was gone, he answered the phone, heard Lakshmi urgently calling his name, and hurried to reassure her he was all right. She explained to him that her security team was aware of the situation and shared with him that what had happened had nothing to do with Jason's performance. She remarked that they were dealing with someone who had major assets and was extremely disturbed.

"Jason Duson will be briefing you on several options," she told him. "Whichever one you choose will be handled accordingly." Pausing, she said, "I'm so sorry, Aric. I truly enjoyed spending time

218

with Miss June and with Eve Rose and Fredeline. They were very nice women."

You'll have to add plaques for Fredeline and Eve Rose next to Miss June's, Aric thought. *Although they may have wanted funerals. God, how many more people will die before this is over?*

Aric finished his conversation with Lakshmi as Jason came into the living room. Once Chelsea had reappeared, he asked her and Aric to sit on the couch and listen to what he had to say. The two of them sat side-by-side while Jason perched on the arm of a chair.

"There's something we have to get straight right away," Jason began. "You both need one-on-one protection. I'm obviously with Aric, but since Miss June died, Chelsea hasn't had anyone like that with her. I really didn't want to bring in anyone new, but we have no choice at this point. A female Agent will be arriving any minute. She's going to be stuck to you like glue, Chelsea. If you don't like her and want a replacement, then tell me and we'll discuss the problem." Once Chelsea had agreed to this, he went on, "You have some decisions to make. Let me tell you your options; then you tell me what you want."

"We're listening," Aric said. "What should we do?"

"That's up to you. Your first option is to go into hiding. You put someone else in charge of the business and disappear until we find the persons responsible for whatever is going on regarding both of you."

"Next?"

"You sell your company, Aric. Both of you disappear and go into something similar to the Witness Protection Program. We'd still work on tracking down the perpetrators, but you'd have new identities, a new location, and new careers."

"Next?"

"You stay and continue on as you are. I shadow you, and the new Agent shadows Chelsea. Our people keep working the case. The President is willing to give us any help she can, but we continue to be at a standstill regarding the overall investigation. I've got no idea how long it will take to crack this case. No matter which option you choose, we're not giving up."

"That's comforting," Aric said sincerely. "I want these bastards found and not just because of the threat to Chelsea or me. Who knows how many other people have been hurt or killed by them for sinister reasons?"

"So, what do you want to do?"

"The choice is clear," Chelsea announced, startling both men. "We have to choose the last option."

Curious, Aric asked her why.

"Because this is your home, and you're making such a huge difference in people's lives with the work you do at your company. You can't abandon it, although I'm sure a part of you wants to and take the opportunity to get a new life and go to medical school like you planned before the D Plague. Even if you did that, you wouldn't be happy. You'd always feel like you let your family down somehow. You've been letting go of your depression little by little. I don't want to see you suffer more again."

"This isn't only about me," he pointed out. "What about you?"

"I've just been figuring out who I really am. If we move and hide, then I have to change that. I like Chelsea and don't want to have to be someone else. I honestly don't know if I could manage it."

"Door Number Three it is," Aric declared. "We need to be very careful though."

A knock at the door stopped Chelsea from commenting. Jason rose and went to open it. A black-haired woman who looked to be around Aric's age stepped in and smiled at them. She was Chelsea's height but didn't have many curves. Her athletic build was attractive in its own way although Aric much preferred Chelsea's ample breasts and backside to the female agent's toned, tight frame and small breasts. Her hair was pulled into a bun behind her head, and she wore jeans and a green sweatshirt. Her brown eyes seemed to absorb everything in the room as she scanned it, but there was only warmth in them when her gaze returned to him and Chelsea.

"Agent Paula Jennings, this is Aric Rodrigue and Chelsea Capra."

The woman gently shook Chelsea's hand then grasped Aric's more firmly. She had a tight grip, and Aric sensed she was actually holding back somewhat. He was impressed and pleased that Paula would be protecting the woman he loved. Still, he had questions and asked the agent to tell them about herself.

Once they were all seated in the living room, Paula Jennings said, "I'm an accomplished agent who's been with the FBI for four years. I'm well-versed in use of weapons and hand-to-hand combat. I also speak French, know how to cook, and am a fitness junkie. Both of my parents and three of my four sisters worked in law enforcement."

"Why do you want to work with us?" Chelsea asked once Paula had finished.

"I'm well-suited to this assignment. You and I are both in our twenties, and people could readily accept that we're friends. I speak French as well as English, so I consider that a plus since the two of you also speak French. I don't know Haitian Creole. I'm a decent cook, and I understand that you're trying to cook more."

"They know we need help cooking because of Eve Rose and Fredeline's being gone," Chelsea observed. "You're physically strong, and I'm not. You could help me work out at home because you're so into fitness."

"Yes."

"Have you ever worked with someone like me who's had a brain injury?"

"I haven't."

"That could be a problem," Aric noted.

"Possibly. I do have other experience that may be very helpful."

"Such as?"

"My older sister is an autistic savant. It's not the same as a TBI victim, but there are similarities."

"Tell me about your sister," urged Chelsea. "What is she like?"

"She's disconnected from the world in many ways, but she's an amazing violinist and mathematician. She likes repetition a lot. She could outperform any calculator, but she can't function as an adult. She can't function in society, period. Her personal care assistant helps her to dress, bathe, and eat properly."

"I used to be fixated on repetition," Chelsea confided. "That's all but disappeared since I've been with Aric. I'm excellent with computers, math, the piano, and sex."

"Oh, Chere," Aric said with feigned exasperation. "Remember what Jason and I told you earlier about discussing sex?"

"If Paula's going to be with me all the time, then she has to know everything she can about me." Looking back to the woman,

221

she went on, "I still have trouble with simple math, but I can do all sorts of complex math. I take things literally sometimes when I shouldn't, but I feel like I'm getting better overall. I'm getting physically stronger, too. Aric tells me I can't get too strong or I'll accidentally kill him during sex."

Jason attempted to cough in order to hide his snicker, but it was a very unsuccessful attempt. Aric decided to let the last remark go and allow Chelsea to take the lead. The FBI agent would be her protection after all.

"I get migraines, although those are getting fewer and fewer the longer I'm with Aric. When I have one, I take medicine, and sometimes that's all I need. Other times, Aric has to do special massage on me to relieve the pain." Cocking her head, she said, "You know all of this, I'm sure. Do you know about my accident and about Aric?"

"Yes, I do. It was part of my briefing. It's still good to hear from you what you feel is important."

Aric nodded and glanced at Chelsea. She looked rather faint, and he realized that none of them had eaten during the course of the evening of shocking revelations and changes. He wondered if a migraine was imminent. He asked Chelsea in Haitian Creole if she was hungry, to which she nodded.

"We have to eat," he told Jason and Paula. Looking to the female agent, he added, "If Chelsea is stressed, doesn't eat, or gets overtired, then she's more likely to develop a migraine."

"I could cook something," Paula offered. "Or we could just make peanut butter and jelly sandwiches. That would be quicker."

The four of them sat at the large table in the kitchen eating peanut butter and grape jelly sandwiches and drinking milk. Once the meal was over, Paula asked, "Would you like for me to stay or go?"

"Stay," Chelsea insisted. "As long as you realize that I'm not developmentally delayed or a child. I'm a woman with a brain injury and don't want to be treated like I'm a little girl." Staring at her lap, she added, "Well, what I imagine a little girl would be treated like." Shaking her head, she added, "Sometimes I wish I could be treated like a little girl so that I'd know what it felt like, but I'm an adult and want to be in control of my life. It can be frustrating."

"I can only imagine," Paula told her. "Maybe we can do things that little girls do but as grown women. People would just think we're being silly, but who cares?"

Chelsea looked hopeful and nodded. Paula asked Aric if he would brief her on what she should and shouldn't do physically with Chelsea from a medical perspective, and he told her he'd like to speak with her at length the following day. He wasn't about to allow Chelsea to be inadvertently injured by someone with no medical knowledge regarding TBI aftereffects.

"Where should I sleep?" Paula asked. "The attic?"

"No, Jason said quickly. "I want you in the main house with us in case any trouble arises. You can take my bed, and I'll sleep on the couch for tonight."

"Why not let her sleep in Fredeline or Eve Rose's room?" asked Chelsea.

"They just died today," Aric said with a hint of shock in his voice. "I think it would be disrespectful."

Reaching out to touch his jaw, Chelsea said, "Aric, they're gone. They weren't killed in their rooms. Jason took Olga's room right after he killed her."

"She was trying to kill me," Aric pointed out. "She wasn't an innocent person who got murdered."

"We need Jason and Paula to be well-rested," she countered. "Sleeping on the couch won't help with that. I think Eve Rose and Fredeline would want Paula to have one of their rooms."

"I agree," Paula proclaimed. "I think I should take Fredeline's room. We won't move anything until tomorrow, but I can put on clean sheets and sleep in there. Then we can move Fredeline's things to Eve Rose's room for now. Will you have a service in their honor?"

"They'd want a voodoo ceremony and a Mass," Chelsea declared. "Tante will arrange it all, I'm sure. I'll go talk to her while you're at work, Aric. That way, Paula can come with me and meet her, too."

"If you're certain."

"I am. I'm also exhausted. It's been a hard day and a sad day. It's very ironic that Eve Rose and Fredeline were killed on All Souls' Day. Somehow, I don't think that was a coincidence."

"I don't think it was either," muttered Jason. "Paula, why don't you and I review things in more detail? Then we can get you situated in Fredeline's room."

Aric and Chelsea bid the two agents goodnight and went to the master suite. Once they were there, Aric closed the door behind them and pulled Chelsea into his arms. He gently kissed her then led her to the bed.

"When you were scared at my office earlier today, you wanted me to make love tenderly to you tonight. Do you still want that, or are you too tired and upset?"

"I need it, Aric. I need you."

"And I need you more than you know."

Taking his time, Aric undressed her, planting soft kisses on each area of exposed flesh as her clothing was removed. His fingers lightly caressed her body as he did this. The combination was eliciting the little sounds of pleasure from her that he so adored. She whispered his name as he guided her back onto the mattress.

Aric slowly removed his clothing before joining Chelsea in the bed. He was thankful for the months he'd spent being intimate with Lakshmi. She liked only tender lovemaking, and he had learned a lot during their time together. It was actually not an easy task to be only tender the entire time one was having sex. It had been years since he'd done this, and he wondered if he would still be able to carry it off. Chelsea typically enjoyed intense sex or a combination of gentleness and forcefulness. Would she tire quickly of only tenderness?

To his surprise, the answer was no. Chelsea responded instantly to what was for her a novel sexual technique. She lay docile and expectant as he used his mouth, hands, and body to tenderly worship hers. She came three times in an hour and begged him not to stop. He sank into her very deliberately, expecting her to raise her hips to meet his. She surprised him again by remaining still, although she whimpered with pleasure, closed her eyes, and bit her lip in order to suppress a groan.

Aric fought the natural urge to thrust and instead moved his hips in a circular motion with delicious slowness. He could tell that Chelsea was on the verge of climax again and laced his fingers with hers. That was all it took. She bowed her back and called out his name as she came, and he spilled into her without uttering a sound. Then he collapsed on top of her and kissed her throat.

"That was so moving," Chelsea murmured with what sounded like reverence in her voice. "It was so different. I never knew that tender could be so intense."

"You liked it then," he chuckled, knowing full well how much she'd enjoyed it.

"I did, although I bet that took some practice to perfect. I think making love like that would be difficult to learn. Who taught you?" When he didn't answer, she conjectured, "I bet it was Lakshmi. She seems to be the type of woman who would focus more on tender rather than primal."

Not confirming or denying her supposition, he asked, "Which do you prefer?"

"So far, I haven't found any type of sex I don't like," she admitted. "At least not with you." Kissing his hair, she said, "Everything will be all right, Aric. I don't know when, but this bad person will be found. Then we won't have to worry about all of the scariness and can concentrate on the beautiful things in life."

He flexed inside of her, making her squeal, and said earnestly, "We shouldn't wait. You are the most beautiful part of my life, and I intend to concentrate on you every chance I get."

Chapter Thirty-one

Aric had spent all morning with his staff in the labs at Rodrigue Pharmaceuticals and the afternoon embroiled in business meetings. It had been productive and rewarding, yet he couldn't quite enjoy the satisfaction he typically felt after such days. He was worried about Chelsea, who'd gone with Nadine LaFleur to visit the elementary school in order to participate in Thanksgiving activities. Despite how well Chelsea had reacted to the Halloween party, he was concerned about her response to being in a school filled with students. Would it satisfy her curiosity about what it was like to be a child in school or would it make her feel more alienated from mainstream society? All he wanted to do was get home and see that she was emotionally all right.

He'd asked Jason if the man could contact Paula periodically to get updates, but Jason had flat out refused. He declared Paula's job was to protect Chelsea and that she would be working intensively with the Vice-President's wife's Secret Service team and didn't have time to call and give Aric reassurances. He reminded Aric that if Paula thought Chelsea was becoming overwhelmed, she would remove her from the situation and bring her home. Aric wanted to protest but kept silent. Jason was right, and he'd tried to relax. It had been a rather unsuccessful attempt.

He'd found out from Chelsea the previous day that Jason and Paula were sleeping together in Jason's room each night. When he'd asked her how she knew this, she had explained that she'd been waking up hungry at 3:00 a.m. every morning for the last two weeks and had been going to the kitchen for a glass of milk and a peanut butter and jelly sandwich. Each time she'd done so, Paula and Jason had both been in Jason's room.

"How do you know that?" he'd asked.

"Because I peeked in Paula's room the second night and she wasn't there. I listened carefully, and I could hear them having sex in Jason's room. I checked each night after that, and Paula's never in her bed. They're together in Jason's room."

Aric had sighed. Chelsea's naturally inquisitive nature was useful. However, it was also probably what had almost gotten her killed a year and a half earlier.

Aric wasn't bothered at all by Jason and Paula's involvement as long as it didn't interfere with their ability to do their jobs. He speculated as to whether or not the relationship was purely physical or if the two agents were romantically interested in one another. As he and Jason rode the streetcar home, Aric reminded himself that it was none of his business.

Government vehicles were parked along the curb in front of the Creole House when they arrived, and Aric deduced that Nadine was still there. A part of him was displeased. He wanted to be home with Chelsea and hear about her day as he held her, and he still didn't like Nadine. However, if the woman remained at the house, then Chelsea obviously wanted her there. Perhaps that was a good sign.

When he and Jason entered the main room of the house, they could hear Chelsea and Nadine laughing hysterically in the kitchen area. Aric grinned and relaxed. Chelsea sounded so happy, and so did Nadine. He realized he'd never heard the older woman laugh that way before even when her three daughters had been alive.

The two men walked toward the kitchen. As they came around the fireplace, they froze. Chelsea and Nadine were standing near the pantry dusted from head to toe in flour, and flour was splattered all over the floor around them. They were wiping tears from their faces, thus inadvertently smearing the flour in patterns on their cheeks. Paula was standing across the room from them looking bemused.

"Aric!" Chelsea cried when she saw him. Beaming, she said, "This has been the *best* day! It was so much fun at the school! Then we came back here and made a pumpkin pie. Nadine and I decided we'd try to make a cake, but we couldn't get the bag of flour open. We were trying to tear it, and it just ripped! Flour flew everywhere. It was just so…unexpected, and we looked so silly! I can't wait to tell you about everything we did earlier!"

Grinning madly at her, he walked over to where she stood and kissed her lightly floured lips. He whispered into her ear that he wanted to hear all about her day and wished he could have her for dessert right then. She threw her arms around his neck and kissed him earnestly then stepped back and said with a smile, "Later." Frowning, she stated, "Now I've gotten flour all over your suit."

"It'll come off. Even if it doesn't, I don't care."

She suggested they clean the floor before she and Nadine took showers. Paula volunteered to sweep up the mess so that the women could get cleaned up. Chelsea looked uncertain, but Paula smiled reassuringly at her and told her that it was no trouble. Chelsea thanked her then turned back toward Nadine and hugged her tightly before leaving to go to the master suite. Aric looked at Nadine as Chelsea left and saw that tears were still streaming down her face, but they were now tears of sorrow, not humor. He knew she must be thinking of the daughters she'd lost in the D Plague and swallowed the lump in his throat.

"I feel like God's given me a second chance," Nadine said suddenly. "You have no idea what a blessing today has been for me."

Not quite certain what to say to this, Aric remarked sincerely, "I'm happy for you. You certainly seem to have had a profound effect on Chelsea. It's evident she loves being around you."

Nadine nodded, covered her mouth with one hand, and turned away from the other three. Nobody moved as she struggled to get herself under control. Finally, she straightened and said quietly, "This is my chance to make things right. I don't intend to let it slip away."

Unable to believe that he was actually going to ask, Aric inquired, "What are you and Buddy doing for Thanksgiving? Do you want to spend it with us?"

Nadine whirled around, her eyes wide with shock and her lips parted in a silent "Oh." Her eyes were shimmering with tears of gratitude. It made Aric feel both uncomfortable and pleased at the same time.

"You...you wouldn't mind if we came by?" she asked. "We have family we're meeting for lunch, but I'd love it if we could come by for dinner. If Buddy can't come, then I'll come alone. Thank you so much for the invitation."

He smiled and nodded. This was not the Nadine he'd known for so long, the one who was a loving wife and mother but not genuinely nice to most others. He liked this new, improved version of the woman and hoped the change in her was permanent. If Chelsea continued to benefit from their interactions, he would welcome her presence on a regular basis.

Nadine excused herself in order to get a member of her staff to bring her a change of clothing. Jason also left the room to take a call. Aric proceeded to help Paula clean up the flour. As they did this, he asked her how Chelsea had handled her visit to the school.

"Very well. She did a lot with the children and appeared to have a wonderful time. She's dying to tell you about it."

"And I can't wait to hear it all."

Jason stepped out of his room and motioned for Aric and Paula to come closer. Once they were clustered in the center of the kitchen, he told them that he had some news. Paula stood a little straighter, and Aric tensed.

"Our people gave me a summary of the Medical Examiner's report on the bodies of Eve Rose, Fredeline, and our agents. All died of gunshot wounds. Eve Rose was held and raped in a similar way to Chelsea, and the DNA in the semen was a match to that of Chelsea's attacker."

Aric gritted his teeth and clenched his fists. He decided that later he might have to make use of the punching bag in his workout room. He had to take out his anger and feeling of impotence on something.

"What else?" Paula prodded.

"Those virtual photos of Chelsea that I ran through all the national databases turned up nothing." Pausing, he checked to make certain that no one was approaching; then he said, "However, I decided I'd follow a hunch and forward them to a friend in Haiti. He found something." Looking at Aric, he suggested, "I think a trip to Haiti after Thanksgiving might be in order for the four of us."

"We're supposed to fly to Atlanta week after next to be examined by the government's doctors. Perhaps we can go to Haiti before then. I'll rearrange my work schedule so that we can all go as soon as possible."

"Good. I'll explain more tomorrow when we're really alone."

Chelsea and Nadine returned, clean and in fresh clothing. Nadine reluctantly announced that she had to leave soon, and Chelsea asked her if she'd like to hear her play something on the piano before her departure. Nadine smiled and mutely nodded then followed the woman to the living room. The others joined them there.

The piece Chelsea selected was by Handel, and they all sat transfixed by her performance. When she was finished, Nadine rose from her seat and went over to hug the younger woman.

After telling her how beautifully she played, the wife of the Vice-President said, "I had a lovely day with you Chelsea. I'll be returning with or without Buddy on Thursday night for Thanksgiving."

Chelsea's face was radiant with joy, as she said, "That would be wonderful! Today was amazing, Nadine."

Once Nadine had said her goodbyes and left the house with half of the pumpkin pie she'd made with Chelsea, the others went back to the kitchen and ate Caesar salads with grilled chicken that Paula had prepared earlier. Chelsea devoured hers before Aric, Jason, and Paula were halfway through theirs.

Aric asked playfully, "Hungry?"

Of course, she took him literally and responded, "I was until I ate all of my food."

Smiling, he said, "I'm glad you'd developed more of an appetite in the past couple of months and had gained some weight."

"Fifteen pounds," she said with a smile. "I'm still six pounds lighter than I was when I had the accident, but that's okay. I do feel stronger and can do more now that I have the extra weight on me and keep exercising."

"I'm happy to hear it. You were too thin."

They each ate a piece of the pumpkin pie, which was delicious. Then Jason and Paula went outside to stand in the cold November air and talk while Aric and Chelsea headed for the couch. Chelsea sat beside him and tucked her feet underneath her before leaning across his chest and slipping her arms around his waist. Aric wrapped his arms around her and asked her to tell him about her day.

"Well, you know how I've been going to the Buddhist temple to chant every morning? I couldn't today, because Nadine said they'd be picking us up at 8:00. So, Paula and I went with her to the school and…."

Aric relaxed as he listened to Chelsea's description of the Thanksgiving festivities at one of the local public schools. There had been a Thanksgiving program put on by the children, a craft session in which Native American headbands and Pilgrim hats had been created from construction paper, a luncheon, and parties in several classes. She and Nadine had taken turns reading stories to the children and interacting with them. It was all very "normal," and Chelsea had loved it. She told him she'd made him a present and extricated herself so she could retrieve it.

She passed him a tracing of her hand that she'd transformed through her artistic efforts into the likeness of a turkey. He'd made more than one of these as a boy for his parents. Children had been doing the same thing for generations.

But not Chelsea, he mused. *Not that she can remember anyway. Perhaps she never made one.*

He smiled at her and rose from the couch. Thanking her for his present, he brought it to the kitchen and tacked it to a cork board that hung over the built-in desk at one end of the counter. Chelsea had followed him and said she was happy that he'd liked the drawing. Aric turned and pulled her close to him, leaning down to bury his face in her chestnut hair.

"We're going to Haiti," he told her as he nuzzled his cheek against her head. "Jason thinks he may have a lead on your past."

"That kind of scares me, but we should go."

"Yes."

"Aric? Do you like Nadine?"

"Yes, I think I do."

"It makes me happy to be with her. She treats me like a child but in a good way. You know, like I'm hers but an adult, too. It's nice."

He squeezed her tightly and was grateful that he'd asked the woman to have Thanksgiving dinner with them. He, Chelsea, Paula, and Jason would prepare the meal together. It was certainly going to be an odd grouping, but it was a spectacular improvement on the Thanksgivings he'd avoided celebrating after the D Plague. He felt the anticipation and smiled.

Nadine and Buddy joined them that Thursday for dinner. They all spent a wonderful three hours eating, chatting, and relaxing. Once the LaFleurs had gone, those remaining cleaned up before Jason and Paula retired to their rooms and Aric and Chelsea went to the master suite. Aric sat at the desk to do some work, while Chelsea curled up on the bed with a book.

Aric was deeply engrossed in company business when Chelsea suddenly appeared naked beside him and leaned down to kiss his lips. Before he could formulate a coherent sentence, she was unbuttoning his fly and pulling down his boxers. He wasn't about to protest and was soon buried deep within her. When she ran her palms over his muscular chest and arms and began to rock her hips, he groaned loudly and brought his hands to her full breasts.

She was driven and wild, and he was aroused to the point of no return within minutes. He came hard, and she followed quickly. Then she sagged against his chest and begged him to hold her tightly.

"You were feeling scared tonight? Did you want me to hurt you?"

"I haven't wanted that since right before I hid under your desk that day in your office. I just needed to be in control this evening so I wouldn't feel so scared. I wish I knew what made me anxious tonight. Today was great. I loved seeing Nadine."

It struck Aric as odd that Chelsea didn't mention Buddy, and he asked, "What about the Vice-President?"

Chelsea shifted slightly in his lap, which brought with it some extremely pleasant sensations. He tried to ignore them and repeated his question.

"I find Buddy kind of intimidating," she admitted. "I don't know why, but I feel like there's something wrong with him."

Aric was perplexed. Buddy had behaved rather oddly on the date of the barbecue, but it had been on the same date as his dead daughter's birthday and so was perfectly understandable. Typically, he was friendly, knowledgeable, and seemingly sincere. During their Thanksgiving dinner that evening, he'd been his usual self and was charming and apparently happy to be at the Creole House.

"You may never get completely over having these episodes, but at least they're not so bad," Aric pointed out. "If having sex makes you feel better, then I'm all for it."

"Hold me tighter," she directed. "I love you, Aric."

He told her that he loved her, too. He shut off his computer and suggested they shower and go to bed. After all, they'd be leaving for Haiti in the morning.

Chapter Thirty-two

They were in their hotel in Port-au-Prince the following evening. The temperature was in the mid-eighties, and Aric wore khaki pants and a green Polo shirt. He stepped out onto the balcony of the connecting suites that they were sharing with Jason and Paula, raked his fingers through his brown hair, and surveyed the waters of the Gulf of Gonave. Aric hoped that whatever they discovered during this trip would answer many questions and not elicit disturbing information. Chelsea was doing so well, and he didn't want to cause her any undue distress. Her psychiatrist and neurologist had assured him that she could handle whatever she learned and reminded him she had an excellent support system in place.

"Aric, we'll be late."

Chelsea was standing near the door wearing a simple yet lovely sleeveless dress that had a flared skirt. Her almond-colored skin seemed to make the sky blue of the dress stand out more prominently. Her hair was loose, and her bright blue eyes shone with expectation. Her tiny pearl earrings matched the strand of pearls around her neck, and she wore his sister's ring. She hadn't taken it off except to clean it since the night he'd shared it with her.

"You look divine as always, Chere."

They were soon seated in the hotel restaurant on one of the expansive porches that ran around the old gingerbread-style structure. Jason and Paula sat at the next table, and Aric knew there were other agents scattered around. He sighed. Someday, he and Chelsea would have privacy without fear.

They ordered their food and drinks and enjoyed the evening breeze. Chelsea pensively stared out into the garden just off the porch. He knew she was nervous but also pleased to be in Port-au-Prince. They would have to come back and spend more than a few days in Haiti sometime in the not-so-distant future. He wanted to explore it with her and to experience the culture on a more profound level.

After dinner, they walked hand-in-hand through the garden. When they came upon a bench, Aric took a seat and gestured for

Chelsea to sit in his lap. She did so and draped her arms around his neck, while he cradled her against him.

"I have something for you," he said in a low voice.

"I thought you might. That's why I didn't wear any underwear."

He laughed and shook his head before telling her that was *not* what he meant. She pouted, which made him laugh again. He put his lips close to her ear and whispered that he would like nothing more than to slip his hand up her skirt.

"So, why don't you?" she asked seriously.

"I can think of several reasons. Two of the main ones are named Jason and Paula. I don't know how many others are hanging around, plus unsuspecting guests."

"But I wouldn't care if they saw," she proclaimed. "There's nothing wrong with you doing that."

"First of all, there is. I know you don't understand it, but most people aren't as comfortable with sex as you are. Second, what if some children happened to be playing in the garden? It wouldn't be good for children to see us having sex. Third, I don't want anyone to watch my fiancée come except me."

"Oh. Okay. So, what do you want to do if we're not going to have sex?"

"Sit up and let me see your hands," he instructed.

She immediately complied, and he removed his sister's ring from her finger. She objected – until he slipped a simple, round-cut diamond engagement ring on in place of it. He then took the other ring and slipped it on the finger of her right hand. She stared down at the diamond as if not comprehending what it meant. His heart sank, as he considered that she didn't like his choice of the one-carat diamond with its plain gold band.

"If it's not to your taste, then you can pick out something different," he offered.

"Something different?" Aric, I love it."

"Then why don't you look happy?"

He frowned as a tear slid down one of her cheeks. He caught it with the tip of one finger then lifted her chin until she was looking at him. Uneasy, Aric asked her why she was crying.

"Because you deserve more."

"What?"

"I'm damaged."

"Chelsea, it isn't your fault you had a brain injury."

"Maybe. Maybe not. It doesn't matter. That's not what I was talking about."

"What then?"

Another tear.

"The rape. I know you think about it."

"How would you know that?"

"You...you talk in your sleep sometimes."

"I do?"

She nodded.

"And you hear me talking about your rape?"

"You're yelling for them to stop. You say you're going to kill the man who's raping me and all the others who helped. You don't sound like yourself when you're saying those things. You sound like you mean it. Then you...it's like you're talking to me."

Stunned, Aric asked, "What do I tell you?"

Altering her voice slightly, she said, "I'm so sorry, Chere. It's my fault. I'm here now, and everything will be all right."

"I had no idea. Do I say other things in my sleep?"

"Yes, but I don't understand most of that. You talk to your family a lot. Sometimes you laugh, and sometimes you cry. I rub your back when you cry, and it seems to help calm you."

Still in shock, Aric asked, "Have I done this for as long as you and I've been sleeping together?"

"Yes."

"Why didn't you tell me?"

"I didn't want you to worry over it. You do that a lot, and you've been so much better. It's been nice for you not to be depressed all the time."

"Why do you think that is, Chere? It's because of you. Not only have you loved and comforted me, but you've forced me to deal with the loss of my family as much as I can. If I hadn't met you...." Kissing her forehead, he said, "I do not think of you as damaged because of your rape. You *were* viciously attacked by a sadistic bastard and his henchmen, but that doesn't affect the way I feel about you or your body. It does make me more furious than I've ever been before in my life."

"Would you kill the man if you ever found him?"

"I'd want to. I doubt if I could really kill another human being unless it was to save someone's life. I'd definitely want to beat him senseless and have him sent away for as long as possible."

"He raped Eve Rose, didn't he?"

For several moments, Aric couldn't breathe. When he was able, he asked Chelsea where she'd heard that piece of information. She told him no one had said anything. She'd simply deduced that this was part of the reason why everyone assumed the person who'd killed Fredeline, Eve Rose, and the FBI agents was the same man.

"There's no assumption. It was the same man. The…biological evidence confirmed it."

"Oh. I wonder how many other women he's raped. What kind of people would help him do that?"

"Other bad men. Probably hired thugs."

Chelsea stared disconsolately down at her engagement ring. In a barely audible voice, she said, "I'm so glad I don't remember that."

Aric kissed her and murmured, "Let's not talk about it anymore tonight. Right now, I want to get married."

Her head jerked up as she echoed, "Married? Now? How?"

"I don't know. Let's go ask the people at the hotel. I don't want to put it off any longer. I love you, and I want to marry you tonight."

"But what if we find out something horrible about me tomorrow when we go wherever it is we're going with Jason?"

"I've told you that it doesn't matter to me what you were like before the accident. I love Chelsea and always will."

"Then there's no reason to wait."

An hour later, they were standing in the backyard of the home of a Haitian man who had the authority to perform marriages. The gentleman and his wife were a friendly older couple, and it was clear to Aric that the man was a local favorite for those who wanted to get married quickly and casually. His wife did have a digital camera in order to take photos of the couples, but there was no other fanfare. The tiny backyard had lovely landscaping but was not professionally maintained. The setting was comfortable and personal. He thought it was perfect.

"Is this okay with you?" he asked Chelsea. "We could go somewhere else if you like."

"I think it's just right," she told him. "It suits us. There's only one problem."

"Which is?"

"I don't have a ring for you."

"We have rings," the Haitian man hastened to inform them. "You want to see?"

Of course they have rings, Aric thought. *This is where people come for quickie weddings. Most probably don't have any rings when they show up.*

There was not much selection, but Aric didn't care. All he needed was a simple wedding band. Chelsea selected one for him similar to the one he'd shown her that went along with her engagement ring. It was fourteen-carat gold and plain. Aric paid the man for the ring and for the service he was to perform and added a generous gratuity. The man thanked him with words and a broad smile.

Jason and Paula were the only guests at the wedding. The ceremony was short but moving. The Haitian man was good at taking care of business but in a way that emotionally touched those gathered.

Once the vows had been exchanged and the kiss between the new husband and wife had ended, the officiator put one arm around Aric and the other around Chelsea and announced, "You are married! May you have a happy, healthy, and long life together."

Jason and Paula congratulated them as the older woman went into the house. She emerged minutes later with photos from the ceremony. They were of good quality, and Aric was very pleased. Chelsea was ecstatic.

The four of them returned to the hotel. They went to the restaurant and ordered cake and coffee to celebrate. Once they'd finished, they went back to their suites and Aric immediately scanned what he considered to be their precious wedding photos into his computer. He then forwarded the images to a company that would print them on quality paper and make them look even more professional. As he did this, Chelsea retreated to the bathroom in order to take a shower.

There was a knock on the connecting door that separated the suites. Aric opened it to find Jason smiling at him. The FBI agent held out his right hand, palm up.

"I need your marriage certificate," he told Aric. "Also Chelsea's State I.D. and her passport. If you give it all to me now, then I can have it back to her within twenty-four hours. Everything will have her married name on it."

"It helps to know the President of the United States?" Aric smirked.

"Something like that. Speaking of the President, you should call her and tell her the good news."

"And Mrs. LaFleur!" Paula called out from somewhere in the other suite.

"Good point. Thanks. I want to call my friend, Maurice, too."

"Congratulations again," Jason said, as Aric handed him Chelsea's documentation and their marriage license. "Try to get some sleep tonight. Tomorrow may be a long day."

When Chelsea emerged from the bathroom, she was wearing knit pajama bottoms and one of Aric's t-shirts. Her hair was damp, and she smelled of jasmine-scented body lotion. He wanted to pull off her clothing and make love to her right then, but he restrained himself and suggested they phone Lakshmi, Nadine, and Maurice.

They reached the two women and the man quickly and were given enthusiastic congratulations via virtual chats. They held up their hands so that their friends could see their rings, spoke of the impromptu wedding, and promised to email the pictures of the ceremony as soon as they disconnected the face-to-face calls, which they did.

Aric went to shower. When he returned to the bedroom, he found Chelsea lying naked on the king-sized bed save for her wedding ring. He expected her to tell him she wanted to enjoy a wild night of sex, but she surprised him by making love to him as tenderly as he'd made love to her the night of Fredeline and Eve Rose's death. She was good at it. Aric smiled against her neck afterward and reflected that she was good at any type of intimate contact.

She's good for me, body and soul, he reflected. *I'm one very lucky man.*

Chapter Thirty-three

After breakfast the next morning, Aric, Chelsea, Paula, and Jason set out from the hotel to meet with Jason's contact. As they walked through Port-au-Prince, Aric pondered whether or not the place would ever change. He knew that the structure of the city itself was laid out like an amphitheater with the businesses existing on the coast and the residences tending to be more inland. Slums remained scattered in various locales throughout Port-au-Prince as well as in the hills on the outskirts. It had been like this for decades. Progress had been made, but it didn't seem like much to him.

At Chelsea's urging, Aric spoke of the time he'd spent in the city on a mission trip he'd taken with his family years earlier. It had been two weeks of hard work but had also been fun and rewarding. They'd gone home, exhausted but with a great sense of accomplishment.

Chelsea smiled up at him as they walked hand-in-hand. When he asked her what was so amusing, she told him she was happy. Confused, he asked her why. He knew she was nervous about where they were headed and what they might learn about her past.

"You're talking about your parents, grandparents, and sisters, and you're smiling and laughing. You're not sad about remembering. You're not depressed. It makes me feel so relieved."

Aric stopped walking. She was right. It was the first time since the D Plague that he hadn't felt overwhelmed with grief when he'd thought about his lost loved ones. It was liberating. He kissed Chelsea and thanked her, telling her that he never could have come so far without her help. He kissed her again before they resumed their journey through the streets.

"Here we are," Jason announced, as they reached an apartment building that appeared to be in fairly good condition. "Everybody ready?"

Jason led them to apartment #3 and knocked six times. A short, compact Haitian man opened the door and ushered them in with a warm greeting. He directed them to sit on the long, tan couch in the living room and sat across from them in a worn orange chair. Jason introduced him as "Toussaint" and explained that the man was trustworthy and would keep everything in confidence.

Looking at Chelsea, Toussaint said, "I understand you have no memory before June of 2033. Are you sure you want to hear about your life here in Haiti? It may not be…pleasant." When she nodded, he sighed and continued, "All right. Just remember that you asked me to tell you."

Aric took Chelsea's right hand in his left, and she gave him a grateful smile. As they waited, she rubbed her thumb back and forth across his wedding band. It seemed to soothe her somehow, and he found it was rather soothing for him as well.

Toussaint began, "You were born on June 8, 2010."

Chelsea gasped, and Aric stiffened. Toussaint nodded knowingly and said, "Yes, your accident happened on your birthday."

"Where was I born?"

"New Orleans, Louisiana. Your birth certificate lists your name as Soleil Estelle Laurence. Sound familiar?"

She shook her head and kept rubbing her thumb across Aric's wedding band.

"Your father's name was Maxime Laurence. Your mother's name was listed on the birth certificate as Constance Chatterly. You arrived in Haiti alone with your father when you were only three months old. He was an engineer."

Chelsea's thumb stopped moving, and she bit her lip.

"What is it, Chere?" Aric asked gently.

"I thought maybe she left us because my father couldn't provide for her, but if he was an engineer…."

"He was a fine engineer from what I've learned," Toussaint assured her. "He moved here with you to take a very lucrative job. I spoke with several men and women who worked with him, and they all admired him. They also said you were the center of his world and that he was a devoted father. They said you were a very happy and sociable child."

"Do you have a picture?"

Toussaint handed her a printed photograph of a handsome black man who was tall and well-built. He was smiling and holding a little girl who was obviously Chelsea. She looked to be about five in the picture. She was also smiling.

"Where did you get this?"

"One of his co-workers took it at a family day party at the engineering firm. This person was the unofficial company photographer at such events and had pictures of lots of people participating in that day's activities."

"May I keep it?"

"It's your copy."

Chelsea stared at the photo and blinked rapidly then murmured that it made her very sad not to remember her father. After remarking that he looked like a loving parent and a nice man, she asked where he was.

"He died when you were twelve. Although he was only forty at the time, he supposedly died of a heart attack. Several of his friends said they wanted to petition to adopt you out of respect for your father and because they genuinely wanted to help you. They said you were an extremely bright student, especially when it came to math, literature, and computers. You were also an accomplished pianist. Mainly, they said you were a sweet and happy girl who was devastated by your father's death."

"Did one of them adopt me?'

Toussaint frowned and hesitated before answering, "They never got the chance."

"Why not?"

"You were temporarily placed in foster care. Before anyone could even begin to fill out the paperwork required in order to start the adoption process, you were adopted by someone else."

"Who?"

Toussaint looked uncomfortable and angry, and Aric's stomach muscles tightened involuntarily. Whatever Toussaint was about to say, it was *not* going to be good.

"You were adopted by a single self-made billionaire from France named Michel LeClerc. Your father worked for one of his companies. At the time he adopted you he was thirty-one."

"Who in the hell allows a thirty-one-year-old single man to immediately adopt a twelve-year-old girl?" snapped Aric.

"Someone whose greed overrides his human decency," Paula muttered. Staring pointedly at Toussaint, she asked, "Do we know how much of a bribe he paid?"

"Ten million dollars."

241

Chelsea gripped Aric's fingers and asked, "I was…sold for ten million dollars?"

"That's the way I'd put it," Toussaint agreed. "I located a few of his former household staff members. According to them, LeClerc doted on you, took you around the world, gave you the finest education and piano instruction money could buy, and took you with him when he visited the disadvantaged. Helping those living in poverty was one of his pet projects, and he wanted you to assist him in aiding those living in squalor. He'd come from extreme poverty. You yourself had never lived in poverty. Your father made good money, and Mr. LeClerc was obscenely rich."

Obscenely something, Aric thought grimly.

"He had my father killed, didn't he?" Chelsea asked quietly. "He wanted me and did what he had to in order to get me."

Toussaint glanced at Jason, pursed his lips, and then said, "We have no proof, but that's what we suspect."

Aric felt Chelsea begin to tremble beside him and withdrew his hand from hers in order to put that arm around her shoulders. He asked her if she wanted to stop. She looked up at him with wide, blue eyes and told him that she had to hear everything they knew, no matter how upsetting it was. He kissed her forehead, and she turned back to Toussaint and asked, "Do you have a picture of this man?"

He produced a photo of a handsome, physically fit, blonde-haired man in his mid-thirties. A sense of power emanated from him, even through the photo. He was smiling, but Aric could see the calculating look in the man's brown eyes.

"What did he do to me?" Chelsea inquired anxiously. "Did he abuse me?"

"Yes, but in an insidious way," Toussaint replied. "He nurtured your intelligence and talent and gave you the finest of everything. The staff said you were very happy living with him after you recovered from the death of your father. LeClerc was tender with you and took great pains to ensure your safety and happiness."

"Then, how did he abuse me?"

The man briefly shut his eyes then reopened them and said, "Because he was grooming you to be exactly what he wanted. According to one former staff member, he started taking you to bed with him when you turned sixteen. The woman said he gave you quite a sexual education, although she refused to say how she knew this. You didn't seem afraid of him or distressed. She felt he'd manipulated you so you'd want to please him because you loved him and knew how much he cared for you. She was disgusted."

"Then why did she stay in his employ?"

"Because she said Michel LeClerc was a brilliant, handsome, dangerous man, and she and the others on staff wanted to make sure *you* remained safe. Plus, they feared for their own safety."

"How long did I live with him?"

"You graduated from college at the age of twenty with a degree in computer science. You were gorgeous, smart, well-heeled, and witty. LeClerc was thirty-nine by this time and seemed very content, running his empire and having you as his companion."

"And then?"

"Everything continued on as before until one night in September of 2030. The staff heard the two of you arguing, something that had never happened in the eight years you'd lived in the household. They heard you tell LeClerc you'd figured out what he'd done to your father and to you and that you hated him. Then you cried out, and the next morning at breakfast you had a bruise on your cheek. They said you were very subdued but refused to talk about the argument. A few days later, you disappeared, and LeClerc was furious. It appears that you hacked into his computer system and dispersed his fortune to charities around the world that helped the impoverished. All he had left was his property and his companies. His wealth was gone, and so were you. He ranted and raved to the staff that he was going to find you and kill you."

"He obviously didn't."

Toussaint smiled darkly and said, "That's because the staff took preemptive action."

"What does that mean?"

"It means they agreed that they had to stop him. Most of them had known and loved you for eight years. They hatched their own little plot and killed him."

Chelsea gaped then stammered, "K-killed him? But how? Are they in jail?"

"No. Michel LeClerc was deathly allergic to peanuts. The kitchen staff prepared him a nice meal and added a very small amount of peanut oil to the sauce for the pasta dish that was served. He died fairly quickly, and the staff claimed ignorance and swore they didn't know how he'd somehow managed to ingest something with peanut oil in it. Of course, those involved had gotten rid of the oil and the pans used to cook his meal. The police listed his death as accidental, and the staff moved on, happy to know that they had protected you from the man they'd secretly despised for years."

"And where was I?"

Shaking his head, Toussaint confided, "I have no idea. You disappeared without a trace. You were very bright, resourceful, and had taken some of LeClerc's money so that you could flee and start over. I tried everything to find out if there was a trail of any sort, but I came up empty-handed."

"At least we have general information about the time period from when Chelsea was three months old until she was twenty," Aric pointed out. "Now she's only missing three years."

"Very true," the man agreed. "I just wish I'd had a nicer story to tell you."

Chapter Thirty-four

"The Tale you told explains a lot," Chelsea said after a moment's pause. "May I keep the picture of Michel LeClerc?"

"Why would you want to do that?" Aric asked angrily. "After what the man did to you –"

"The photo might be useful in the future," Chelsea interrupted. "Maybe someone who knew me when I lived with him will have more information. I'll scan it and put it away in case we need it later."

Afraid to speak for fear he might make things worse, Aric nodded curtly. The mere thought of Michel LeClerc and what he'd done to Chelsea was enough to make Aric almost crazed with rage. He wondered how Chelsea was handling this disquieting information and considered whether or not he should ask her or wait for her to approach him.

"Do you have any more questions before you go?" Toussaint asked them. "Jason and Paula have a file of what I found out and can review this information again with you, although they can't release all the details or sources."

Chelsea thought for a moment then asked, "What was I like?"

Toussaint shrugged and asked her for clarification.

"What was my favorite color? What kind of music did I like? What kinds of books did I enjoy? Did I like to attend plays, symphonies, and ballets? Did I prefer watching television or listening to music? Did I go to church or a temple or a mosque? Did I have friends?"

Aric caught the pained expression that momentarily crossed the Haitian man's face before he replied, "I only know what the staff of the house told me regarding most of those things. Blue was your favorite color, and you loved all types of music. You enjoyed all kinds of books as well. Yes, you enjoyed the theater, ballet, and symphony performances. You weren't much for television but loved listening to music. When your father was alive, you attended both the Catholic Church and voodoo ceremonies. LeClerc didn't take you to any religious services. You had many friends at the private school you attended and at college. His staff said you were very kind-hearted and polite to everyone you met."

"Thank you so much," Chelsea said sweetly. "Thank you for all of your hard work. It's helped me."

"I'm glad," he told her, although he sounded sad. "It's too bad I couldn't track your movements after you ran from LeClerc."

"That's okay. If I'm meant to know about those three years, then I'll find out someday. Is there something I can do for you?"

Toussaint blinked in surprise and asked, "What? Why?"

"To show my gratitude."

"It's my job."

"I know. I'd still like to do something special for you."

"Jason tells me you and Mr. Rodrigue got married yesterday. Be happy in your marriage and your life. Pray that I have the same with my family."

"It'll be my intention when I chant tomorrow morning. I do Buddhist chanting every day."

"I thank you for the intention. Take care of yourself, Mrs. Rodrigue."

At the mention of her new last name, Chelsea grinned and glanced shyly up at Aric, who grinned back. Everyone rose, said their goodbyes, and left Toussaint's apartment. It was lunchtime, and they stopped at a small, dirty Haitian restaurant that had wonderful food. Aric figured Chelsea wouldn't want to eat, but she did. He was glad to see that she continued to have an appetite.

"I've gained four more pounds since Thanksgiving," she announced with satisfaction. "Soon, I'll be back to my old weight. Then you can stop worrying about that so much, Aric."

"I just want you to be healthy," he remarked.

"I am healthy. Those samples I sent to the doctors at the CDC earlier this month confirmed that things are looking great like they did last month."

"I'll still feel better once you've been examined in person next week when we go to Atlanta." Reaching over to brush a crumb from one corner of her mouth, he asked, "Are you okay with what you learned this morning?"

"I'm still processing what he said. I don't want to talk about it for a while. Don't be hurt."

"I'm not. I won't take it personally. We'll talk when you're ready."

She nodded distractedly and returned to eating her lunch. When they got back to the hotel, Chelsea asked Aric for a migraine pill and said she wanted to go with Paula up to their suite. Before they headed for the elevators, she suggested that Aric and Jason have a drink or wander the gardens. Aric wasn't happy about this, but he decided that perhaps she wanted time alone with another woman to discuss what Toussaint had told them.

"Let's walk," Jason directed. "She needs a breather and some rest."

As they went outside to the gardens, Aric asked, "What didn't Toussaint tell us?"

"You wouldn't believe the amount of material he uncovered. I can't tell you most of it. It crosses over into Classified."

"Classified? LeClerc was working for the U.S. government?"

"Not as such. Many of his companies did contract work with the Department of Defense."

"What can you tell me?"

"Aric, you really don't want to go down that path. Toussaint hit the high points. Leave it."

"Leave it?!?" Aric snarled. "The sick bastard probably had Chelsea's father killed so that he could adopt her and mold her into the perfect mistress! She was twelve years old! He started having sex with her when he was thirty-five and she was sixteen! What else did he do, Jason? I know there's more to it than your friend was telling us."

They were standing by the water, and Jason spent a long time staring out into the Gulf before saying, "I'll tell you on the condition that you never tell Chelsea."

"Done."

"One of the staff members revealed that LeClerc often…offered Chelsea to men he wanted to do business with in order to solidify deals. Because of the way he'd brainwashed her, she was more than happy to oblige. He assured her that the men were told it was their job to please her and if they harmed her in any way, he'd not only call off their deals, but he'd also have them sent to jail. I'm sure he told those men he'd have them killed. Guys like that don't call the cops when they're offering other men their under-aged mistresses. None of the men were older than he was. They were all fit, vain, powerful men and were ordered to give Chelsea as much pleasure as they received. LeClerc told them he'd know if they strayed from their agreement with him, and none of them did."

Aric was too shocked to speak. He wanted to ask how the man could have known if the terms of such vile agreements weren't met.

"The staff member who confided this to Toussaint said LeClerc was able to verify that everything went well, and no one crossed the line."

"How?" Aric managed to choke out.

Glancing at Aric, Jason said, "He had a secret room with monitors and cameras. He watched. He also reviewed digital recordings of himself and Chelsea having sex."

Aric whirled and threw up his lunch into a nearby flower bed. He was shaking with rage and revulsion. How many other rich men were still alive doing similar things or worse because they had the means? Had the U.S. government been aware of LeClerc's predilections and still done business with the monster?

As he straightened, Aric announced quietly, "I'm going up to my wife now." When Jason objected, he said, "I won't tell her."

"You look like crap. She'll know something's wrong. She's very intuitive."

"I'll tell her I'm sick to my stomach. It's the truth. She doesn't have to know it's because of what that creature did to her. She can assume my lunch didn't agree with me."

Chelsea lay asleep in a nightgown, the sheet pulled up to her waist. Paula was reading in a chair. She instantly rose, nodded to Aric, and went through the door to the room she was sharing with Jason. He followed, told Aric to summon them if there was a problem, and closed the door.

Aric brushed his teeth, put on pajama bottoms, then stretched out on the bed beside Chelsea. She was so precious to him. He fought the impulse to stroke her brown hair and caress the almond-colored skin. He longed to bring her some peace.

He imagined her father, Maxime, watching protectively over her until his untimely demise. He shuddered as he thought of Michel LeClerc watching over her and more. He tried to suppress thoughts of the man seducing sixteen year-old Chelsea, teaching her everything there was to know about sex, and then offering her to other young megalomaniacs like himself and witnessing them violating the girl he supposedly adored.

Sexually abused as a girl then raped as a woman, Aric thought dejectedly. *And what happened in-between? Did Chelsea use her wits and body to stay alive? How did she end up in that taxi?*

Chelsea's eyelids fluttered open. She didn't return the smile he gave her. Instead, a single tear trailed down one cheek.

"What is it, Chere?"

"Do you want a divorce?"

Lines etched Aric's forehead, and he asked her what would make her think such a thing. She chewed on her lower lip then asked him to hold her. Once her head rested on his chest, she sighed and wrapped her arms tightly around him while he stroked her hair.

"I don't know how you could still want me," she admitted. "My father and LeClerc were killed because of me. All of these people have died because of me, and I still don't know the whole story about everything and the missing years. I know you think about the rape, and now you'll think about that man having sex with me when I was a girl. Why would you want to touch me after all of that?"

"You were a victim. None of it affects the way I feel about you! What do I need to do to convince you that I love you and want you no matter what others did to hurt you?"

"I wish I'd been fat, ugly, and stupid. At least then no one would have gotten killed because of me."

"Chelsea, stop. You're a wonderful, amazing woman and are *not* responsible for any bad deeds done by others. Remember when you told me early on that maybe it was better that you had no memory? Well, I'm thinking you were right."

"Jason told you more about my life with LeClerc, didn't he?"

Aric remained mute. He didn't want to lie, but there was no way he could tell Chelsea about the other men and LeClerc's voyeurism. He explained that Jason had shared some details, only on the condition that Chelsea not be told.

"Did more people die because of me?" she whispered.

"No. I can assure you of that."

"That's all I needed to know. If Jason asked you not to explain the rest, then I know he has good reason. I don't want to know." Beginning to cry, she admitted, "I only wish I remembered my life before my father died. Sometimes I feel so alienated from the rest of the world. I feel like nobody even when I try to remember I'm somebody now."

"You were always somebody. From what we learned today, you were always somebody special. I'm sorry you don't remember that and don't remember your father. I wish we could locate your mother. Maybe that would make you feel better."

"She didn't want me," Chelsea cried. "She wanted her rich family more than my father and me. How could she do that? How could she leave her lover and her little helpless baby?"

"I don't know. People do the wrong things sometimes for various reasons. If your mother's still alive, she may have regretted her decision for the last twenty-four years."

"Or she may never have cared."

"I doubt that. According to Old Helene's story, your mother would barely let you out of her arms from the time she had you until the day she left. She loved you."

She quieted and nodded, her soft cheek rubbing against Aric's chest. She lowered her hand and rubbed it against the front of his pajama bottoms, and he groaned her name. Her nightgown was off in a matter of seconds, and she was ardently kissing him and telling him that she loved him.

"I love you more than anything," he breathed, as he pulled her tightly against him. "I'll always love you for who you are. You're my life, Chelsea Rodrigue."

"And you are mine," she declared. "My husband."

Chapter Thirty-five

"What a week," Jason muttered. "First, we had Thanksgiving in New Orleans with the LaFleurs. Then, we flew to Haiti where you got married and we met with Toussaint. Then, we flew back to New Orleans for a few days. Now, we're in Atlanta."

"We'll leave the hotel at 7:00 tomorrow morning to go to the CDC," Paula told Aric and Chelsea. "We'll be there until 5:00 and then fly out of Atlanta at 10:00 the following morning."

Aric watched his wife pick at her salad. It was 7:00 p.m., and she'd barely eaten anything all day. When he'd asked her what was wrong, she'd said she didn't know and simply wasn't hungry. What little she had ingested had only been the result of his gentle, but persistent prodding.

Chelsea's been eating much more in the last month or so than she has since I've known her, so why am I stressing about one day? She's probably just exhausted. This has been a hard week for her, he reminded himself. *The trip to Haiti resulted in our marriage and was filled with unsettling revelations. We only had a brief time at home before we turned around and flew here for these exams, which she's been nervous about from the beginning. Christmas is coming, and I'm sure she's thinking about Fredeline and Eve Rose not being here to celebrate it with her like they did last year. She'll start eating more again once we get home.*

Aric knew he was making excuses. Everything he'd been thinking was true, but Chelsea had been doing fairly well until that morning. She hadn't been acting like herself all day. He wondered if a migraine was imminent and was almost hoping she'd develop one of the bad ones she hadn't had in a while. That way, the CDC doctors could examine her while the episode was occurring.

"I'm tired," Chelsea quietly announced. "I think I'd like to go up to our room and get ready for bed now that Paula's done with her sandwich." Leaning over to kiss Aric, she said, "Please stay here and finish your dinner with Jason."

"I could go up with you."

"No. You eat. I...I'm just tired."

Once the women had gone, Aric stared at his half-eaten cheeseburger. He was no longer hungry. He remained inexplicably uneasy and resisted the urge to rise from the table and follow Chelsea upstairs.

"She'll be fine once all the poking and prodding is over tomorrow," Jason assured him after he'd finished his cup of chicken soup and club sandwich. "It's probably making her think about all that time in the hospital after the accident and then the months spent living in the rehab facility. Plus, this has been a very tiring week. You look beat yourself."

Aric nodded but felt anxious. They talked of the next day's schedule, paid their bills, and headed upstairs. As in the hotel in Haiti, they were in adjoining suites separated by a connecting door. Jason escorted Aric to the entrance to his rooms and wished him a good night before going to his and Paula's suite.

A small lamp was on in the empty living area when Aric entered. He left it on and headed for the bedroom. It was deserted, and Aric frowned. Where was Chelsea? Perhaps she'd developed a migraine after all and was in the bathroom, which was also dark.

"Chere?" he called out softly as he stepped across the threshold into the bathroom. Turning on a dimmer light, he saw Chelsea lying curled on the floor near the large tub. She was still wearing the jeans and sweater she'd had on at dinner and was facing away from him.

"Chere?" he repeated. Edging around her and sitting next to her on the floor, he asked, "A migraine?"

Chelsea looked up at him and said in a voice tinged with pain, "No."

"No? What then?"

"It hurts. Please, get someone to make it stop hurting, Aric. It hurts so much."

"Where?" he asked, his pulse rate quickening.

"My abdomen."

Aric touched her right side and prompted, "Here? Does the pain move? Maybe your appendix is inflamed."

"No. Lower. It feels like…like cramps when you have your period but much worse. I don't understand. I don't have periods. I still have five more months left of the birth control shot. You don't have periods when you're on the shot."

"I know. Are you bleeding?"

"I don't feel like I am," she said weakly. "The pain keeps increasing, and –" Gripping his wrist with one hand, she mewled, "It feels like I'm dying."

"You are *not* dying! You hear me, Chelsea? You're going to be fine!"

Chelsea cried out and drew her knees up higher. Aric withdrew his phone from his jeans' pocket and commanded it to call Jason. When the man answered, he told him it was an emergency and to call the CDC. After explaining that Chelsea was in physical distress, he ended the call then asked his wife if her bones and joints hurt.

"It's not the D Plague. Whatever this is –"

She cried out again and blindly reached for him. Aric knew he shouldn't move her but couldn't stop himself from responding. He carefully lifted her into his lap and held her in his arms as she clung to him. Her skin was clammy with perspiration, and she moaned continuously. Aric felt powerless as he held her and told her that help was on the way.

Jason and Paula burst into the bathroom and crouched beside him and Chelsea. Paula laid a hand on Chelsea's shoulder and gingerly squeezed it, as Jason turned up the light and relayed his conversation with their contact at the CDC. He assured Aric that an ambulance filled with government doctors would arrive any minute. When Chelsea began to cry, the man touched her arm and stated that he wished there was more he could do for her.

If she dies, then my life is over, Aric thought desperately. *I'll end it. I can't go back to before. I won't.*

"Aric, listen to me," Paula said firmly. "I'm going to ride in the ambulance and be with Chelsea as she's taken care of at the hospital. You're going to ride with Jason and meet us there."

"What? No! I'm staying with her!"

"No, you're not," Jason countered. "It's Paula's job to protect Chelsea. She needs to be watching over her and seeing what they're doing. Do you understand what I'm saying? They won't let you in with her, but they can't refuse Paula. We're under direct orders from the President of the United States to safeguard the two of you. No one can refuse Paula and me access to either of you without basically committing treason. We have to do it this way. We have no other choice."

Aric automatically wanted to argue but saw the logic and necessity of what Jason and Paula were suggesting. He nodded to each of them then kissed Chelsea on the top of her head and told her that he loved her as someone pounded on the door of the suite. Jason hurried out of the room in order to let the doctors in. Aric heard the man talking to someone and exchanging what sounded like security codes. Then, the large bathroom was filled with medical personnel. Aric kissed Chelsea again and reluctantly allowed the doctors to take her from him. She was now unconscious.

He listened intently as they checked her vital signs. Her pulse and blood pressure were high, probably due to the pain. Her temperature was one hundred and two degrees Fahrenheit. Her oxygen levels were on the low side but not dangerously so. At the lead doctor's request, Aric repeated what Chelsea had told him after he'd found her on the floor. He also informed them of her lethargy and lack of appetite that day. He was thankful that these physicians knew both his and Chelsea's entire medical histories, so he didn't have to rehash all of it.

As they worked on their patient, one of the paramedics deftly removed Chelsea's wedding ring set and her earrings. These items were handed to Aric, who accepted them in stunned silence. During his preparation for medical school, he'd only heard of this act being immediately performed on those who might need resuscitation by cardiovert, the use of electrical stimulation to restart the heart.

Jason was saying his name, but Aric ignored him. He pocketed his wife's jewelry and watched as the men and women dashed out of the bathroom with her as hastily as they dared. Paula was right beside them, and that gave Aric some comfort. He grabbed Chelsea's phone and both of their computers and placed them in the pockets of the coat that Jason handed to him as they ran after the medical team.

Jason followed the ambulance as closely as he could while they drove through town. When they arrived at the hospital, he refused to let Aric out of the vehicle at the Emergency Room entrance and insisted they park the car and hurry together to find out where Chelsea was being brought for treatment. The moment they stepped inside, another man Aric didn't recognize called out to Jason, and they darted down several corridors after him to a private waiting room.

"Where is Chelsea?" Aric demanded. "Where is she right now?"

The other man said authoritatively, "You and Agent Duson will be updated as soon as possible. The doctors are examining your wife to discern the cause of her current condition. Agent Jennings will remain with her at all times for now. I need to get back there myself." Looking at Jason, he said, "Imahara will be outside the door if you need anything."

Once he was gone, Aric asked, "Who is Imahara?"

"Part of our team. She'll stand in the hall while we wait in here."

"I can't just stay here and wait!"

"What in the hell else are you going to do? Are you going to go find Chelsea and assist the doctors? I don't really think they're going to let you in the fucking room!" Lowering his voice, he said more calmly, "Call the President. Call Maurice Moreau. Make some business calls. Do something to occupy yourself while we wait."

Aric withdrew Chelsea's phone from his coat pocket. He lowered himself into a chair, gave the security code override, and scrolled through her Contacts list. He then ordered the phone to call Nadine LaFleur. The woman answered on the third ring.

"Hello, Chelsea," she answered with obvious delight in her voice. "How are you?"

"Nadine, it's Aric."

There was a long, long pause.

"Aric, why are you calling me on Chelsea's phone?" she asked in a hoarse whisper.

"Because she needs you. We're at the hospital in Atlanta, and I think...I think she might...." Unable to control himself any longer, he broke down and admitted, "They don't know what's wrong with her, and I'm afraid that...I'm afraid. Please, come."

"Oh, God. I will."

Aric could hear Nadine crying as she told him she was in D.C. but would be there as quickly as she could. She asked him what had happened, and he briefly explained. She begged him to call her if there was any news before she arrived. He promised he would.

"Hold on, Aric. She'll be all right. She has to be all right."

Once they'd disconnected the call, Aric pulled out his own phone, followed the protocol, and left a message for Lakshmi. Then he phoned Maurice, who declared he was going to take the next flight to Atlanta. Aric didn't try to dissuade him. He needed his friend to be there. Jason took the phone from Aric's hand and told Maurice that an escort detail would meet him at the Louis Armstrong International Airport and get him to the hospital in Atlanta as fast as they could. Then he ended the call and sat beside Aric. He used his own phone to make several other calls regarding Maurice's trip then slipped the device into his pants pocket.

"You should take off your coat," Jason suggested. "I get the feeling we'll be here a while."

Lakshmi called ten minutes later. She spoke to Aric about what had happened then asked him to put Jason on the phone. Aric half-listened as the man kept repeating, "Yes, Ma'am." Eventually, he handed the phone back to Aric, who assured Lakshmi that he understood why she couldn't come right away. She was in the midst of delicate peace talks between the United States and several other countries. She uttered comforting words, told him her people would keep her informed, and promised to call as often as she could. He thanked her, disconnected the call, and stared at the wall in front of him. Time passed.

When Nadine and her entourage arrived, Aric hugged the woman tightly and said, "Thank you for coming."

"Nothing could have kept me away," she said through her tears. "I was about to leave for a public appearance tour in South America but have indefinitely postponed the trip."

Aric was touched and impressed. Again, the woman had surprised him.

"How long has it been since they brought Chelsea here?" asked Nadine as she took a seat between the two men.

Aric shrugged. He was withdrawing into himself and was not paying much attention to the movement of the hands on the clock. He knew the longer they waited for word, the worse things must be. Therefore, he'd decided not to think about it and to focus instead on getting from one second to the next.

Someone knocked on the door, and Aric, Nadine, and Jason were instantly on their feet. A young woman of Asian descent, presumably Agent Imahara, stepped into the room and said, "I have an update, although it's not much. Mrs. Rodrigue is in surgery, but I'm not quite certain why. Agent Jennings is still with her but isn't in a position to give us status reports. I'll let you know when I get more news."

Jason thanked her. She exited the room as Maurice hurried in. As he pulled Aric to him in a brotherly hug, he whispered in French, "She'll be fine. You two will be back upstairs playing pool at the restaurant in no time." As Aric nodded against him and tightly squeezed his eyes shut in order to staunch a flood of tears, his friend added, "Have faith."

"I haven't had that luxury since the D Plague," Aric said before stepping away from Maurice. "Thank you for coming."

They all sat in the small waiting room and drank coffee that someone from Nadine's staff brought for them. When Aric finished his, he threw away the cup and fished out Chelsea's wedding ring set and the diamond earrings from his pocket. Nadine stared at the jewelry in his palm, while Maurice excused himself to use the restroom.

"The diamond ring is beautiful," she murmured. "As for those lovely earrings, Chelsea wasn't wearing them the last couple of times I saw her."

"These were her mother's. The woman left them behind when she left Chelsea and her father behind. Chelsea was struggling with things and hadn't worn them in a while. She's still struggling."

Nadine nodded sadly and said, "She spent three hours on the phone with me while you were at work after your return to the States. She told me everything she'd learned about her first twenty years of life. It was…heartbreaking." Looking up at Aric, she asked, "She doesn't know everything, does she?"

"No. I don't know everything either. The sick bastard who had her father killed and adopted her did work with our government, so a lot is Classified."

Nadine lifted the earrings from Aric's hand and asked, "What made her put these back on?"

"I convinced her that her mother must have loved her even though she left her. I told her people did things they regretted for various reasons. I guess she decided to give her mother the benefit of the doubt. She started wearing the earrings again every day once we got back home from Haiti."

"What you told her is very true." Nadine returned the earrings to his palm and said, "She'll want them once she wakes."

Maurice returned to the room, and the foursome waited for news. Someone brought food, but none of them ate. They waited some more. Aric felt as if the waiting would never end.

Chapter Thirty-six

Aric hadn't realized he was dozing until the door to the waiting room opened, and he jerked awake. When he saw Paula standing in the doorway, he leapt to his feet and let out an anguished cry. Paula rushed forward and exclaimed, "Aric, she's not dead! I was so tired that I didn't think! Someone else is with her for a while. I'm so sorry I scared you."

"She's not dead," he repeated shakily. "Not dead."

Jason released a sigh of relief, while Maurice muttered a prayer of thanks and Nadine began to cry quietly. Paula, who looked pale and beyond exhausted, asked if they could sit down while she explained. Nadine hastened to request fresh food and drink for the FBI agent. While they waited, Aric asked how Chelsea was doing and what was wrong with her.

"The head surgeon's coming to talk to you. Let's hear what he has to say. I'll fill you in on anything he…leaves out."

Tension was radiating from the woman. Everyone in the room seemed to sense it, and Aric suspected Paula wished she'd had time to talk alone with Jason before the doctor's visit. All Aric wanted was to get information and to see his wife.

The surgeon was a middle-aged, black-haired man with a slight paunch. He looked as if he'd recently finished a marathon and was about to collapse. Dressed in clean scrubs, he took a seat across from Aric and introduced himself as Dr. Orr; then he explained that Aric's regular internist was with Chelsea at the moment and, therefore, couldn't be present.

"What was wrong with my wife?" Aric asked, relieved that his voice sounded reasonably level. "What did you do to help her? How is she now?"

Orr cleared his throat and said, "We checked her out from head to toe very quickly once she was brought in but concentrated on her abdomen. That was, indeed, where the problem was located."

"What problem?"

Dr. Orr shifted in his seat before announcing, "Mrs. Rodrigue was pregnant."

"Bullshit," Aric shot back vehemently. "Tell me the truth, you lying son of a bitch! "She was on the birth control shot! My company produces the medication in the injection. She could *not* be pregnant. The shot allows for ovulation but not for fertilization. It causes subtle physiological changes that make the uterus toxic to sperm. Conception can't occur if the sperm can't survive."

Orr swallowed hard and said, "For normal human beings, that's right. The shot is totally effective. You are *not* a normal human being, and your contact with your wife has enhanced her immune system somehow. We think that because of what happened to you five years ago…the physical mutations that occurred altered your sperm as well. Like you, it became impervious to attack, except that it wasn't being attacked by illness but by toxins produced as a result of the birth control shot. The fact that Mrs. Rodrigue's immune system was also altered probably weakened the effects of the medication in the injection. The combination led to the fertilization and implantation of an embryo."

"Those at the CDC who were studying me knew this might happen?"

"There was…speculation."

"You fucking bastards!" Aric shouted, as he got to his feet. "Chelsea was right! You were using us as empirical subjects! If we'd known this was even remotely possible, then we would've used condoms! We never would've taken a chance!" Enraged, he continued, "You've been taking samples from Chelsea for the last couple of months. Did you know she was pregnant?"

Orr grimaced and admitted, "We did."

Aric launched himself at the surgeon. He hit him square in the jaw before Jason, Maurice, and Paula could grab him and pull him back. He fought against them and said, "What did it do to her? She's still alive, but will she stay that way? Is she still pregnant?"

Rubbing his jaw, the surgeon slowly got to his feet and said, "We don't know if she'll live or not. There were complications."

Breathing hard, Aric strained to free himself from Maurice and the two FBI agents before admitting defeat and asking, "What sorts of complications?"

"Mrs. Rodrigue could have only been about eight weeks into the pregnancy, but what she was carrying wasn't a baby."

"What the fuck is that supposed to mean?" growled Aric.

"It was fetal tissue but not an actual fetus. It was about the size of a fetus at twenty-three weeks. We're not certain if the abnormal growth rate is what caused the threat to Mrs. Rodrigue's life or if there was some sort of incompatibility between her body and the developing mass. Regardless, once we got her in here, determined what was happening, and performed some hasty tests, we knew we had to remove the fetal tissue. However, when we initiated the surgery, we realized that it was as if her uterus was protecting her from the mass. It had basically collapsed and encased the tissue as if it was trying to save her by destroying the invader. She was bleeding internally, and we knew we had to remove the mass and get the bleeding under control if we were going to save her. We had to take out the tissue and uterus at the same time and were forced to also remove the rest of her reproductive organs." Looking at the floor, Orr said, "Her heart stopped once during surgery. We were able to resuscitate her in a short amount of time, but her vitals are still not as stable as we'd like. She's on a ventilator at the moment. Her brain activity is good, but we have her sedated for obvious reasons."

"She could still die?" Nadine asked weakly.

"Yes, although the odds are now in her favor. Because of her intimate contact with Mr. Rodrigue, her immune system and physiology are in much better shape than those of the average woman."

"Except she's not the average woman," Aric hissed. "She's a TBI victim with a much greater risk of stroke and further brain damage."

"True," Dr. Orr conceded. "The neurologists will check her out once she comes to."

"If she comes to," Aric said grimly. "You may have killed her because of your little experiment. What were you going to do? When were you going to tell us she was pregnant?"

"The team agreed that once we'd examined her personally during your visit and determined the state of her pregnancy, then we'd discuss the situation with the two of you. Believe me when I tell you that we didn't anticipate this happening. We'd been studying your sperm since you survived the D Plague, but we had no idea that the changes in you would result in...this. We feel terrible."

"Well, as long as you feel terrible," Aric said sardonically. "I know you'll do a complete dissection of the fetal tissue and try to determine what went wrong. I want to see a full report, and I want you to think about the horrible thing you and your team did to me, my wife, and what should have never been allowed to happen. You think about what should've been our baby as you carve it into tiny pieces and study the tissue under a microscope. Then, you go home to your kids and picture the mass of fetal tissue that should have been our child." Shaking his head, Aric said, "God, Chelsea was so right. I was such a fool to trust you people. You can believe that we'll never, ever trust you again. I'll be speaking at length to President Jitesh about all of this. What you did was an abominable thing. I hope it haunts all of you until you die."

The surgeon nodded and said, "We deserve that. I am sorry, Mr. Rodrigue. We're supposed to do our jobs in order to help with 'the big picture' but often forget the individuals involved."

Aric glared at him and said nothing. Orr reddened with what Aric hoped was shame and left the room. Once he'd gone, Aric turned to Paula and asked, "Was he lying to me?"

"Not that I could detect. I'm no doctor, Aric. I don't claim to understand what all the medical jargon was or exactly what they were doing to Chelsea, but it fit with what Dr. Orr was saying. It was very difficult for me to watch, but I made myself because I knew it was of the utmost importance. I thought I was going to throw up a few times. I've never been too good with blood and needles. There was a lot of blood, and there were scalpels, needles, and other things."

"How big was the mass they took out of Chelsea?"

Giving him a half-shrug and paling further at the memory, she offered, "About the size of a grapefruit or a small cantaloupe. It was kind of hard to tell because of everything they were taking out. It wasn't like seeing a C-section on TV where there's a baby being born. It was sort of awful-looking, and Chelsea was losing so much blood. That was when her heart stopped."

"How many times did they have to shock her in order to restart her heart?"

"Twice. They tried medication first, but it didn't work."

"Did you hear them talking about removing anything else besides the mass and her reproductive organs?"

"No. They were frantic in the Operating Room, which surprised me. I always thought doctors were trained to be cool and calm under stress. These men and women were frazzled."

262

"Because they knew what they'd done," Aric said wearily. Sinking into a chair, he asked no one in particular, "How am I going to tell Chelsea about this? We'd agreed early on that we were never going to have children since we didn't know what might happen because of my unusual condition. Now, she gets to find out that she was pregnant with a mutant monster and that it damn near killed her."

This is my fault, he reflected. *My sperm did this. My bodily fluids did this. I did this.*

"She's unconscious for the time being," Jason reminded him. "Even when she wakes, she may be too out of it for a while to understand. You can think about it after you've had a chance to sleep."

"You think I can sleep?" Aric asked bitterly. "Are you an optimist or a fool?" Getting to his feet, he said, "I don't even know if I can trust you or Paula. You could have been placed with us by Miss June to spy on us and feed me and Chelsea misinformation. Hell, for all I know Lakshmi could be lying to me at this point."

Nadine rose and said steadily, "Lakshmi Jitesh is the most honorable woman I know. She would never lie to anyone, least of all you." Extending her hand to him, she commanded, "Take a walk with me, Aric."

"But Chelsea –"

"You know they won't let us see her until she's situated in the Critical Care Unit. We have a few minutes. Agent Jennings needs to eat and drink, and Agent Duson needs to explain to Mr. Moreau about your…condition and the need for confidentiality. I need for you to come with me."

After a member of her Secret Service detail had swept another room down the hall for threats, she walked inside with Aric, closed the door, and asked him to sit on the small loveseat in the room. He did so, wondering what she was going to say. He didn't feel like talking anymore to anyone. All he wanted to do was lie down and die. He'd hurt the person he loved more than anyone else in the world, not that it had been intentional. But it was still his fault.

Nadine sat beside him and declared, "You are *not* to blame for surviving the D Plague or for what happened to Chelsea because of your contact with her. I may not be able to give you an explanation as to why these things happened, but I'm certain there is one and it has great significance. Promise me you'll stop with the self-loathing. That's not who you were before 2029, Aric. It's not who you are." Placing her hands on his shoulders, she said, "You're a good man, and you torture yourself way too much. Please don't give in to depression or despair.

"I know we weren't always the closest of friends, but I've come to depend on you and trust you more than you can know. Chelsea's had a great effect on both our lives, and we've had a great effect on hers. You are her world. You have to keep going for her and for yourself. She loves you so deeply."

"She loves you as well. You're like the mother she never had."

Nadine wiped at the corners of her eyes and sat up a little straighter as she said, "I lost three daughters in the D Plague. I don't intend to lose Chelsea. I also don't intend to lose you."

Aric smiled for the first time all day. *This* was more like the Nadine he knew, the one with the backbone of steel. He realized that she was very similar to Miss June. She was simply more direct.

"I am going to handle this," she declared. "And you are going to let me."

"Handle what?"

"What these medical people have done to you and to that sweet girl who almost died today. I'll talk to the two FBI agents assigned to protect you and Chelsea, gather the documentation required, and have these doctors' medical licenses revoked. You're a very intelligent man, but you're guileless when it comes to how things work within certain government agencies. I lost that innocence a long time ago, and I'm very savvy when it comes to the ways of the political world. I'm not just a trophy wife, Aric. I have a degree in political science from Tulane and have learned quite a lot in my forty-something years on this planet. I know how to play the system for everything it's worth."

"Would Buddy approve of you doing this?"

"Buddy and I haven't had a true marriage since our children died. The only thing holding us together is our common desire to make the world a better place. He and Lakshmi are doing an excellent job of making that happen. I won't leave him and put the fate of the globe at risk because we don't love one another anymore. We work well together as a political team. It keeps us going."

"If you do this and take care of things regarding these doctors, then who will look after Chelsea and me?"

"Other doctors who can actually be trusted to do their jobs in a morally acceptable manner."

"I'll be kept appraised of our health information, experiments, and changes no matter what?"

"If I have my way."

Sighing heavily, Aric said, "All right. We can try it." Standing, he asked, "Can I trust Jason and Paula?"

"Totally. Lakshmi and I had them checked out. They're as incorruptible as they can be. They also care about the two of you." Smiling slightly, she said, "Once this is over, I think they want to quit the FBI and settle down together. Agent Duson is very good as your top administrative assistant. You might want to offer him a permanent job."

"I'd love that, but I don't know if that's what he wants. Perhaps Jason would rather work at his family's security firm."

"Never. He and his brother despise one another. Julian is efficient and ruthless."

"Have you ever met him?"

"He did some private security work for Buddy years ago. I demanded that Buddy fire him. I could tell what kind of a man he was and didn't want him anywhere near my family. Buddy pitched a fit but capitulated."

They walked back toward the other waiting room. Before they reached the door, Nadine stopped him and asked, "May I make a suggestion?"

"I thought you were telling me what to do."

She flashed him a knowing grin then said, "It's not about what you and I were discussing regarding the healthcare professionals involved with you and Chelsea. It's about you."

He eyed her suspiciously and asked, "What's your suggestion?"

"I know you'll insist on reviewing all of the documentation from Chelsea's treatment here today and during her recovery."

"Definitely."

"Don't examine the images of the mass or watch the digital recording of the dissection of the fetal tissue. It will tear you to pieces emotionally."

"I have to see it. I have to know if they were telling the truth and what really happened. It wasn't a baby, Nadine."

"It wasn't and it was. Please reconsider. If you don't, then you'll regret it. Believe me. Listen to me."

"I'll think about it. Will you listen to a suggestion from me?"

"Of course."

"Don't request the details of what happened to Chelsea while she was in LeClerc's care. Get the summary and be satisfied with it."

"I don't believe I can do that. I have to know."

Aric cocked his head and said, "Perhaps the reason you and I didn't get along well in the past is because we're too much alike."

Nadine appeared pensive then said, "Perhaps you're right. I'm so glad we're friends now."

"I am, too. I never thought I'd say this, but I need you, Nadine."

The woman's eyes filled with tears, as she said, "I need you, too. And Chelsea needs both of us. I pray she'll be all right. We both need her as well. We all deserve to be happy."

Chapter Thirty-seven

Aric sat by Chelsea's hospital bed in the CCU and held her right hand in his left. He watched her sleep. He was glad the ventilator tube had been removed. He'd seen Chelsea like that on the digital recordings from her hospital stay after the taxi accident, and it had been unnerving. Seeing her with it down her throat in person was much, much worse.

At least her vitals have stabilized, and she's shown no signs of stroke, Aric thought gratefully. *But when will she wake up?*

Everyone had been urging him to return to the hotel room to rest. He'd refused. Jason, Paula, Maurice, and Nadine practically had to force him to eat. He hadn't tasted anything they brought him but had managed to take in enough food to satisfy them. Except for brief trips to the bathroom and the occasional walk around the room, Aric hadn't left the chair for two days. He was wearing the same clothing, hadn't shaved, and had only used mouthwash Maurice had brought him in lieu of a toothbrush and toothpaste.

Maurice still seemed awed by the knowledge that Aric had contracted and survived the D Plague. It was clear he wanted to ask Aric questions about his experiences but recognized that now was not the time. He'd sworn never to reveal the truth to anyone. The enormity of Aric's predicament had dawned on him within the first few hours of his briefing by Jason, and he had told Aric in a voice thick with emotion that what he'd learned had explained so much regarding the past five years. Aric had been slightly confused by this statement but was past caring at that moment. He would talk with his friend later and find out what he'd meant.

Jason and Paula had been taking turns staying with Aric in Chelsea's room. Nadine came in and out and was very attentive to both Aric and the still-unconscious Chelsea, but Aric could tell that she'd found out what Jason had told him regarding Michel LeClerc's perversions and his offering of young Chelsea to other powerful men. The woman was bristling with suppressed rage. He understood. LeClerc was dead, and there was no one on whom to focus her anger. Unlike Aric, Nadine did not engage in daily exercise and couldn't exorcise her fury by pummeling a punching bag each morning.

Aric wished he had a punching bag in the hospital room. He was caught in the odd position of alternating between feeling numb and feeling livid as he sat beside his wife and held her hand. Nadine had followed through with her pronouncement to make the physicians involved pay for their transgressions, and Chelsea and Aric had a new team of doctors who'd thoroughly reviewed all of their records. They would have to prove themselves to Aric, not only as medical personnel but also as trustworthy individuals.

"Aric?"

He looked across the room at Jason, who was holding out his phone. Aric shook his head.

"But it's the President."

He shook his head again and said, "I can't. Not right now. Tell her I'm sorry and that I appreciate the call."

Aric heard Jason explain and then a lot of "Yes, Ma'am's" before the FBI agent switched off the device. Once he'd pocketed his phone, he said, "She's really worried about you. *I'm* really worried about you."

He wasn't listening again. He was mulling over what he was going to tell Chelsea when she woke. He was at a total loss as to how much he should say and how she would react to any of the facts.

Against everyone's advice, Aric had viewed the entire digital recording of Chelsea's care from the time she'd been brought into the Atlanta hospital until she'd been moved into her current room. He'd had no desire to see any of it but hadn't trusted the government's doctors or Paula's inexperienced observations. He'd sat beside his wife's bed and reviewed the materials, even though what he saw sickened him.

Paula had been correct in her assessment that the government doctors were panicked by Chelsea's physical condition. They'd scrambled to perform necessary tests before quickly determining that what they'd thought was a normal fetus was not and that it had to be removed. Aric battled the natural urge he'd felt to close his eyes when they'd operated on his wife and taken out the mass from her abdomen. The amount of blood loss had been staggering. He'd had to remind himself to breathe when *she* stopped breathing and flat-lined, and they'd had to bring her back to life with the Crash Cart.

She'd been cleaned up before she was prepared for movement to a post-operative area.

Aric hated that he'd had to watch, but he didn't regret it. He'd seen what kind of care his wife had received, what had been done and not done, and caught a glimpse of the uterine-encased mass. He'd heard the doctors and nurses speaking of their research and about how to proceed. Several important questions he'd had about what the CDC was doing with his and Chelsea's data had been answered.

He and Nadine got into a heated argument in Chelsea's room once he'd finished viewing the recordings and demanded to be present for at least part of the dissection of the fetal tissue. At one point, the Vice-President's petite, blonde wife looked as if she'd wanted to tackle him to the floor in order to prevent him from attending the examination. Jason and Agent Imahara had interceded and demanded that both Nadine and Aric walk away for a while and calm down.

"I could stop you from doing this!" Nadine had cried, as Agent Imahara and one of the Secret Service people tried to lead her in the opposite direction from Aric. Tears streaming down her cheeks, she begged, "*Please.* Don't do this."

Aric had turned his back to her and focused on the still form of his wife. He was acutely aware of how his presence at the dissection might affect him, but it was like the recordings he'd had to watch. He had to know the whole story if he was going to protect Chelsea. In truth, what he learned might safeguard others in the future from being tormented because of misuse of his previously-collected sperm and other samples.

"Mr. Rodrigue?"

Aric looked up and saw the middle-aged female doctor who was now in charge of the CDC team responsible for him and Chelsea. She wore green scrubs and a somber expression. He couldn't recall her name.

"We're going to begin in an hour. Are you certain you want to do this?"

"I most certainly *don't* want to do this, but I have to," he replied dully. Glancing at Chelsea, he asked, "Were there any changes on her last EEG or EKG?"

"No changes." When he got stiffly to his feet, she said, "You'll have to shower and put on scrubs before we start. If you'll come with me...?"

Jason stepped forward as Aric moved toward the door, but Aric said, "Stay where you are."

"It's my job to protect you."

"I don't give a damn about anyone's protection except Chelsea's." After reminding Jason that Chelsea was literally helpless at the moment, Aric said, "If it makes you feel better, I'll allow another agent to accompany me as long as the person waits outside the door of the room I'll be in during this...evaluation of the fetal tissue."

With obviously monumental effort, Jason refrained from arguing or trying to dissuade Aric from going with the doctor. He'd already attempted this earlier that day after Nadine's outburst. Instead, he directed Agent Imahara to go in his stead and protect his headstrong charge.

Aric conceded that it did feel good to shower and put on clean clothing. He emerged from the bathroom wearing fresh green scrubs and disposable paper shoes. He walked behind the doctor, whose name he now remembered was Leah Levine, to the room where his "non-baby" was about to be dissected. Imahara positioned herself beside the only entrance as he and Levine went inside.

After undergoing the requisite decontamination procedures and donning hats, masks, and gloves in an anteroom, the two of them joined five others in a small chamber that held a rectangular stainless steel table, a bright overhead light, medical instruments, and computers. Aric knew that everything was being digitally recorded and was glad of it. He hoped it would help Levine and her team when they reviewed the dissection in the future.

Aric was introduced to the others and was once again strongly advised against witnessing the dissection. Although he was already feeling sick, he insisted he had to stay. No one appeared pleased, and he couldn't blame them. He just didn't care.

His heart pounded hard as someone brought out the box that contained the mass. The lid was lifted, and then the contents were withdrawn and placed on the table. Despite the somersault his stomach performed, Aric was fascinated. The uterus had literally tightened around the tissue like old-fashioned shrink-wrap. What lay on the table was approximately eight inches long and seven inches in circumference.

The medical examiner began his dictation and reviewed the origins of the mass as he withdrew a tool that looked like a Phillips screwdriver. Because of Aric's love of medicine and former plans to become a neurosurgeon, he knew this was actually a laser used by surgeons and coroners. The man set to work and deftly cut away the uterus in order to reveal its contents.

Bile rose in Aric's throat as he stared at what should have been a normal eight-week fetus. That fetus would have been half an inch long but would have begun to resemble a human baby. The large mass of fetal tissue on the table was unrecognizable as anything human. As the doctor rotated the mass, Aric caught a glimpse of what looked like an eye. When the man turned the tissue in order to view it from another angle, a miniscule hand appeared to be tucked between part of the malformed mass.

"I've seen enough," he announced before the medical examiner could begin the dissection. Addressing Levine, he asked, "You'll discuss the general findings with me later?"

"Yes, Mr. Rodrigue. Would you like for me to go out with you?"

"No. I want you in here. I want you to see what those people did to me, my wife, and this thing that should never have existed. Then I want you to make sure it never happens again."

"It won't as long as I'm in charge. Go back to your wife. We'll talk again soon."

He nodded and forced himself to thank her and the others for their efforts before walking back out into the anteroom. Removing his hat, mask, and gloves, he disposed of them in a hazardous waste bin then returned to the hallway. Imahara eyed him uncertainly.

"Do you need assistance?" When Aric shook his head, she said, "Agent Duson arranged for one of the other agents to send up a bag filled with clean jeans, a long-sleeved shirt, underwear, and socks."

"Great, where's the bag?"

"In the same bathroom where you washer earlier."

Aric showered again in an attempt to wash away the feel of the dissection room. He then dressed in his own clothes pulled from the bag before putting his tennis shoes back on. His dirty clothes were gone. He assumed the unseen agent had taken them away while he'd been attempting to scrub the memory of the fetal tissue from his mind while cleansing his skin.

As he stared at his reflection in the bathroom mirror, Aric ran his hands over the brown stubble on his face. He wondered if Jason had gotten someone to retrieve his razor. He needed a shave.

Like a shave will change everything, he thought darkly.

Imahara walked with him back to Chelsea's room. When Jason saw him, he asked whether or not he needed anything. Aric shook his head and resumed his seat next to Chelsea and took her right hand in his left once more.

"The President called again while you were gone," Jason informed him. "She was distressed by your decision to attend the dissection."

"It was pretty distressing to me, too."

"She wants me to keep you under constant surveillance."

"I thought we were already under constant surveillance."

"Suicide watch," Jason clarified.

Aric studied Chelsea's beautiful profile and said, "You don't have to worry about that as long as Chelsea lives. If she dies, then you don't have to worry about that either. I *will* kill myself."

"You don't mean that."

"I most assuredly do."

"Suicide's a goddamned selfish choice to make."

"I've spent most of my life trying to be as selfless as possible. If Chelsea dies, then I'll be selfish for once." Sitting back in the chair, he said, "I'm tired. I'm going to rest my eyes for a while. Will you wake me if there's any change?"

"You know I will."

"Yes. I do trust you and Paula. If this ever ends, would you consider working for me full-time?"

Aric was asleep before Jason could answer.

Chapter Thirty-eight

Aric's sister, Aurelia, and her unborn son were dying. As he, his parents, and her husband stood by helplessly, she screamed and begged for someone to help her and save her baby. After more screaming and thrashing in the bed, she died. They watched as her body disintegrated before their eyes, knowing that her baby was enduring its own horrible, slow death. When there was nothing left of his sister, a wailing shape moved underneath the sheet where his mother had lain only minutes before. Aric reached for the sheet and pulled it away. Lying on the bed was what should have been a healthy baby. Aric knew he didn't have long and gently lifted the tiny, blood-covered infant and cradled him against his chest as the boy lived for several more excruciating minutes. Then, there was only dust all over Aric's shirt.

"Aric! Wake up! *Aric!*"

Aric woke feeling disoriented and nauseated. Nadine was standing in front of him looking extraordinarily pale and agitated, and he glanced frantically around, trying to pinpoint his location. He was still in Chelsea's room but was no longer in the chair, holding her hand. Instead, he was halfway across the room. Jason was behind him with one arm wrapped firmly around his chest and the other pinning his left wrist to his back.

Continuing to feel confused, Aric slowly looked down at his shirt. No dust. No little Aric. No dying Aurelia. No sobbing brother-in-law or grieving parents. A nightmare then.

"Are you awake?" Jason asked softly.

He nodded dumbly and stared at Nadine. She looked so upset, and he wondered what he'd done in his sleep to disturb her so deeply. He'd have to ask Jason later. Right then, he had other more pressing concerns.

"Let me go to the bathroom *now*," Aric said urgently.

Jason instantly released him, and he rushed for the toilet. He threw up the contents of his stomach then washed his hands, rinsed his mouth first with water then mouthwash, and wiped his face with a damp paper towel. He was visibly shaking. Placing a hand on either side of the sink, he closed his eyes and tried not to think of his dream. He wished he were in bed with Chelsea. Chelsea would make it better.

When he returned to the room, Aric found Nadine standing by the bed on Chelsea's left side. She was crying, stroking the younger woman's hair, and pleading for her to wake. Chelsea didn't move, and Aric resumed his seat in the chair and took Chelsea's right hand in his left again as Jason watched.

Buddy LaFleur appeared in the doorway. He scanned the room, assessed the current state of affairs, and walked over to his wife. He laid a hand on her back and said her name, but she shrugged him off. He stiffened and looked down at Chelsea then shook his head and sighed.

"Is there anything I can do?" the Vice-President asked Aric.

"Not really."

"Aric –"

"I'm not up for talking, Buddy. Do you mind if Agent Duson fills you in?"

"No. I understand." Glancing at his wife, LaFleur looked at Jason and asked, "Could we step out into the hall for a couple of minutes?"

Once the two men were in the hallway, Nadine kissed Chelsea on the forehead and murmured, "You have to live. I can't lose another child. I'm so, so sorry."

Aric was about to ask Nadine what she had to be sorry about, but movement on his hand stopped him. Chelsea was rubbing her thumb back and forth across his wedding band. For a moment, he thought he was imagining it. He wasn't.

"Nadine, get help," he said evenly. "She's coming to."

The woman immediately pressed the Call Button on the wall behind the bed. Then she took Chelsea's free hand in both of hers, as Aric rose, leaned down over his wife, and murmured her name. Chelsea kept rubbing her thumb over his wedding band but didn't open her eyes or say anything. He kissed her lips.

"Aric?" she said hoarsely, her eyes still closed. "Where am I?"

"A hospital in Atlanta. Try not to talk. You were on a ventilator for a while. I'm sure your throat hurts."

"Why am I in a hospital?"

"It's a long story. Doctors are going to be in here in a minute and will want to examine you. Once they've gone, then I'll explain what they don't."

Dr. Levine and others rushed in along with Jason and Buddy. Levine demanded that everyone leave. Aric and Jason refused and were allowed to stay, but the LaFleurs were forced to exit. Aric thought Buddy was going to have to physically pick Nadine up and carry her out. Chelsea finally opened her eyes and assured Nadine that she would be fine and would see her soon. The older woman smiled wanly and left with her husband.

Once they'd departed, Levine bent over the bed and said gently, "Chelsea, my name is Dr. Leah Levine. I'm your new doctor. You have all new doctors. We're going to take very good care of you from now on."

"Am I going to be all right?" Chelsea's brow furrowed, and she said, "I remember some things. There was so much pain. I thought I was dying, but Aric told me I wasn't. Then it was all dark. What happened?"

Aric sensed that Levine was going to tell Chelsea about the surgery, the complications, and the mass of fetal tissue. He was surprised to realize how relieved he was. He would still have to decide how to explain a lot to his wife, but Levine was going to lift the greatest burden from him. He would always be thankful for that and gave her an appreciative nod. The doctor nodded back.

"Chelsea, we need to examine you; then I'll tell you what happened." Turning to Jason, she suggested, "Mrs. Rodrigue might feel more comfortable if you waited outside during the exam."

Once the agent had stationed himself outside the door, the doctors set to work. The sheet and blanket were pulled down and Chelsea's gown was untied so that it opened at the front. She looked up at Aric and asked, "Are you sure you want to stay and see me like this?"

Unable to tell her that he'd seen everything on the digital recordings, Aric merely nodded and squeezed her hand. Except for the thin line that extended along her abdomen where the incision had been made, she looked remarkably healthy. She had lost weight, but that was understandable.

The physical and neurological evaluations went well. Once the physicians had finished conducting their exams and Chelsea was secured in her gown and back under the sheet and blanket, all of them left the room except for Dr. Levine. She suggested that Aric have a seat and took Chelsea's free hand before beginning her explanation. Aric felt Chelsea's thumb begin its rhythmic movement across his wedding band once more and knew she was anxious. Well, he was anxious, too.

He listened as the woman spoke frankly about Chelsea's treatment, surgery, complications, and the withdrawal of the mass of fetal tissue. She expressed her disgust at the behaviors of the previous medical team in regards to their misuse of the confidential data, samples, and research. She told Chelsea of the removal by that team of her reproductive organs in order to save her life. Chelsea's thumb stilled.

"So, I can't ever have any babies? That's a relief."

Levine appeared startled and asked, "You're not upset or angry?"

Shaking her head, Chelsea said, "I wish it hadn't come about this way, but at least we don't have to worry anymore about me getting pregnant and what might happen. We know now what will happen, and it's bad. Will you destroy the remaining samples of Aric's sperm so it won't be misused like before?"

"If that's what the two of you want."

"I won't be procreating, so there's no need to study my sperm any further," Aric said firmly. "I'm still hesitant to trust anyone at the CDC, no offense intended."

"None taken. We know we'll have to work hard to earn your trust. We want to prove to both of you that we have your best interests at heart. Mrs. LaFleur declared it one of her life's missions to make certain that the two of you are not misled or maltreated by anyone in the government. The wife of the Vice-President is a formidable force to be reckoned with."

"Tell me about it," Aric muttered. "I'm glad she's on our side."

Levine snorted and patted Chelsea on the arm before saying, "We'll start you on ice chips. Once we know you can keep those down, then you need to drink some broth then rest. If all goes well, then I'd say you could go home in about a week. Any other questions?"

"The fetal tissue you removed...."

"Yes?"

"That was why I was so hungry for the last few weeks?"

"Probably."

"Did it look like a baby?"

Levine darted a glance at Aric before saying, "No. We're going to study it and see what we can learn from it. Your husband gave us permission. Do you have any objections?"

"No. I don't want us to have gone through all of this for nothing."

"It wasn't for nothing. It was a much-needed revelation for some people. Any other questions?"

"Will we still have to give blood and urine samples every month?"

"For the next six months at least. I want to monitor you very closely as you recover to make certain you're healing well. Providing there are no problems, then I believe I'll recommend cutting back to quarterly samples and a yearly exam for each of you. If things remain stable for twenty-four months, we can simply have you fly in for a yearly physical and blood work."

"Like normal people."

"Yes, just like normal people. Unlike normal people, you could always call your personal CDC healthcare team at any time if you had physical issues or concerns."

"How soon can Aric and I have sex?"

"Chere, how can you even be thinking about that?" Aric asked incredulously.

"Because we like to have sex, and I had major surgery and want to know how long it will be before I can have you in me again. We both need to be able to make love, but we can't do it too soon or it'll hurt me. That would make you feel depressed, and you're depressed enough as it is."

Aric smiled in spite of his exasperation, exhaustion, concern, and sadness. Literal, sex-loving, pragmatic Chelsea was back.

"No intercourse for six weeks," Dr. Levine proclaimed. "Even then, you'll need to be cleared for sexual activity by one of the team first."

"Can Aric touch me as long as he doesn't enter me?"

"Yes."

"Good. And I can still touch him and take him in my mouth?"

Levine's face was suddenly flaming red, and she seemed torn between amusement and shock. Finally, she grinned and agreed that those things would be fine as long as Chelsea was careful not to overexert herself.

"I'm going to go order that cup of ice chips for you," the doctor said as she headed for the door. "I'll tell the others to wait outside a little longer to give you two some time alone."

Chapter Thirty-nine

"So, what does your intuition tell you about Dr. Leah Levine?" Aric asked once the physician had left the room.

"She seems completely honest. I like her. I liked the other doctors who were in the room, too. They actually seemed to care."

"Good. I'm still leery of all the government doctors, but I feel somewhat reassured by this new group."

"You watched the recordings of my surgery, didn't you?"

Aric looked away and nodded.

"And you saw the fetal tissue?"

"Yes."

"In person?"

"Yes."

Chelsea placed her hands on either side of his face, turned his head until he was looking at her, and said, "My poor, sweet man. That must have been terrible for you."

"It was, but I had to do it."

"I know. Did the tissue really look just like a bunch of tissue or did it look like a baby?"

"Mostly tissue."

"Mostly?"

"I saw an eye and...and a tiny hand in random locations. I had to leave after that. I don't have the report, yet."

"Oh, Aric," Chelsea said as her eyes filled with tears. "You want to know if it had a brain and was suffering, don't you?"

He said nothing. Chelsea urged him to bend and kiss her, then rubbed at his back for a while. He murmured that he loved her and had been so afraid she would die.

"I have no intention of dying anytime soon, but I am hungry, tired, and sore." Looking around, she asked, "Where is Paula?"

"At the hotel. She and Jason and others have been taking turns watching over us. Paula stayed with you during the surgery and afterward in Recovery."

"That must have been hard for her. She *hates* medical stuff. She won't even watch medical programs on TV that show lots of blood. Was there a lot of blood during my surgery?"

"Lots."

"Poor Paula. I'm glad she went back to the hotel. Promise me *you'll* get some sleep," Chelsea urged. "You and Jason both look awful. Nadine looks bad, too. Who else has been here with us?"

"Maurice flew in the same night you were brought to the hospital. He finally went back to the hotel earlier today."

"Buddy hasn't been here long."

Aric looked quizzically at her and asked her how she knew that.

"His clothes aren't all wrinkled, and he looks well-rested and clean-shaven." She paused then added, "I don't think he and Nadine have a good marriage."

"I believe they used to before their girls died."

"So, why do they stay together?"

"It's complicated. Could we talk about it later? You need to rest."

That evening, Maurice and Paula stayed with Chelsea while Aric, Jason, and Nadine went to the hotel to rest. Aric spoke to Lakshmi once he was in his suite and updated her on Chelsea's progress. She seemed relieved, but he knew that she remained worried and disapproved of his viewing of the recordings and being present for part of the dissection. He refused her suggestion that Jason sleep in the same room with him and promised he wouldn't harm himself.

"Do me a favor then," Lakshmi said. "Leave the doors open between your suite and the one being shared by Agents Duson and Jennings. It would make me feel better."

Too tired to argue, he agreed and told her he was going to bed. She bid him goodnight and said she'd come to see him and Chelsea as soon as her schedule allowed. He told her they would both be looking forward to it.

After offering Jason a brief explanation regarding Lakshmi's request that he leave the door between their suites open, Aric donned his pajama bottoms and a t-shirt, brushed his teeth, and fell into bed. It felt so good to lie prone after days of restless sleep in a hospital chair. He could barely keep his eyes open, but he lay awake for a while and thought of how odd it was to be alone in the bed. He missed his wife lying beside him.

He slept fitfully and had disturbing dreams. Some involved the deaths of his family. One involved his own affliction and survival of the D Plague. A few detailed the repugnant Michel LeClerc's abuse of Chelsea's trust and the taking of her virginity. Several highlighted a young and innocent Chelsea offering her body to powerful men at LeClerc's direction.

Each time Aric woke from one of these nightmares, he vowed to get up but was simply too tired. He needed sleep but couldn't find peace. It seemed as though the night would never end as he dreamed and woke, dreamed and woke....

Aric finally came fully awake at 9:00 a.m. He got out of bed and padded to the living area of the suite. He was surprised to see Jason stretched out on the couch, wearing jeans and a sweater as he read a book. When he raised an eyebrow at the FBI agent, Jason said, "You were talking in your sleep. At first, I thought someone had gotten past Security and was in here. Scared the shit out of me. Instead, I found you alone, asleep, and threatening to kill Michel LeClerc. I tried to go back to bed, but you kept waking me up."

"Chelsea told me not too long ago that I talked in my sleep. My family never mentioned it. None of my previous partners ever said anything about it. I guess I only started doing it after everyone was gone, but I wasn't sleeping with anyone and didn't know about that."

"You should've said something to me before. If you had, then I never would've told you about Michel LeClerc prostituting Chelsea to his business associates. If you haven't already nocturnally spilled the beans, then you will eventually."

"Damn it!" Aric snapped. "That never occurred to me."

"You can't think of everything. You've had a lot on your mind for the last five years, especially the last few months."

"What did I say while I was sleeping at the hospital?"

"When?"

"You know when. When I got out of the chair and you had me in some sort of hold and Nadine was freaking out. What did I say that was so upsetting to her?"

Jason closed the book, which turned out to be an old David Baldacci novel, and placed it on the coffee table beside him. He sat up slowly and rested his elbows on his knees then stared at his hands before stating, "You said something about poor baby Aric and prayed that he would die quickly. You said he'd be going to a place where there would be no more pain and that you wished you were able to go with him. I thought Mrs. LaFleur was going to come unhinged. When you got out of the chair and started walking toward the door, she swore you were going off to kill yourself. I didn't believe that, but I did know that I had to stop you from walking around in your sleep. My hand on your arm did nothing to slow you down, so I put a little muscle into my efforts and grabbed you. That's when you woke up."

"Where is Nadine now?"

"In her rooms with the Vice-President. She knows she'll have to resume her duties now that Chelsea's going to recover. She'll probably be on the phone with her every day."

"I'm fine with that. Nadine's changed since she met Chelsea. She was always kind of stand-offish around me until Chelsea became part of my life."

Jason's phone buzzed, and he removed it from the pocket of his jeans. He listened for a minute then swore and said grudgingly, "Go ahead. I'm in Mr. Rodrigue's suite."

"Problem?"

"Yes. I apologize, but I'm going to use you as an excuse. Play along with me. Okay?"

Aric was intrigued. Jason was not in the habit of making excuses. He wondered why the man would need one now. He didn't have to wonder for long. Julian Duson, Jason's older brother, was soon standing in the living room of Aric's suite.

Julian was tall with light brown hair and sharp brown eyes. His stature and bearing were impressive and intimidating, and Aric was reminded of Michel LeClerc's photo. The words "powerful, calculating, and remorseless" came to mind as he studied the man. Although he and Jason shared a strong resemblance, Aric knew that they were nothing alike. He instantly loathed Julian and could see why Nadine would insist that he not be around her or her children.

"What do you want, Julian?" Jason asked tightly.

"I got the papers regarding Gran's estate."

"And?"

"And I don't give a fuck that she left everything to you. I don't need what little money and property she had. I have plenty of my own. Dad left me the security firm."

"Yeah, yeah. Dad liked you best, and Mom liked me best. Gran liked me better than she liked you, but that was only because I took after her and Mom and had a heart and a conscience. Too bad you took after Dad."

Ouch, Aric thought. As he tried to gauge Julian's reaction he realized, *He doesn't care. I think he's pleased with what Jason said. God, how do people get like this? Was he born that way or did he become like this?*

"You came all the way to Atlanta to tell me how you don't care about Gran's estate?" Jason asked his brother. "I doubt that."

"No, I happened to be in town and wanted to drop by and tell you to fuck off."

"Mission accomplished. I have work to do."

Julian looked at Aric and said, "Oh, that's right. You're a secretary for Mr. Rodrigue. And Mom always said you were so smart. Well, who owns his own company and who's a secretary?"

"Who saves the world every day and who likes to rape and pillage it?"

"I don't typically rape or pillage," Julian said coolly. "I just protect those who do. It's a very lucrative business."

"You'll burn in Hell someday for everything you've done."

"I think Hell's always gotten a bad rap. We sinners have a lot more fun than you saints."

When he made to leave, Aric said, "Wait."

Obviously surprised, Julian stopped and turned. He was attempting to look bored, but Aric could sense his interest. He made the man stand where he was while he went back to the bedroom and retrieved his phone. After quickly scrolling through the pictures stored on it, Aric found the one he wanted and returned to the living room. Holding out the phone to Julian, he asked, "Did you ever protect anyone who had sex with this girl?"

Jason stiffened but kept quiet. Julian looked at the picture of sixteen year-old Chelsea for a long time then said, "Yes."

"Who?"

"That's confidential. I can't tell you."

"Did they know she was a minor at the time?"

"Of course. That was part of the appeal." Handing the phone back to Aric, he said, "I can't tell you who my clients were, but I can tell you that I protected two of the men who slept with her before she turned eighteen. They told me she was the best fuck they'd ever had." When Aric blanched, Julian laughed and said, "Later." Then he was gone.

"What in Heaven's name happened to him?" Aric muttered. "Was he always such a prick?"

"Yes. Our father wasn't quite as bad as Julian's become, but they were definitely cut from the same cloth. Gran couldn't stand either of them. Why Mom married Dad I'll never know. Julian was her greatest disappointment, and I was her greatest success. That was always a huge thorn in my brother's side. I guess it still is."

"Thank God you're nothing like him."

"I do that every day." Walking toward his rooms, he suggested, "Why don't you get dressed. We'll eat and go back to the hospital."

"Jason?"

"Yeah?"

Did you consider my idea about you working for me?"

The man grinned and declared formally, "When all of this is over, I would be proud to be your secretary."

Aric grinned back before heading for the shower.

Chapter Forty

"You can't do this!" Nadine insisted furiously. "Aric, you could die!"

"I doubt if anything could kill me."

"Don't be flippant," she shot back. "You don't know what will happen."

"Probably nothing. No drugs have worked on me since my bout with the D Plague. This may have no effect on me either."

"Or it could kill you! No one knows how your body will react. What if you die? What would Chelsea do then?"

Mentally groaning, Aric said, "Chelsea was with me when Dr. Levine proposed this. She agreed I should try it. If, on the off-chance I should die, then I know you, Jason, and Paula will take good care of her."

"But –"

"Nadine, I'm a grown man and am going to do this! I appreciate your concern, but it's my decision!"

Dr. Levine approached the woman and said, "We need to attempt this, Mrs. LaFleur. The other team studied Mr. Rodrigue for over five years. No medication seems to work on his post-Plague body. Alcohol does have some effect, so that's promising. However, no one has ever tried anesthesia on him. We need to know if it will work or not."

"Why? Give me one good reason!"

"I can give you several. Car accidents. Muggings. Falls. Anything that might require surgery. Would you rather we not try this and perform something like a triple bypass on him someday without the benefit of anesthesia or painkillers? We have to know if anything is effective."

Nadine looked panicked but nodded. Aric relaxed slightly. He was uncomfortable with the unknown, the uncertainty of what might happen to him during this medical experiment, but he agreed that it would be foolhardy not to try. He had no desire to wait and see what might occur should he need surgery at some point in the future. The thought of undergoing any invasive procedure without anesthesia was nauseating.

"Why don't you go sit with Chelsea in her room?" Aric suggested to Nadine. "Jason will be with me during this little test."

"Please, Mrs. LaFleur," the doctor prodded. "We'll let you know as soon as we're done."

Nadine reluctantly went with a member of her Secret Service detail toward the elevators. It had been three days since Aric's wife had been moved from the Critical Care Unit to a regular room. If she continued to do well, then she would soon be flying back to New Orleans with Aric, Jason, and Paula. Forced to leave the day after Chelsea had awakened in order to deal with some issues at Moreau's, Maurice called to check on the state of affairs each afternoon. Lakshmi phoned as often as possible. Aric was thankful for the long-distance support.

"You sure you're up for this?" Jason asked as Aric was prepped in the Pre-Op Unit. "You could still back out."

"No, I can't. I'll be curious to see the digital recordings of the surgery after it's all done."

"I'll be watching over you."

"I know. That's part of why I agreed to this."

Jason gave him a small smile and said, "See you later, Alligator."

"After while, Crocodile."

Since nothing else had worked in the past, Aric was fully prepared for the anesthesia to have no measurable effect on him. Therefore, he was surprised to find himself waking up groggy and sore with Jason by his side.

"It worked?"

"Like a charm. You were out as soon as the anesthesiologist started to put you under. I think all the doctors in the room breathed a collective sigh of relief."

"Then what?"

"Then they did what they set out to do. They inserted several needles into you and took tissue samples. Once they were certain you weren't going to come out from under the anesthesia, they made an incision on your right side and removed your appendix."

"Why? Was it inflamed?"

"No. They said they wanted something significant to study that might give them insight about how your body was working and the cells and all. You don't need your appendix, so they took that.

Again, they were relieved you didn't wake during the operation. It was kind of entertaining to see how excited they got about you not coming around. I heard several of them say that they've been very concerned about what might happen if you were seriously hurt and couldn't have anesthesia. I guess your experiment today was a hit."

"I'm glad, but now I hurt like hell where they stuck me and cut out my appendix. Too bad painkillers don't work on me. Maybe I should ask for a beer."

"In this case we might just oblige," Dr. Levine said as she came over to the bed. "I'm sorry you're in pain. I want to give you a painkiller you've never had before and see if it helps. If not, then at least you can rest assured that you'll heal at an abnormally fast rate. You'll most likely be fully recovered by tomorrow. Your cells are still amazingly healthy and resilient. We're thrilled to be able to examine your appendix."

"I'm glad I didn't let the members of the old team operate on me. They probably would have taken my kidneys, pancreas, liver, stomach, intestines, brain, and heart for study."

Levine sobered and said, "Probably." Holding out a cup that contained one bright red pill, she said, "Try this."

"What is it?"

As the doctor detailed the physical properties of the medication, Jason looked on blankly. Aric, with his medical background and work in pharmaceutical development, understood every word and was intrigued. This painkiller was traditional but with an unusual chemical twist.

"The success rate on normal human beings is 100% in our trials," Levine confided. "That includes a diverse group of adults ranging in age from eighteen to ninety-one."

"Side effects?"

"The usual. 1% suffered from upset stomach, diarrhea, headache, blah, blah, blah. I will tell you that this medication was used in tests with your samples and showed no detrimental results. If it had, then I wouldn't be suggesting you try it."

Aric shifted in the bed and winced. He was in a notable amount of pain and did want relief. He took the pill, and Levine and Jason sat in chairs near the bed.

"You're going to wait with me?" Aric asked the physician.

"Of course. You're my top priority. I want to monitor you and draw blood from the line every five minutes whether you feel the medication is having any impact on your pain or not. It may help us learn how to help you better in the future."

After twenty minutes, Aric said, "The pain is easing somewhat."

Levine was instantly on her feet, her eyes bright with excitement. She asked Aric to describe how he felt.

"Kind of sleepy. A bit light-headed. It feels like I'm drunk."

The doctor lowered the head of the bed and called for the other members of the team. Aric asked her if something was wrong.

"Not at all. This is a very positive result. Most people were unconscious within a few minutes. The drug's taking a little longer to work on you, but at least it seems to be working."

"Oh. Good. I want to sleep now."

"Then sleep."

He slept. When he woke, someone was holding his hand. His first thought was that it was Chelsea, but Aric quickly realized that it couldn't be her. She was still relegated to bed rest and wouldn't be allowed to come to wherever he was. He squeezed the hand and was rewarded with a return squeeze.

When he was finally able to pry his eyes open and turn his head, Aric saw Nadine LaFleur seated beside him. She smiled with relief and thanked God that he was all right. He told her that she worried too much. As he drifted back to sleep, he imagined he heard her say, "I've earned the right to worry too much after losing four children."

Four…? he thought hazily. *Did she say four? She only had three girls…*

He slept again and woke feeling perfectly fine. Dr. Levine appeared with her team and performed a complete examination, along with several scans, and then she requested more blood work. The medical personnel were awed by Aric's quick recovery. His surgery had taken place only twelve hours earlier, but his wounds had almost completely healed. He was no longer in any pain. He was wide-awake and ready to get out of bed and go to Chelsea's room. The doctors agreed to this, but only if he promised to lie on the couch there and rest for the next twelve hours. They would check on him periodically, draw more blood during that time, and then make a final determination as to whether or not he was deemed healed.

When Aric walked into Chelsea's room with Jason, his wife practically squealed with delight and opened her arms to him. He carefully leaned over and kissed her, and then he did as the disapproving nurse ordered and took his position on the couch.

Paula, who was seated in the chair beside Chelsea's bed, asked, "Do you need anything, Aric?"

"No thanks. I'm fine." Shocked to realize that he was disappointed that Nadine was not in the room waiting for him, he asked, "Where's Nadine? I figured she'd be with Chelsea."

"She and the Vice-President are having it out in a lounge somewhere," Paula said quietly. "He's demanding she stop shirking her duties as the wife of the Vice-President, and she's telling him that the lives of people one loves are more important than public appearances. They were getting pretty vocal in here and were asked by the nurses to take their discussion somewhere more private. Mrs. LaFleur is quite the spitfire."

As if on cue, Nadine burst into the room. She glanced frantically around, but then she instantly relaxed once she saw Aric lying on the couch. She gave him a brief smile then went over and kissed Chelsea on the forehead, took her hand, and announced that she was going to have to leave the following morning for D.C.

"I'd like to drop by your house during the Christmas holidays when Buddy and I are in Louisiana," she added. "Perhaps we could celebrate together, although it may not be on Christmas Day. I'm not sure of our exact schedule, yet."

"Would you decorate the tree with us?" asked Chelsea. "I don't remember decorating a Christmas tree before. Maybe we could string popcorn, and Aric and I could take turns playing Christmas carols on the piano."

"That would be divine. Buddy and I really haven't had much in the way of Christmas spirit since we lost our daughters. It would be nice to try to recapture it." Brushing some hair away from Chelsea's face, she said gently, "You call me any time before then. I love our talks."

"I will. Me, too. Be safe."

Nadine smiled at the younger woman and bent to hug her. Then, she came around the bed and sat on the edge of the couch beside Aric. He looked up at her and waited for her to speak. She brushed the fingertips of one hand across his forehead and said softly but firmly, "You be good and take care of yourself and our girl, you understand? Christmas is only a couple of weeks away. I want you both well by then."

"We'll do our best. You're pretty demanding, you know that?"

"So I've been told."

Chapter Forty-one

Once Nadine had departed, Aric looked over at Chelsea and asked, "What do you want for Christmas?"

"I want to be home at your house."

"Chelsea, it's *our* house."

"Okay, I want to be home at *our* house. I have everything I need. I've got you, Paula, Jason, Nadine, a roof over my head, clothes to wear, food to eat, my computer and phone, the piano, and my routine." Sighing, she said, "I'll have to modify my routine for a while. The doctors say I can't do my exercises for a whole month and can't kneel to chant. After that, I have to be careful. I don't want to be careful. I was feeling so strong."

"You'll get there again," Paula said encouragingly. "Think of it as a holiday break. You can still do some stretching, remember? The doctors showed me how to help you do that. As for your chanting, you can chant at home for now in a chair until you can get back to the Buddhist Temple to chant every morning. Other than that, you'll have to content yourself with reading and being on the computer."

"It's a good thing she's addicted to both," Jason muttered under his breath. Then he said more loudly, "You could probably play the piano as soon as we get home. Ask your doctors before we leave."

As the others spoke of Chelsea's restrictions and approved activities, Aric was struck by her complete lack of a desire for material goods. True, she adored her computer and phone and the piano and would be sad if they were taken away. However, other than that, she appeared totally unconcerned about owning anything. For a woman who'd supposedly been fortunate enough to grow up having every privilege and convenience, Chelsea didn't appear to desire material possessions.

She doesn't recall her life before the accident. Is that why she doesn't care about owning things? Or is it some buried remnant of having had those things but learning that they'd come at the cost of her father's life and her innocence at the hands of Michel LeClerc? Is it because she found Buddhism after she ran away and adopted the attitude that worldly possessions were of no consequence in the scheme of one's true intentions?

Aric stopped trying to figure it out. Chelsea may not care, but he wanted to give her some meaningful gift for Christmas. He wanted some semblance of his pre-Plague holiday celebrations. He needed to think of what he should get Jason, Paula, Maurice, Lakshmi, Buddy, and Nadine. He smiled. He was not really certain if he even believed in God anymore, and he was trying to figure out what to give his Buddhist wife, Hindu ex-lover, and Christian friends for the Christmas holiday.

"Aric, what do *you* want for Christmas?" Chelsea asked suddenly.

"You know how I love anticipation. I'll look forward to being surprised."

"I'm sure I can manage something," she said mischievously. "After all, I have lots of extra time on my hands."

"*That* could be dangerous," Aric said with a smile. "Behave, Chelsea."

He was declared completely recovered from his surgery later that night. Paula and Jason returned to the hotel to rest, leaving Agent Imahara and a male FBI agent Aric had never met standing at the door to Chelsea's room. Aric opted to sleep on the couch, which was actually comfortable. If he couldn't sleep with Chelsea, then at least he could sleep near Chelsea.

The sound of his wife calling his name roused Aric from a disturbing dream regarding the dissection of the fetal tissue. His heart pounding from the remembered feeling of revulsion and fear, he opened his eyes and asked Chelsea what was wrong.

"I need one of my pills," she moaned. "My head hurts so badly."

Going over to the bed, he asked, "Why didn't you wake me sooner?"

"Because you had surgery yesterday and needed to rest. I know they said you were better but –"

She broke off and moaned then begged him for a pill. Knowing how she was going to react, he steeled himself in preparation for her tears and told her, "No."

"N-no?" she stammered. "But why not?"

"Because Dr. Levine and her team asked me not to if you developed a migraine while you were in the hospital. They want to see what's happening as your migraine occurs, so they can try to work on a drug that will help you without things escalating and requiring the addition of massage."

She began to cry and begged him for a pill as he pressed the Call Button. Kissing her temple and taking her hands in his, he told her, "No," and apologized. In the few seconds he had before the doctors flooded the room, he explained that this was something that needed to be done and asked her to trust him.

Whimpering, Chelsea said, "I do. I won't ask for a pill again tonight."

Over the course of the next few grueling hours, Chelsea was examined by multiple doctors, subjected to brain scans, and given a ground-breaking migraine medication the CDC had developed. Unfortunately, it had no effect on her. Aric stayed with her throughout the ordeal and held her off and on as she cried, vomited, and shook with pain. Finally, she was given one of the pills she normally took, and Aric was asked to perform the massage that typically brought about an end to the migraines. However, after thirty minutes of his usual ministrations, Chelsea was showing no signs of relief.

"It's been too long," he said grimly. "She usually takes a pill at the onset of the migraine; then I perform the massage Olga taught me as soon as possible. Afterward, she sleeps deeply, but then wakes pain-free. This time, everything's been delayed for hours."

The neurologist sighed and said, "I agree. We had to do this, but I think you're right about the result. We're going to have to give her something to render her unconscious."

"No!" Chelsea protested as vehemently as she could. "I hate that! Please, Aric. Don't let them do that."

"They need to, Chere. Your blood pressure's pretty high. If it keeps climbing, you could have a stroke. I'm sorry."

"I don't like it when anyone makes me go to sleep in a hospital while I'm having a migraine."

"Why not? You'll wake up without a headache."

She startled him by beginning to sob. Attempting to soothe her, he stroked her hair and asked her why she was so terrified.

"Because when they did that in the hospital and rehab facility, I'd wake up sometimes and…and…and I'd know that someone had…violated me. I didn't remember what sex was like, but I knew what it was. I could feel that someone had used me while I was unconscious. I felt so sick and dirty afterward. Please don't let them do that to me again."

Aric struggled to process this information and knew that the others present were also stunned. He managed to tell Chelsea that he was not going to leave her alone and unprotected for a minute while she was unconscious, and the doctors hastened to reassure her as well.

"We'll see to it that there's a full investigation of the hospital and rehab facility where you were treated after your accident. The digital recordings in each room should show if someone harmed you," the neurologist pointed out. "If they did, then their careers are over and they'll be prosecuted."

"Everything was erased except the highlights in her main file," Aric pointed out. "No assaults were on that. I watched all of it."

As one of the nurses injected something into his wife's I.V. line, Chelsea asked Aric, "How can you want me after what Michel LeClerc did to me and how he had me sleep with those other men? I was raped before the accident then used by the people at the hospital. You saw the mass and know now it was growing inside me. How hideous. How can you want me?"

"Oh, Chere. I've been talking in my sleep, haven't I?"

She nodded, tears streaming down her cheeks. He kissed the wet skin and told her that he would always want and love her. He reminded Chelsea that she'd been a vulnerable child who'd been used by LeClerc. He insisted he wasn't disgusted by her but was enraged by the behavior of her adoptive father and the other men.

"As for the growing mass of fetal tissue, it's my fault."

"It's not," she protested as she began to sink into unconsciousness. "It just happened. It should have been our baby...."

Once the team of doctors had left the room, Aric asked Agent Imahara to sit beside Chelsea and guard her while he took a walk. The other FBI agent followed him to a deserted office. Aric stepped inside, closed and locked the door, and then sat in the desk chair in the darkened room.

Our baby, he thought, remembering the tiny eye and little hand that had been part of the malformed mass. *Our baby.*

Aric withdrew his phone from his pants pocket. He didn't hesitate to give it the verbal command to phone Nadine LaFleur.

He'd added her number after Chelsea's health crisis. When she answered, he asked, "Are you free to talk for a few minutes?"

"Of course. Aric, what's wrong? Is Chelsea okay?"

He explained about the migraine and what had transpired during the previous several hours. Swallowing hard, he told her of Chelsea's disclosure that she'd been used for sex by some of the medical personnel at the Orlando hospital and rehab facility when they'd drugged her during her migraine attacks. Nadine's fury was palpable.

"She asked me how I could want her after LeClerc's molestation, the molestation of her by the other men, the rape before the accident, the later assaults, and knowing...seeing what had been developing inside of her. I tried to reassure her before the medication knocked her out, but I don't know if she believes me. How can I convince her that I want her no matter how she was hurt? It wasn't like she wanted any of that to happen. I hate that it did more than anything, but I separate my love and desire for her from all of that. What more can I do?"

"I don't have an answer for you. Perhaps something will come to me. Chelsea's situation is unique. The poor child has been so treasured and so damaged, but she remembers none of it. Plus, she's still missing those three years and doesn't know what triggered the rape, the accident, and the deaths of those other doctors who saved her life. That weighs heavily on her. As a woman, I'm sure she feels like she's let you down by allowing herself to be abused."

"But she didn't *allow* any of it!"

"I know that, and so do you. It's different for her. She has no frame of reference, Aric. Maybe you could talk to her psychiatrist?"

"I'll have to. I have permission from Chelsea to talk to the woman at any time. I've already spoken to her once since Chelsea's surgery."

"Call her again. Perhaps you could talk to her about your own feelings, too."

"What good would that do?"

"Aric, you've been chronically depressed since the D Plague, yet you constantly refuse professional help. I myself have suffered from depression since I was in my late teens. I know how badly you need a therapist or medication, and you can't take anti-depressants."

"Chelsea is the best therapy for me."

"I understand that. The moment I saw her that first time…saw the two of you together…I realized that you were doing better than you had been since 2029. She's your miracle. The problem is that she can't always be your miracle. Take a look at yourself right this minute. Chelsea is incapacitated, and you sound so depressed. You're under a lot of stress, and who knows when that will end? On top of everything, you push yourself to your limits physically and emotionally."

"I can handle it."

"Can you?" she demanded. "How stressful was it for you to watch the recordings of Chelsea's surgery, see her die on the table, and see the mass removed? How unbearable for you to see part of the dissection of your baby."

"It wasn't a baby. It was fetal tissue."

"It was a baby gone wrong, and you are so blaming yourself. You should never have seen it. I wish you'd listened to me. You keep going on and on about Chelsea needing to let go of feeling sullied by her sexual abuse by men, but you shoulder the blame for unwittingly fathering a baby that was destined never to be born."

"Nadine, please stop."

"No. You need to hear this. You grew up with a big, loving family, and I know you wanted to find the right woman, get married, and have lots of children someday. From what Chelsea told me, you both have made your peace with choosing not to have a family because of your physical condition and Chelsea's brain injury. You'd accepted it. Then this happened. What those other doctors did to the two of you was unforgivable. At least you know it will never happen again, but it can't take away the memory of your child's existence. You have to allow yourself to grieve for it and for the lost opportunity it represents."

"Nadine, I told you it wasn't a child. It was fetal tissue."

"I saw photos, Aric. I know you and know you can't get the image of the hand and eye out of your head. It should have been a normal baby, and you blame yourself for its abnormal growth and development and the fact that its existence almost killed Chelsea. Please, don't."

"It didn't have a brain, thank goodness," he said softly. "At least it wasn't suffering."

"*What* wasn't suffering?" Nadine pressed him.

"Our baby," he whispered. "At least our baby wasn't suffering."

He covered his mouth with one hand and muffled his sobs as Nadine said soothing words to him and promised him that it would get easier as the days passed. He would never forget, but the loss would become less biting over time. He cried until he was spent and thanked Nadine for helping him even though he was resistant to help.

"You called me, Aric. You were calling for help. I would never refuse you or Chelsea anything. I've made some major mistakes in my life, and I don't want to make any more blunders if I can avoid them. I told you that when Buddy and I first came to your house, I felt as though God had given me a second chance. I don't intend to blow it. I told Chelsea to call me anytime, and that offer extends to you as well. Remember that."

"I will."

"Rest and take care of yourself and your wife."

"I'll try. You get some rest, too. Take care, Nadine."

"Take care, Aric. Forgive yourself for being a survivor."

Chapter Forty-two

Aric sat on the couch in the Creole House and held his wife in his lap. A roaring fire crackled in the double-sided fireplace, and wonderful smells were wafting from the kitchen into the living area. Paula and Jason were chatting and laughing as they cooked the Christmas dinner. A huge fir tree stood barren in one corner of the main room.

Chelsea, who wore a long blue dress but no shoes, nuzzled one cheek against Aric's chest and asked, "What time is it?"

Hugging her a little more tightly to him, he replied, "Almost 5:00. Nadine will be arriving soon."

His wife hadn't been herself since the night she'd had the migraine in the hospital. Chelsea had awakened from her drugged state; terrified that someone had sexually assaulted her, and it had taken Aric almost an hour to calm her down and convince her she hadn't been left alone while unconscious. Even once she'd been reassured, she remained fearful and begged Aric to have sex with her, so she could feel as though she was in control again. He'd reminded her they couldn't have sex for several more weeks because of her surgery, and then she'd become hysterical. The doctors had finally insisted on giving her a mild sedative in order to help her relax. It had worked, but she'd been forced to remain on the medication continually ever since despite engaging in a virtual session with her psychiatrist and then several visits to the woman's office after they'd returned to New Orleans.

"Sex is Chelsea's ultimate coping mechanism," the psychiatrist had told Aric when they'd met alone after one of her sessions with his wife. "Until you're able to successfully have intercourse again, she's going to need the medication."

"What do you mean by successfully?"

"Chelsea has been the victim of sexual abuse for almost half of her life. The fact that she doesn't remember participating in it doesn't mean she's not greatly affected by it. She's lost this potential child she'd never expected in the first place, and on top of that, now she has no reproductive organs. Many women associate those organs with their womanhood. All of this combined is definitely having an impact on her self-image, which was still developing due to her loss of identity after the accident in 2033. She's not only afraid you won't want her; she's also afraid *she* won't want her. Understand?"

"Sort of."

"Keep giving her reassurances that you love and want her. Call me if you get stuck and don't know what to do."

Aric had followed the psychiatrist's advice. Every weekday when he was at work, he'd texted or called Chelsea at random times to talk and declare his love and desire for her. She'd responded but in a rather lackluster fashion. Paula confided to Aric that Chelsea seemed anxious and depressed most of the time and hadn't played the piano, been on her computer, or done much reading while the men were at Rodrigue Pharmaceuticals. Whenever they were at home, Chelsea spent most of her time clinging to Aric, although she'd made no move to touch him in any sexual way. The entire state of affairs made Aric feel helpless.

What if she doesn't come out of this? He wondered. *I can't stand to watch her be frightened and sad all the time.*

There was a knock on the front door, and Paula hastened to answer it. Nadine entered with several members of her entourage in tow. They were carrying bags and boxes and did as Nadine directed by placing them near the fir tree before exiting the house. Nadine removed her coat and gloves and handed them to Jason before coming over to sit on the edge of the wooden coffee table. She rested a hand on one side of Chelsea's head and greeted her and Aric. Chelsea didn't move or reply.

"Oh, Sweetheart," Nadine said softly. "You've lost a lot of weight since I saw you in Atlanta a couple of weeks ago."

"I'm not very hungry," Chelsea said in a small voice. "I was so hungry before when I was…when I…when I had the…the mass growing inside me."

"When you were pregnant."

"Aric and the doctors said it wasn't a baby."

"What do you think?"

Chelsea answered tearfully, "I think it was a baby that didn't develop properly. I think I was pregnant, and no one except my psychiatrist will let me say that. I want to talk about it, but Aric's already so depressed about everything that I don't want to make him worse."

Nadine stood and said resolutely, "You come with me to your room so we can talk. I've lost all my children, and it helps to be able to verbalize how you're feeling so you can heal."

Chelsea went with the older woman, while Aric stayed on the couch. Jason and Paula seemed uncomfortable and returned to the kitchen. Aric stared into the fire and knew that he and Nadine were about to have a huge argument.

"What are you doing?" she demanded once she returned alone from the master suite. "That poor girl is grieving over the loss of your baby, and you're not doing anything to help her!"

"Not doing anything? I've talked to the psychiatrist both with and without her and have talked to Chelsea and tried to be as supportive as possible. I call her off and on all day when I'm at work and spend most of my time at home attempting to comfort her. This isn't just about the mass of tissue, Nadine!"

"No, but that's an enormous part of it! Did you ask her if she wanted a funeral?"

"A funeral for what?" he shouted. "The...the pieces of tissue?"

In his mind, he envisioned the small eye and small hand and thought of perfectly formed unborn baby Aric dying during the D Plague. Two potential lives that were never meant to be. He hadn't had a funeral for little Aric either.

"Aric, lower your voice," Nadine hissed. "Chelsea's resting. Come outside with me for a while."

"It's dark and cold."

"We both have coats, and neither of us is afraid of the dark."

They were soon sitting on the swing that Aric had made with his grandfather so many years earlier. Nadine tentatively reached out and took Aric's right hand, and he allowed her to hold it in both of hers. She asked him if he remembered their phone conversation when he'd called her from the hospital after Chelsea's migraine episode. When he replied that he did, she asked him why he was regressing?

"You admitted that what the doctors removed from Chelsea was a baby. Tonight, you're back to calling it tissue. Did you change your mind?"

"No. It just hurts too much to think about what I saw."

"What you never should have seen. You're so bull-headed!"

"Yes, I am. And so are you."

"You won't get any arguments from me there."

They sat in silence for several minutes before Aric asked, "How can I help Chelsea? What did you do that made her feel better?"

"I did what I would have done with my daughters. I held her and told her to give it time and that I'd always be there for her. I let her talk without interrupting or trying to rephrase what she was saying. I told her to talk to you and to tell you what she needed because men were just plain dense a lot of the time. That got a smile out of her. It was good to see." Dropping her head, she said, "It's so rewarding being with Chelsea, but it saddens me, too. I should be doing things with my three girls. I should be celebrating their graduations, accomplishments at work, engagements, weddings, babies, and comforting them during life's tragedies. Thank God for antidepressants. I've been on them for so long. The ones I take now are actually made by your company. They work better than any others I've used previously. I do continue to struggle with depression, but I function well and talk regularly with my therapist."

"What made you start taking antidepressants in the first place?"

"I lost a baby. I was young and thought I could move on, but I couldn't. I tried to kill myself, and my family didn't understand. They did get me some professional help. I started taking the antidepressants. It was such a relief to feel human again."

"I wish I had that option. I didn't know that you and Buddy had lost a child before the girls."

"We didn't. It was before I met Buddy. He doesn't even know about my baby. You're the first person I've told besides my therapists since it happened."

Aric wondered how he should respond to such an admission. He felt both honored and confused. He also questioned the LaFleur marriage. How good could it have been from the start if Nadine had never told her husband that she'd lost a baby before they'd met?

Unsure as to whether or not he was overstepping his bounds, he asked hesitantly, "How far along were you when you lost your baby?"

"My baby was full-term."

Aric was heartsick for her. What had happened to him and Chelsea was horrible, but what had happened to Nadine was perhaps even worse. He tried to imagine a woman carrying a healthy baby for nine months and then having it die right before or during birth.

He wondered if the child's father had been there with Nadine to share her grief and comfort her or whether she'd suffered through the loss alone.

Nadine looked up at Aric and said, "I don't think I can talk about my baby anymore tonight. It's Christmas, and you need to go figure out how to make things right for you and your wife. This should be a happy time. You go, and I'll attempt to help Paula and Jason in the kitchen."

Once she'd returned to the main house, Aric went through the French doors into the cottage and found Chelsea lying on her side on top of the bed staring at nothing in particular. He removed his coat and draped it over the desk chair. Then he slipped off his shoes, climbed onto the bed, and spooned his body against hers. She didn't react. Lightly draping one arm around her waist, he kissed her neck and asked, "May I touch you?"

"If you want," she replied dully.

Aric moved his hand and covered the place where her scar was located. Chelsea stiffened and asked him what he was doing.

"I don't know. I want to touch you all over, but I wanted to start here."

"Why?"

"Because I wanted to know that I wouldn't hurt you if I did. Is it sore?"

"A tiny bit."

"Talk to me about the baby."

"I thought you said it wasn't a baby."

"Technically, it wasn't. It was a mass of fetal tissue. I can't help but think of it as a baby though."

"Me neither. I feel so badly because you saw it."

"Nadine tried to stop me, but I wouldn't listen. I needed to make sure the government people weren't lying again."

"I want to have a funeral for our baby."

"How? We don't have anything to bury."

"We should go to Tante's shop tomorrow and ask her. She'll know what to do."

"If you think it will help."

"I do."

"Then we'll go, assuming she's open the day after Christmas."

Chelsea breathed what sounded like a sigh of relief and murmured, "Thank you. I need this, and I think you do, too."

Aric wasn't sure what either of them needed, but he seemed to have nothing else to offer and was desperate to help his wife in any way he could. He thought of Nadine's confession to him about her lost baby and wondered why she'd shared that with him and not with Chelsea. He decided it was futile to try to understand women. He put aside all of his troubling thoughts and slid his hand lower.

Chapter Forty-three

"Aric, what are you doing?" Chelsea asked, as he eased her onto her back.

"I need to make love to you, and I need you to make love to me."

"But the doctors said we can't have sex for at least another two weeks."

"Dr. Levine said we could touch as long as we were careful."

"You want to touch me?"

"Oh, Chere. Of course. I love and want you more than anything else in this world."

"After everything I've done?"

"What have you done?"

"Had sex with lots of men."

"Because you were manipulated or assaulted. I wish I could make you see that you were the victim and not the perpetrator."

"I see it. I still think you'd find it off-putting to be with me. And what about the baby. You said you saw how…grotesque it looked. It was growing in me."

"Because I put it there."

"Not on purpose. I was the one carrying it. It was living because my body was allowing it to grow. When they took it out of me, the doctors removed all of my reproductive organs. How can you think of me as a woman without them?"

"Chelsea Rodrigue, you are the most beautiful woman on the planet. They took out my appendix while I was in the hospital. Do you think I'm less of a man because I'm missing an organ that you couldn't see and never thought about when I had it?"

"It's not the same," she protested.

Aric was done talking, thinking, rationalizing, and explaining. He carefully but quickly removed Chelsea's dress and made love to her with his hands and mouth as fiercely as he dared. He didn't want to hurt her still-healing body, but he wanted to erase all doubt from her mind regarding his desire for her despite the men, the malformed baby, and her missing female organs. She climaxed once then again within minutes and begged him to enter her.

"I want to, Chere. You don't know how much I want to, but it's too soon. I'll hurt you. We have to wait."

"We won't wait a minute longer than we have to."

"You don't need to convince me, Chere."

Aric stroked Chelsea's hair, and she rubbed his chest with one palm. Finally, they rose, showered, dressed and went back to the main part of the house. Chelsea was smiling as she hugged Nadine, Paula, and Jason and thanked them for taking care of making the Christmas dinner. They all seemed to relax, as they smiled back at her.

"Next year I want to cook the dinner," she declared. "But I think we should do something for others at lunch."

"Like what?" asked Paula.

"My family and I used to serve lunch at a homeless shelter every Christmas," Aric volunteered. "We'd hand out presents to the people there, too. Then we'd go back to the house and have our own family dinner."

Nadine smiled rather sadly and said, "That is a wonderful idea. Your parents did a great job with you and all of your sisters."

"They did. They always told us never to take anything we had for granted. Our grandparents used to say things like that, too. They were all wonderful role models."

"My mother and my Gran were like that," Jason noted. "Too bad my father and Julian were always such self-centered bastards." Looking pensive, he added, "I wish Gran were here. Mom's been gone for a while, but this is my first Christmas without Gran. It's odd not to have her around."

"I wish Miss June were here, too," commented Aric. "And my family."

"And Fredeline and Eve Rose," added Chelsea.

"And my daughters," said Nadine. "I think they're all here because we're thinking about them. It's not the same, but it's something. We should make this a happy time and celebrate what we have together tonight."

They ate the turkey, oyster stuffing, sweet potato casserole, green bean casserole, and chocolate mousse that Paula, Jason, and Nadine had prepared. Then they all sat around the large table and strung popcorn, which was something Chelsea had wanted to try. Once they had enough strands to decorate the large fir tree, they strung them around along with white lights and hung the gold, green, and purple ball ornaments that Nadine had brought with her.

"I knew you didn't have the time or energy to buy decorations this year, so I figured I'd bring balls that represented Mardi Gras colors. Next year, you can make your tree your own."

"I like this theme," Aric declared. "The lights, popcorn, and balls look great. We can buy other ornaments and personalize our tree as we want each year."

"It's too bad we don't have any ornaments with sentimental value to hang tonight," Chelsea stated, as Jason spread a gold tree skirt around the stand at the bottom of the tree.

"I do," Aric said suddenly. "Jason, do you mind coming with me to the shed in the backyard?"

As the women exchanged quizzical looks, the two men walked outside and across the yard to the newly completed shed. The structure looked as if it had been constructed at the same time and in the same style as the house and was four hundred square feet. A workshop had been situated on one half to accommodate Aric's grandfather's tools. The other half held the containers Aric had kept from the storage unit.

He and Jason returned to the main house carrying four small boxes each. Chelsea, Nadine, and Paula watched curiously as they were placed on the coffee table. Aric opened the first one and said, "Aurelia, my eldest sister, had us make ornaments for our parents when I was three. Each one embodies the personality of each of my sisters and me."

"Tell us about them as you hang them," Nadine suggested. "I want to know more."

He started with Aurelia's beautiful oval ornament that had an Impressionistic landscape scene delicately painted on it. After he'd explained, he handed it to Chelsea and asked her to hang the ornament on the tree. He did the same with each of the others until he got to Alycia's amazingly intricate spiral pattern of rainbow colors.

"Aric?"

He looked across the room at Nadine and saw her through a haze of tears. He haltingly spoke of the sister who had been closest to him in age and of her free-spirited ways. He handed the ornament to Chelsea. He noticed she was wearing not only her wedding ring but also the ring he'd selected for Alycia's sixteenth birthday. Wiping away his tears with the heels of his hands, he smiled and withdrew the last ornament, the one with a heart on it that he'd made when he was three.

Once it was hung, he looked at the tree and nodded with satisfaction. It was a good first tree. He took a picture of it, and then he asked Jason to take a photo of him, Chelsea, and Nadine standing beside it. For a moment, he thought Nadine was going to burst into tears, but she remained composed and stood smiling between him and Chelsea as they posed for the photo. Then the woman insisted that Jason and Paula stand with Aric and Chelsea so that she could take a picture of the little group.

"I'd like for you to text me these photos," she told Aric, as she handed him back his phone. "This has been a lovely night."

"You can't be going!" cried Chelsea. "We haven't even opened the presents, yet."

"I'm not," Nadine said reassuringly. "I was just making an observation. This has been a very unusual but rewarding Christmas evening."

"I have an idea, Aric," Chelsea offered. "How about if we make ornaments for the tree each year? It could be our own little tradition. We could make our first ones once we've been to Tante's shop tomorrow. It'll be after Christmas, but they'll be ready for next year. Maybe Paula and Jason could make ornaments, too."

"We might, considering next year we intend to have our own tree," Jason announced. Glancing at Nadine, he implored, "Please don't say anything to anyone outside this house. Paula and I have known each other for several years now. I've asked her to marry me, and she's accepted."

After congratulations had been offered by Aric, Chelsea, and Nadine, Aric asked, "Why can't we say anything?"

"They wouldn't be allowed to work on the same assignment if their engagement was common knowledge in the Bureau," replied Nadine. "Don't worry. Your secret's safe with me."

"But how do you know you'll have your own tree by next year?" Chelsea asked. "What if this mysterious stuff drags on forever?"

"None of us wants that," Paula said. "We're thinking positively."

"But I don't want you to leave!" Chelsea insisted. "You're my best friend!"

Paula looked genuinely touched and said, "You're my best friend, too. Even once this is over, I won't go far. We'll find a place close by. We'll see each other all the time. Someone has to keep you out of trouble, right?"

Chelsea grinned and nodded. Aric was grinning, too. Jason would continue to work as his personal assistant. If there was a place for Paula at Rodrigue Pharmaceuticals and she was interested, then the job would automatically be hers.

"How about some Christmas carols?" Chelsea suggested. "People seem to like that on TV shows and movies. Why don't we try it? Aric and I can take turns playing the piano."

They spent the rest of the evening singing, opening presents, talking with Lakshmi via the computer, and eating more chocolate mousse. At midnight, Nadine said that she had to leave but added that she wanted to take everyone out for dinner the following evening and asked where they would like to go.

"Moreau's," Aric said instantly. "We haven't seen Maurice since we were in Atlanta, and I promised him we'd drop by for dinner the day after Christmas."

"But we can't go upstairs and have sex like we usually do," Chelsea pouted.

"Chere, remember how we're not supposed to talk about sex so freely around other people?"

"But this is our family, isn't it? Aren't you supposed to be able to talk about *anything* to your family?"

Before he could comment, Nadine asked stiffly, "Could we go somewhere else tomorrow night? Maybe you could meet Maurice for lunch at his restaurant?"

"No, he's expecting us for dinner. I promised him this weeks ago. His schedule is crazy at this time of year, and we agreed that this would be the only evening he could take off and enjoy a meal with us. I'm sorry. If you don't want to go, then maybe we could have lunch with you somewhere else."

Nadine shook her head and said, "Buddy and I have other obligations. I – I just haven't been to Moreau's in a long time. I'm sure it will be fine."

Aric caught Jason's eye, and the agent raised one eyebrow. He obviously sensed Nadine's discomfort, too.

Nadine gave them what was a blatantly forced smile and assured them everything would be all right. After agreeing to meet them at Moreau's at 6:00, she hugged Chelsea and Aric then bid them and the two FBI agents goodnight and left.

"I wonder why she doesn't want to go to Moreau's," muttered Paula once the wife of the Vice-President was gone.

"Maybe she doesn't like the food there," Jason said with more than a hint of sarcasm in his voice. "Unless she tells us, we'll never know. Nadine LaFleur has always managed to keep things close to the vest. How she does it, I have no idea. Even her own people say they know she keeps secrets from them, but they can't find any skeletons in her closets."

Like the little skeleton she mentioned earlier, thought Aric. *Her own husband doesn't know about the baby she lost, so how could anyone else be aware of it? If she –*

He froze. Nadine hadn't actually told him that her baby had died. She'd merely said she'd lost a baby. What if…?

Aric looked at Chelsea, who was helping Paula and Jason to straighten the living room. Chelsea was twenty-four; Nadine was in her forties. Chelsea had been told that her mother was white, rich, and had abandoned her and her mixed-race father to return to her wealthy family. Nadine had spoken of having been given a second chance when she'd met Chelsea. Perhaps it wasn't just a reference to the loss of her three younger children. Perhaps Nadine was being literal. It would certainly explain her maternal feelings toward his wife and her desire to spend as much time with her as possible. It would also explain why her attitude toward Aric had softened since she'd met Chelsea in October.

"Aric? Are you okay?" Chelsea asked anxiously.

"Just tired. We should get to bed. I have a feeling tomorrow will be a long day."

"Yes, but it will be a good day in a lot of ways. At least I think it will be."

He smiled at his wife and nodded, studying her features and build. She didn't look like Nadine, although they did both have blue eyes. How would she react if it turned out that the woman was her biological mother? Would she be ecstatic or feel betrayed?

"Let's get some sleep and see what happens tomorrow," he told the others. "I can't even think straight anymore tonight."

As the two women went to put their presents away, Jason turned to Aric and asked quietly, "Are you really okay?"

"Maybe."

"You want to share?"

"No. Not yet. If I do, then I know you're not far. Thanks again for that."

"It's what they pay me the big bucks for," Jason shot back. "Merry Christmas, Aric."

"This has been the best and most unusual Christmas I've had in years. I'm hoping next Christmas will be even better. I don't think they could get any more unusual."

"You're tempting fate there," Jason told him. "Stop while you're ahead, will you?"

Chapter Forty-four

Jason and Paula refused to leave Aric and Chelsea alone with Tante in the rooms behind her shop. When Aric tried to explain that he'd known the woman for as long as he could remember and was certain they'd be safe, Jason snorted derisively.

"The last time two protectees went to a voodoo event, they and the agents assigned to protect them all ended up dead. That's not going to happen to you, Chelsea, me, and Paula. We're staying."

Tante courteously invited the FBI agents into her living room with Aric and Chelsea. A young Haitian woman minded the store in the front. All of them sat, and Tante addressed Chelsea and Aric in Haitian Creole.

"I understand why this man and woman need to be present, but this is private and painful for the two of you. They don't need to hear it. It's between you and me. We'll just talk in Creole until we're done." After they'd agreed, Tante said, "Chelsea told me on the phone that the two of you lost a baby and can never have any more. I was very sorry to hear that. Did you know the sex of the child?"

Chelsea looked uncertainly at Aric. She hadn't asked him, and he'd been too emotionally disturbed by seeing the fetal tissue to discuss this with her. He told both women truthfully that he didn't know if the baby would have been a boy or a girl had it been normal.

"Do the two of you have a sense of what you think it was?"

"A boy," they said in unison then looked at each other in surprise.

"A boy then." Rising from her chair, she said, "I'll be right back. While I'm gone, I want you to think of a name for your baby."

While she was out of the room, Chelsea asked Aric, "Did you ever think about names you'd want to give your children if you ever had any?"

"I don't think guys do that like girls do. Did you?"

She shrugged and said, "I don't remember what I did before the accident. I had a hard enough time picking out my own first name afterward."

"What boy names do you like?"

311

"I don't know. Whatever we choose, I think it should start with an A like all the other members of your family."

"The only names I can think of are Albert and Abner, and I don't care for either of those."

"What about Aaron?"

Nodding slowly, he said, "I like that."

Tante returned to the room carrying a brown cloth doll that had no features, hair, or clothing on it. It was about a foot long and was very simply made. As she sat, she asked the couple if they'd picked out a name for their baby.

"Aaron," Chelsea answered.

"That's a good, strong name," Tante remarked. As she handed the doll to Chelsea, she directed, "You hold this like it was your baby, close your eyes, and tell him everything you wanted for him."

"I don't understand what I'm supposed to say."

The older woman smiled gently and said, "Anything you want. Anything at all."

Chelsea cradled the doll in her arms, shut her eyes, and said, "Aaron, I wish you'd lived and been normal. I wish I'd been able to have you and nurse you and keep you forever, not like my mother. I wish I'd been able to watch you take your first steps and hear your first words and get you ready for your first day of school. I wish I'd been able to hear you laugh and see you play with your father. I wish you'd had a chance to grow up. We would have loved you so much."

When she opened her eyes, Tante nodded approvingly and said, "Kiss your son and give him to Aric."

Aric accepted the doll but admitted, "I don't think I can do this. It seems...weird."

"Your Tante Marie trusted me with every fiber of her being," the Haitian woman declared. "You not only can do this, but you have to. Trust me."

He stared down at the nondescript brown doll. No twisted mass of tissue, little hand or tiny eye. He lifted the doll to his shoulder, lowered his eyelids, and pictured the Aaron who should have been. He had light brown skin, brown hair, and Chelsea's blue eyes. He told this Aaron how he'd wanted to hold him, read to him, teach him how to play baseball and the piano and build things.

"I wish I'd been able to watch you develop into a generous man like my father and grandfathers. It makes me sad that you weren't able to be born healthy and whole. I would have loved seeing your mother nurture you. Our lives would have been so different if you'd lived."

When he was finished, Tante said, "Kiss your son and hand him to me."

Aric reluctantly did so. The woman placed the doll in a polished wooden box and said, "Be with God, Aaron Rodrigue." Then she put the lid on the box and directed the couple to follow her out the back door. When they stood, Jason hurriedly got to his feet and asked what was going on.

"We're following Tante outside."

"Why?"

Aric whirled around and yelled, "Why the hell do you think? We're here to try to lay our child to rest! Will you just give us some fucking space?"

"If I give you some fucking space then you could fucking die! Not only is it my fucking job to keep you alive, but you're my friend, Goddamn it! I don't want to see you die, too! You think it's easy for me and Paula to have to stand by and watch the two of you hurting so badly? You don't think it affects us when you and Chelsea are going through so much pain? If that's what you think, then fuck you, Aric!"

Everyone in the room stared dumbfounded at Jason, who was breathing hard. Aric looked at the man and saw only anger and pain. He apologized to Jason for his part in their argument and asked him what was going on. Jason shook his head, and Aric knew that whatever it was would be discussed with him later. He nodded, and Jason apologized to everyone else in the room for his outburst.

The little group went out into Tante's yard. Aric hadn't known that it backed up to a small cemetery. They walked through a graveyard dotted with crumbling raised tombs until they reached a dilapidated stone building. He expected the inside of the place to smell of death and mold, but it only smelled like herbs and flowers. There was an opening on one wall.

"There never was anything in this one," Tante said. "I have wondered since I discovered it whom it was waiting for. Today, I realized it was waiting for your baby. He'll be safe here. You can let him rest in peace."

She slid the polished box into the hole and directed Aric and Jason to put a heavy stone that had obviously been cut to fit the opening in place. Then she said a prayer in Haitian Creole and asked those gathered to say "Amen" at the end, and they did.

"Aaron will always be with you, but things will be easier after today," Tante told them. "Go, celebrate life, and love each other with all your heart."

When Aric tried to pay Tante for her time, she looked indignantly at him and said, "You go help some poor children somewhere with that money. Your son may be gone, but there are plenty of boys and girls in this world who need what the two of you can give."

"Thank you so much, Tante," Aric said sincerely as they left. "Thank you for everything."

"I'm here for you as long as I live," the woman said as she hugged him. "Have some faith, Boy."

Aric, Chelsea, Jason, and Paula walked without speaking to the pottery shop. When they arrived, Chelsea asked the clerk if she still had Christmas ornaments available for painting and firing. The woman showed them half a dozen shapes. Jason and Paula declined to participate, citing the need for them to be alert to any danger. As they retreated to a nearby table, Aric asked Chelsea what kind of ornament she wanted to make.

"I don't know if I'm any good at art," she admitted. "Could we make one together?"

"Sure. What do you want to paint?"

She chewed on her lower lip for a moment then said, "I want to make an ornament for Aaron. He should have an ornament on the tree."

"Which one would you like?" the clerk asked brightly.

"The one that's round," Aric told her.

"What colors will you need?" she went on.

"Black, blue…." Aric floundered. "Yellow?"

"And brown," Chelsea added.

For the next hour, they worked on the ornament. Chelsea was not much of an artist. Aric ended up drawing a nondescript doll like the one Tante had given them and then putting stars around it at the top. At the bottom, he wrote "Aaron" in block letters. Then Chelsea painted the doll brown, the background light blue, and the stars yellow. Aric outlined everything in black and painted over "Aaron" in black. Once the ornament was completed, they agreed that it had turned out well and took it to the counter.

"Oh, that is just too cute!" the clerk exclaimed. "Did you two just have a baby?"

"We just lost a baby," Aric said solemnly.

The clerk's face fell, and she hastened to ask their forgiveness for her unintentional faux pas. Chelsea assured her it wasn't her fault and that they hadn't taken offense. The woman told them the ornament would be ready for pick-up the following week.

They arrived at Moreau's early and sat at a table in a far corner of the main room. Maurice soon joined them and asked where Nadine was.

"She should be here at 6:00," Aric said, handing him a square box that held his Christmas gift.

As Maurice passed his friend an enormous box, he sat and said, "Merry Christmas Aric and Chelsea." Nodding to the two agents, he added, "To you as well."

Maurice's gift was a signed first edition of what Aric knew was his favorite book, *All the King's Men* by Robert Penn Warren. The man was amazed and pleased and thanked Aric and Chelsea profusely for the gift. Then he told them to open his gift to them.

It was a beautifully carved antique mirror. Everyone at the table oohed and aahed over it, and Chelsea asked if they could hang it in the living room as soon as they got home. Aric didn't hesitate to say, "Yes. We'll hang it right away."

"Do you know what Aric got me for Christmas?" Chelsea asked Maurice. "It's kind of ironic."

"I'm all for irony," Maurice told her. "What did he give you?"

"A little table and everything I need to make my own Buddhist shrine in our bedroom for my chanting when I do it at home. He went to the Buddhist Temple and asked them what I should have, and they explained it all. He got everything I need. It's perfect. I was so happy when I opened my gifts!"

Aric kissed his wife and said, "I'm glad I made you happy by giving you sone Buddhist items I thought you'd like as your Christmas gifts."

"I'll put this in the back where it won't get damaged," Maurice said as he lifted the mirror. He carried it and his treasured book out of the room, returning to the table just as Nadine arrived.

The Vice-President's wife seemed wound so tightly that she might violently uncoil at any moment. However, she tenderly hugged Chelsea before giving Aric a brief hug and greeting the others. As she took her seat, she asked how the visit to Tante's shop and the pottery store had gone.

"I'd rather tell you later," Chelsea confided. "It was good, but very sad today."

Nadine reached out and tucked some loose strands of hair behind one of Chelsea's ears and said, "We'll talk privately about everything later."

In an effort to redirect the conversation, Aric asked, "Did your day go well, Nadine?"

"Oh, yes," she said, but Aric could tell she was lying.

He considered that Buddy was fed up with Nadine's insistence on seeing Chelsea and wondered whether the man suspected that Chelsea might be Nadine's illegitimate daughter. Buddy had always paid a little too much attention to Chelsea. Maybe that was why.

He was like that with Eve Rose when she was alive, Aric recalled. *Maybe he just has a thing for black or mixed-race women. That would be a twist if Nadine was Chelsea's mother and had given herself to a mixed-raced man and her husband preferred mixed-raced girls. Yet, Buddy married a little blonde-haired, blue-eyed Southern belle. I suppose most mixed-raced girls aren't as well-placed with old family money and don't get you into higher office within the government.*

Aric chided himself for letting his mind wander in that direction. Unless he was going to confront Nadine, he doubted he could confirm his suspicions regarding her role in Chelsea's parentage. As he watched Nadine, he wondered whether or not she would even be able to make it through dinner. Stress was radiating from her.

After they'd ordered their food, Aric asked Nadine if she'd mind going up to Maurice's office with him for a moment so that they could talk. He was shocked to see fear in her eyes for a few seconds, but she agreed. He kissed Chelsea and told her he'd be back soon. She frowned but merely nodded.

Once they were upstairs, Aric asked, "Are you alright? You seem really stressed about being here at Moreau's. Do you want to leave?"

"I'm not all right. I appreciate your concern. Yes, I want to leave, but I'll stay because it's the right thing to do. It's no one's fault here that I'm…that I want to leave this place."

"Why *do* you want to leave?"

"Don't, Aric. I can't explain."

He stared at her for a long moment before asking, "Are you Chelsea's mother?"

"What? No! Why on Earth would you think that?"

Unless Nadine was a consummate actress, she was totally sincere. He shook his head and admitted that he was very tired and had been made more than a little paranoid by the past several years' experiences. Her expression softened instantly, and she came forward and laid a hand on his arm.

"I understand," she said soothingly. "It was heartbreaking to see you after the D Plague. You were like the shadow of your former self. I know how that feels. We all wanted to help you but didn't quite know how to approach you. You were so…different."

"We were all different after the D Plague."

"You have to admit that your situation was unique."

He sighed and rested his backside on the edge of the pool table. He was so, so tired. Nadine looked tired, too.

"Let's go back and eat, so you can return to Buddy," Aric said as he straightened. "I'm sure he's already telling you that you're spending way too much time with Chelsea."

"He is, and I'm ignoring it. As I told you, we haven't had much of a marriage for over five years."

"Forgive me for being blunt, but did you have one before? If so, then why didn't you tell him about the baby you lost before the two of you got together?"

"Because I relive that nightmare almost every waking moment of my life. Buddy and I loved each other very much from the first night we met. If I'd told him what had happened, then he would have thought about it every day, too. I didn't want our marriage to be overshadowed by my tragedy."

"He has to know about the antidepressants."

"He does. I told him about them early in our relationship. I said I had a chemical imbalance. He assured me it didn't matter to him and that he loved me regardless. End of story."

"Will you tell me what happened with your baby?"

"It's enough that you've lost your own child. You don't need to know about the horrors that took place when mine was born."
Taking his hand, she said, "I need to go back downstairs. I need to go, period. Thank you for trying to help. You're such a good man. Buddy used to be a good man, too."

Aric kept replaying that last sentence over and over in his mind as he lay awake later that night. If the wife of the Vice-President no longer felt that her husband was a good man, then where did that leave Lakshmi and the United States of America?

Chapter Forty-five

Chelsea was screaming, and Aric was loving every second of it. It was the middle of January, and the doctors had deemed her fully recovered. She and Aric had gone to the master suite Friday after dinner and had only emerged periodically to eat over the course of the following two days. Aric had never had sex so often in such a short time, not even with Chelsea. They were exhausted, sore, and completely happy.

Aric hadn't thought about anything else all weekend. He hadn't checked his emails, business, accounts, or phone. Nothing mattered except being with his wife. She was insatiable, and so was he. He wondered how much more either of them could take, but neither of them wanted to stop. Their weekend of physical intimacy had emotionally reconnected them.

Admittedly, things had been better between them and for each of them since Christmas Day and the day after. Chelsea had been less anxious and had gotten off the mild sedative she'd been on since her hysterics in the hospital. She'd gone back to exercising, working on the computer, reading, chanting, and playing the piano on a daily basis. She and Paula had been cooking dinner most evenings. Paula had told Aric that Chelsea was back to her old self, and he'd been greatly relieved. She'd had only one bad migraine, and her pill and Aric's massage had worked effectively to stop it quickly.

As for Aric, he'd been less depressed and less worried about Chelsea since the holiday. Their encounter with Tante and the funeral for Aaron had somehow lifted much of the guilt and pain from him. Now when he thought of the child that never should have been, he thought of the ordinary doll, not the mass of tissue. The Christmas ornament for Aaron lay in the box with the other ornaments that had been made by Aric and his sisters twenty-five years earlier. He was still saddened by what had happened, but his guilt and grief were no longer almost paralyzing.

Of course, there remained some very major issues in their lives. No one believed that the threats to his life and Chelsea's had vanished, and Jason and Paula continued to be their constant companions. Aric and Chelsea were still dependent on the CDC and FBI but weren't certain to what extent they could trust anyone in the government, except for the President and the couple living with them. Chelsea's missing three years were worrisome on a variety of levels, and what she knew about her past was damaging to her and, therefore, to Aric. Although she'd come far in her recovery over the last six months, Chelsea remained a TBI patient with limitations and challenges that frustrated her at various times. Nadine had been remote with the two of them since their dinner at Moreau's, which had bothered them both.

Nadine's private conversations with Aric during the holidays had also greatly troubled him. He'd talked to Lakshmi in a general way about Buddy and asked how he was doing in his role as Vice-President. She'd told him that she was happy with her political partner and his behavior. He knew she suspected there was more behind his inquiries than idle chatter but hadn't pressed him for details. Aric was glad, since he wasn't sure what he'd say if she did.

"Aric?" Chelsea murmured.

"Hm?"

"I don't think I can have sex anymore today."

The corners of his mouth twitched, and he said, "We should note that on the calendar. I never thought I'd hear you say those words."

"I never thought I'd say them either. This weekend has been so wonderful. It felt so good to be with you like this. I've missed it." As she snuggled against him, she sighed and said, "I love you."

"I love you, too."

Aric breathed in the sweet perfume of sex and glanced at the clock. It was almost 7:00 p.m.

"Why don't we shower, put on some clothes, and order a pizza to share with Jason and Paula?"

"That would be good. I want to chant for a while before we eat though. I haven't had any routine all weekend."

"You can't say you haven't had lots of repetition," he chuckled. "We both came again and again."

She giggled, and he kissed her on the top of her head before saying, "I wish we could stay in here forever."

"That would be nice, but I think your company would probably go bankrupt if we did. I wouldn't want that to happen. Lots of people depend on the medications made by Rodrigue Pharmaceuticals."

"That they do."

Once they'd showered and put on jeans and sweaters, Aric left Chelsea kneeling in front of her little altar, preparing to chant. He padded barefoot down the hallway to the main part of the house. Jason and Paula were nowhere in sight. Perhaps they were sleeping or reading.

Aric wandered the empty rooms of the house, including what should have been Paula's room. Her personal articles were there, but it was obvious she didn't sleep in the room. Aric looked at the photo of her with her parents and family. He instantly spotted the autistic sister and noted that Paula was standing protectively beside her. The Jennings clan didn't seem to be a very close-knit group if one studied their expressions and positions in the photo, and he wondered if that was why Paula hadn't asked for leave to go home for Christmas.

There were noises coming from Jason's room. Aric frowned. He could hear the couple having sex a little too clearly. The walls in the old house were thick, and he shouldn't have been able to hear much of anything. He remembered Chelsea telling him months before that she'd heard the couple having sex on more than one occasion, but he hadn't thought much about it and hadn't mentioned it to either agent. Now, he was intrigued.

He quietly moved around the room trying to find any opening that might allow the sound to filter through unhindered. It took him a few minutes to find it. There was a narrow space along one side of the built-in desk attached to the wall connected to Jason's room. That room had been Olga's. Since he'd designed the spaces with Chelsea, he knew there was an identical built-in desk on the other side of the wall. Crouching down, he peered through the crack. What he saw shocked him.

There were some sort of optics connecting the two rooms. By moving his eye, Aric was able to view the entire space through a camera mounted somewhere else besides next to the desk. Jason and Paula were definitely having some pretty intense sex, and Aric couldn't stop himself from watching for several seconds. Then he shook himself and thought, *You're not a teenaged boy stumbling across your sister and her lover in the woods. Get a grip and move on.*

He did so and went to the other side of the room where he found more optics. Odds were that there was a central viewing location for optics that had been run through every room in the house. He left the bedroom as he heard the couple on the other side of the wall climax.

Aric sat on the couch, stared into the cold fireplace, and weighed his options. He wasn't certain if he should tell Jason and Paula about his startling discovery. Jason had assured him when they'd moved in that the house was the one place no one could harm them and that there would be no internal cameras or bugging devices placed without notification. Was Jason lying to him? If not, then how had the devices been planted there? Had they been installed during the renovation of the house? If so, by whom? Were there more devices that had allowed someone to see into the other rooms as well? Had the government done it without notifying Jason? Had Olga and her boss orchestrated it? Who was spying on them and why were they trying to kill them? Could Aric really trust anyone except Chelsea?

Nadine, he thought. *Of all people, you know you can trust Nadine.*

Withdrawing his phone from his pocket, he called her. Buddy LaFleur answered the phone, and Aric stumbled over his words as he greeted the man and asked where Nadine was.

"She's getting ready for a State dinner," Buddy said coolly. "She just got in the shower." He paused then asked bluntly, "Are you having an affair with my wife?"

"What did you say?"

"You heard me," Buddy replied. "Are you screwing my wife? Is that why she wants to spend so much time at your house?"

Furious, Aric growled, "Your wife wants to spend time with *my* wife, whom I love very much and would never cheat on. I suspect *you* don't have quite the same scruples I do. I saw the way you were looking at Chelsea and Eve Rose the first time you met them, and you pay a little too much attention to Chelsea whenever you're around her. Thank God, that hasn't been often."

"Your wife enjoys spreading her legs for powerful men, Aric. You're a powerful man. So am I. I can't help but be attracted to her."

Aric was rendered mute by Buddy's words. He wondered whether or not he was talking to the same man he'd known for so many years. He'd always liked Buddy. Was he that bad at judging someone's character?

"I've seen how Nadine looks at you ever since we first met," Buddy snapped. "Nadine's always gone on about your accomplishments and was a little too concerned about you after you survived the D Plague and were so damned depressed. You're good-looking, smart, well-off, and have that added bonus of being a genuinely nice guy. Women can't resist that."

Seething, Aric said, "Nothing ever happened between me and your wife. We didn't even like each other until she took a shine to Chelsea in October. I've come to appreciate her as a good friend. That's all. After what you just said about me, your wife, and most of all Chelsea, I'm no longer *your* friend."

"Fine by me," the Vice-President said nonchalantly. "By the way, Nadine won't be talking to you or Chelsea any more."

"Nadine is very much her own woman. She'll talk to whomever she damn well pleases."

"We'll see about that," Buddy said in a chilling tone before disconnecting the call.

Aric screamed an obscenity at the phone before following the protocol and calling Lakshmi. Odds were that she was going to be attending the same State dinner, but he left a message for her anyway. When he finished, he looked up and saw that Chelsea, Jason, and Paula were all standing near the fireplace staring at him. Jason asked him what was wrong.

"I can't tell you."

"Why not?"

"Because I don't know if I can trust you or Paula."

"Since when?"

Aric shrugged and avoided looking at the man.

"Since when?" Jason repeated more insistently. "I thought we were friends."

"I don't know who my friends are anymore. All I know is that I don't seem to know much of anything and am really, really tired."

His phone rang. It was Lakshmi. He excused himself from the living room and went back to the master suite. He and Lakshmi logged onto their computers, and he stared at her worried face on his virtual screen. She was wearing a yellow evening gown and her long, black hair was pinned up in a very sophisticated fashion. He wondered what time the State dinner was scheduled to begin.

"Tell me as much as you can quickly," Lakshmi urged.

"I called to tell you that I won't be calling for a while."

"Aric, what are you talking about?"

"Everything. I'm really not sure whom I can trust anymore."

Lakshmi gasped and asked, "And that includes me?"

He nodded.

"But…but what have I done?"

"Maybe nothing. Maybe everything. I'm really not sure. One thing I am sure about is that Buddy LaFleur is not the man I thought he was and that I won't be voting for your ticket during the next election if he's your running mate." Sighing, he said, "I'm sorry, Lakshmi. Perhaps I'm wrong about everything. If so, I hope you'll forgive me. If not, then I'm assuming you'll pull everyone off this, and Chelsea and I will either be dead by morning or imprisoned by some CDC goons. If that happens, I'll find a way to get to Chelsea and kill us both."

"Aric, you're talking crazy!"

"Maybe whatever the D Plague did to me is driving me insane. Maybe I'm just finally wising up."

He ended the conversation before she could argue. When she tried to reach him again, he didn't answer.

"Aric? The pizza's here."

"I'm not hungry."

As she came over to stand in front of him, Chelsea asked, "What changed since you and I took a shower together an hour ago?"

"A lot of things."

"Tell me."

"Not here."

Her mouth fell open slightly, and he realized that she immediately knew what he was intimating. She sat in his lap and whispered, "Jason and Paula are very hurt right now."

"I'm sorry for that. I just hurt Lakshmi, too. I had to." Burying his face against her neck, he asked, 'Is it wrong that I want to just end it all and have some peace?"

"Yes."

He smiled in spite of his confusion and said, "My lovely, literal wife."

"Why don't we go to Moreau's? We can have sex on the pool table, and you can tell me what's bothering you."

"I thought you said you couldn't have sex again today."

"I can always make an exception for you."

"There's pizza here."

"The pizza will keep."

The ride to the restaurant was unbearably tense. Jason and Paula looked angry and hurt and were all business as they escorted Aric and Chelsea from the Creole House to Moreau's. They waited at a table near the foot of the stairs while Aric made love to Chelsea on the pool table and told her about the optics and his conversations with Buddy and Lakshmi. Once they were both sexually sated, Chelsea held him and declared that Jason and Paula were not capable of deceiving him and encouraged him to bring them upstairs and explain what was going on. He wanted to do exactly that but remained mistrustful.

"Aric, you've said all along that I have an extraordinary ability to sense people's integrity. I don't know if that started after I found out the truth about Michel LeClerc or after the accident. Will you trust me on this? Please? We need Jason and Paula. If they're not on our side, then we're done for. I'd rather find out now rather than later."

"I'm glad we agree on that point," he told her. "Let's do it."

Jason and Paula were soon seated stiffly on the couch in Maurice's upstairs rooms. The more Aric explained, the more their expressions toward him softened, yet they grew rigid with what Aric assumed was frustration and rage.

"Thank you," Jason said once Aric finished.

"For what?"

"Believing in us enough to trust us. We were pretty hurt earlier, but what you did was understandable now that you've told us the details."

"Do you think I should call Lakshmi back and reveal everything to her, too?"

"No," Paula replied. "I don't see the President as being the mastermind of some evil scheme against you and Chelsea, but someone in her inner circle might be responsible. If they're made aware of what you did to her tonight, that might force them to act."

"You know Nadine will call. What do we tell her?" Chelsea asked nervously. "I love Nadine like I think I'd love my mother. I don't want to lie to her."

"Me neither, but she may be under surveillance herself and be unaware of it. Let's see what happens once she calls."

"Until then we act as though nothing has changed," Jason directed. "We'll find out if the FBI is involved. If Paula and I are ordered off this job or given instructions to do something inappropriate, then we'll know it's time to move."

"Move where?" Chelsea asked blankly.

"Jason and I created an escape plan when he first started working for me. Better to be safe than sorry. If things get too bad, then we'll all have to disappear and assume new identities."

"But we agreed we couldn't do that!" Chelsea exclaimed.

"It's our last resort," Jason told her. "It'll only happen if we have no other choice."

"I don't think it will come to that, Chere," Aric said soothingly. "I don't want to leave our home, friends, or the business any more than you do."

She nodded, but her eyes were filled with tears.

"Let's go downstairs and have some dinner. I want to talk to Maurice and enjoy some crawfish stew."

Nadine called Aric as he was washing his hands in the restroom at Moreau's. He answered, asked the woman to hold for a moment, and nodded to Jason before hurrying up the stairs to take the call in private.

"Aric, what's going on?" she asked frantically. "Buddy and Lakshmi were talking and said you'd gone off the deep end!"

"Interesting. I can understand why Lakshmi might think that since I kind of cut off our contact. However, it's odd that Buddy would say the same thing considering my conversation with him earlier tonight."

"What conversation?"

"I called to ask you for advice. Buddy answered the phone, accused me of having an affair with you, and said that it was perfectly normal for him to want to have sex with my wife since he said she liked to spread her legs for powerful men, and he and I were powerful men. Then he said he'd see to it that you never called me or Chelsea again."

"Oh, my God! Oh, Aric! What awful things for Buddy to say! You have to know that I *never* led Buddy to believe you and I were having an affair. That would be preposterous!"

"I never believed you'd do that for an instant."

"Why did you cut off contact with Lakshmi?"

"We're under surveillance that wasn't disclosed to us or Jason or Paula."

"Good Lord. You think it was *our* people?"

"The truth? I think it was either someone in our government or someone working with someone in our government. There's no way all of this could have been orchestrated without inside contacts. I understand why they want me. I'm Mr. Miracle and am very valuable to a lot of researchers. What I still don't understand is why they want Chelsea. How does she fit into all of this? Is it something totally unrelated? I think that would be way too great a coincidence, don't you?"

"Yes. What can I do?"

"Keep your eyes and ears open and let me know if you hear anything you think is worth passing on."

"Do you have an escape plan set up just in case?"

He said nothing, which gave her his answer.

"If it comes to that, then I want to come with you. Once all of this is over, I'm going to file for divorce from Buddy anyway."

"I'm glad to hear it. Watch yourself. Buddy sounded…different when he said he would prevent you from talking to us. I don't want anything to happen to you."

Nadine laughed bitterly and said, "I've lost all of my children. It doesn't matter what happens to me."

"Well, it certainly matters to me and Chelsea."

She started to cry, thanked him, and hung up. Aric looked around Maurice's pool room one last time, then went downstairs. He wondered if he would ever see the place again. If not, then at least he and Chelsea had great memories of the times they'd spent there. If they survived whatever lay ahead, he planned to return and shoot some pool with Maurice on a regular basis. He hoped to be given the chance.

Chapter Forty-six

Chelsea phoned Aric in the middle of the afternoon the following day. He and Jason were reviewing some information regarding drug trials run by Rodrigue Pharmaceuticals. It was an inopportune time for Aric to take the call. He took it anyway.

"I did it!" she cried excitedly. "Oh, Aric! I really did it!"

"What did you do?" he asked and grinned. "You sound very pleased with yourself."

"I am! I found me!"

"What do you mean?"

"For a long time now I've been thinking about how I was attacked and was in the taxi accident in Orlando. I began to search Buddhist Temples and communities in Florida, and I found myself! I stayed at a place near Miami. I arrived there around the time I would have fled Haiti and asked for refuge. The people there took me in. They said I liked Buddhist practices and living in their community. I had been put in charge of their computer system and the business part of the organization. I was a member of the community until I accepted a job in Orlando. No one there knew that I'd had the accident or what had happened to me because I wasn't living in Miami anymore. They thought it was odd that I didn't keep in touch because they said that wasn't like me. However, they said people do that sometimes. It happens. So they didn't know I was in trouble and needed help. They were so sorry that they hadn't known and didn't come to help me!"

"Slow down," Aric directed, as he switched on the speaker phone mode so Jason could hear what Chelsea was saying. "Who are 'they' and where exactly is this Buddhist community? And what name did you use while you were there?"

"The man I spoke with is named Matthew. He's studying to be a Buddhist teacher. He said I was a nice, young woman who embodied the spirit of Buddhism even before I knew anything about it. He said I told them I was running from someone who wanted to hurt me. Guess what I told them my name was?"

"I have no idea."

"Sunshine! Oh, Aric. It was me!"

"It certainly sounds like it. What was the name of the community?"

"I'll email you the link." She paused for a second then said, "Okay, I sent it. We should go there. Perhaps they can tell us –"

Chelsea shrieked, and the call was suddenly disconnected. As Aric and Jason jumped to their feet, Jason phoned Paula. She didn't answer, and he swore furiously and began to make other calls. Aric grabbed their coats and told his startled receptionist as they passed there was an emergency and that he and Jason would be in touch.

"Shit!" Jason swore as Aric hailed a cab and gave the driver the address for the Creole House. "Nothing! Other agents are on their way, but there's no response from anyone guarding the perimeter. Damn it!" After they'd gone about another quarter of a mile, he ordered the cabbie, "Turn around!"

"What?" Aric cried. "No!"

Jason said quietly, "If someone got to Chelsea and Paula, then they're either already dead or else they've been taken. I'm thinking kidnapping is more likely. However, either scenario spells trap for you and me!"

"Where are we going?"

"To the airport!" Jason ordered the taxi driver. Then to Aric he said, "We need to get to the Buddhist community Chelsea was telling us about before we got disconnected. Hopefully, we can get to this Matthew guy before anyone else does and maybe catch a break."

"But it's near Miami!"

"No shit, Sherlock!" Jason snapped.

"What the hell is wrong with you?" Aric asked angrily. "You don't have to lash out at me when you can't control everything! You've done it before."

"I suppose I have. I'm sorry. It's an old habit. My brother, Julian, was always cruel. When our parents weren't around to see, he used to wail on me every chance he got. I was younger and smaller and could only mouth off at him when he was pushing me around. I hated feeling helpless. I've been feeling helpless in certain ways since Gran died."

"No one likes to feel helpless. I know I'm pretty pissed off at how helpless I feel right now. I –"

"Not here," Jason interrupted. "We'll talk more when we're at the airport. Got it?"

"I got it."

Jason's phone rang, and Aric clenched his hands into fists in his lap and waited. He tried to discern the state of affairs at the Creole House by listening to Jason's side of the conversation but couldn't ascertain much. By the time Jason pocketed his phone, he looked grim but determined.

"No Chelsea or Paula," he said tightly. "The other agents around the house are cold, and I don't mean because it's below freezing outside."

Neither of them spoke until they were out of the cab. As they stood in line to purchase plane tickets to Miami, Aric ruminated on what had happened at his house that afternoon. Did this prove that Lakshmi was responsible for everything? Surely not. If she was going to pull their protection, then she would have done exactly that. She wouldn't have ordered the murders of FBI agents to cover up…what?

"I don't think the Head Gardener is responsible for this," Jason muttered as they inched forward. "She's not the type, even if you and she didn't have a shared history. Plus, she cares too much about the Tree."

"Did you learn that analogy from Miss June?"

"Yes. That was how Gran explained the U.S. government to me when I was small. The imagery works well."

"If not the Head Gardener, then who? Who are our suspects?"

"Others in the government who want you for your body and Chelsea for her mind or, rather, what was in her mind. Perhaps they think they can access that area of her brain again while they study you in a lab somewhere."

"That's a lovely thought," Aric said wryly.

"Yeah, I know."

"Who else?"

Jason shrugged and said, "A wild card? Someone we aren't aware of with motives we don't know about."

"Another lovely thought."

"My main thought right now is to get to Matthew and see if that leads us to a more productive line of thinking that will take us to Chelsea and Paula. I'm praying that whoever has them isn't planning to hurt them. If he'd wanted to kill them he would have probably done so at the house."

Once they were seated in the plane, Aric admitted nervously, "If they hit Chelsea in the head or if she falls, it could be physically devastating for her. It could kill her or cause greater brain damage."

"I know. I'm sure whoever took them knows it, too. That might mean they'll take better care not to harm her, depending on their ulterior goals. Paula may not be so lucky."

"Paula's in great physical shape."

"She's also pregnant." When Aric gaped at Jason, the man confided, "We just found out last night using a store-bought home pregnancy test. When you saw us having sex, it was sort of...make-up sex."

"Make-up sex?"

"We had an argument about the pregnancy once it was confirmed. The timing definitely sucks. I wanted Paula off the case. We're in the middle of a dangerous assignment, and you and Chelsea just lost Aaron. Paula didn't want to leave. We argued about what to do. We both agreed that neither of us wanted to end the pregnancy. We weren't really sure how we were going to proceed but decided we'd talk about it more tonight. Then we had make-up sex, which is when you happened upon the optics." Sighing heavily, the man said, "We should have talked about our plans last night. Someone else could have taken her place temporarily. Paula might not have been home with Chelsea today, and she and the baby would be safe. At least if they hurt her and anything happens, it is early on in the pregnancy."

"How early on?"

"We guesstimated she's about eight weeks along."

"I'm sorry, Jason."

"It's not your fault that we miscalculated or that we opted not to take advantage of the birth control shot your company developed. That was our own stupid fault. I just want Paula back alive. If we lose this baby, then we'll have another." Grimacing, he said, "Now *I'm* sorry."

"It's not your fault that I am whatever it is I am or that the CDC people played me and Chelsea and allowed Aaron to be conceived and to develop. It's *their* fault that Chelsea almost died and that we can't have any more children, although I doubt if we'd try because of my…condition. You and Paula shouldn't plan your family around trying to spare our feelings. Actually, it might be great for the two of you to have lots of kids. Then we can play aunt and uncle and enjoy some parenting even though we can't do it on our own." When Jason simply stared out of the plane window, Aric said resolutely, "Chelsea, Paula, and your baby will be fine. We're going to figure it all out. We have to. If Chelsea dies, then I die, remember?"

"I can't let you do that."

"You won't have a choice. Help me save Chelsea, and you'll save me. It's as easy as that."

"Easy, eh?"

Their flight was uneventful, and they were soon renting a car in Miami. The Buddhist community where Chelsea had lived for almost three years was thirty minutes from the airport. It was part of the city but was shielded by an area that greatly resembled a nature preserve. The wooden buildings located on the sprawling grounds were lovely in their simplicity.

Since Aric had called ahead before their plane had left New Orleans, they were expected. A young woman who had a shaved head and was wearing the robes of a Buddhist nun met them at the front door. She never stopped smiling and asked them to follow her to a room where they could speak in private with Matthew. She offered them food and drink, which they accepted. Neither of them felt like eating, but they knew it was necessary. The nun left them with tea and some delicious type of cake Aric had never tasted before. As if he'd planned it, Matthew entered once the tea and cake were gone. Introductions were made.

Matthew was a slim, middle-aged man with sandy brown hair and a gentle smile. He was wearing hospital scrubs. Aric asked him if he was a doctor.

"A nurse," he answered. "If I were a doctor, I wouldn't have time to hone my Buddhist practices the way I feel I should."

"We don't have a lot of time here ourselves," Jason said tensely. "The woman you knew as Sunshine and another woman are in danger. We're trying to save them. Any help you can give us would be greatly appreciated."

"We all want to help," Matthew declared as he took a seat. "Sunshine was just like her name. She was like the radiant light of the sun contained in human form. We'd love to see her again, although I understand from what little she told me that she has no memory before June of 2033 and doesn't remember us."

"I'm sure she'd like to spend time with the people here regardless," Aric said sincerely. "She may have lost her autobiographical memory, but she retains certain things. She chants every day and goes to a Buddhist Temple where we live to chant with others."

"That's good to hear. I'd like to know all about her life since she left us, but I understand that now's not the time. What can I tell you that might help?"

"It sounded like Chelsea was happy here," Aric began. "Why did she leave?"

"She was very happy with our community. However, running our computer system and organizing our administration were like child's play to her. She loved Buddhist practices but had no desire to become a nun or a teacher. She craved the intricacies of complex databases and similar things. We understood. She had her own path to follow. We supported her efforts to find a more challenging job."

"And she found one?"

"It didn't take her long. If her abilities weren't affected by her accident, then you know how amazing she is with computers and the piano."

"She did suffer brain damage, but all of that remained intact," Aric told him.

"Good."

"Did she tell you where she was going to work?" asked Jason.

"Of course. She was very excited. She was hired by a company called Gulf Global Green, Inc."

Aric thought he might throw up the cake and tea he'd recently ingested. Jason looked sharply at him and asked, "You've heard of it?"

Nodding, Aric said, "Buddy LaFleur founded it with several other wealthy, environmentally conscious businesspeople. Their aim was to make the world a better, more eco-friendly place by studying how nature and technology could be blended in the most effective manner."

"And you know about this company because…?"

"I was one of its founding members in 2030."

"Holy shit!" Jason exclaimed. Looking at Matthew, he said, "Sorry about that."

Matthew smiled and said, "I'm not offended. I choose not to curse, but I don't project my choices onto other living beings. I accept everyone as they are. We're all striving for enlightenment, whether we realize it or not."

"Will you and the others here in your community pray that we find Chelsea and Paula and all make it through this alive and whole?" Aric asked. "Could you make it your intention?"

"It will definitely be one of our priorities," the nurse assured them. "Please let us know the outcome. If you have other questions or need our help, don't hesitate to contact us."

"You may all be risking your lives because of your involvement."

"Everything is transitory. If I'm killed tonight because I've helped you, I'm completely at peace with it. I did what I was supposed to do. Anything less would be morally unacceptable."

Aric thanked him and said, "We appreciate your help and your prayers."

As they returned to their rental car, Aric asked Jason, "Can you trust anyone in the government to help us without doubting their motives?"

"No. We're going to have to lose our FBI Protection Detail."

"If you say so. Then let's make a stop and head for Orlando."

"A stop for what?"

"Firearms. I know darn well that you can shoot, and so can I. If Buddy LaFleur is somehow responsible for this, then I don't think too many others will be involved. He's the Vice-President after all and wouldn't want a lot of people to know his dirty secrets. No matter what, I think we should both be armed."

"No arguments there. But if there are a large number of corrupt government people involved then he could have a whole frickin' army waiting to ambush us."

"Like Matthew said, if I die tonight because I was doing the right thing, then I'll be at peace. Do you see any other way?"

"No," Jason admitted sourly. "But I think we should have a safety net of sorts."

"Like what?"

"I know you and the President have an encrypted method of communication in case of emergency. Between the two of us, we should be able to set up some sort of delayed message. That way, if we go in and get killed, she can at least be aware of the situation and handle things to avenge all of us."

"Maybe we should contact her first."

"And risk being exposed if there's a mole in close proximity to her?"

"What about Nadine?"

"Same principle. We can't tell either woman up front without risking their lives as well as our own."

Aric groaned and acquiesced. Then he and Jason set out to lose their Protection Detail and buy some guns.

Chapter Forty-seven

Aric pulled into the parking lot of Gulf Global Green, Inc. at 1:00 a.m. He and Jason had purchased firearms and bullets through a less-than-reputable dealer. Then, they set up the delayed message for Lakshmi and stopped at a Walmart Supercenter to buy jeans, long-sleeved dark knit shirts, black socks, and tennis shoes. They'd changed out of their business clothes in a truck stop restroom and had stashed them in the trunk of the rental car along with two blankets, pillows, protein bars, and bottled water they'd also bought while at Wal-Mart.

Although he'd only been to the headquarters of Gulf Global Green twice in four years, Aric had access to the building due to his status as a founding member and co-owner. The company had advanced research in its target area and had begun to earn a profit, although money had never been Aric's concern. He wanted to help the world.

As they approached the doors of the darkened four-story office building, the only thing Aric wasn't certain of was whether or not the security system would allow him access but refuse Jason. There was only one way to find out. If an alarm sounded, then so be it. They would either be taken prisoner or the police would automatically be summoned and save the day.

Like that will ever happen, he thought dryly. *Cops are great, but we're dealing with the big boys here. Jason and I already know we're pretty much walking into an ambush, but what choice do we have? Our only hope is to find out what Buddy wants, give it to him, and pray he lets Chelsea and Paula go unharmed. Why do I have the feeling I won't be walking away from this place?*

After identifying himself, giving the proper access codes, and submitting to a retinal scan, Aric was rewarded by having the doors to the building slide open. He and Jason walked in, guns in hand. Everything was quiet and seemingly deserted.

They moved through the first floor but found no one lying in wait. The same held true for the second floor. When they reached the third, Buddy LaFleur was sitting in a chair on the landing of the stairwell. Beside him stood Julian Duson.

Aric instantly aimed his gun at Buddy's chest, while Jason leveled his weapon at his brother. The other two men already had guns trained on Aric and Jason. No one spoke or moved for several seconds. Then Buddy lowered his weapon into his lap.

"Let's get real," he said. "None of us wants to end it this way. No one gets what he wants if we all kill each other here. We need to talk."

"So, talk!" barked Jason. "Where are Chelsea and Paula?"

"If you'll come with us, we'll be happy to show you," the Vice-President said with saccharine sweetness. "Which one would you like to see first?" When neither Jason nor Aric replied, he smiled politely and said, "Let's go up to the fourth floor. That's where the private apartment is. That's where they are."

Aric's stomach did a nauseating flip-flop. He thought of Chelsea's fear of his former apartment at Rodrigue Pharmaceuticals and Jason's speculation that she'd been taken to a similar place for her brutal rape. Had that place been the top floor of Gulf Global Green? He suspected he knew the answer, and he wanted to shoot Buddy LaFleur on the spot. He began to raise his gun.

"Don't even think about it," Julian hissed. "If either of us gets shot, then both of the women die in very unpleasant ways." Looking at his younger brother, he said, "You know I like to inflict pain. I'd love to hurt your woman very slowly for my own amusement. Don't tempt me."

Surprisingly, Jason held his tongue. Aric knew his friend was well aware that Julian was capable of anything. Losing his temper and responding to his goading was only going to hurt Paula and the baby.

The entire fourth floor was a sensibly decorated, fully functional apartment. Aric had toured the place the first time he'd visited the building but had never stayed there. He knew other co-owners and donors were frequent guests, but he'd felt an odd sense of discomfort when he'd visited.

"Hm. Why don't we start with Agent Jennings?" Buddy suggested. "Julian, if you'll lead the way."

It was only as they walked toward the hallway that Aric noticed the four armed men who were standing at attention in various locations. He understood that if he made any unexpected movements, he would be riddled with bullets. He speculated that these men were part of Julian's private security team and would have no qualms about shooting him, Jason, or anyone else if ordered to do so.

There was a deadbolt on the first door they came to. Julian withdrew a set of keys from his pants pocket and unlocked the door. Then he pushed it wide and said officiously, "After you, little brother."

At first glance, no one seemed to be in that bedroom. However, as they scanned the space, Aric caught a glimpse of Paula's still form slumped in one corner. Jason was already hurrying toward his partner. He knelt beside her, said her name, and gently touched a purple bruise on one of her cheeks. She winced, and Aric relaxed slightly. At least she was alive.

Jason took her pulse than lifted her chin so that he could look into her eyes. His mouth became a thin, hard line as he said, "She's been drugged."

"No shit, Sherlock," Julian said sarcastically. "She put up one hell of a fight. We finally just gave in and shot her up with something that would make her more compliant." Grinning maliciously at his younger brother, he said, "I was sorry about having to do that."

"I'll bet."

"No, really. I wanted to see how feisty she'd be to fuck, but taking her like this wouldn't be any fun."

Jason lifted his weapon once more and pointed it at his brother's head. Buddy LaFleur placed the muzzle of his own gun to Jason's temple before stating, "You shoot him, then I shoot you. That won't help your girlfriend, will it?"

Jason instantly lowered his weapon and said, "The two of you are unbelievably perverted. At least I can take some comfort in knowing that you'll burn in Hell with Michel LeClerc when you die."

"I've told you several times before that Hell has always gotten a bad rap. I think we'll have a blast," Julian said casually. "Too bad you'll be pushing up daisies and playing harps with stupid angels."

"If Gran could see you now," Jason muttered. "What a disappointment you were to her and Mom."

Before Aric realized what was happening, Julian raised his gun, pointed it at Paula, and shot her in the right shoulder. Despite being heavily drugged, she cried out with the pain and arched her back. Jason shouted obscenities at his brother, placed his gun on the floor between him and Paula, and pulled off his shirt. He applied pressure to her wound and told her to hold on, that everything would be fine.

"Sure it will," Julian said and shot Jason in the side of his torso. The man howled and pitched forward, bracing his hands against the wall on either side of Paula's head. Buddy trained his gun on Aric, who was preparing to shoot Julian.

"Don't be ridiculous," Buddy offered. "If you do that, then I'll shoot you, then Jason and Paula, and finally your precious Chelsea."

"What do you want?!?" Aric growled. "What is the point of all this?"

"We'll get to that. Let's leave the two lovebirds alone for a while, and I'll take you to Chelsea. First, give Julian your gun, then go pick up Jason's weapon and hand it to his brother as well."

Despite Jason's protestations, Aric did as he was told. Neither of them was in any position to refuse. He prayed that the gunshot wounds suffered by the two FBI agents weren't life-threatening. However, he understood that Julian and Buddy would come back for the kill later unless Aric could somehow think of a way out of their current predicament.

As they left the room, Aric looked back at his wounded friends. Jason sat on the floor and cradled Paula against him. When Aric and Jason's eyes met, Aric could *feel* the message Jason wanted to verbally convey: *Do whatever it takes to kill these bastards.* Aric nodded, then the door closed behind him.

He walked between Buddy and Julian toward a door located at the far end of the hallway. Julian used a different key to unlock that deadbolt. He gestured with his gun for Aric to open the door and enter what turned out to be the master suite of the apartment. Chelsea lay on the bed with her eyes closed. He could instantly tell that she was suffering from a bad migraine. Her head rested in Nadine LaFleur's lap.

The older woman stiffened when she saw Aric, and the fingers of her hand that were stroking Chelsea's hair stilled. Her eyes widened slightly, and she swallowed hard. Looking between Buddy and Julian, she asked nervously, "What is this? Buddy, what is going on? What are you doing?"

"Wrapping up loose ends I should have taken care of in June of 2033," he said flatly. "How lucky for me that everyone's here together. It makes things so much easier. You, Aric, Chelsea, Jason, and Paula can all die, and I can publicly grieve then move on. Lakshmi will meet with an unfortunate accident, and I'll grieve again then assume her role as President."

"Have you lost your mind?" Nadine asked in disbelief.

"Not at all. As a matter of fact, everything has become very clear."

"Nothing seems clear to me," Nadine shot back. "I don't understand."

"Well, that'll never do. I can't just kill my wife without letting her know *why* I'm killing her and her friends."

"Yes, you can," Julian put in. "Who cares if they know why? The end result will be the same."

"I've been married to this woman for a long time. We had three beautiful daughters together. She's stood by me and sacrificed a lot so that I could become the Vice-President of the United States of America. She should know."

"And the others?"

"I suppose I'd feel guilt if we simply shot them without telling them why. I'll let you explain it to your brother and his girlfriend."

Julian nodded curtly, and Aric knew that the man would not offer any explanations before murdering his brother and Paula Jennings. Purposefully ignoring Buddy and Julian, Aric walked over to the bed and frowned as he studied the swollen area on Nadine's forehead. Her eyes flitted to Julian, and Aric clenched his jaw before hugging Nadine tightly to him.

"We have to figure a way out of this," he whispered into her ear. "Jason and Paula are hurt and locked in one of the other bedrooms." Before she could comment, he broke away, bent to kiss his wife on the temple, and said, "Chelsea, I'm here."

Chapter Forty-eight

Chelsea moaned, and Nadine said, "She's in so much pain. They have her pills, but they won't give them to her."

"When did the migraine start?" he asked Nadine.

"About an hour ago."

"Aric, make it stop," Chelsea pleaded. "Help me."

Aric straightened and demanded, "Give me her pills."

"Why? So she doesn't go to Heaven with a headache?" Julian quipped.

"If you're going to kill us all anyway, then what difference does it make if she has some relief?"

"He does have a point," Buddy said smoothly. "Julian, give the man the bottle and some water."

Aric coaxed Chelsea into swallowing a migraine pill and then used the massage technique Olga had shown him the night she'd tried to kill him. Chelsea sagged onto the mattress but didn't sleep. The ingestion of the medication and his ministrations had been delayed too long for her to sleep and wake pain-free. He lifted her into his lap and kissed her hair.

"Aw, isn't that sweet?" Julian taunted. "The lovely brain-injured girl and her champion. If only you'd seen what I've seen. It'd either make you want her more or never want to touch her again."

"And what have you seen?"

"Your exotic woman there bringing some of the most powerful men in the world to their knees. I worked for two of those men and got to watch along with Michel LeClerc as his little girl did anything and everything with my employers. Talk about a turn-on. Seeing a gorgeous, naïve sixteen-year-old giving and getting some of the best sex you could ever imagine."

Aric shut his eyes in disgust. He was disgusted with the men and with Julian Duson, not Chelsea. She'd been an innocent victim.

"Who were the two employers?"

"The only two men older than LeClerc who were allowed to fuck his concubine. One was Olga Knudsen's long-time lover and the father of her son. The other was Buddy LaFleur here. Damn that was some good sex to watch, although I personally enjoyed

341

watching her screw all those younger guys more. No offense, Mr. Vice-President."

Buddy shrugged and said, "None taken. I was only forty, and Olga's partner was in his fifties. We were both in great physical condition. It wasn't like we were old, fat guys, but I guess everyone has his preferences."

Nadine was gripping Aric's arm so tightly that he wondered whether or not she would cut off his circulation. She put her free arm around Chelsea's head and shoulder in a protective gesture and said, "Buddy, you slept with a *child?*"

"She wasn't five, Nadine. She was sixteen. She loved sex and was very accomplished at it."

"Because a pedophile had defiled and manipulated her! My God, Buddy! How *could* you?"

"I could because I could. I was doing business with Mr. LeClerc, and he offered me Little Miss Sunshine to solidify the deal. If it's any consolation, that's the only time I ever slept with another woman."

"She wasn't a woman," Nadine said as she began to cry. "Oh, my poor girl."

Aric was becoming more and more resolute in his decision to kill Julian Duson and Buddy LaFleur. He wanted them both dead but needed answers first. Even if they all died in this room, he had to know the whole story.

"Olga was working for you?" he asked Buddy.

"No. Olga was working for Julian. Why don't we go back to the beginning, back to when your wife was sixteen and content with her adoptive father. She would have done anything for him. She pretty much did. She was the best fuck I've ever had." Looking at his wife, he said, "Sorry, Nadine."

The woman pressed her forehead against Aric's shoulder and refused to look at Buddy.

"As I said, I was doing business with Michel. He offered me Soleil, and I took full advantage. Julian was in charge of my security team at the time. He was supposed to never let me out of his sight. So, he watched with Michel via the cameras."

"You said you watched others with Chelsea," Aric remarked to Julian. "If only Buddy and Olga Knudsen's lover were under your protection, then how'd you see the younger men with her?"

"I did business with Michel LeClerc myself, although it was a different type of business. At that time, I didn't have the money or power the other men had. He wouldn't let me fuck Soleil. He would, however, let me watch the recordings. It was part of my Bucket List to have sex with Soleil before I died. Then she ran away, and *he* died. I was furious and thought I'd missed my chance."

"And?"

"And then Soleil turned up working for Gulf Global Green, Inc. as Sunshine. Of course, she had no idea that Buddy LaFleur was one of the founding members when she was hired. She didn't know I still had ties to him even if his bitchy wife had made him fire me. I continued to work for him behind the scenes. For the first couple of months Sunshine was here, neither of us was even aware of it. That was an oversight on our part."

"What tipped you off?" asked Aric.

"You," Julian answered coolly. "They say that curiosity killed the cat. Well, Sunshine got a little too curious about what Gulf Global Green was doing through their research. She was a whiz kid when it came to computers. I guess she saw something that didn't look right and started digging. She turned up all sorts of indiscretions that we'd managed to keep hidden from pretty much everyone else. The biggest indiscretion was Buddy LaFleur's scheme to use you and then kill you."

"Me?" Aric shook his head and asked, "Why me?"

"Because you survived the D Plague, and my daughters all died. I bribed the people on the original team at the CDC who were hired to work on your case so they'd feed me the information they gleaned on you. I had them experiment with your samples. I wanted to know why you'd lived when my daughters had died. I wanted to find a way to make you suffer, although Nadine kept whining that you were suffering so much because you'd survived and lost everyone else in your family. Poor Aric. He's lost everyone. Boohoo. You were still alive, and our girls were gone. I found it impossible to feel sorry for you."

"So, Chelsea found out about your machinations and, therefore, about you running the company. She knew you'd been with her at Michel LeClerc's. She knew you were the Vice-President. What did she do? Did she threaten to expose you?"

"Yes. She called me and asked if we could meet here at the office after hours to discuss what she'd unearthed. So bright but yet still so naïve. She thought I'd come alone. I didn't."

"It was almost comical seeing her try to persuade him to stop what he was doing," Julian chuckled. "She was so idealistic. She thought she'd get him to realize the error of his ways. When he refused, she threatened to go to the authorities or the press. Bad move. I ordered my men to grab her, and she darted under a desk. Like that would protect her."

Chelsea was weeping quietly in Aric's arms. She asked him to make them stop, but he shushed her and told her they had to hear this and know the truth.

"What did you do next?" Aric asked Buddy.

"I told Julian to take care of the situation and left the building. *That* was a mistake. I should have stayed to see that things were handled to my satisfaction."

"What happened?" Aric asked Julian.

"I finally had the chance to fuck the little girl I'd been denied before. She'd changed her tune, of course. She didn't want to have sex with anyone else until she fell in love and was in a mutually exclusive relationship. My men dragged her up here kicking and screaming. They stripped off her clothing then held her while I raped her. I'd always liked rough sex, but I could never be as rough as I'd wanted. No woman would stand for that much forcefulness, even if she liked it rough herself. Here was a beautiful girl I'd wanted for several years, and I didn't have to be careful with her because I was planning to kill her afterward. I took my time with her. When I was done, my men and I released her. She could barely stand. We made her dress and took her downstairs where a cab was waiting. I told her I'd give her an hour head-start then the hunt would begin. I gave her cash and told her I was looking forward to catching up with her. I said if she confided in anyone that I'd personally see to it they were killed, too. We tracked her to Disney Springs, and we were on our way in her wake as she fled to SeaWorld. That was a blunder on her part since SeaWorld closes earlier than most parks. As it turned out, it was irrelevant. My men and I actually witnessed the taxi accident. How ironic and how frustrating. We couldn't get to her in the hospital. We decided to wait. Once she woke and we found out about her brain injury, I decided we'd see if she was faking or if she really had lost her memory. Her amnesia was genuine, but I eventually ordered all of those who'd treated her killed just in case she'd inadvertently told them anything that might incriminate me or Buddy LaFleur. We recruited Olga, who had been floundering and searching for some purpose in her life after the loss of her lover, son, and grandchildren, and we placed her at the Serenity Resort and Spa to spy on Chelsea."

"And then Fate had you attend a conference at the resort. We made sure Olga was set up as your masseuse. Fate smiled on us again when you met the girl who didn't remember that you were the catalyst for her rape, accident, and brain injury," Buddy said with a shake of the head. "And she fell in love with you and you with her! It was the perfect foundation for me to have my revenge against the two of you. The only problems were that we knew you had FBI protection and that Olga kept vacillating between wanting to kill you and wanting to save you. We had devices installed in your house while it was under renovation and used them to spy on you, the others, and on Olga, since we weren't sure where her loyalties rested. Her feelings for those in the house ended up costing the woman her life."

Aric asked, "Why didn't you just kill me and Chelsea? Why kill Fredeline and Eve Rose and the others?"

"I wanted to torture you with loss like Nadine and I had been tortured by the loss of our girls." Shooting a displeased look at Julian, he said, "Although I didn't ask Julian to recreate Chelsea's rape. I didn't ask him to rape Chelsea in the first place. Raping her and Eve Rose was his idea."

"My little brother and his people certainly got the message," Julian pointed out. "We just kept biding our time and waiting for good opportunities to advance our personal agendas."

"And what about the baby Chelsea and I created?"

"You mean the monster?" Buddy corrected. "My CDC people predicted that, although they weren't sure what would happen to a fetus that developed from your sperm. It was a valid experiment and caused you more suffering, so I was pleased."

"You sick, sorry excuse for a human being!" Nadine shouted. "Both of you!"

"I am sorry, Nadine," Buddy told her with what sounded like genuine remorse. "You're the mother of my children, and I'll always love you for that. But you've chosen these two here over me, and I can't let that transgression go unpunished."

"I'd rather die with them than look at you for another minute!" she spat. "You're the monster!"

"Don't be like that," he chided. "Remember the good times."

Julian approached the bed and said, "This is way too much chit chat. You've had your little say, Buddy. You've rubbed it in. Now, let's finish this. You have funerals to plan and soon a country to run."

"With you right beside me," Buddy agreed. "We make a good team."

"Yes, we do. How do you want to dispose of these three?"

"What do you recommend? You are the security expert after all."

"I'd also like a little revenge. I say we take them back to where my brother and his girlfriend are and shoot them one by one. Since you want Aric to suffer and I want Jason to suffer, they can watch the others die first."

"Excellent idea." Pointing his gun at the three of them seated on the bed, Buddy said, "Get up and get moving."

"Can you stand, Chere?" Aric asked Chelsea before brushing his lips across hers. "It would be good for you to stand."

She opened her eyes and stared up at him. He saw that she understood he had something in mind and said in a small voice, "I think I can stand if you and Nadine help me."

Aric lifted Chelsea up and kissed her passionately then murmured that he loved her. He felt as if his life was coming to an end and hoped that his wife would survive and that Nadine would take care of her. He wondered if Jason was alive and if Paula was still pregnant. Then he helped Chelsea to sit up and to stand. Nadine put her arms around the younger woman and steadied her.

They went to the other bedroom, and Julian unlocked the door. The room appeared to be empty.

"What the fuck?!?" Julian screamed. He called for one of his men just as Jason lunged at him from the side, grabbed his gun, and shot Julian in the head. Chelsea and Nadine screamed, and a look of shock crossed Buddy's face. In that moment, Aric tackled him, wrestled the gun out of his hands, and shot the Vice-President of the United States in the face. As the man slumped to the floor, one of

Julian's hired henchmen materialized in the doorway. Aric pivoted and raised his gun as the man raised his own weapon and aimed it at Aric's chest. The hitman staggered back as a round hit him in the neck, but it wasn't Aric who'd shot him. It was Jason.

Aric's chest suddenly felt very heavy. He stared down and saw a gaping wound and blood spreading across his shirt. He looked at Chelsea and Nadine and said, "I'm sorry." Then he collapsed.

"Aric, no!" Chelsea cried. "No! No!! No!"

He heard more gunshots but couldn't see where they were coming from. Aric stared straight ahead and saw Paula lying unconscious under the bed. He assumed Jason had put her there in order to protect her from further harm and hoped she would live. He doubted he would be so lucky.

The heaviness in his chest was quickly being replaced by agony. It was as if his heart had been ripped apart and was radiating waves of gripping pain with every labored beat. He heard himself scream and felt as though it was 2029, and he was living through the D Plague again. The only difference was that this pain was localized.

"Aric, you can't die!" Nadine was yelling. "I lost you once before. I will *not* lose you again! *Aric*! I love you!"

"I love you, too," he mumbled automatically, and Nadine began to sob. "Chelsea...?"

"I'm here, Aric! I love you, Cher! Always!"

The room was suddenly filled with people, but he was too far gone with the pain to be aware of anything save for Chelsea repeating over and over that she loved him and Nadine brushing her lips across his forehead. He prayed to Jesus Christ and Loa Eshu and asked for protection of his loved ones and a quick death for himself. Then all was dark.

Chapter Forty-nine

Searing pain shot through Aric's chest, and he screamed and reared off the bed. People were shouting, barking orders, and trying to hold him still. He couldn't open his eyes. He sounded like a mortally wounded animal and wished that someone would shoot him and put him out of his misery. Then he remembered that he'd already been shot in the chest at point-blank range. Why wasn't he dead?

Someone was putting something over his face, and everything mercifully went black again.

Aric woke screaming. He was strapped down to a hospital bed and was reminded of his affliction with the D Plague. He cried out in pain and frustration and called for Chelsea to help him. She was instantly there, holding his hand and stroking his cheek with the backs of her fingers.

"Make them let me up!" he cried, as tears of pain ran down his temples.

He felt tears from Chelsea's eyes fall onto his face as she attempted to soothe him. He screamed again and begged her to get someone to release him from his bindings.

"They can't. Your chest is all open. You were shot in the heart. A normal man would have died instantly. You can't move or you'll stop healing. Your wound will never close. They'll make you sleep again as often as they can."

"Now!" he demanded. "Please!"

"It won't work that frequently," Dr. Levine said sympathetically from his other side. "We figured that out early on once you were brought in. We can only use the medication and anesthesia intermittently if they're going to retain their effectiveness and not kill you."

Aric moaned loudly and tried to twist against the restraints. He couldn't move at all. He screamed again.

"I wish I could do something for you," Chelsea lamented.

"You...do," he said through the haze of pain. "You...always...do. I just...I don't...I can't do this forever or I'll go insane."

348

"Hold on," Levine told him as she lifted the dressing on his chest. Sighing, she said, "It's time for more digital images and recordings."

"I don't understand," Aric managed to say, as a woman in scrubs approached them with some sort of camera.

"You will when you recover, and you'll be fascinated," Leah Levine assured him. "We're not being callous here. What we're doing is imperative."

After what felt like hours, Aric was once again given anesthesia. He lost consciousness, listening to Chelsea say that Jason and Paula were alive. She told him Paula was pregnant, which, of course, Jason had already told him. The doctors weren't certain about the condition of the fetus.

For what felt like eternity, Aric was caught in a cycle of agony, medication, agony, anesthesia, and more agony. Chelsea was always with him, but Nadine was nowhere around. When he asked about her, Chelsea told him that the doctors had given the woman something to calm her down and wouldn't let her see Aric in his current condition.

"I have to talk to her," he told Dr. Levine through gritted teeth. "When can I talk to her?"

"You have to be healed a bit more before she can see you. She's been on the verge of a breakdown ever since the…incident at Gulf Global Green. Witnessing the shootings has left her emotionally unstable right now. She's begged us to let her come to you, but we can't permit it, yet. We fear that it would undo her."

"But you could keep the dressing on my chest. I have to talk to her."

"Aric, your chest was literally blown open in front of her eyes. You can barely speak because of the pain. You have to be in better shape if you don't want to make things worse for her."

More days followed, and the cycle repeated itself. Finally, Aric woke and found that he was no longer restrained. The pain was still intense, but it was bearable. He was stiff and sore, which was probably not a bad thing. It deterred him from moving around much.

"Chelsea," he murmured without opening his eyes. "Chere?"

"She's finally sleeping soundly," Nadine said softly. "Once the doctors allowed me in your room, she agreed to go into the next room and get some real rest. I'm amazed she hasn't had a bad migraine with everything that's happened in the past five days."

"It's only been five days?" he asked with astonishment as he opened his eyes. "It feels like it's been five years."

"Yes, it does."

"Nadine, I…I'm confused about things."

"I know. You're still in so much pain. I think we should wait a little longer to really talk. I'm just extremely thankful that you're going to live. We all are."

"How are the others?"

"Chelsea is fine other than being desperately worried about you. She refused to leave you, even though your wound was pretty…horrific to see."

"What about Paula and the baby?"

"Paula will be fine. They're not certain what to do about the baby."

"What do you mean?"

"Buddy and Julian had her drugged with something very powerful that will definitely cause significant birth defects although they didn't know she was pregnant. I doubt they would have cared even if they'd known. I…I can't get over what they did and how Buddy acted. I wasn't surprised about Julian. You know how I felt about him. But Buddy? We didn't have the best marriage after we lost the girls, but I'm in shock that he could be so narcissistic, cruel, and callous. It's shaken me up pretty badly."

"So, Jason and Paula don't know what to do about the pregnancy."

"I think they do. They're just coming to terms with it. They know they shouldn't bring a baby into the world who will be deformed and brain-damaged, but you know all too well how difficult it is to lose a child no matter what the circumstances."

"Yes. Are they okay otherwise?"

"Recovering. None of their wounds were life-threatening, thank God."

"How is Lakshmi handling all of this?"

"She's rather devastated. She got your delayed message and sent in the cavalry, but it was a bit too late. She's had to put a lot of spin on events in order to keep her job and keep her agenda going.

There was a mole in her staff, and that person has now been identified and…relocated."

"What is the official position on Buddy's death?"

Nadine stared at her lap and said, "Suicide. The stress of office became too great for him, and he shot himself. They couldn't come out with the truth unless they wanted to compromise the people's faith in Lakshmi. Lakshmi wasn't about to make up some elaborate cover story but knew she had no option but to allow the staff in the Public Relations Department to fix things. Otherwise, she would have had to step down as President. She actually wanted to, but we convinced her that resigning would destroy all of the wonderful things she's accomplished. She's already said she won't be running for a second term though. She's very shaken herself. She came to see you right away, which was probably a mistake. I think that seeing you like that solidified her decision not to run for office again."

"Where is she now?"

"D.C. She's having to get the Speaker of the House acquainted with his new duties as Vice-President. Lakshmi's been calling several times a day to check on things here."

"How are you doing?"

"Now that I know you'll live, I'll be fine." She rose and bent to kiss his forehead before saying, "You look like your pain has worsened a lot since we've been talking. Close your eyes and rest."

"It hurts too much to rest."

"Then I'll see if the doctors can give you something to help. You need to sleep a little more. I'll be right here when you wake."

Aric woke feeling sore in the center of his chest. He smiled tiredly at Nadine and asked, "How long did I sleep?"

"Two hours. Chelsea remains sleeping in the next room."

"I'd like to talk now."

The woman looked anxious but nodded and took his hand.

"Tell me the whole truth, no matter how bad it is. I have a feeling I know nothing about the truth of my entire life."

"Oh, but you do," she said reassuringly. "You grew up in a wonderful household with loving parents, grandparents, and siblings. You had the phenomenal Tante Marie and the benefit of a normal childhood and a great education. You were a smart, happy, handsome boy. If the D Plague hadn't struck, then you would have

351

gone on to be a happy, fulfilled neurosurgeon probably married to some smart, lovely woman. The two of you would have had your own large and loving family. I'm so sorry that things turned out the way they did. It was better when I was the only one who had to deal with such crushing loss and depression at such a young age. I never wanted that for you."

"You're my mother," he stated evenly.

"Yes," she said with a little sob.

He squeezed her hand and asked, "How? Were you Alycia's mother, too? She and I were different from our other siblings somehow."

"No, Alycia wasn't my child. You were the only baby I lost."

"Will you please explain it to me?"

"Of course. Now that you know, I could never keep it from you. Before, I was trying to protect you. I didn't want you to suffer. At present, not telling you would be worse."

"So, tell me. Please, Nadine."

She sat up a little straighter before beginning, "By all accounts, the Rodrigues were a wonderful couple who were devoted to each other. They were successful in their home, their work, and in the community. They kept having beautiful daughters on a frequent basis and seemed more than content with their lives. Then, in 2004, seemingly happy Mrs. Rodrigue and Maurice Moreau's father had a one-night stand. She was obviously very fertile and somehow managed to get pregnant during their one encounter. Her husband was very hurt but loved his wife and forgave her. He agreed to raise the baby as his own child. Mr. Moreau, who had recently married, was relieved by this news and vowed he'd never interfere."

"How did they know Alycia wasn't a Rodrigue?"

"Mr. Rodrigue was out of the country on business when his wife got pregnant. She confessed and begged him to forgive her."

"So, Mom has Alycia, and everyone thinks she's Dad's daughter. Who else knew the truth? How'd you find out? And how'd I end up a Rodrigue?"

"Tante Marie knew the real story but kept her mouth shut."

"Until?"

"Until nine months after Mr. Moreau seduced a nineteen-year-old college student named Nadine and got her pregnant. His wife was pregnant with the baby who would turn out to be Maurice

Moreau. He didn't want his indiscretions exposed and his own seemingly happy family destroyed."

"Why didn't you just have an abortion?"

Nadine looked shocked and said, "I loved you, Aric. From the moment I knew you were living in me, I loved you. I could never have aborted you. Mr. Moreau said he wouldn't help me, so I planned to keep you and bus tables if I had to in order to raise you myself."

"Why didn't you then?"

"It started with Maurice's father. He told me that it wouldn't be fair to our baby for me to raise it alone. He said it needed a family. He had an idea of how our child could have an idyllic life. This plan would allow Mr. Moreau to keep his standing in the community and his own family and for me to finish college and have a better life of my own. I told him I didn't want to hear anything he had to say. He'd charmed himself into my heart and was now talking about giving up our baby. I felt betrayed and totally confused."

"What changed your mind?"

"Mrs. Rodrigue visited me with Maurice's father. She said she and her husband had agreed not to have any more children together after the recent birth of Alycia, but Mr. Moreau had approached her about his bastard child and how he wanted it to have a loving, happy home. She said she'd been immediately taken by the idea of their infant daughter growing up with her half-sibling. If she didn't take the baby and raise it, then Alycia would never know her flesh and blood. She'd talked to her husband about it, and he'd agreed to take in one more child that wasn't his. That man must have been a saint."

"So, you agreed."

"No. I refused. I told them I'd do whatever it took to keep my baby. I asked them to leave."

"How far along in the pregnancy were you when they approached you with this idea?"

"About six months. I was fortunate not to start showing until around that time. Luckily, I was out of college for the summer and told my parents I'd decided to simply stay in New Orleans for the break and look for a summer internship. They didn't question it since we weren't very close. You were due at the end of August, so I figured I'd have time to get a job and perhaps return to college in the fall at least part-time. The problem was that you were late and didn't arrive until September. Throughout the summer I'd looked for work, but no one wanted to hire a very pregnant nineteen-year-old girl who'd never worked a day in her life before, especially knowing that she'd soon have a newborn to care for. I kept thinking I'd work something out, but nothing worked out at all. I was so desperate." She began to cry as she continued, "I went into labor at 12:30 a.m. on Labor Day. I called Maurice's father, hoping that he would have changed his mind and would help me. Maurice was only a month old. I stupidly thought his father's paternal instincts would be stirred by his feelings for his new son. They weren't. When there was a knock on the door at 2:00, I opened it and there was your Tante Marie. I wanted to ask her to leave, but instead I burst into tears and asked for her help. I was all alone and in pain and had nowhere to turn. She put her arms around me and told me that everything would be all right. She suggested I let her take me to the hospital, but I refused. I think I knew the moment I saw her that I wasn't going to be able to keep you. If I didn't have you in the hospital, then your parents could file for a birth certificate with their names instead of having to adopt you. No one would know outside of me, Maurice's father, and your family. You wouldn't hate me, and you wouldn't go through life feeling like you weren't a natural-born Rodrigue. You and Alycia would have your place in the sun. I told myself it was the best thing I could possibly do for you."

"You had me at home?" Aric asked hoarsely.

"No. Tante took me to Moreau's. Mr. Moreau knew that she'd helped her mother deliver babies in Haiti. I guess he anticipated what would happen and had insisted on giving her a key. The room upstairs that Maurice has converted into a pool room used to be an efficiency apartment. That's where I was seduced. That's where you were conceived. That's also where you were born."

"Good God. Was it…terrible?"

She nodded, the tears streaming down her cheeks. Refusing to look at him, she said, "It was terrible on so many levels. I was in labor for only six hours, but it was a very difficult labor. It was my first birth; I was a small woman, and you were a big baby. Tante was so wonderful, kind, and knowledgeable, but that didn't help ease the pain. There were times when I thought you'd never come. Plus, the entire time I was irrationally hoping you *wouldn't* ever come because I didn't want to give you up."

"And when I was finally born?"

"I was awed by how beautiful and perfect you were. I changed my mind. I told Tante that I couldn't do it. I had to keep you. She said she understood completely and that I had to decide what was best for me and my baby."

"But you didn't keep me."

"No. As I nursed you, I realized that I could never give you everything you needed. We would be scraping by in the slums, and you'd have no father in your life. You did deserve the life the Rodrigues could give you. I held you for a long time then handed you to Tante Marie and told her to take you to your parents. I only had one request."

"Which was?"

"That your first name be Aric. That's what I'd been calling you from the moment I'd found out I was pregnant. I knew you were a boy somehow. I could sense it."

What happened after she took me away?"

"I lay in the apartment, crying for days. Tante came back to tend to me, but Mr. Moreau never set foot upstairs while I was there. I think he was too ashamed and rightly so. When I was finally healed enough to go back to my place, Tante took me. The semester had already been going on for a few weeks by then, so it was too late to attend that term. My rich parents kept paying my bills and had no idea that I wasn't in school. I became more and more depressed. I went to a doctor and complained of severe back pain. He wrote me a prescription for a very strong narcotic. Not a very good doctor, obviously. That night, I downed the entire bottle. My next-door neighbor heard me stumbling around in my apartment and called the police to make sure I was okay. By the time they got me to the hospital it was almost too late. They saved my life and called my parents, who were shocked and horrified that someone in the family was suffering from emotional instability. They had no idea about you. I told no one – not the internists, psychiatrists, or my family. I was institutionalized, put on antidepressants, and sent to therapy. Slowly, I recovered. I went back to school the following summer, finished college, got a great job, fell in love with Buddy, married, and had our three beautiful girls. I tried getting off the antidepressants several times, but I couldn't. The memory of losing you was always too great of a weight for me to bear. I eventually decided I would simply have to be on them forever."

"Did you ever see me or try to find out about me?"

"After Buddy and I were married, we started running into your parents at different functions. I was polite but always avoided being alone with them. I was told by everyone what great parents they were and how their kids were wonderful. I was very glad to hear it but it was torture, too. I needed to distance myself from the Rodrigues as much as possible."

"And Maurice's father?"

"The last time I saw Maurice's father was when he and Mrs. Rodrigue came to see me when I was pregnant."

"And when you met me for the first time when I was an adult?"

"I almost lost it. You were so wonderful. You were highly intelligent, caring, handsome, and fun. I wanted to rush over and wrap my arms around you and tell you how proud I was of you. When Buddy and I were with you and Lakshmi, you spoke of your great family and happy life. I realized I'd made the right choice, even though it had nearly killed me. I loved you so much but couldn't allow myself to get close to you. I had to maintain my distance."

Aric frowned and said, "I always assumed you didn't like me. It never occurred to me that you loved me and that's why you were staying apart from me."

"Why would it? For all you knew, you were born and raised a Rodrigue." Shaking her head, she said, "And then the D Plague hit and everyone died, but you lived and became so depressed that I wanted to comfort you so badly. I wanted to tell you everything but feared that it would make things even harder for you. I couldn't get near you without wanting to tell you that you were my baby."

"Were you interested in my welfare?"

"Of course! Because of my position as the wife of the Vice-President I was privy to all sorts of inside information about you. I wanted to make sure you were safe after you survived the D Plague. I knew someone would want to experiment on you. I thought I was keeping tabs on things and taking care of you. What I didn't realize was that my own husband was trying to harm you. I can't believe he blamed you for living! You didn't ask to be different any more than our girls asked to die in 2029."

Sighing, Aric said, "You were always standoffish, and now I understand why. What changed things?"

"Chelsea. The day we met her at the Creole House I saw how much happier you were. I also saw a young woman who had been so physically and emotionally damaged and needed a mother. I decided that I should help her. By doing so, I could actually be close to you without it being too obvious. I loved spending time with Chelsea, and it allowed me precious moments with you. I could handle being around you while mothering her. Somehow it was bearable, and I didn't feel the overwhelming need to tell you the truth. I had a second chance to be your mother and to help a lovely young woman who was so lost herself. What a gift."

Aric nodded. He was exhausted although grateful to finally know the truth.

"You should rest again," Nadine told him. "You look so tired."

"Should we tell Maurice I'm his half-brother?"

"I can't think that far ahead," Nadine admitted. "I've wanted to tell you the truth for so long. Why don't we wait and decide later what we should or shouldn't tell Maurice? He's a very nice man. I like him a lot."

"Okay," Aric said sleepily. "I'm sorry I hurt you."

"When?" she asked worriedly.

"When I was born."

Nadine smiled and kissed him on the cheek before saying, "All the pain was worth it to bring my perfect little baby into this world."

The next time Aric woke, Chelsea was sitting beside the bed once more. He smiled at her, and she grinned back and told him he looked better than he had in a week. He told her he wanted to kiss her, and she didn't waste a second before slanting her lips over his. Afterward, he asked her where Nadine was. She frowned and said she'd gone to be with Jason and Paula, who'd had a miscarriage.

"When we get home, things will be better for all of us," Chelsea told him. "Jason and Paula will finish healing and will have to grieve for their baby like we grieved for Aaron. You have to finish healing, although I don't think that will take much time. You and Jason will go back to work, and Jason and Paula will get married. They said they want to try to have another baby as soon as possible after that and have lots of kids. Paula wants to stay home and raise them and has asked if we'd be Auntie Chelsea and Uncle Aric to the children. Nadine can be Granny Nadine."

"Gran would suit her more," Aric suggested. "Do you think you can be Auntie Chelsea and run the IT department for Rodrigue Pharmaceuticals at the same time?"

"I could try. If not, then I could be your IT consultant."

"No hacking the government from our database, right?"

"Not from work anyway," she said mischievously. "But I'll always be checking out the systems to make sure you, me, and the others are safe. You're a miracle, Aric. You're so lucky to be alive, and I want to keep you that way."

Two weeks later, Aric was sitting on the couch in the Creole House reviewing the digital recordings of his surgery and the treatment that had followed. Chelsea was playing Strauss on the piano. It was interesting background music for the images on the screen.

Dr. Levine had been right in her supposition that Aric would find the entire documentation of the condition of his initial wound, emergency surgery, and recovery fascinating. The bullet that had pierced his chest had done so much damage that he should have died within seconds. His mangled heart had seemed beyond repair. Yet, it had somehow managed to keep beating and pumping blood. As he'd watched the recordings, he'd seen his body literally knitting itself back together during and after surgery. The process was remarkable and inexplicable. It made him feel as though all those years of study by the CDC had been worth the trauma he'd had to endure. Whatever had mutated in his body during the D Plague was of enormous significance and would hopefully provide modern medicine with huge advances.

"You've watched that so many times over the last few days," Chelsea said, as she came to sit beside him on the couch. "It's so gory. I could never have been a doctor. It's amazing, but ugh!"

He laughed, shut off the computer, and tucked it into one pocket of his jeans. Then he scooped Chelsea up in his arms and pulled her sideways onto his lap. She kissed him then wove her fingers into his brown hair, while he fisted some of her chestnut curls in his hands. Gently tugging her head back, Aric drew his tongue along the nape of her neck.

"I love you, Chere," he murmured. "I'm the luckiest man alive."

"We're both lucky," Chelsea said, her breathing quickening. "So lucky to...oh, Aric!"

Aric felt joy surge through him. After the D Plague, he'd thought of his survival as a curse. Now he understood that it had been an opportunity that had led to the greatest blessing of all. Aric knew real love, the truth about his past, and had found what he'd been searching for since 2029 – peace.

ABOUT THE AUTHOR

Lauren Cutrera, who also writes under the name Barbara Cutrera, has published over 20 contemporary romance, romantic suspense, paranormal romance, mystery, and fiction novels. Diverse people and plots highlight her works, drawing readers into the characters' unique journeys as they navigate their way through their struggles and triumphs. Lauren and her husband, Budge, are the proud parents of a grown son. They live in southwest Florida and have a cute and naughty Yorkie, Hadrian, who sleeps next to Lauren as she writes each day.

Explore other published works by the author at amazon.com and goodreads.com

Check out all things Lauren (and Barbara) at www.laurencutrera.com

And connect with her there or on

Facebook: https://www.facebook.com/profile.php?id=100063631654302

Instagram: https://www.instagram.com/laurencutrera/

Pinterest: https://www.pinterest.com/laurencutrera/_saved/

OTHER BOOKS BY THE AUTHOR:

The Essential Elements Series

Kindred Spirits
Scorched Creek
Spirits Corner
Memory Lane
Homeward Bound

The Limitless Series

Sight Unseen
Better Left Unsaid
Unheard Of
Under Her Skin
Brain Storm
Out On A Limb

The Seneca & Michael Duet

A Lovely Dream
A Lovely Reality

The Gift Series

The Healer's Gift
Jordan's Way
Bound by Grace
The Nameless

The Real World Series

Over, Under, Across & Through
A Good Man's Life
Mercy
Unfinished Business (Final Chapter)

Barbara Cutrera

<u>Standalone Novels/Short Stories</u>

In A Manner of Speaking
Prim & Proper
Lucky
Compromising Positions
True: 3 Short Stories